ORTOG

ORTOG

by
Kurt Steiner

translated by
Brian Stableford

A Black Coat Press Book

Acknowledgements: We are indebted to Jean-Luc Rivera.

Aux Armes d'Ortog Copyright © 1960, *Ortog et les Ténèbres* Copyright © 1969 by André Ruellan.
English adaptation Copyright © 2010 by Brian Stableford.
Introduction Copyright © 2010 by Jean-Marc Lofficier.
Cover illustration Copyright © 2010 by Mariusz Gandzel.

Visit our website at www.blackcoatpress.com

Introduction

André Ruellan, born August 7, 1922, was first a teacher, then decided to become a medical doctor. He began his literary career in 1948 when, during his first year as a medical student, he published a few articles and poems in a student magazine, *Hebdo Latin*, including a dark and satirical pamphlet in which he suggested that the students were so badly fed by the University restaurant that they would soon be forced to eat the cadavers they were dissecting. This macabre, yet funny, take on ordinary life would become his literary trademark.

In 1950, the newspaper *Le Hérisson* published his first short story, *Méfiez-vous des Veuves* [Beware of Widows], again a dark-humored, twisted tale, whose theme he later expanded in his first horror novel for Fleuve Noir. More crime stories followed, including *La Chaise Infernale* [The Infernal Chair] in *Voir Magazine*.

Ruellan's first published novel was *Alerte aux Monstres* [Alert, Monsters], published in 1953 under the nom-de-plume of Kurt Wargar by the small press Flamme d'Or as No. 6 in their new science fiction imprint, *Visions Futures* [Future Visions]. That same year, Ruellan also wrote a thriller, *Du Sang jusqu'au Coude* [Blood Up To the Elbows], published by Faucon Noir, a publisher specializing in lurid, spicy thrillers. Interestingly, its cover was drawn by Jean-Claude Forest, the creator of *Barbarella*, moonlighting as a commercial artist.

In 1954, publisher Fleuve Noir, which had been founded in 1949 by Armand de Caro and Guy Krill, and published cheap paperback imprints devoted to police thrillers, espionage novels, and science fiction, decided to launch a new horror imprint called *Angoisse* [Anguish or Anxiety]. Their first novel in the new imprint was a translation of Donald Wandrei's 1948 dark fantasy, *The Web of Easter Island*.

Fleuve Noir's editorial policy was to rely on a stable of house authors, whose pseudonyms were owned by the publisher. Ruellan, who, at the time, was finishing his fifth year of medical studies, immediately wrote a horror novel which he submitted to the new imprint. It was *Le Bruit du Silence* [The Sound of Silence], which was accepted two weeks later by Fleuve Noir.

A meeting was hurriedly arranged between Ruellan and the editors, including José-André Lacour who had already penned a few of the first horror titles under the house pseudonym of "Benoît Becker." [1]

Ruellan was told that not only would *Le Bruit du Silence* soon be released—it was *Angoisse*'s 13th title, published in late 1955—but he was commissioned on the spot to write more. Since Fleuve Noir demanded ownership of his pseudonym, he decided to adopt that of "Kurt Steiner."

Despite Krill's death in a car accident, Fleuve Noir grew by leaps and bounds, adding new authors to their roster and new imprints to their catalog. Ruellan had been writing six horror novels a year, becoming one of *Angoisse*'s most prized authors.[2] Perhaps because of his medical background, the strength of his novels lay in their detailed, almost clinical, atmosphere of heavy, oppressive, bludgeoning horror, which anticipated the stronger, gorier, books of the next decades.

In total, Ruellan penned 22 novels for *Angoisse*, mastering all the classic themes and creating some new ones as well. One of his books, *Le Seuil du Vide* [The Threshold of the Void] (1956) featured modern-day vampires, and anticipated many of the themes of *Rosemary's Baby*; it was made into a low-budget horror film in 1971.

---

[1] That pseudonym was later taken by renowned screenwriter Jean-Claude Carrière who used it to write seven, critically-acclaimed novels featuring Mary Shelley's Frankenstein Monster.

[2] Other significant writers included B.-R. Bruss, Anbdré Caroff (the creator of the character of Madame Atomos) and Marc Agapit, whose novel *La Bête Immonde* was adapted into a English-language screenplay entitled *Despair* and published by Black Coat Press (ISBN 978-1- 932983-06-7).

The same editor, François Richard, [3] was in charge of both the science fiction imprint, *Anticipation*, and *Angoisse*. *Angoisse*, however, was only selling 6000 copies of each title on average, while *Anticipation* was selling nearly 15,000.[4] So, in 1958, having established himself as a valuable author, Ruellan was invited to contribute novels to the science fiction imprint as well.

For *Anticipation*, Ruellan wrote a total of 11, no less remarkable, novels. *Salamandra* (1959) featured a love story between an Earthman and a Mercurian woman. The groundbreaking *Le 32 Juillet* [July 32] (1959) described how a man found himself in another dimension and explored the vast insides of a giant, living entity. *Les Improbables* (1965) told of a time war between two future cities, and the attempts made by their descendents to manipulate events to increase the probability of their existence. *Les Océans du Ciel* [The Oceans of the Sky] (1967) was a colorful space opera featuring cosmic cross-fertilization between worlds. *Les Enfants de l'Histoire* [*The Children of History*] (1969) was a thinly-disguised allegory of the political events of May 1968 recast in futuristic terms. *Le Disque Rayé* [The Scratched Record] (1970) was the complex tale of a complicated time loop. *Brebis Galeuses* [Black Sheep] (1974) was the story of a medical dystopia.

Ruellan was also the first writer to introduce modern heroic-fantasy in the *Anticipation* imprint with his *Aux Armes d'Ortog* (1960), and its sequel *Ortog et les Ténèbres* (1969), featuring a futuristic Earth where sophisticated science cohabits with a pseudo-medieval society.

In the 1970s, Ruellan's writing skills, vivid imagination, and ability to pen fast-paced thrillers drew the attention of film directors and he found himself increasingly involved in film writing collaborations, including a low-budget adaptation of

---

[3] Richard was also the partner of young, prolific science fiction writer Henri Bessière who wrote under the nom-de-plume of Richard Bessière.

[4] *Angoisse* was, in fact, cancelled in 1974, with its 261st title.

his *Angoisse* novel *Le Seuil du Vide*. Other genre films included the surreal sci-fi picture *Hu-Man* (1975) and a remarkable modern horror movie, *Les Chiens* [The Dogs] (1979), in which an attack dog trainer, played by Gérard Depardieu, uses people's fears about safety to slowly take over a town. Ruellan also wrote the novelization of his own screenplay.

Other books of note include *Tunnel* (1974), published under his own name, which depicts the hopeless flight of a man through a garbage jungle surrounding a bleak, futuristic Paris. The hero drags his dead lover's body with him, as he searches for a way to resurrect her. In 1984, Ruellan wrote *Mémo*, a novel in which a scientist's experiments with a new drug intended to stimulate memory end in a nightmarish disaster. His latest novel, *Big Crunch* (2009), is a Robert Sheckley-like dark and satirical journey through the end of our universe and how it affects a neighboring universe.

A full bibliography and filmography of André Ruellan, as well as a selected cover gallery, is appendixed at the end of this volume.

Jean-Marc Lofficier

Aux Armes d'Ortog

KURT STEINER

★

ANTICIPATION

Editions
"Fleuve Noir"

Book One: Ortog's Arms

Chapter One

"In those times, a mortal night fell slowly over the universe of humankind, in which all consciousness was engulfed. Toward the thousand cardinal points of space, invisible and venomous, spread the winds of desolation that the race had unchained for its doom, and obscurity of mind corroded the efforts of those who had kept open the eyes of reason..."
Song of the Perfecti
Psalm IV, Verse 18

The Sun had just disappeared behind the arborescent ferns. A vapor rose from the humus, in which gilded flies the size of a hand were whirling.

Dal paused at the foot of a tall sigillaria. He looked at the pernicious fog of the undergrowth and raised the nocturnal mask that served three different functions over his face. Only then did he advance into the dale, in the direction from which the trumpeting seemed to be coming.

The mask reacted to individual photons. Externally opaque, its material became transparent inside, and more than transparent, stimulating the retina by sending it thousands of luminous particles for every one received, always maintaining the original trajectory. It made night into twilight and twilight into broad daylight—but its role did not stop there; the filter with which it was provided destroyed the miasmas. Finally, it served as a shield against the flies.

The trumpeting resumed. Dal reached the swarm and the insects hurled themselves upon him. In an instant, his head was covered with them, which impeded his vision—but he would have been much worse than inconvenienced if he had ventured forth without protection: each one armed with a proboscis with cutting edges, the flies would have dug through his eyelids, attacking the corneas and emptying the orbits. The herdsman swatted them away with the back of his hand; they only attacked the eyes.

He found the stray behind a clump of horsetails. The megatherium, rearing up mightily on its hind feet, was presenting its jaws to a hybrid creature even taller than it was itself. Dal unhooked the coagulant from his belt and directed its spray toward the beast. It vacillated, then fell, making the ground shake. The weapon triggered the transformation of fibrinogen into fibrine in all kinds of normally-coagulating blood; the entire circulatory system immediately became the site of a vast embolism.

The megatherium remained on its hind feet briefly, and then resumed its natural position, sniffing the cadaver. Dal threw a clod of earth at it. The beast turned its dark muzzle toward him, trumpeted, and went into the forest, following the herd.

It was necessary to hurry. The perils of the night were silently prowling around the young herdsman, who went into the pass. From the gloomy dusk the mask drew an orange light, in which pairs of green lanterns danced. Dal recognized the presence of big cats. His weapon could not simultaneously sweep the areas before and behind him; the safest thing to do was rejoin the animals. He could not imagine a wild beast bold enough to attack an entire herd of megatheria. On the other hand, the animals knew their herdsman; he had no fear of them.

Dal rapidly rejoined the herd and perched on the neck of a large male. Accustomed since childhood to the irregular gait of the megatherium, he maintained himself there without difficulty, scanning the flanks of the column with his gaze. As he had anticipated, though, no carnivore risked coming too close.

A river appeared. Through the mask, the water resembled mercury. It was shallow, and the animals traversed the obstacle rapidly. From that moment on the ground began to slope upwards, but the vegetation became thinner.

It was long after nightfall when Dal reached the plateau. The landscape had no secrets for the herdsman in spite of the darkness. He could make out the basalt outcrops and blocks of pumice stone quite clearly, follow the distant progress of an ill-defined beast, and register the presence of a stalk agitated by the warm and humid wind. Like moving rocks, the megatheria were still advancing beneath the dull turquoise sky. Sometimes, they trumpeted, and then the silence regained possession of the volcanic plateau, interrupted solely by the footfalls of the giant mammals.

In the distance, Dal saw the steel walls of the village of Galankar. They were gleaming, with a harsh and somber glow. He called out, and the masked sentinels whose silhouettes stood out on the ramparts opened the vertical gates. Dal went into the village with his animals, slightly surprised by the silence and darkness,

As soon as he was inside he leapt down on to the flagstones. As the animals crowded into the enclosure reserved for them, at the foot of the wall, the herdsman saw a man clad in a white cape standing before him: one of the noblemen attached to the Country House of Galankar.

"You're late back, herdsman," the man said.

"One of my animals was separated from the herd," Dal explained, with a genuflection. "It was nearly killed by a hybrid."

The man in the cape nodded his head gravely. "Strengthen yourself against the misfortune that has overtaken you," he said, "for you have missed your father's final moments."

Dal suddenly felt weak at the knees. "My father!"

At first, Dal could not believe what the man had said. He had left his father at sunrise to take the herd out, as he did every morning.

While watching the animals, the herdsmen gathered vegetable and mineral specimens; they brought them to the village, where they were studied in the local laboratory with a view to biological applications. That practice had been common for decades, for the war had destroyed the majority of species and—by virtue of a modification of the climate and the intensity of radiation—had given birth to a large number of others. Some of them represented an abrupt regression to the Miocene, others a mutational leap to more-or-less variable forms that were incorrectly termed "hybrids." The herds of herbivorous megatheria were less than 100 years old.

That day, Dal had not found any specimens worth collecting. He had spent hours daydreaming in the red ferns, listening to the wind that was tormenting the tips of the horsetails, imagining all sorts of things. For him, the day had been bathed in a singular climate, in which formless hope was mingled with a confused apprehension—but that apprehension had evidently had a basis, since a catastrophe had been waiting for him on his return: a catastrophe incomprehensible in its suddenness. His father had been perfectly healthy when he had left him.

Dal collected himself, took a step forward and said: "Tell me, Jaral Kerr Jaral, how my father died." He had a commanding presence for one of the common people, even at barely 18 years of age.

Jaral's ample movement caused the wings of his cape to flap. "Natural causes…senescence."

The abyss grew even deeper. Dal had imagined a fatal accident, but it had been bound to be a natural death. They were the most difficult kind to understand, and the hardest to accept, since their premature character revealed a malady of the entire race—a genetic malady, involving the appearance of mortal factors or some sort of progressive exhaustion of embryonic vital potential. Senescence! Always that euphemism;

no one ever mentioned "old age." By virtue of its biological reference, the term they used took on an impersonal significance. It transformed death by premature aging into a scientific observation.

Dal rebelled against it: what was scientific about that mock-resignation? "But my father isn't…wasn't yet 60!" His gaze was blurred by tears. What could be done, in Lassenia, against this constant shortening of human life? Despairingly, he added: "My father's father died at 66."

"I know," said Jaral. "And before him, people lived to be 100—and the generations of previous centuries lived longer still. God's curse has weighed upon the race of men since the Blue War. Soon, the last generation will die before having reproduced. The race will die, and the three planets will be returned to the animals and plants."

Dal remained silent. He did not accept the necessity of dying at 45—and, if he had a son one day, seeing him die even younger. With a kind of mental pain, he made a connection between the death and the stars that dotted the sky above his head.

That dated from his childhood. He had been scarcely ten years old, and often accompanied an old herdsman who told him long, exciting and colorful stories. One day, the old man had talked about the Blue War, about which he possessed information of a terrible verity—information handed down orally within his own family. The patriarch had not been trying to frighten the child, but he had allowed himself to be carried away by his own memories, and Dal had been overwhelmed by a profound terror that had ended up making him run away.

The child had then followed a circular route through the forest, returning to his point of departure as night fell. The fear of darkness and wild beasts had directed his footsteps toward the old man, whom he had left in a clearing—but when he found the clearing again, the old man was no longer there. Gripped by increasing anguish, he had searched for him, calling out without receiving any reply—and suddenly, as he climbed a slope in the darkness that had already fallen, he had seen two minuscule gleams directly in front of him, which seemed unearthly.

Immobilized at first, he had eventually gone closer, to find the herdsman's inert body at the top of the slope. The faint gleams that he had seen were the reflections of the moon in the old man's eyes, staring into eternity.

Dal had run back to the herd, which was grazing nearby. He had succeeded in gathering the megatheria together and returning to Galankar under he animals' protection—but the shock had been rude; ever since that night, Dal had assimilated, as if in a vast cloud of multiple significance, the eyes of wild beasts and those of the old man, the disasters of the Blue Wars and the luminous points of the stars. Since then, he had been unable to avoid feeling physically ill at the thought of the gulfs of space—an anxiety that he had never connected specifically with the psychic shock caused by his nocturnal discovery.

And now another catastrophe had overtaken him...

"Well," said Jaral, "the gerontologists are working on the problem night and day, even though the Priesthood is getting excited and crying heresy. Even the noblemen are divided; many of them are putting pressure on the Sopharchy to have gerontologists and geneticists imprisoned. You're not unaware of that, herdsman. The Manicheism of the priests is finding more echoes every day. How could it be otherwise? The Blue War was a great sin; it's not surprising that God is afflicting the descendants of the guilty."

Dal shook his head. He had no sentiment of guilt. The sins of his forefathers were not his; in his view, it was not just that the divinity should make him expiate them. The audiovisual education he had received fifteen years before had fortified him in this opinion.

"Go, herdsman," Jaral Kerr Jaral concluded. "Vigil is being maintained on your father in the Temple."

Bleakly, Dal headed slowly for the Temple. He thought about the audiovisual education imposed by the Sopharchy, decried by many noblemen and vilified by the priests. The terrible news of his father's death caused him to return to it inwardly, and to reconsider through that disastrous lens the indelible memories imprinted in his mind by the photosonic cells. It seemed to him that a part of his personality, still veiled by innocence until that moment, was beginning to emerge from the shadows under the impact of new evidence.

It was the dawn of the 50th century, and that dawn resembled a dusk. The Blue War dated from scarcely 250 years before. If the priests could be believed, that was the cause of everything.

That war had obliterated the traces of the 2500-year-old civilization that had preceded it. By chance, a rocky redoubt had been discovered on Titan, which contained books, magnetic and cinematographic tapes, and various other things—but the cavern must have been sealed at the end of the 22nd century. After 20 years of effort, these vestiges had been translated, and historians possessed fairly abundant information about humankind's past up to that era. On the other hand, they had the collected testimony of survivors of the War, which had permitted them to pick up the threads of history in the second half of the 47th century.

It was beyond doubt that present-day civilization was almost entirely due to the Titan vestiges—which, in spite of everything, amounted to a regression of more than 2000 years, if one did not take account of certain fundamental discoveries, whose applications—such as the Star Drive—had subsisted without anyone being able to rediscover the principles. Historians were inclined to think that those two millennia had passed peacefully, favoring the population of Venus and Mars and economic expansion—but for some reason or other, the problem of traveling beyond the Solar System had only been resolved shortly before the war, for only one meagre colony of exploitation had existed in the Alpha Centauri system, from which little information had been received concerning the cataclysm.

In the black hole of those 2000 years, the three planets had seen their populations increase to such an extent that it was reasonable to imagine the Blue War as a sort of auto-regulatory mechanism that had exceeded its role to an insane extent—and which had, furthermore, occurred at the exact moment when the problem of overpopulation had become soluble by interstellar emigration, thanks to the perfection of the Drive. Political passions had doubtless taken speedy advantage of the method of salvation thus offered to them, however. From the mouths of survivors it had been learned that Mars, Venus and Earth had maintained a dangerous political balance for more than a century, in which alliances had been continually overturned. Supplemented by the formidable plethora of human beings, such a situation was bound to end in conflict.

That conflict had cost, at the lowest estimate, 30 billion lives, in the course of an Apocalypse that had only lasted a few months.

Like some inferior species, humans had been almost annihilated. Scarcely a billion remained after the cataclysm, and although that number had doubled in three centuries, counting the populations of all three planets, the proportion of adults over 60 had considerably diminished. Whether it was a consequence of the war or a divine curse, the human lifespan was shortening. After a new explosion of births, the race was heading for extinction.

Since the Blue War—so named because of a Venusian weapon that had disintegrated entire cities in a bluish halo—two tendencies had confronted the precocious senescence, both of which had sought support in the divine.

The fanatical pessimism of the priesthood which sprang from the chaos referred back to certain religions anterior to the conflict. The priests preached resignation in purificatory practises. The majority of the common people extracted a sort of anesthesia from that, and many noblemen were content with it. The noblemen represented the descendants of those who had reconstructed society of the bases of a sort of communitarian aristocracy on the one hand, and scientists and philosophers on the other. The latter still exercised a collective authority, constituting themselves as a "Sopharchy," in which supreme power was vested in wisdom. In fact, the Sopharchy were in contention with the priests, who did not address themselves to reason, and, in consequence, manipulated crowds very easily.

In the beginning, the nobility had been recruited from men of action and good will. It still included some, but a rapid decadence had debased many of them, making them ineffectual individuals, though very liable to arrogance and cruelty. With them, too, the Sopharchy had to contend.

One last bastion of men of honor remained, however. That was the Star Corps of Knight-Navigators, ranked among the petty nobility, but possessed of a great elevation of mind and sentiment. Although very pious, the Navigators opposed the priests, because they remained men of action and could not resign themselves to the prospect of gradual extinction. They supported the gerontologists, and the still-enormous power of the Sopharchy rested, in large measure, on them. Their Star Corps represented the ultimate means of action of the Sopharchy, which affected to believe in the utility of their expeditions, but actually placed all its faith in the geneticists, even more than the gerontologists.

The Expeditions of the Navigators...everyone had dreamed about them at least once in recent years, for the goal of their enterprise was conducive to dreams. The Star Corps of Navigators had been given the mission of searching the galaxy for the Planet of the Archangels, and questioning the Immortal Prophet who was said to live there.

In addition to the technologies that had come through the Blue War, the rites of a religion had survived, the origins of which had been lost to human memory. Only the colony of Alpha 3, which had not been affected by the War, and whose generations had preserved a link with them, were able to shed a little light on them—but the pioneers who had founded it had been recruited from sectors of the population in which unbelief had triumphed, and the people of Alpha knew no more

19

than those of the Solar System about the significance of the Archangels and the Prophet. The priests sent to Alpha at the same time as the pioneers had only had a very slight influence, and had died without being replaced.

At present, the Navigators were investing their hope in a sort of recovery of the profound myth on which the religion emptied of its meaning reposed: a myth whose elements subsisted in oral tradition, in such enigmatic forms as the notion of an Immortal Prophet guarded by Archangels, on a planet lost in the Galaxy.

As he went through Galankar, plunged in the gloom of grief, Dal understood more fully the definitive and implacable character of the loss he had experienced. The shadow and silence of that little agglomeration, ordinarily illuminated and noisy, rendered the detestable news more concrete.

He recalled with amazement that he had not asked Jaral Kerr for any precise information about the dead man's last moments, about the moment of his death, or anything else that would permit him to make the person he had lost live again, to some small degree. He had been crushed by the news, deprived of all reaction. On the other hand, he had immediately felt, in the depths of his inner being, the insulting injustice that the collective limitation of life represented. The traditional mourning of the entire community on the occasion of a single death suddenly appeared to him in all its symbolic significance: a symbol of despair gradually installed in the people, and respected by their leaders, in spite of the ineradicable hope of the Navigators and the Sopharchy. At the same time, he identified his father with that gigantic drama, and plunged himself into it via his father. The determination to do something himself, by whatever means, inundated him like a revelation. It was with a sort of violence that he approached the Temple.

Dal had pushed his mask back to the nape of his neck. He had no more need of the artificial nyctalopia, for the Temple was surrounded by a blue luminescence, that color having been chosen by the priests in order to remind the faithful of the war, in order to render present in their minds, during every ceremony, the guilt of their ancestors and the necessity of mortification.

The Temple stood next to the Country House, where the three Lords of Galankar were usually lodged. Its pyramidal mass shone in a sinister fashion in the starlight. Dal went in through an archway in which the perfume of ozone floated—the odor of ionic death—and was surrounded by chanting. The arched corridor led to a large square room lit by the same cold steely light. In the center, on the altar, the dead man's corpse had been laid out. Standing around him was a crowd of relatives and friends, which Dal joined silently. The priest Akar extended his hands over the body, his blue and white robe reminiscent of a shroud.

"Consider this man," said Akar, "who was a model of courage and piety in our midst. In an instant, the breath of his life was snuffed out, and his soul has rejoined the One who lent him existence. Let this dolorous separation incite each of us to turn the severe gaze of his conscience into the depths of his heart. Let this new departure be a reason for you to abandon the fallacious love of terrestrial life, for human nature is coming closer to that of God as the race approaches its end. Marvelous redemption, that of a species condemned by its excesses, while its creator receives its representatives more generously in His bosom as the fatal terminus draws nearer! Supreme generosity, that of fusing with the Immortal Prophet in divine Nirvana, rejecting the heavy vestment of flesh whose multiplication has soiled Space!"

Akar made a circular gesture, and the faithful resumed the rosary of the Psalms of Resignation.

Dal moved away from the audience and went to place his hand on his father's cold forehead. He looked the motionless priest in the eyes, and began speaking in a slightly tremulous voice.

"I swear to fight for my race," he said.

21

Silence hung beneath the vault. Dal left the Temple in the midst of the scandal.

In the half-light of the parvis, he met Jaral Kerr again—whom the common folk called Jaral Kerr Jaral, his noble entitlement being distinguished from plebeian names by the repetition of his forename. The radiation of the Temple vaguely revealed the sharpness of his features.

"Have you left the funeral ceremony, then?" Jaral said.

"Lord of the House," said Dal, "I cannot tolerate an attitude of resignation in the face of my father's death. I'm not the only one—you said as much yourself, since the Sopharchy is protecting genetic research."

Jaral was pensive. "The Housemasters," he declared, finally, "do not all obey the Sopharchy…and they are often enemies of the Navigators. I don't approve of the attitude of the majority of my peers, even though I admit the guilt of the race. It's a jealous attitude unworthy of their rank, which is superior to that of the Navigators. But that's a power-struggle in which you are not involved, herdsman. You'd have done better not to set yourself apart—Akar is vindictive."

Dal shook his head. "Life is now so short that it scarcely demands heroism from those who dream of revolt," he said.

Jaral looked at him with interest. "Would you speak like that to a Housemaster other than me?" he asked.

"No," Dal admitted. "That would rob me of any means of action in advance."

Jaral smiled. "Any means of action!" he repeated. "So you're thinking of *acting?* And you've chosen me as a protector?"

Dal looked him in the eyes. "I've known for years that you're a good man," he declared, "and I wouldn't say the same of the other two Lords of Galankar. I don't know how I can make use of my weakness, but I think you'd be disposed to help me in a just cause. That's what I've been thinking about since my father's death—it's suddenly taken possession of my mind, for my grief has made me indignant."

Jaral looked him straight in the eye. "We shall see, Dal Ortog," he said. "We shall see…"

The monotonous calls of the sentinels sounded in the depths of the darkness.

Dal went back to his habitation unit without having witnessed the atomization of his father's body. At the door, he ran into two armed men who shone a bright light into his eyes.

"Surrender your coagulant!" one of them said, brutally. "Orders of Housemaster Jaral Kerr Jaral."

Dal Ortog took a step back. He had placed his trust in an enemy, then! As he considered making use of the device, he was pinioned and disarmed.

"Follow us," said the man.

They took up positions to either side of him and dragged him away. Dal saw their embroidered badges, and did not resist. On the way, they met a company abundantly equipped with xenon lamps, in spite of their masks. It was led by Akar. In the wavering light, there was something hideous and terrible about the completely-hidden heads. Akar was the only one not wearing a mask.

"Where are you taking young Ortog?" the priest demanded.

"To the Country House," was the reply. "That's the order."

Akar made a gesture of annoyance. "He's committed sacrilege!" he said. "He must the handed over to the Temple guards."

"He's committed another crime," said the soldier. "Everyone will get their chance."

The two armed men shoved Dal in front of them, and drew away from the indecisive company.

As soon as they crossed the threshold of the Country House, their attitude changed. "We're Jaral Kerr's bannerets," said the one who had not yet spoken. "He ordered us to take possession of you, in order to forestall the arrest that awaited you. Here's your weapon—you have nothing to fear."

Dal, astonished, recognized Kerr's cunning. "Is the lord here?" he asked.

"Yes. This is the way to his apartment. We'll be standing guard."

Dal thanked them and went along a sumptuously-decorated corridor, at the end of which a door slid open before he reached it. He went into a room furnished with refined taste, where Jaral Kerr was waiting for him, smiling.

"I've got myself into trouble," he said. "Everyone will know by tomorrow that my order was a subterfuge to forestall the man who was going after you. You'll have—or, rather, we'll have—all night to flee Galankar. I don't have enough men to oppose those of two other Housemasters and the priests combined, but I'll have to fight if I don't go into exile, for the incident will give my enemies a pretext. They're all angry with the government—I'm the only one still loyal to the Sopharchy. I would have had to cut and run soon…"

"I don't know how to thank you, Lord," said Dal.

"Keep it to yourself, then."

The company had gone quietly through the Western Gate, which was guarded by sentinels loyal to Jaral—who had joined the column.

Jaral had eighty men at his disposal, led by four bannerets, all provided with specimens of *Equus viridans*. The zoologists had given that name to a horse with a dark green coat that had arisen by mutation. They often made use of such Latin terms, by reason of the cultural habits of the 22nd century, assimilated via the Titan vestiges.

Dal had also been given an equus, and marveled at the facility with which he could ride it. Accustomed to megatheria, on which it was much more difficult to maintain his equilibrium in spite of their rather slow pace, he soon adjusted to his rapid mount.

The bannerets had moved quickly and skillfully; their men had left their billets quietly and collected the equus without a whinny being raised. The inhabitants of Galankar were confined to their homes by virtue of the mourning, and that had also contributed to the success of the enterprise. Now, the gleam of the steel door that had been closed behind the fugitives was a patch in the darkness. Jaral Kerr was riding at the head with Dal, and a trail into the wilderness opened up before them. The reconstruction of roads had hardly begun; the manufacture of vehicles had only been resumed in large cities. The men advanced into the woodland, riders and mounts alike masked against the darkness.

"How far do we have to go to reach Lassenia?" the herdsman asked Jaral.

"I don't know," Jaral said, through his mask, "but it takes four days by equus, if we don't run into any difficulty—which is doubtful. Every time I've made the journey, I've been delayed by various obstacles, particularly attacks by the Mlols."

Dal said nothing. He was thinking about the Mlols: nyctalopic half-humans who lived in nomadic bands scattered through the forest. They used very primitive weapons, but they were skilled in setting ambushes, and their temerity was unparalleled. There were not only Mlols, but also hybrids and felines. By virtue of that troubling proximity, all small townships like Galankar were entrenched behind high steel walls—some hybrids could dissolve stone—and maintained well-armed militias.

Unfortunately, rural society was taking on an increasingly feudal aspect; it was not uncommon to hear of the men of one village raiding another, with the aim of carrying off provisions and women. In these incidents, the attacked village saw its walls melted, and what remained of its inhabitants left at the mercy of Mlols and wild beasts. No crop-grower or herdsman ever indulged in such misdeeds, against which all the priests railed, but noblemen and their liegemen often succeeded in avoiding audiovisual education, and no conditioning fought within them against their instinct for pillage. The priests had criticized their crimes strongly and published the names of the guilty parties, likening them to those responsible for the Blue War, but it always happened again, because only force could have stopped it. Sometimes, a space squadron commander by a Navigator landed somewhere in the wilderness and devastated a Housemaster's troop, but that was rare; the Navigators had more important missions to fulfill.

The scent of humus and sap-filled stems seeped through the masks. Dal, who had always lived amid that powerful perfume, found it richer than usual, charged with significance. Did the melancholy sensation that it produced stem from the tragic disorder of the night, in which grief was mingled with the consciousness of exile? Dal had only abandoned distant relatives, and flight to Lassenia marked a new beginning as well as the end of a phase in his life. Was it, then, the memory of beasts dead in the jungle, whose remains were beings slowly reabsorbed into the earth, that memory fusing with that antique methods of burial to give the nocturnal perfume the face of death? Dal would have preferred it had his father's body not been atomized, but placed instead within the bosom of the robust earth that he had helped to fecundate.

He was riding close beside Jaral, and their masks were pressing the darkness like a fruit to extract rare droplets of light therefrom.

"Don't you think, Lord, that the darkness is becoming denser?" said Dal.

"God is amassing a storm over our heads," said Jaral, in a hoarse voice, "and rain makes the entire forest into a vast marsh at this time of year."

At that moment, a rider coming forward from the column came level with them. He spoke rapidly to Jaral: "I'm part of the rearguard, Lord. We need to increase our pace; the infrasonic detectors indicate a numerous company pursuing us."

"Already!" cried the herdsman, involuntarily.

"Go back to your post," Kerr told the messenger. "We'll make our animals give all that they can."

The man turned round, and Jaral shouted a curt order. Whinnying resonated in the shadows as the horsemen took up a hesitant gallop. On the one hand, the gloom inhibited the equus in spite of the masks and made it difficult to guide them; on the other hand, that same gloom was becoming almost impenetrable for the similarly-masked men. As the trail was pitted with hidden potholes and thorny vegetation, rapid progress increased the danger of a fall. Nevertheless, the mounts were the result of a fortunate mutation; their qualities of athleticism and equilibrium were comparable to their incredible speed over flat ground—and, indeed, the pursuers would run into the same difficulties.

Dal thought of that, and also of something else. "Don't the Housemasters have a helix at their disposal?" he asked, crouching over the reins.

"I've had it destroyed," Jaral shouted. "We couldn't use it—too noisy—and it's a single-seater."

Jaral had thought of everything. He had been able to issue a series of orders while Dal was at the Temple, and they had been executed with amazing promptitude.

A bluish glow illuminated the foliage and a dull roll of thunder shook the sky and the forest. Before the blue color of the lightning, Dal and Jaral instructively made the sign of protection: a hand on the forehead, then the breast. With the immense sound of a cataract, warm rain inundated the sigillarias.

Lightning-bolts fell in front of the company, cleaving an exceedingly tall tree, whose cracking and fall were covered by the loud detonation of the discharge. The men continued amid an odor of ozone, which chilled them to the bone.

It was not an easy business to overcome the obstacle that barred the trail—but by mustering their strength, the majority of the equus sailed over it with prodigious leaps that took them to the other side. Three of them, however, broke legs, and had to be put down by means of the coagulant. Their riders were given pack-horses, whose loads were abandoned. Dal, for his part, had made the enormous jump very smoothly. Jaral congratulated him on it, which filled Dal with joy and pride; noblemen were not in the habit of congratulating herdsmen....

Arrested by that idea, Dal suddenly understood why he found in Jaral Kerr something of the elder brother he had always wanted—a brother who had, to some extent, replaced his dead father. That a Housemaster could conduct himself in that manner towards him surpassed all his hopes. The nobility did not, however, hold the common people in servitude. Theirs was a sort of functionary category vested with the prestige of a hereditary title, in addition to their administrative role. Dal had always envied and admired their social status, though—even that of the harshest and most depraved. He compared the other two Housemasters to Jaral Kerr, and was convinced that even if he had been born in their ranks, he would have modelled himself on Jaral.

As the rain diminished in intensity, barbarian howls broke out in the forest, accompanied by the hiss of arrows and spears.

"The Mlols!" cried Jaral. "Maximum speed, and protect the flanks!"

A lightning-flash lit up the trail. For a fraction of a second, Dal saw a group of hairy individuals with green pupils and heavy jaws massing in front of him. He aimed his coagulant and swept the area, while spurring his mount on. He passed over a heap of motionless bodies like the wind.

After a brief gallop, they called a halt and counted their losses. Sixteen men, one of them a banneret, failed to respond to the roll-call. Five others were wounded. Jaral's shoulder had been grazed by an arrow. It would have been futile and perilous to go back. For the Mlols, human beings were prey like any other—a particularly dangerous prey, but one whose flesh was tasty enough to risk the lives of half a tribe in its pursuit. Naturally, they would already have carried the cadavers away, after slaughtering the wounded, without any distinction of race.

Mlols were the result of the only viable mutation that had afflicted humankind, or the only one that had survived. In the same way that *Homo sapiens* had descended, through many transformations, from *Pithecanthropus*, the Mlols, in becoming unhuman, constituted a further branch—but a regressive one, which was not far removed from the race from which humans had issued. Much more distant from humans than the

Neanderthals had been, their morphology linked them to great wild beasts.

In the distance, a chorus of howls rose up.

Separate into two groups and lie in ambush in the bushes to either side of the trail," Jaral ordered. "Hide the equus."

The maneuver was rapidly executed. Dal had followed the Housemaster, and spoke to him in a low voice.

"Do you think the Mlols are chasing us?" he said.

"No," said Jaral. "What I think is that they're very numerous and that they've heard the people from Galankar coming. I think they'll set another trap for them, at the place where the tree came down. In the confusion created by the obstacle, they'll be able to inflict much heavier losses on our pursuers than we've suffered."

Galloping horses made the ground shake. Jaral's men levelled their weapons at an angle that posed no risk to those opposite, on the other side of the trail. When the horsemen arrived, it was a massacre.

"What a disaster," said Kerr, as he reassembled his company. "Whether one likes it or not, it's impossible to escape these battles. If the race were not condemned, it would launch itself into a new Blue War a few centuries hence."

The cavalry of the two other Housemasters had already been mown down by the Mlols, for they could only count a hundred victims on the trail—one of whom was the priest, Akar.

"If the tree hadn't been struck by lightning," Dal said, "and if the Mlols hadn't attacked, the men from Galankar would have caught up with us an annihilated us."

"Without a doubt," confirmed a banneret. "They would have been delighted to be rid of us—and I presume that they would then have fought one another, until the Country House was in the hands of one alone."

"The central power is too weak," said Jaral. "The Sopharchy can still punish any rebellious Housemaster, but they let the degradation continue. Have they lost all hope, or are they entirely absorbed in research related to longevity? The result is dire."

They got under way again. The herdsman's thoughts were taken up by the death of Merrill Ortog. Sadly, he recalled that of his mother four years earlier, accidentally killed in the jungle on the very edge of the village. Now Dal was an orphan—which helped him to envisage exile calmly, for this really was an exile.

There was scarcely any other populated country in the world but ancient Europe, where the migration of initially-scattered survivors after the War had recreated a kind of loosely-populated nation. Decentralization and significant vestiges of the particularity of various importations, however, had made that reformed nucleus a mosaic in which the slightest transplantation was equivalent to a profound rupture. Faced with that rupture, Dal armed himself with his solitude, but also with the reassuring company of Jaral.

He suddenly thought about his own responsibility toward the Housemaster. None of this would have happened if he, Dal Ortog, had not taken it into his head to stand up to Akar, in a fit of pride. He looked into darkness. No, it had not been pride, but indignation. If religion contained virtue, that indignation was based on an error of judgment, but if the opposite were the case...

Now, he thought, *the Lord Housemaster is bound more tightly by his role as protector than I am by my position as protégé. I don't like that. It's good that I'm no longer bound to anyone, but I'd also prefer no one to be bound to me, in any fashion whatsoever...*

The confused character of his associations of ideas did not escape him, but he conserved in his heart the profound conviction that he was now old enough to take sole responsibility for himself. To be sure, if he were to integrate himself into the urban society of Lassenia, it would be easy to call upon the influence of Jaral Kerr Jaral; even so, he felt an enormous need for independence—not for the independence that he had enjoyed in the wilderness in the long days while he watched his animals, but a liberty doubtless less easy to master: the kind that exposes one to the threats of the society of men when one accepts a role therein necessitating contacts. Perhaps that sentiment found its origin in the dread of losing his arbitrary liberty, and in the obscure desire to adapt himself to the new life on which he was embarking.

The night was still covering the forest like a black shroud. In a tight column, the men rode rapidly along the middle of the track, and the bannerets took care to prevent any dispersal: the animal shapes glimpsed in the undergrowth would attack any laggards. No pursuit constrained them to force the pace now, but the goal of the journey remained far away, and the more rapidly they made progress, the better chance the troop had of reaching its destination safe and sound.

They had, however, reached a region in which the deluge of rain had accumulated, by reason of a large natural depression. The trail disappeared into the midst of a marsh, as Jaral had anticipated.

"We'll make camp here," said the Housemaster. "The sun will evaporate this water in the morning, and we'll only lose a few hours—whereas, if we carry on, we risk losing men in the bog."

The wounded, skillfully bandaged after the attack, had been able to remain in the saddle, but they fell into a deep sleep as soon as they lay down on the spongy ground beside the trail. Fires were lit and sentries posted in sufficient number, once the mounts had been organized into a continuous rampart to double the protection.

In the flickering firelight, which evoked the idea of primitive times, Jaral gathered Dal and the three surviving bannerets—Galgo Rank Galgo, Sar Jdanor Sar and Rog Moniz Rog—around him and spoke to them.

"Bannerets," he said, "first of all, I want to remind of what your titles signify, for the benefit of this young herdsman. Originally—which is to say, 4000 years ago—the term designated, without any distinction of rank, a nobleman who could raise a certain number of men under his banner. The structure of social cadres resulting from the war has had the effect of altering its meaning, giving it the value of a definite rank, intermediate between those of a warrior and a knight." He paused, looking around the faces that the flames caused to shift, and then continued: "As Bannerets of Galankar, you are my liege-men, but you have the right to choose your own troops. You see before you Dal Ortog the herdsman, who has shown courage in defying Akar and the faithful, with an objective that the faith might dispute but which reason does not condemn." He paused again. Surprise was legible in the eyes of the three men, and joy in Dal's. "Who will consent to replace one of his men slain in combat with Dal Ortog?"

Galgo was the first to nod his head. "Me, Housemaster," he said. "But you must take responsibility for that change of status"

"Understood," Jaral agreed. He turned to Dal. "You're no longer a herdsman," he said. "You are now under the orders of Galgo Rank of Galankar."

So Dal, who had just promised himself that he would not surrender his liberty at any price, found himself submissive to a commander, and took pride in it. After assuring Jaral of his gratitude, he started thinking again. In reality, his status as a herdsman had only procured him a measure of independence while he acted in that capacity. Was there any need for herdsmen in cities? No. It was necessary for him to assume another role. That of warrior had nothing honorable about it with reference to the recent massacre, but the new ranks specifically excluded that sort of thing from their reference. A soldier had become, first and foremost, a protector of civilians against wild animals and overly powerful scoundrels. There was no denying that a soldier might one day become a powerful scoundrel himself, but it was not always thus. In any case, a simple hormonal cause explained Dal's pride—the same cause that was beginning to bring about the rebirth of war, even though the species was on the road to extinction.

Dal was presented with the jerkin of a wounded man too gravely injured to fight. On the right shoulder the garment bore a badge with the arms of Galgo Rank Galgo: a golden hybrid on a quartered field of sable and silver. Involuntarily, Dal compared that design to the one ornamenting Jaral's breast, and found it much more prestigious; the Housemaster's arms simply consisted of a silver chevron on a field of gold. Jaral's rank was superior, though, and his quarters dated from the original ennoblements of nearly two centuries before. Dal did not know that the ancient Sopharchy had revived forgotten traditions, and that the simplest symbols were, in reality, evidence of descent from one of the original reorganizers.

Dal took his leave of the group and joined the twenty or so men who bore the same insignia as him. He was welcomed with mixed feelings, which ranged from frank sympathy to open hostility.

After a night free of incident, Dal and his companions broke camp at the first light of dawn. Because of the giant flies, they had to keep their masks on.

They held council while waiting for the heat of the day to evaporate the rain water and make the ground firm again. For the first time, Dal did not join the group formed by Jaral and his bannerets, but remained in the midst of coarse warriors, who were beginning to accept him. Only two or three of them still showed some reticence. Paradoxically, Dal felt freer among them than by Jaral's side.

In a circle around their leaders, the men listened to the exchange of words, while the sentries kept watch on the edge of the woods. After a rather long discussion, Jaral addressed the three cohorts—the followers of the banneret who had died in the ambush had been divided between the other three.

"We're a long way from the capital," he said, "and numerous perils still await us on the road we must follow. I appeal to all of you to form an indissoluble body with the others.

33

That's the only means that will enable us to reach Lassenia with minimum losses." He looked around the circle. "Some of you have relatives or children in Galankar, who now only possess the protection of individual weapons like those with which the herdsmen are equipped. None of them knows how to use the great siege-projectors—with the result that the village is now at the mercy of an attack of any sort whatsoever. Those among you who desire to be repatriated to Galankar will be, by the same aerial convoy that will send help as soon as we reach Lassenia. Let that give wings to your mounts." He turned to the marsh, in which a sinuous narrow strip of land and heaped-up stones was already discernible. "It's time to go," he concluded. "Saddle up."

"One moment," said Rog Moniz. "Wouldn't it be better for one of us to go back, with his horsemen, and get his collaborators ready to defend Galankar until the arrival of the reinforcements you mentioned? The Mlols prefer to attack by night, and there's no enemy waiting for us within the village walls, now that we've annihilated your peers, along with the priest Akar."

Jaral's face wore a sceptical expression. "We could do that," he said, "but I fear that your cohort would not be very numerous, by comparison with everything roaming the forest…and I can't reinforce it without weakening my own forces excessively."

Sar Jdanor raised his voice timidly. "Why do we need to go to Lassenia? "You can assume sole control of Galankar. Exile is no longer necessary, since you now have only friends."

"My decision is taken," Jaral retorted, frowning. "I thought at first that it was only Dal Ortog's rebellion that forced me to leave. I know now that my task is no longer sufficient for me. Go back, then, and leave me to continue, with those who remain faithful to me."

There was a deep silence.

"I'm going back," said Rog Moniz, finally, "for I can't bear my wife and child being exposed to the risk of death while I'm far away."

Jaral looked at him benevolently. "That concern does you honor," He said. "Take my cape; I delegate the functions of Housemaster to you. Leave with your men and be the protector of Galankar. I'll send you reinforcements quickly." He took off his cape and held it out to Moniz, who took it respectfully. "What about you, Banneret Sar Jdanor Sar?" he asked.

Called to account in this way before his warriors, Jdanor did not dare retreat, for he had no motive as serious as Rog Moniz's. "I'll follow you, Housemaster Jaral Kerr Jaral," he said, in reply to Jaral's challenge.

"That's good. Let's not lose another second."

The two troops exchanged the sign of protection—hands to the forehead, then the breast—and Moniz's horsemen soon drew away on the trail that led to Galankar. With astonishing agility—Jaral was over 40—the Housemaster leapt into the saddle. The column formed up behind him and they all rode into the green penumbra that descended from the trees. Agitated by a thousand conflicting sentiments, Dal prepared himself for the long road ahead.

They rode until mid-day without their progress being interrupted by anything but a rapid hunt carried out alongside the track, which permitted them to bring down two large birds with multicoloured plumage as well as a kind of zebra. A halt was soon called, and the game roasted before being divided as equally as possible between the men. The absence of flies permitted them to remove their masks. A steam that ran a short distance away quenched their thirst, and they were getting ready to mount up again when the sound of numerous breaking branches resounded in the undergrowth.

The column formed up in battle order, and they listened without anxiety; the racket had to be made by a herd of some sort, because a Mlol tribe would have approached silently. They were astonished, however, when a man appeared on the rail with his arms raised in the air. He was wearing a tattered black jerkin and had a bad wound in his leg.

"Come forward!" shouted Jdanor. "But if your friends are trying to set a trap for us, know that we're well-armed!"

The man staggered and fell in the middle of the trail, while four others came out of the bushes carrying an unconscious female. Dal made as if to race forward.

"Stay where you are!" Galgo instructed him, brutally. "One doesn't forget discipline when confronted by danger."

Dal contented himself with examining the lamentable group, toward which no one made a move. Three more men emerged, one of whom was carrying a new-born child in his arms, followed by two women in rags.

"We're from Malakorjal," shouted one of the men who had just laid the woman on the ground. Our village was attacked by a flying hybrid, which decimated our troops and destroyed our houses."

The weapons were progressively lowered.

"A flying hybrid?" Jaral repeated.

"Yes, it's the first time I've seen such a creature. An immense monster. The village walls were no use, of course, nor were the coagulants."

There was a consternated silence.

"The coagulants…" Jaral repeated, again, stupefied.

"We attacked it with thermic projectors," explained another fugitive, "and inflicted some superficial wounds on it. It had blood that was absolutely black."

Jaral shook his head. "Help them," he said to the two bannerets.

It transpired that the village of Malakorjal, the nearest to Galankar, had been almost destroyed at dawn by a capture that resembled a giant whale, whose fins, adapted for flight, must have covered half the village. To all appearances, the beast had come from the ocean, and had doubtless returned there after a brief incursion inland. It had crushed the habitation units, in which a great many people had perished. Dozens of wounded had been devoured, while the disorganized troops attempted to destroy the monster, which had eventually flown away without sustaining any considerable damage.

Delirious with fear, the survivors had set off into the wilderness in the direction of Galankar in the hope of finding refuge there. Within a few hours, though, many of them had perished under the claws of wild beasts or Mlol spears. Of the numerous population of Malakorjal there remained eight men, three women and a child. The four Housemasters and their bannerets had been killed, unable to put up a fight, and the ruins of the Temple had buried the two priests.

This catastrophe distressed the men of Galankar; their own families had no protection against a similar disaster. It was necessary once again to care for the wounded, and the healthy men were incorporated into Jdanor's troop. There were many warriors who repeated the sign of protection several times over; all of this reminded them of the limitless consequences of the Blue War, and many of them would gladly have welcomed the presence of a priest in their midst.

Only one of the escapees had belonged to the regular troops of Malakorjal. Galgo Rank asked him why he had not followed the trail that linked the two villages.

"There was panic," the man said. "I was unable to influence hem, and they were determined to cut through the forest in order to get to Galankar more rapidly. As I went with them I didn't expect to remain alive until mid-day."

The finally got under way again, and reached Malakorjal as dusk was falling.

In the bluish daylight that bathed the forest, the ramparts of the village loomed up on the edge of an immense grassland. From a distance, there was nothing obviously abnormal, apart from the absence of sentinels on the steel walls.

"The track makes a long detour," said the soldier from Malakorjal. "We're arriving from the direction opposite to that in which we fled. On this side, all the gates are still shut. We'll have to go around the walls if you want to get in."

He was talking to Jdanor, who called Rank and observed: "It would be desirable, in fact, to take advantage of what remains of the ramparts in order to protect us through the night."

"They're intact," said the soldier, "and we can get in through one of the large open gates. It's very unlikely that the incursion of the same hybrid will be repeated."

At the head of the column, Jaral Kerr made an expansive gesture to indicate the direction, and shouted a few words of explanation, which carried to them faintly.

"Yes," said Galgo, "Jaral's right. It's better to move along the ramparts at a respectable distance, in case any enemies have introduced themselves into the place during the day."

Jdanor shook his head. "Mlols?" he said.

"Who knows? Let's keep out of bowshot. By firing from the walls they could decimate us with a single volley."

The horsemen went around Malakorjal in a sinuous line that brought them closer to the forest as it cut across the grassland. At its head, Jaral stopped and shouted: "We've circled the village. There's no open gate."

The entire column stopped. Silence fell, occasionally broken by the whinnying of an equus. Far away in the forest the cavernous growl of some unknown beast was audible. Bor Talak, the soldier from Malakorjal, brought his mount to a trot in order to join the Housemaster of Galankar. Immobile on his equus, Dal scanned the top of the wall.

It was a disturbing enigma. Even if the Mlols had got into the fortified enclosure, they could not possibly have operated the mechanism that closed the doors. That was Bor's opinion, and also that of the bannerets who were conferring with Jaral.

"I'm certain that all the survivors fled at the same time as us," Bor declared, pointing vaguely at the group from Malakorjal incorporated into Jdanor's troop.

Jaral remained momentarily perplexed, then made a decision. "We'll send five men forward to parley. We'll cover them with our long-range weapons, if warriors appear on the ramparts."

A little company was formed. In the declining twilight it moved forward toward the steel walls.

The bannerets debated the opportunities of such an initiative with Jaral.

"We camped all last night without suffering the slightest attack," said Sar Jdanor. Why do we need the protection of Malakorjal, at any cost, tonight?"

"For two reasons," Jaral replied, patiently Firstly because we've had to abandon some of our provisions en route, and have a good chance of finding more in the ruins. Secondly, because we're moving into the savannah, where one encounters the most dangerous hybrids. Except from the flying monster that destroyed the village, none of them can do anything against the walls." He looked at each of them in turn and concluded: "Is that enough for you?"

The bannerets gave in.

Already, the majority of the men had put on their masks, abandoned by day because of the absence of flies in the part of the forest through which they were travelling, which had become indispensable to confront the dangers of the darkness.

Dal had volunteered for the advance party. He approached the walls with two men from Galankar and two from Malakorjal, one of whom was Bor Talek. The last-named, moved by a vague hope, shouted a few words of greeting. From a distance, Jaral's warrior aimed little ultrasonic projectors at the ramparts. To the amazement of the delegation, welcoming cries went up from behind the massive doors, and the steel batten slowly lifted.

Jaral joined the advance guard at a gallop. Several gesticulating silhouettes came through the gate of Malakorjal, one of which was wearing a white cape. Before doing anything else, Jaral gave his instructions.

"Dal Ortog and Bor Talek," he said rapidly, "go back to the men and place yourselves under Galgo Rank's orders. Tell him to enter Malakorjal last, and to arrange his forces on the patrol-way above the gate, whose controls he'll command. The equus can remain outside the walls, but near enough for them to be brought inside if a hybrid appears—provided that all is well inside."

While Bor and Dal went back to the troop, which was deployed in a threatening line a hundred meters away, Jaral saw a masked man coming towards him with his hand extended, whose embroidered blazon he knew only too well.

"Jaral Kerr!" cried the man in the cape. "What a surprise! Doubtless you too have come to the aid of the victims of the catastrophe that has struck Malakorjal?"

"May God grant you long life, Erahrt Melej Erahrt," said Jaral, dully. "Survivors reached your town, then?"

"No," said Erahrt. "One of my helices flew over Malakorjal and the observer returned to Kilnir to raise the alarm. But let's put an end to this palaver. Tell your men to come forward and let's put ourselves under the protection of the walls...."

Jaral made a broad gesture. In the distance, the column reformed and started to move. The Housemaster from Kilnir took his counterpart from Galankar with him. The three guards followed, perplexed.

Kerr was glad he had taken precautions. In fact, Erahrt Melej had a detestable reputation. He had never made any move against Galankar, nor, presumably, against Malakorjal—those being the two villages closest to Kilnir—but other agglomerations had suffered from his visits, even though he had not, strictly speaking, carried out raids on them. Melej had simply pronounced occasional death-sentences on bannerets suspected of impiety. He always traveled with a general staff of fanatical priests, whom no one wanted to encounter.

As they went into the village, Jaral wondered whether Melej knew anything about the events that had taken place in Galankar. His attention was soon claimed, however, by the horrible atmosphere of disaster that reigned within the walls. One might have thought that a rain of rocks had flattened the habitation units. The Temple no longer existed, and nothing was left of the Country House by a heap of rubble.

Melej's men were camping in the midst of the ruins. They seemed abnormally numerous to Jaral.

Erahrt came to a halt, fixed in an attitude of surprise. "What are your men doing?" he asked.

Jaral made an evasive gesture. "Oh, nothing," he said. "Standard tactics…it's become second nature to them."

Melej directed his masked face toward the cohort that was deploying along the walls, but he raised his head. His gaze was evidently following Galgo's men, who had swiftly climbed the steel ladders and were taking up position on the patrol-way. "But…" he began. Then he changed his mind, clapped Jaral on the shoulder, and pointed to Kilnir's warriors. "It's time for prayers," he said. "You'll have to break your strategic habits for once, especially now you've met up with friends. Order your men to come and join mine around the priests.

"No," said Jaral, coldly.

Melej remained silent for a brief moment. The mask hid the expression on his face. "As you please," he said, finally. If you prefer to send them a priest, I'll put one at your disposal, since your troop doesn't appear to include one."

"Thank you," said Jaral, laconically.

Melej went over to the group formed by the four priests in blue and white robes. "I would be grateful if one of the reverend guardians of the faith…" He began, to attract their attention; then, after a pause, he continued: "would consent to celebrate mass for the soldiers of my friend Jaral Kerr Jaral of Galankar."

A heavy silence was gradually established among the troops from Kilnir. Jaral thought, uneasily, that Melej's words had thrust Akar's absence into sharp relief. Everyone remained as motionless as the surrounding rubble.

"That's fine," said one of the priests, eventually. "I'll go." He moved away from the others and came toward Jaral, adjusting his mask. Kerr had an opportunity to glimpse his regular features, his short grey beard and, especially, his bright eyes.

"I am grateful to you, Reverend Guardian," said Erarht, in an ambiguous tone, in which Jaral discerned a worrying hint of slyness.

The priest headed at a leisurely pace toward the men of Galankar, whose alignment at the foot of the walls had not changed. He set himself in front of the gage and raised both arms toward the sky. The wind caused the wings of his tunic to flap. A strange silence still reigned. Suddenly, the priest fell forwards and remained motionless on the ground.

Jaral anticipated the catastrophe and bounded towards his men, crying: "Everyone down!"

Shouts went up: "Priest-killers! Impious assassins!" A woman began screaming in terror

Silent and invisible, the rays of coagulants cut through the air. Jaral fell first, with his three guards. Behind the interior walls of the patrol-way, Dal saw the Housemaster's inert body roll over a broken flagstone. He bit his fist in order not to scream. It was as if he had lost his father for a second time.

Very badly-protected, the men of Galankar were struck down, one by one, but Galgo and his twenty warriors sent forth a murderous downward fire over the ruins, which decimated the men from Kilnir. In the midst of the screaming, Dal heard a familiar voice shouting: "Don't let any of them escape! I saw them kill their brothers and their priest!"

Dal recognized the voice of Rog Moniz, the banneret who had left Jaral. "The criminal!" he said, through clenched teeth.

The man next to him turned his mask toward the ruins. Dal caught the sound of his stifled voice. "A trap!" said Galgo. "Rog didn't go to Galankar but to Kilnir. He knew that our route passed close to Malakorjal—and the disaster caused by the hybrid made things even easier…"

Dal saw a man jumping between two sections of wall. He aimed his ultrasonic projector and the man exploded.

Not far from the walls, the pretended corpse of the priest was crawling toward shelter. Galgo made him a real dead man.

Dal felt his throat closing up painfully. "If Jaral Kerr Jaral hadn't given his orders, not one of us would have escaped."

He fired twice, wrathfully. Rog Moniz's men. The traitor must have chosen them carefully. The voice of Jdanor was heard, crying: "Retreat! Get out of the village!"

Galgo supported the maneuver by ordering an inferno of fire from all the weapons on the patrol-way, and the fire of the men of Kilnir ceased almost entirely for the brief interval that the remains of Jdanor's troop required to slip out through the great gate. When it was certain that all the surviving soldiers of Galankar had quit the village, Galgo had the steel plate moved, amid the howls of Melej's men. Already, from outside, grappling-irons were being thrown up to the battlements, from which long ropes hung down to enable the combatants on the patrol-way to slide down, while the last of them awkwardly held off the assault from the interior.

They regrouped rapidly, and those who had escaped the trap retreated into the darkness of the grassland on galloping horses. There were no women or children with them.

Three more men fell before they were out of range. Dal was riding in the midst of a meager band, reduced to 15 survivors, drowning in hatred and despair.

Chapter Two

*"Capital of the three planets, the gigantic city
existed day and night, all of its millions of inhabitants
promised to the eternal darkness. Villainous intrigues
were born there and withered there like the morbid
flowers of carnivorous worlds..."*
Song of the Perfecti
Psalm VII, Verse 13

Dressed in violet mist, Lassenia, the city with a woman's name, extended slackly within a valley that the rays of the Sun, being too oblique, had not yet reached. Stretched over several dozen kilometres, the vast city was no broader than three or four at its greatest width. Its countless two-story habitations, whose roofs and terraces bore a mosaic of grasses and shrubs, were disposed on either side of the river, and sometimes on the river itself. Slowly, as the sun sank lower, the violet mist became more luminescent. The city came to life at night, just as the scenery and actors had emerged from obscurity in the glare of floodlights on the stages of ancient theatres.

On the edge of the plateau, a few silhouettes stood out against the profound sky: eight men with hard faces, five of whom wore tattered uniforms. On the breast of one of them was a silver eagle in the center of a yellow cross. Another's shoulder was decorated with the effigy of a clawed animal against a black and silver background. Each of them was holding the bridle of a visibly exhausted equus.

"So," said Sar Jdanor hoarsely, "we've reached Lassenia."

His eyes shining, Dal gazed at the city. "That," he said, "is where Lord Jaral had decided to take us, and himself. He has left us, but his shade had protected us. The name of Jaral Kerr Jaral will remain in our memories."

Sar Jdanor turned his emaciated face toward Dal. "He was the best of the men of Galankar," he said, slowly.

The men lowered their heads. A breath of wind passed over their faces, bringing with it a perfume of eternity.

In theory, a mounted company needed to reckon on a four or five day journey to reach Lassenia from Galankar—but the survivors of the Malakorjal massacre had spent nearly a week on a little islet in the middle of a river infested with terrible dangerous fish. The metallic bridge that crossed the river had been carried away by a flood, and the men had had enormous difficulty reaching the islet. They had remained there, as if besieged by those fish of the piranha family, until hunger had chased them away. It was during the second crossing that Galgo Rank had lost his life, with five other companions and a dozen equus. As they looked down on Lassenia, they were no more than eight, and their journey had lasted fifteen days. That very morning, one of Galgo's warriors had died in the grassland, a quarter of an hour after being stung by a fifty-centimeter-long myriapod.

Night had fallen; a luminous halo now enveloped the city, toward which the eight horsemen descended rapidly. In the depths of the sky, the moon displayed its face, ravaged by the Blue War.

"I've been to Lassenia several times by helix," Jdanor observed, "And I know the residential quarters in which I stayed fairly well. I intend to return to the Planetary Foundation of Bannerets, but first I'll take you to the southern suburbs, where you'll find lodgings. It's understood that I consider you as my personal guard, even though almost all of you are wearing badges that don't display my arms, and your upkeep will be assured by me until you're integrated into the city."

There were a few murmurs of approval. Fatigue and lack of nourishment had lowered the men's morale and rendered them incapable of reacting. Dal moved his mount alongside Jdanor's.

"How shall we remain in communication with you, Lord Banneret?" he said.

"The suburban hostels are all provided with optiphones, by means of which one can obtain communication with any building whatsoever."

Dal remained thoughtful. "Why is it that Lassenia isn't linked to the principal villages?" he asked.

"The cables are being laid," Jdanor replied.

They fell silent as they continued their route toward the city. Unlike the villages, the capital was not entrenched behind walls of steel. The presence of an enormous human agglomeration kept wild animals and Mlols away much better than the small rural concentrations. Lassenia did not fear any danger of that sort; there were no ramparts and no guards along the line of the first habitations. The only eventuality that had to be guarded against was that of an aerial attack, which was very improbable. Against that menace, the astroport built on the plateau was equipped with the Blue Weapon of the ancient Venusian colonies. The terror that it inspired had caused it to be completely abandoned, even by stellar expeditions, and it was no longer used except to ensure the ultimate defense.

Followed by his horsemen, Jdanor went into the suburbs, whose habitations were scattered. "Give me your weapons," he ordered. "They're forbidden in the city."

The banneret put the coagulants and ultrasonic projectors in a bag attached to the saddle of a riderless equus. He added his own weapons and resumed the lead.

The habitations were becoming more densely aggregated. A paved roadway appeared, on which the animals' hooves resonated strangely. Coming from the far end of the avenue, an approaching ovoid vehicle, aggressively red in the luminescent air, slowed down to let the horsemen pass. Dal scarcely noticed the suspicious expression of the driver inside the transparent dome; he only had eyes for the machine. Although he was aware of the electro-chemical principle of its functioning, he was burning with curiosity. Nothing of that sort existed in Galankar.

The car turned on to a side-road, while a group of men came out of a horse through a street-level door. They were dressed in patched tunics, wearing long grey beards, and their balance seemed unsteady. They were talking among themselves in thick voices, with coarse accents. A senile clucking and fragments of songs were audible through the open door.

"Let's pass on swiftly," said Jdanor. "It's a pleasure-house for old men. Here, they have special rights because they ought to be dead already. We can't allow them to…"

"Who are they?" said one of the drunkards, in a guttural voice.

Jdanor urged his horse forwards, but the man had already launched himself into the middle of the avenue, where he fell down. He got up again with difficulty, cursing. The others had followed him and were blocking the way. Two of them came forward to meet the horsemen, brandishing stout walking-sticks. Jdanor's equus reared up, while the banneret, standing up in his stirrups, attempted to master the animal. Other half-senile vagabonds surrounded the men from Galankar and Malakorjal.

"Get back, wretches!" shouted Jdanor. "Can't you see my blazon?"

There was a hesitation; then one of the old men, who was wearing a disgustingly filthy long cloak, came forward, pointing to his chest. His tunic was embroidered with a red eye at the center of two overlapping triangles.

"Get back yourself, vassal!" he shouted, in a hoarse voice. "I'm a Housemaster!" Staggering, he repeated: "A Housemaster! Come on, the rest of you! Thrash these fellows for me!"

With a thrust of his heel, Dal threw one of the old drunkards against a wall. Talek's horses kicked, and almost caved in the chest of a second aggressor. As for Jdanor, he had torn the cane out of the hand of the man who had threatened him with it, and was brandishing it over the head of the fallen Housemaster, shouting: "You dare to make use of a title that you're dragging in the mud of the slums!"

A brawl was becoming inevitable when strident sirens sounded, approached at lightning speed, and died out two me-

47

ters away from the from the combatant. Three red cars were blocking the avenue behind them, and six men got out, aiming projectors. Within seconds, there was nothing more than inanimate bodies.

The policemen carried away the aggressors and Jdanor's men together, all plunged into a leaden sleep by the low-power ultrasonics.

When Dal recovered consciousness he was lying on a miserable bunk. The daylight filtering through a little window furnished with bars told him two things: firstly, that he had spent the night in this place—as soon as he woke up he had remembered the details of the quarrel and the intervention of the police—and secondly that the jail in which he was held did not have the slightest element of comfort, not even plaster on the black stone walls.

In fact, he had spent three days there.

He stood up and examined his prison: the bed, the walls, the window and the steel door. There was nothing else.

A nice welcome to the capital! he thought.

What had they done with his companions? Presumably they were locked up in other cells. And the banneret? Would they be giving him special treatment? Of what sort? Better, or even more rigorous?

They must have been watching out for his awakening in some secret manner, for he had no time to ask himself any more questions. The door slid open and a man came in silently. He was dressed in a white jacket and red boots. On his shoulder shone the red sun on a gold background that Dal had always seen on the fronton of the Country House of Galankar: the emblem of the Sopharchy. Bizarrely, the man seemed to hesitate for a fraction of a second; then, as if against his will, he stiffened and gestured to Dal with his hand.

"Stand up!" he said. "You're to be interrogated."

Dal got up, and leaned against the wall momentarily. The inhibition of the brain by the ultrasound left a nauseous vertigo on awakening. The guard was evidently not inhumane. Had

48

the prisoner's youth ameliorated his natural roughness? He supported Dal along the corridor, open to the sky, that gave access to the cells.

"Where are my companions?" Dal stammered, his tongue thick.

"You're to be interrogated separately," the guard said. "But keep quiet—you don't have the right to speak...especially to me."

Dal was beginning to find the guard's attitude odd. "Why not to you?" he said.

"You'll find out later...I hope," the other said, swiftly. "Now, be quiet."

The corridor ended at a black door, which was raised up as they approached. Dal remained on the threshold, unsteadily, while the guard retraced his steps, without saying another word.

"Come forward!" said a voice.

Dal obeyed, with difficulty. The room where he was awaited only had subdued lighting, in the orange part of the spectrum, coming from the ceiling. The prisoner took a few steps, stopped, and made as if to go back. There was a metallic noise. Dal turned round; the door had just fallen shut.

At the back of the room, seated behind a long table, were five men in blue and white robes, framed by four individuals in white capes, with black tunics embroidered with complex blazons. There could be no question of flight. Dal went forward, his tread becoming firmer, until he reached a high-backed chair that stood in isolation between him and the seeming tribunal.

"Sit down," said one of the priests.

Dal went around the armchair and sat down. Immediately, metal hoops closed around his body. He made a movement, quickly suppressed, and waited in silence.

The priest resumed speaking, dryly: "What is your name?"

"Dal Ortog."

"Where have you come from?"

"Galankar."

"By what means?"

"By equus."

"What is your employment?"

"Soldier."

"You're lying."

"I'm not lying. I used to be a herdsman. Lord Jaral Kerr Jaral made me a soldier." Dal felt anger rising within him. "I haven't committed any crime," he added. "Those old drunks…"

"Be quiet," the priest cut in. "the futile brawl of which you speak was certainly the reason for your arrest, but not for your retention in the cells." He fell silent, without taking his eyes off Dal, then continued: "You have to answer for a serious crime, and complicity in a large number of crimes."

Dal frowned, but made no reply.

"That crime is a sacrilegious attitude in the Temple of Galankar. The other crimes are the murders of a priest, three Housemasters and their men. Confess your guilt, and you will only be punished with rapid death."

Dal felt his face grow cold. "I shall admit to nothing," he said. "Some wretched informer has distorted the truth. My attitude in the Temple could not have been different in confrontation with my father's death, and the annihilation of our pursuers was merely the result of their obstinate determination to destroy us. To swear an oath to work for my race cannot constitute a sacrilege, and to defend yourself against someone who is trying to kill you is not a crime."

"You admit the facts, then."

"Not in the manner in which you have presented them."

The priest pressed a button embedded in the table. Dal uttered a cry of pain; an electric current had just passed through the metal hoops imprisoning his neck and wrists.

"Do you admit the facts?"

"No, not in the manner…"

Dal screamed. The current lasted a little longer.

"Do you confess?"

With sweat on his forehead, Dal tried to move his tongue, which was contorted by a painful cramp. He uttered a few scarcely-intelligible words: "You'll never make me confess that..." The remainder was lost in a long scream of pain.

As if for the depths of a nightmare, Dal heard a din from the door behind him, and then a commanding voice which said: "Stop! By the authority of the Sopharchy, I, Karel Arz Karel, Knight-Navigator of Lassenia, call a halt to this trial!"

The metal hoops were opened. Dall strove to remain conscious. Soon, he could see the long table and his torturers clearly. The priests and noblemen, standing up and waving their arms, were gathered in front of a man of athletic build, in a steel-grey costume. Dal was looking at him from an oblique angle, and could not quite make out the design he bore on his breast. While speaking in a dry voice, the newcomer moved slightly, and Dal recognized a red sun horizontally barred with a white stripe.

"He's a criminal!" yelped a priest, above the furious voices of the noblemen, who were replying all at once to the Sopharchy's emissary.

"Be silent," said the Navigator, coldly, "or I shall have the room cleared."

Turning round, with difficulty, Dal saw a compact phalanx of men standing behind him. They were clad in similar costumes, with a steely gleam, wearing metallic helmets equipped with antennae. Each shoulder bore the red sun with the white stripe. Their faces were expressionless, save for a hint of scorn. These men did not seem to be taking matters lightly, any more than their leader. Beside them, the Housemaster's guards that he had provided for Dal's protection, and bannerets' soldiers, all stood like statues.

Silence gradually fell. The members of the tribunal were visibly intimidated. Dal was hardly any more tranquil.

"First of all," said Karel Arz, with increasing iciness, "a guard had to alert the Palace in order for the Sopharchy to discover the conditions under which a trial had begun here, without their being informed. The Sopharchy does not approve of rudeness, much less of premature initiatives."

Murmurs were heard.

"Shut up!" said the Navigator, without raising his voice. "In the second place, an inquiry has been going on for three days at the Palace with regard to the arrival of this company. It has revealed that your witnesses made contact with you six days ago, when they travelled to Lassenia by helix. There were two of them, and their names are Rog Moniz Rog and Erarht Melej Erarhrt. Both are traitors and murderers, and a space squadron left for their refuge in the early hours of this morning, with orders to bring them back, dead or alive."

Cries of indignation broke out. The Knight made a gesture, and his entire phalanx took one step forward, without making a sound. The cries died away.

"The Sopharchy," the Navigator continued, calmly, "is willing to believe that these two rebels have deceived you, on condition that you do not persist in your errors. If not, it will have the painful obligation of exiling all the members of the tribunal to Ganymede."

He stopped speaking. A pregnant silence ensued. The faces of the priests and the City Housemasters were contorted with fury.

"Oh, I forgot," said Karel Arz. "The Sopharchy has already forbidden the use of this chair. They observe with regret that their orders have not been respected, and they have decided to have them carried out by my men. Stand up, Dal Ortog."

Dal got to his feet unsteadily, his throat dry but his eyes shining with joy. Immediately, the helmeted guardsmen surrounded the chair. They had slender cylinders in their hands, each as long as a finger. Defeated, the tribunal looked on.

The instrument of torture disappeared in a blue-tinted halo. At that horrible sight, two priests fainted and collapsed, along with a Housemaster. Dal leapt backwards with a cry of terror. Even Karel Arz went pale. Several guardsmen trembled.

"Follow us, Dal Ortog," said the Navigator, finally.

Dal, his legs shaky, accompanied Karel Arz and his men. The door fell shut behind them.

In the orange light, the members of the tribunal began to moan fearfully.

Flanked by the Knight-Navigator's guards, Dal tried to compose his thoughts, but could not do it. Like all those who had witnessed the disintegration of the torture-chair, he remained frozen with fear. Actually, the operation was very similar to the atomization of corpses, but it had been much more rapid, and, more importantly, the halo that it had produced was irresistibly reminiscent of that of the Venusian death.

Eventually, he dared to say to a guard: "It's frightful. So you're making use of the weapons of the Blue War! I thought they were reserved for the defense of astroports."

The guard did not reply, but Karel Arz had heard. He turned to Dal. His was the brown face of a Spaceman, tanned by short-wave radiation. "You've been able to observe at your own cost how much evidence the clergy and Terran nobility presents of insubordination. Their audacity is growing every day, and the Sopharchy has been forced to the extremity of inspiring terror, in order to avoid a revolt showing their strength in order to avoid having to make use of it.

Dal considered these words. They had just reached an iron staircase that led to the gallery of an interior courtyard, when the white-clad guard to whom Dal had spoken after waking up appeared and came over to Karel Arz.

"Lord," he said, "I'd like to make a request of the Sopharchy. If I remain attached to the Relegation unit, my death will not be long delayed. I'd like to be transferred to another post, and I'd like to leave immediately."

Arz looked at him, and then observed: "Your uniform indicates that you're under the direct orders of the Sopharchy. I suppose that it was you who warned them what was happening here. Join my men."

"Thank you, Lord!" said the guard, with a sigh of relief.

The troop went down the staircase. In the courtyard, Dal asked the Knight in his turn: "What will happen to my companions?"

"They'll be set free," said Arz.

"Will I see them again?"

"I don't think so."

Dal fell silent, disappointed and vaguely anxious as to his own fate. The Sopharchy's means of communication seemed to be considerable, since they had been informed of everything concerning Dal and the massacre at Majorkal within three days. Might he be about to fall out of the frying-pan into the fire? The Palace must be equally well-informed bout the annihilation of the Housemasters of Galankar. If Jdanor and his men were to be set free, and Dal had been snatched away from the vengeance of the Priests and Housemasters, why did the Navigator doubt that he would see them again? What sort of liberation was this, after all?

Dal watched Karel Arz surreptitiously. So this was one of the Knights whose renown extended everywhere? They obviously corresponded fairly closely with the idea that people had of them.

Six red cars were lined up in the interior courtyard. A policeman in a black uniform was standing next to each of them. Karel Arz's men climbed into five vehicles, and Dal was placed in the last with the white-clad guardsman. The Navigator murmured something to the policeman, who made the sign of protection and sat down at the controls. He moved off after the others, and turned in the opposite direction once they had emerged from the gateway.

In the car, the young provincial marveled silently at the comfort. He looked at the pilot; the controls were reduced to a single lever, which served as a steering-mechanism, an accelerator and a brake according to its position. The guard, sitting in the back with Dal, did not move and did not say a word. The pilot was also silent.

Dal was waiting impatiently to find out where they were bound when a curious phenomenon drew an exclamation from him: the vehicle changed color. While passing down a deserted side-street, it had suddenly turned grey—an anonymous grey. Dal suspected that the colour of the bodywork was due to a special lighting system hidden in the very substance of the vehicle: a different fluorescence, according to the frequency of certain waves emitted from the dashboard.

The policeman drew the control lever toward his body, and the car stopped smoothly. He turned to Dal.

"Get out, and continue in the same direction until you reach a shop situated on your right," he said in a monotonous voice. "It has a sign on which you'll read the word *Paleos*. Go inside—someone's waiting for you." He fell silent, and Dal hastened to obey.

The car set off again with an infernal acceleration. Beneath the dome, the white-clad guard turned round. Dal started walking, without having any inkling as to the reason for the bizarre instructions.

For the first time, he found himself in a relatively busy part of the city in broad daylight, and one surprise followed another. He was walking on a pavement only slightly raised above the level of the roadway, where city-dwellers dressed in multicoloured tunics, with short-cropped hair, were passing in both directions. The women, in ample dresses or very short tunics, wore their hair quite long. All of them seemed strange to Dal, for the fashions of the big city bore only a remote resemblance to those of the villages.

After a brief interval, he observed that every kind of profession had a preference for a particular color—a preference, that is, unless it was compulsory. He noticed this while crossing over a side-street where shiny machines were digging up the pavement in order to install a moving walkway; the workmen who were operating the machines were all dressed in green—a green one-piece garment with no emblem. In the crowd, there was almost no one to be seen who wore a coat of arms on his breast, except for the occasional soldier whose shoulder was decorated with the red sun of the Sopharchy. The crowd in front of him was composed of civil servants, techni-

55

cians, workmen and salesmen. Everything was as peaceful as in the time of the Historic Gulf.

Dal cut across other streets that were much busier, and thought about the number of people who must live in Lassenia. Audio-visual education spoke of 24 to 26 millions. Lassenia represented a whole universe to a young herdsman from Galankar—a village that scarcely had 1000 inhabitants.

Sometimes, a passer-by darted a curious glance at the armorial shield of Galgo Rank that Dal still wore on his shoulder. Others looked at his dirty and ragged jerkin with disdain. Three young girls turned to look at him, and burst out laughing.

Be careful! Dal instructed himself. *Given the precautions with which the Knight has surrounded the rendezvous that's been arranged for me, I shouldn't allow myself to be noticed...but the poor banneret's accursed blazon is enough to attract attention. I should have ripped off the epaulette on which it's embroidered. Where can this shop be hiding?*

He had to cross over the bridge that spanned the river Senia before he saw the metal plate bearing the name *Paleos* oscillating above the heads of the crowd. He darted a furtive glance behind him. No one seemed to be particularly interested in what he was doing. Rapidly, he opened the door, went in and closed it behind him. The batten was presumably carefully soundproofed, because the noise of the street suddenly died away, as if the entire city had been transported on to the plateau that overlooked it.

Dal looked around in amazement. There was a yellowish light, produced by electric bulbs covered with little cones of light fabric. Thoughtfully, Dal recalled optical illustrations of archeological expeditions or extra-solarian technology. The light illuminated curious objects, the majority of which remained devoid of significance so far as Dal was concerned. His gaze was primarily held by an assembly hanging on the wall, composed of three tubular triangles and two circles provided with a large number of radii, all in rusty metal. He wondered whether it came from a distant planet or was of earthly origin. He thought about traders from other worlds; he had not yet seen one—but they mostly stayed in the business district, the closet to the astroport.

As he was examining a bronze statuette representing a female nude, who had an electric light-socket on her head, he heard a slight scraping noise behind him and turned round.

She was also a woman, but a living one—or, rather, a girl of Dal's own age. She was dressed in a short tunic, which left her bronzed arms bare. Her black hair extended down to her waist. "Dal Ortog?" she said.

Dal did not reply immediately; he was admiring her appearance, especially the green eyes that were fixed on him. "Yes," he said, finally. "I was sent by…"

"Shh!" She put a finger to her lips, and darted a suspicious glance toward the door. "I know," she said. "Follow me."

Dal darted another rapid glance around the marvelous trivia with which the shop was filled, and followed the girl into a small dark room at the back of the shop. The same archaic lighting rendered the ambience mysterious, and the tattered red velvet curtains extended over the walls added to its singular character.

The young woman showed Dal to a low couch upholstered in an incredibly ancient fabric. Above the couch, attached to the curtains, was a crown of Martian emeralds. Dal sat down; his hostess remained standing in front of him.

"My name is Kalla," she said. "Housemaster Jaral Kerr was a good friend of my father." She paused, fixed her gaze on the crown of emeralds, and then continued: "My father is a Sopharch."

Dal got up, painfully. He was astonished by this declaration. "Forgive me," he said, for remaining seated in your presence. Even if you were not so highly born, in fact, I…"

"Never mind," she said, with a smile. "I see that some herdsmen are not content to become soldiers—it's also necessary for them to adopt the courtesy of language and manners by which the fops at the Palace measure their worth…"

Dal fell silent, full of confusion.

"I'm nor reproaching you for it," she added, softly, "for I can tell that you're a weightier individual than those marionettes."

Dal's confusion increased. To cap it all, she had just at down in her turn, and drew him down next to her by his wrist.

"Let's talk seriously," Kalla said. "I need to tell you a few things." She paused momentarily for though. The noise of the city reached them through the walls like an infinitely distant murmur. "First of all," she said. "Know that the Council has been told what happened in Galankar, thanks to Jaral Kerr, who had the use of a personal optiphone channel linked to the Palace. As for the battle of Malakorjal and he Housemaster's murder, the enquiry carried out three days ago enabled us to obtain numerous details of it. For the first time, I saw my father carried away by anger. These events are not unconnected with the Council's decision to arm the Knights with the Blue Weapon."

Dal listened meekly. He understood that he had been correct when he had declared that Jaral Kerr was continuing to protect them after his death.

"The Housemaster," she continued, "went so far as to affirm that you were the only one, among the people of Galankar, who has stood up against the general mood of resignation for several years. He claims that you suddenly infused him with young blood by your rebellious attitude."

Dal wanted to sink into the ground.

"The Sopharchy was, therefore," Kalla concluded, "informed of your coming. It was decided not to send you any reinforcements, in order that you might be hardened to strife, in view of the task that had been reserved for you. My father deeply regretted that decision when he learned that his friend had been killed by traitors."

There was a long silence; then Dal tried to restore more accurate proportions to the part of the speech that had offended his modesty. "It's because my father had just died," he said. "I'd never thought before of making a stand against the customs…"

She smiled. "Many young men in the same situation would have kept their heads down," she declared. "It doesn't matter. My father and the entire Council are nurturing grand plans with regard to you. That's why you're here—which is to say, in a place better protected from spies than the mot secret rooms in the Palace."

Dal looked at Kalla. He felt as if he were moving through a dream. "What about my companions?" he said.

"We'll know before the day is out what is to become of them."

She got up and opened an ancient item of furniture, a triangular chest of drawers encrusted with reptilian scales, which had been fashionable a hundred years before. She took out a folded garment, which she handed to him.

"This is one of the radiation-proof suits used at the University during practical sessions in physics," she said. "It will provide you with safe conduct, for the students and the professors are allowed access anywhere. It will forestall any indiscreet questions—which is important, for you must prepare yourself for certain trials that would confound any commoner and the majority of noblemen. University people form a special caste. It's not unusual to encounter them in the most unexpected paces, or to see them taking part in activities for which they're unsuited."

Dal spread out the suit on the couch, while Kalla continued in a falsely-detached tone: "Provided that you still retain the same enthusiasm to serve the cause of Humankind."

He straightened up. "I've never been more determined," he said, in a rather uncertain tone.

Chapter Three

"Then the seekers of the impossible distinguished themselves, and among them, one who shirked none of the direst perils, one who exchanged the silence of his humble condition for dazzling renown..."
Song of the Perfecti
Psalm IX, Verse 3

The sky of flame shaped the arena, and those whom fate had designated prepared themselves for the tournament. An immense murmur ran through the terraces, where more than two thousand spectators oriented their teleoptic screens, feverishly debating the respective chances of various champions.

Constructed on the edge of the plateau, facing the apron of the astroport, which they separated from the profound valley of the Senia, the titanic arenas overlooked the city. The crowd that had flocked into them in the early hours of the day was composed of privileged individuals, the remainder of the population following the Games by optiphone. That method of transmitting sound and images was derived from the ancient three-dimensional color television, considerably simplified.

On the official platforms the 12 red-robed Sopharchs had taken their places. They could be seen from a long way off, thanks to the bright hue of their clothing, which they alone could wear among men—although a few women had chosen the same shade for their dresses or tunics; but they generally only attracted ridicule, even though it was the color of prestige itself.

On the edge of the arena, in front of the platforms, a large metal canopy enameled in blue and gold protected the young men who were about to enter the lists from the blazing sun. It was time for the fourth bout, and it was the turn of Dal Ortog, the ultimate hope of the Sopharchy.

Since the singular conversation that he had had in the back of the antique shop, Dal had seen Kalla, the daughter of Sopharch Karella, twice more—only twice, in the course of a month dedicated to an intense cultivation of body and mind, and already the young Lassenian woman occupied all his thoughts. In the hardest hours of training, in the midst of the most complex hypnagogic dreams, the image of Kalla arose within him. Her presence multiplied the efforts that he had to accomplish, while giving them a greater justification.

Dal had no shortage of reasons, however, for putting everything into his work, in view of the victory to be obtained. In addition to a certain weakness that Kalla had shown in his respect, the proposition that had been put to him exceeded his wildest hopes: he had been given to understand that, if he did not disappoint the confidence that had been placed in him, it would not be impossible that he would be able to take part in an Expedition. Furthermore, in the course of the tournament he would be the Sopharchy's final candidate—a signal honor, greater still when one understood the occult significance afforded to the Jousts.

By means of these periodic tourneys, the Sopharchy, whose authority was only really effective over the Navigators, attempted to solidify their influence over the people by the methods of prestige, confronting in the lists the factions of the Upper and Lower Nobility, as well as those of the Clergy. If the champion of a Housemaster were defeated, the title itself was tainted in the eyes of the people, while the victory of the Sopharchy's candidate elevated itself over them.

Every contest comprised several distinct trials, from which it was necessary to emerge victorious in order to be admitted to face an opposing champion. Thus, by successive elimination, an overall victor emerged, who was presented, amid great pomp, with the Oriflamme of the Games. The honor granted to Dal Ortog was something remarkably unusual, when one considered the importance that the Sopharchy attached to the worth of their champion.

Dal was thinking about precisely that importance, and that honor. He thought about it all the more because he did not feel that he was in the requisite physical condition or possessed of the desired mental agility. It seemed to him that his strength and lucidity had suddenly been stolen away, at the very moment when he had the greatest need of them.

The fanfare of Sonorous Structures flooded the air. It was the song of metal and stone, rockfalls and gongs, in a pit through which a furious wind was blowing, over an enormous rustling like an ocean swell. A gigantic ovation mingled with the fanfares, and spread from the tops of the terraces to the center of the arena as Dal Ortog advanced. A few paces, and he was visible to everyone; his slender silhouette stood out against the white soil of the circus, for he was wearing a garment similar to that of Knights. His grey costume with a metallic sheen was ornamented on the breast with the red sun of the Sopharchy.

Originally, the trials had had a purely Olympian character, but the nobility had gradually succeeded in rendering them dangerous, sometimes even ferocious. They had introduced combats between beasts and humans, and had reduced the armaments of the latter to the minimum. They had added duels between champions which often terminated in the death of one of the adversaries. Similarly, a candidate was sometimes provided with such awkward materials that he had every chance of being killed. The Sopharchy had never been able to inhibit murderous turn that the Games had taken. On the contrary, it had often been necessary for them to increase it further, in order not to lose face and give the impression of a power on the wane. That was why Dal was advancing at a measured pace toward what might be his own death.

He replied to the ovation by shaping his arms into a cross and turning around slowly, as custom demanded. While he accomplished this courteous rite, he darted a glance at the distant terraces, as if he might be able to recognize a few individual faces in that human ocean....those of his companions from Galankar. He had been told, 48 hours after his liberation, that

62

all of them had been similarly set free, but that only one of them had undertaken the preparations for the Games. The others had immediately bee distributed to various employments in the city; some had been judged worthy of undertaking technical studies. Dal thought about those who had already crossed his path in his as-yet-brief existence, and a melancholy overtook him on finding himself so far removed from the witnesses and companions of his new life: the only people in the enormous city who had originated from his own village. Even the men from Malakorjal had been closer to him and more familiar than the foreign and anonymous population, accustomed to a way of life so different from the one he had known.

He bowed toward the rank of Sopharchs, especially toward Karella.

Torol Karella was one of the oldest; he was nearing the age of seventy, and did not know whether death awaited him in the course of the next few weeks. Having been prepared for his annihilation for a long time, he remained lucid, his mind entirely devoted to the interests of the human race. He smiled at Dal Ortog.

"We are putting our trust in you," he said. "Show yourself worthy of that trust, and bear the emblem of the Great Council bravely."

Dal bowed again, then raised his eyes once more toward the Sopharch's bald head and sharp-featured, deeply-wrinkled face.

"God will come to my aid..." he said.

Torol Karella's smile was a trifle ironic. "May it be thus," he approved, darting a rapid glance at one of the priests sitting motionless at the far end of the platform.

Dal had already had dealings with the priests of the Palace. Chosen by the Sopharchy, they represented the most effective tendency of the Clergy. Mostly young, they did not consider the efforts of explorers and laboratory workers as heresy. They constituted a kind of bond, made of warmth and confidence. Some of them had even taken part in Expeditions. If Torol Karella had permitted himself a skeptical smile with respect to the Divinity, it was because he placed more hope in laboratory work than in metaphysical research—and also because, in spite of the efforts of the Council, the Palace Clergy was not entirely loyalist. Priests of a Manichean stripe had already infiltrated it, and the ravages they contrived were observable on a daily basis.

"One moment," Karella added, as Dal made as if to step back. "You will only have two champions to fight. The first has already triumphed over all his adversaries in trials of attack and defense with naked weapons, and in those of skill in the handling of weapons. The second, a specialist in sensory acuity and intellectual culture, has not yet fought. Do you feel sufficiently well-prepared to face masters of such different disciplines? I would be desolate to lose a man whom my friend Jaral Kerr thought worthy of distinction from others…"

"I shall do my best," said Dal, growing impatient with these preliminary speeches.

"Go," said the Sopharch, simply, addressing the sign of protection to him.

Three waves of acclamation greeted the combatants. Dal, the Sopharchy's candidate, had been the only one standing in the shadow of the canopy. His two adversaries entered the arena from different points, and Dal could not make out their features from so far away, for the circus was immense.

Two oriflammes rose simultaneously along a mast placed in the center of the arena. One bore the sun of the Sopharchy on a grey background, the other a strange blazon. Dal used his hand to shield his eyes in order to make out the backcloth and figures in the dazzling light. Standing out against a background of green and gold stripes was a silver hand with fingernails curled like claws. The crenellations that surmounted the figure and its two sections showed that they were the arms of a Housemaster—probably a Lassenian nobleman, a flag-bearer of the turbulent caste spurred on by the most fanatical elements of the Central Temple. Dal was astonished once again at having been permitted to fight a nobleman; the Sopharchy's champions were almost all recruited from the ranks of the Knights. The Council had doubtless used all its authority to make a nobleman agree to meet an obscure provincial without a title.

One of the men in the distance began to move forward. Dal advanced to meet him, while a profound silence was established in the crowd of spectators.

Not far from the mast with the oriflammes a deep ditch opened up in the ground of the circus, over which a metal grille had been fixed, whose criss-cross bars were about a meter apart. The two adversaries stopped on either side of this ditch, seven or eight meters apart. Dark forms were moving in the depths of the pit, and a deep growling was frequently audible.

"Housemaster Gorl Amoktar Gorl of Lassenia!" cried the other man. His voice, captured by hidden recorders, thundered along the terraces.

"Dal Ortog of Galankar!" Dal shouted in response. He studied the Housemaster. The other was a man of tall stature, with powerful shoulders and heavy features. He wore a gaudy golden tunic embroidered with his arms, which allowed a sight of his legs, muscular but a trifle short. The man looked Dal up and down with scornful arrogance.

The fanfare of Sonorous Structures burst forth, then died away. It was followed by a few words pronounced by a herald from the roof of the official platform.

"In this pit are four famished hybrids!" the herald cried. "Each of the two combatants will endeavor to throw the other into it!"

Dal felt his heart beat more rapidly. He peered into the depths of the ditch and saw a scaly beast with six legs, armed with claws, which fixed him with its scintillating eyes and opened its enormous mouth. Other monsters were stirring in the gloom, from which a noxious stink emerged.

Gorl Amoktar burst out laughing and set his foot on the bar nearest to him. Dal did likewise. His tongue was dry and his hands were icy.

In a profound silence, the man and the adolescent advanced toward one another, moving their feet from bar to bar. In the depths of the pit the growling resumed, louder than before. Dal mastered the tremor that had gripped him.

They were face to face, two meters apart. One more step, and it was a hand-to-hand struggle in precarious equilibrium, in which a fall....

"Come on, coward—son of a wretch!" cried Amoktar.

Dal thought about his father. He became livid, and placed a foot on the bar that separated them. Gorl threw himself forward and delivered a brutal punch to the chest that sent Dal reeling backwards. Dal, winded, turned as he stumbled, hanging on to the intersection of two bars. Carried forward by his momentum, Gorl also vacillated, but he remained upright and burst out laughing again. Hatred and scorn were legible in his brutal features.

Dal recovered his breath, though. Slowly, he got back to his feet on the intersecting bars, watching his adversary all the while. *It's essential that he doesn't lay a hand on me*, he thought, rapidly, *or I'm dead. He weighs half as much again as I do, and is three times as strong.*

Gorl leapt from one bar to another and threw a punch. Dal avoided it with a feint, but his movement caused him to lose his balance again. He fell, missed one bar but seized another in mid-air and remained suspended by one hand over the pit. The clicking of jaws resounded, level with his heels, at the same time as Gorl advanced a foot to crush his fingers.

With an agile swinging movement, however, Dal had already grabbed a bar with his other hand, released the first to ensure his leverage, pulled himself up and recovered a kneeling position on an intersection. A tempest of enthusiastic howls was unleashed.

"Vile insect!" yelled Gorl, amid the tumult. "I'll throw you to the hybrids!" He bounded from one bar to another—but Dal, repeating the maneuver that he had just performed, let himself fall, while holding on to the metal and flexing his legs to keep them out of range of the beasts. At the same time, and with the same pendulum swing, he reached a position beneath Gorl' feet, seized him by an ankle, dislodged the foot and re-established himself a meter away.

Amoktar fell, with an anguished howl, but he too caught hold and clung on. Dal was on him before the Housemaster had time to change his grip. It seemed unsporting to crush the other's fingers beneath his heel, but the other had not hesitated to do so, and had been intent on throwing him to the hybrids. He struck.

Amoktar had solid and muscular fingers. He did not lose his grip, and escaped Dal's stamping feet, re-establishing himself two meters away. They both paused momentarily to draw breath. The crowd was rapt.

Gorl's rage had something bestial about it. He launched himself at Dal again—who drew him towards him this time by seizing one of the flaps of his gaudy tunic. Impelled by his momentum, Gorl fell, and Dal—who had made a bridge between one bar and the next, accompanied his fall with a thrust of the heel to the black of the neck.

A hideous scene unfolded in the depths of the ditch. Dal, white and trembling, came back from bar to bar to the edge, in the midst of hysterical acclamations.

Slowly, Amoktar's blazon descended the flagpole, while a black pennant rose up. Dal straightened up, saluting the crowd. *In fact*, he thought, *it's that sadistic mob which constrains the Sopharchy to make the games so ferocious*. Cries of fury were emitted from the terraces where the most sumptuous costumes were displayed, but they were almost entirely drowned out by the howls of joy. Dal turned to the official platform and bowed.

Gradually, silence fell. One of the Sopharchy's White Guardsmen was detached and came toward Dal, at the same time as a man advanced whose appearance caused the former herdsman to frown. As the silhouette came closer in the blaze of noon, Dal recognized the emblem embroidered on his tunic: a plunging silver eagle on a cross of gold.

"Sar Jdanor!" he murmured, nonplussed.

The fanfare burst forth. For the second time, the herald's voice resounded.

"Dal Ortog is the victor in the trial of strength and agility," he cried. "He will now fight Banneret Sar Jdanor Sar of Galankar, champion of the Temple, replacing Housemaster Gorl Anoktar Gorl, by God's will!"

Sar approached.

"So it's you, Lord," said Dal, dully, "who takes up arms against the Sopharchy! You, Jaral Kerr Jaral's banneret!"

Sar did not defend himself with any arrogance or mocking laughter. "I understand your astonishment, herdsman," he said. "I was freed the day after you and installed myself, as I had intended, in the Foundation of Bannererts. I met a priest of great wisdom there, who knows that evil is rooted within us and that the human race is vermin within the galaxy. I'm now convinced that to struggle against its extinction is to offend God. Rather divine oblivion than a second Blue War."

Dal listened, bewildered. He remained silent momentarily, but eventually replied: "If that's your conviction, defend it."

The White Guardsman led them to two poles about ten meters high, terminated by narrow platforms. They were separated by a distance of fifty meters, and on each platform a copper vessel was releasing a spiral of smoke.

The Guardsman gave each of them a bow and three arrows. "You must shoot flaming arrows," he said. "The bitumen burning up there will permit you to do that. But of one of you is only wounded, the game will be terminated, to the advantage of the other. He drew away.

"I shall try not to kill you, herdsman," said Sar, with a protective smile.

"I give you the same assurance," Dal replied, with a respectful smile.

They climbed the masts amid an attentive silence.

Between the ages of six and twelve, Dal's principal plaything had been a Mlol bow similar to the one he had just been given. Very probably, Jdanor had only been firing a bow since a much more recent date. He must have learned how to handle the primitive weapon during his training period.

They reached their respective platforms at the same time and plunged an arrow into the flaming bitumen. Dal took rapid aim and attempted to hit Sar in the shoulder rather than the leg, in order to maximize the chance of sparing him a fall. His arrow had scarcely departed when a brand arrived with a hiss, heading straight for his chest. He ducked with lightning rapidity. The arrow went past, level with his head. To judge by the trajectory, he would have received it in the throat or at the top of a lung.

Amazed, he fixed his gaze on Jdanor, whose shoulder had been grazed by the projectile that the herdsman had dreaded embedding in his flesh. The banneret plunged a second arrow into the bitumen and straightened up, shouting: "You're vermin, like all the rest, and the best moment for you to die will be the soonest!"

Dal nearly fell from the height of his platform avoiding the second arrow, which he would have received in the abdomen. He drew his blow and fired with a single movement. In the distance, Sar collapsed, with a flaming arrow in his heart. His body remained on the platform for a moment, then rolled off and fell to the floor of the arena.

Stunned and distressed, Dal did not hear the acclamations or the cries of rage.

He was overcome by a great bitterness. Of all those who had left Galankar, pursuers and pursued, there remained only a handful of warriors, who had been incorporated into the Lassenian Guard. The others were dead, and Galankar was condemned to destruction. Dal had contributed to those murders himself. Of all the people from Malakorjal, only a few men remained. Dal remembered Bor Talek, and regretted never having seen him again. He felt that he was now an exile, alone in the world, his hands already steeped in blood.

White Guardsmen came to take Sar Jdanor's body away. Dal, rooted to the spot, watched the banneret's arms slowly descending the central mast. He also followed the long ascent of the black pennant. The red sun of the Sopharchy now floated between two black flames, all the blacker for fluttering in the bright light.

The memory of Kallla made the victor shudder. He threw down his bow and went down rapidly to the bloody floor of the circus.

After the fanfares, the herald continued his announcements.

"Dal Ortog, vanquisher of Sar Jdanor Sar, will meet, for the trial of sensory acuity..." He fell silent, and waited for the oriflamme to mount the central mast. From afar, Dal saw the banner, and the cotises on a field of ermine: an ancient lineage. The herald resumed: "...will meet Housemaster-Baron Zoltan Charles Henderson de Nancy."

At the announcement of these titles and these extraordinary names a stupefied silence descended upon the arena.

The herald continued: "The Housemaster-Baron is one of the very rare heirs of those noble families whose origins go back far beyond the Blue War, more than 3000 years..."

He was interrupted by an ocean of acclamations, in the midst of which a few ironic or malicious cries of "Liar!" and "Buffoon!" were almost inaudible.

On the first row of the terraces, a Housemaster in a silver robe shrugged his shoulders. He was from a very old family ennobled immediately after the Blue War—two centuries of true nobility!

Dal shared the general astonishment. The White Guardsman returned with a tall, thin man who wore a thin line of black hair above his lips. *A moustache!* Dal thought. *A primitive fashion...the man is some kind of Mlol. I'll have to be wary of him.*

The Housemaster-Baron bowed slightly to Dal, with a wry smile. "Delighted to meet you," he said.

Dal remained silent.

"Yes, I know," his singular adversary went on. "Our era only uses the formal version of *you* in the plural. Don't take offence—just remember that I'm very *old Earth*."

"You've….read many old books," said Dal, his tongue half-paralyzed, and using the informal version of *you*. "Books from Titan…"

The other smiled again, in a disquieting fashion. "And many others," he said, by way of completion.

Dal recovered his aplomb. "If you're so knowledgeable in archaeology, why are you fighting the Sopharchy?"

"Oh, I don't know what to say. Tradition, perhaps."

The guard interrupted rudely. "You're not here to engage in conversation but in competition," he said, dryly.

The Housemaster-Baron raised his eyebrows. "All right, my friend, all right," he said, in a reedy voice. "We'll take due note of your admonition."

Dal was becoming increasingly wary—but the fanfares sounded again, and the herald resumed his announcements.

"As you all know," he cried—and his voice was carried to the ear of every spectator—"the trial of sensory acuity takes place in the labyrinth that you see over there. According to his position in relation to the exit, the candidate will find himself between wall of greater of lesser distance from one another, and he will hear a sound of higher or lower pitch. The separation of the walls will increase in a scarcely-perceptible manner, as will the frequency of the vibrations. The labyrinth is provided with a roof that renders it airtight, and its atmosphere contains a toxic gas that will become mortal by accumulation in the blood. In order to be victorious, it is necessary to emerge from the labyrinth in less than fourteen minutes—a duration that varies, according to the individual, between twelve and sixteen minutes; if not, one remains there. It is also necessary to emerge first. There are several routes, more or less dangerous because they vary in distance."

Dal darted a glance at the standard with the paired slanting stripes of its cotises.

"After you, if you please," said the Housemaster-Baron, slightly slyly.

Dal looked him up and down, and then remembered that he was, after all, dealing with a nobleman. His conditioning took over. "After you, Lord," he said.

All the way across the arena that bizarre individual talked, in a precious fashion, and Dal did not understand half of what he said. As they arrived at the doorway of the large, flat building, he not longer had the impression of being beside an adversary. The encounter had something dreamlike about it. Dal hardened himself. He had need of all the means at his disposal, and this clown with the unpronounceable name and ridiculous title, this living fossil, seemed prodigiously self-assured.

It was not until they were at the entrance to the labyrinth that Dal noticed the Housemaster-Baron's clothes. He had seen similar ones in the course of audiovisual education. That outfit surely dated back to the 21st century…

His mind blank, Dal went into the labyrinth after the anachronism.

Zoltan quickly turned a corner that took him out of Dal's sight. In the white light that reigned there, the herdsman was aware of the separation of the walls. A faint sound, very high-pitched, seemed to saturate the corridors. Dal went forward, taking one corridor after another, retraced his steps and took yet another, and hurried on.

The deadly gas affected the mind and troubled perception, which made the test even more uncomfortable and even more perilous. Dal though he could see the walls drawing in, when they had been diverging a moment before, without having branched. As for the sound, it seemed to be varying constantly. Dal summoned up his keenest attention, and turned another corner.

He was now advancing through a luminous mist, and hallucinatory images were appearing at every step, while the high-pitched sound changed its frequency strangely. Dal hung on desperately to his visual and auditory sensations, the only things that could save him. Among the data they furnished, however, he had to perform a triage, and concentrate his waning attention on the useful elements. The labyrinth was a clever trap from which it seemed impossible to escape.

Dal moved through the light wispy mist, from which the impalpable form of a monstrous hybrid sometimes emerged, born of the wandering of his mind, poisoned by the deadly vapor. At first, he was able to recognize their artificial character by grasping their hallucinatory nature—especially because the forms were modified with every passing moment and often appeared in such dimensions that that could not really be contained within the corridor he was following.

Soon, though, they were of a volume compatible with the space into which Dal was advancing, and their boundaries became more precise and stable. At the same time, false auditory images, initially heterogeneous and incoherent—the sound of distant voices, insulting words whispered in his ear, fanfares deformed by an imaginary journey over a sheet of water—became narrowly accommodated to the visual hallucinations, enhancing them and conferring a terrible plausibility upon them. The monsters disappeared, and Dal saw his father coming to meet him, accompanied by Jaral Kerr.

He stopped, petrified. In the tumult of his disorderly thoughts, antique beliefs surged forth again, ancient terrors of the time when humans believed in ghosts. He struggled, with his last remaining strength, against an almost irresistible desire to retrace his steps. He conquered it, and went on. The two phantoms disappeared into the walls of the labyrinth—but there was soon a sequence of items of advice murmuring in his ears, and inside his head.

"Take that corridor there, to the left. You can clearly see that its walls are further apart than those of the corridor along which you're walking!"

Dal examined the corridor rapidly. Was it wider or not? It seemed identical—but no; it was wider…

"Wider," said the voice. "Obviously wider."

Dal went into it, and had the impression that the faint sound dropped an octave. He went back. The sound did not change. Disorientated, started forwards again, and observed that his ears were playing multiple tricks, as were his eyes. He paused, breathless, with sweat on his brow. How long had he been in the labyrinth? Eight minutes? Ten? The moment was approaching when he would slowly topple, along the wall, insidiously asphyxiated by the attenuated gas that had been mixed into the atmosphere. Never again would he see the color of the sky. He would never be able devote himself to the struggle to save the human race. He would never see Kalla again, with her eyes like black lakes and her hair inundated with the most subtle Martian perfumes.

Tottering, Dal turned into a corridor visibly wider that the one he had been following. A few meters away, a thin man leaning against the wall watched him approach. He swayed slowly to keep his balance, and looked at Dal lifelessly. Beside him, the corridor described a sharp bend, which ended in a doorway.

"I was 15 seconds ahead of you," said Zoltan, thickly. "I tried to turn back to help you, but I can't move from here."

Amazed and admiring, Dalm summoned the last vestiges of his strength in order to support Zoltan, draw him away from the wall and help him to reach the door of the labyrinth.

They collapsed, one atop the other, in the bright sunlight.

The acclamations made the ground shake. The unleashed fanfares increased the din, which was reminiscent of a storm. In the open air, the two "adversaries" recovered consciousness.

"Don't breathe a word of this," Zoltan murmured rapidly to Dal, on seeing the White Guardsmen approaching. "It's forbidden to help one another. I must say…"

He broke off. Dal got to his feet, painfully. *Either he told the truth in the labyrinth,* he thought, *and I'm dealing with an exceptional individual...or, having arrived at the exit before me, but more exhausted than I was, he told me a lie in order that I would help him get out. One or the other.*

In the same way, the advice he had just been given could be interpreted in to ways. At any rate, Dad decided to follow it.

"How is it that you came out together?" asked the nearest Guardsman.

"We arrived by two different corridors," said Dal, his voice still weak. "I think one of us took a more direct route than the other, but the second hesitated longer at each junction…"

"For once," said Zoltan, "my thoughts find themselves in accord with those of my inestimable enemy."

The Guardsmen looked at one another suspiciously, but the herald was already crying toward the sky: "The trial is a draw. The adversaries are sound. They will, therefore, go on to the final trial, that of knowledge, which will take place without delay."

The refined and barbaric sound of the Sonorous Structures burst forth, ad died away again immediately.

"The contestants will be placed in the presence of two robots, whose programming they will be required to discover within a time-limit of four minutes. After that limit, each machine has orders to destroy its observer. Before then, it will be sufficient for the champion to make his solution known to the guardsman accompanying him, and the machine will be immobilized. I have faithfully transmitted the decision of the Great Council of the Sopharchy."

The silence was only troubled by a few distant exclamations. A Guardsman was attached to Zoltan, and led him to a point on the circumference of the circus. Dal was led to a diametrically opposite point by a second White Guardsman.

Next to each of them was an opening in the ground, from which emerged a shiny being perfectly similar to a man, but whose stature reach almost 2.50 meters.

The one that appeared before Dal began to rotate, describing strange figures. It was obviously a dance—but what kind? As he wondered vainly whether he was dealing with the ritual dance of some religious sect or the primitive dance of a mutant people, or even one of the steps currently fashionable in the suburban pleasure-spots, something thundered in his skull. A whirlwind of energy forced him to look at the point of the arena where another robot was whirling in front of Zoltan and his guard. In spite of the distance, a name immediately sprang to mind: *the gait of a megatherium!*

An internal voice, like those he had heard in the labyrinth, but mocking in tone, sounded inside his head: "Thank you. I'd never have found that on my own."

Bewildered, he looked around, encountering nothing but the sullen mask of the Guard and the large, shiny and inexpressive face of the robot.

"Come on, my dear chap," the voice went on, "let's not give ourselves away. In order that all will end well, I can inform you that your machine is dancing a step that was all the rage in the remotest antiquity; it's called a waltz."

There was a pause, during which Dal wondered whether he might suddenly be enjoying the favour of the Divinity. "It's me, Zoltan," said the silent voice, then. "Let's help one another. Don't be suspicious and give the reply to the guard. We only have a minute left."

That man, Dal thought, *is...* He could not find the he was seeking, and concluded: *...not a man.* He turned to the Guardsman. "It's a very old dance, which is called a waltz!" he said.

The Guardsman stepped back in amazement. With an automatic gesture, he pressed a switch on the telecommunication box he was wearing in his belt. The robot stopped abruptly, with one leg in the air, and fell heavily to the ground.

In the distance, the machine that should have destroyed Zoltan had already collapsed.

The ovation was gradually transformed into a concert of screams, in which insults and imprecations were mixed. Many people considered that they had been cheated of the delightful spectacle of a massacre, of the death of a man crushed by a machine. Some saluted the worth and science of the combatants, others questioned the regularity of the trial in terms too obscene to repeat.

"Citizens of Lassenia," cried the herald, "Noblemen and Technologists, the Tournament is terminated, and you have the honor of two victors instead of one. Thank the Creator and Destroyer of All Things for that!"

Fanfares punctuated these words in a deafening manner. On the central mast, the wind was making the four standard flutter in unison. Two of them descended slowly: the black pennants of the dead.

Then, a very rare event was seen to occur. Three Sopharchs left their armchairs and came down into the arena, where they came toward the victors with an imposing dignity. On the teleoptic screens looming over the highest terraces, their scarlet robes looked like drops of blood rolling slowly across the arena.

The champions hastened to meet them and bowed to them. Dal recognized Torol Karella. He had never seen the others before today.

Torol spoke, and his voice filled the air. Dal remembered the hidden recorders and realized why Zoltan had murmured; the floor of the arena was one vast microphone. *But telepathic exchanges are undetectable*, he thought, with satisfaction. He laughed inside himself.

"Several champions have died in the course of these difficult trials," said Karella. "The Council salutes in you the same valor that it recognized in the others whose destiny was less fortunate. It is to their memory that we dedicate the rewards to which your superiority has rendered you worthy."

It was not customary to applaud the words of Sopharchs. Their echoes persisted for several seconds and died away into the crushing silence of the motionless crowd. Divided as it was in its opinions, with regard to the Council, the crowd had never permitted itself—as yet—to transgress the rule of profound deference that had surrounded the person of a Sopharch for two centuries.

"To you, Zoltan Charles Henderson de Nancy," Karella continued, "whose strange name excites the hilarity of fools and the melancholy admiration of history-lovers, will be given a proper and legitimate fief on Titan, with all its wealth, in the assurance that we shall see it maintained by the most able hands as the fundamental patrimony of our threatened race."

Zoltan bowed elegantly. He still had a slight smile on his face, ambiguous in its significance.

That man, Dal thought, *does not believe in anything, or take anything seriously... except, perhaps, for the lives of others—while his peers have the opposite attitude; they attach importance to a host of vain things, but hold every life cheap—sometimes even their own—for futile reasons.*

Karella turned to Dal. "As for you, Dal Ortog, whose birth was obscure, you spent your childhood in a remote village. Your youth was that of a herdsman, but you were picked out by a brave man before the end of your adolescence—for Housemaster Jaral Kerr Jaral made you a man of war. That precocious maturity led you to choose to defend the emblem of the Sopharchy, and the brilliant results that you have just obtained demand a proportionate reward. I am authorized by the Council of Three Planets to bestow upon you the title of Knight-Navigator." He paused momentarily and smiled. Dal, unsteady on his feet and blushing, could not believe his ears. "Henceforth," Karella resumed, you shall be named Dal Ortog Dal, Knight of Galankar and Malakorjal. These names and titles will be the property of your descendants, and common people will call you *Lord...*"

The Sopharch was still speaking, but Dal lost the thread of the speech. Later, he remembered the clamors of the crowd, Zoltan's smile, and the blazing sun burning down on the arena. He recalled the Navigators' march blaring out of the Structures, and the chanting of the priests, as well as the bright colors of the Oriflamme of the Games that was given to him...but at the time, all that was blotted out, and his mind was carried away by a formless whirlwind.

The end of that memorable day saw the preparations for a sumptuous reception, which would be held at the Palace until the following dawn. Dal was taken to the luxurious barracks of the Knights, whose multicoloured building flanked the Sopharchy's Palace. He was given a bizarre apartment, in which splendor and rigor were mingled, with an enormous conservatory with a transparent hemispherical ceiling, along with a training-room, a drawing-room and a laboratory.

The White Guardsmen who had escorted him there respectfully abandoned him on the threshold, with out forgetting to address the sign of protection to him. Dal found himself alone at the entrance to an immense room and took a few steps forward, darting admiring glances around him. He had the impression that he was entering a habitation unit that was not his own, of penetrating into the home of a nobleman who had not invited him. He had not yet adjusted to the idea that he had become a Knight, and that the entire population of Lassenia and the Three Planets would consider him one from now on.

He was reaching out for an optiphone when he heard a discreet cough behind him. He turned round and uttered an exclamation of surprise. A man was standing in the doorway, dressed in a steel-colored jerkin. He was smiling broadly.

"Bor Talek!" Dal exclaimed.

"At our service, Lord," said Bor Talek.

"Oh, no!" said Dal. "I forbid you to call me that. We're companions, and you participated with me, at the same rank, in the expedition to Lassenia."

"Yes," said Bor, "but you have distinguished yourself since our arrival—something that I have not done, and would not have dared to attempt. It's right that our respective positions have been modified—but I shall call you *Sire*, if you prefer that title."

Dal burst out laughing, but did not protest. Although the joy that had been selling in him since the end of the games turned to pride that he knew to be legitimate, he did not forget that chance had worked in his favor in the course of that incredible social success—which avoided his being blinded by vanity. Nevertheless, it was the first time that anyone had called him by his newly-obtained titles, and Bor's words were music to his ears.

"But that's not the question, Dal Ortog Dal," Bor went on, mischievously emphasizing the repeated pronoun. "I'm attached to your person in the capacity of bodyguard. While you were in training for the Games, I was improving my weapon skills and would have entered into the service of some other knight if you had not triumphed. It was at my own request that the Sopharchy sent me to you. If you'd prefer another guard, you're free to choose one—but you can't do without one, for Navigators are all in constant danger, because traitors and hired killers of every sort are swarming in the city and the Palace."

Dal clapped him on the shoulders. "God forbid that I should put myself in the hands of a stranger, when an old friend offers to watch over me!" he said.

Bor's smile widened. "In that case," he went on, and as I took the liberty of anticipating your acceptance, I've already brought a message for you."

Dal raised his eyebrows. Can't you guess who the message is from?" said Bor, darting an oblique glance at him.

Dal felt his heart beat more rapidly. "Tell me..." he said, hesitantly.

"Kalla Karella," said Bor, "asks whether you can grant her a few minutes."

Dal started. "Where is she?" he cried.

Bor Talek stepped back and left the room. "Protection, Sire!" he said, as he went.

Kalla Karella was standing on the threshold. She was wearing a moss-green dress made of algex, a fabric that bore a hallucinatory resemblance to human skin. She had swept back her long black hair, and fastened it with a double golden triangle. Her beauty and regal bearing took Dal's breath away. She came toward him with a smile that revealed dazzling white teeth.

"Congratulations, Sire!" she said, echoing Bor—whose footsteps could be heard drawing away.

Dal blinked. She did not seem entirely real.

She advanced further, coming very close to him, her head raised and her lips half-open. Dal took her in his arms, with an almost brutal gesture.

He had little time to devote to Kalla; he had to prepare for the impending consecration, for the ceremonial program would begin with the enthronement of the new Knight-Navigator. The late afternoon was taken up with trying on the ceremonial garb that Dal had to wear.

The ceremonial costumes of Navigators had nothing in common with the various fripperies of Housemasters or Bannerets . It was traditional among them to reject excessive whimsy, including exaggerated individuality. In other words, one found in all Knights the fundamental elements of the uniform of the Stellar Corps, even in ceremonial dress.

A bronze-colored outfit was cut, fitted and assembled in record time for Dal, tightened about his figure by a broad belt and prolonged from the neck to the forehead by a semi-metallic skull-cap with a coppery gleam. A white circle on the breast had been reserved for future arms. Two symmetrical holsters attached to his belt accommodated the personal weapons from which the Navigators were rarely separated: the coagulant and the ultrasonic projector. For this exceptional evening, Dal was offered weapons with butts delicately carved by the finest artists in Lassenia, mortal jewels extracted from the stores of the Palace goldsmith.

Evening arrived.

The Council Hall was abuzz with the noise of conversations, against a distant musical background distilled by camouflaged optiphones in the walls. Richly clad, the guests were standing in groups commenting on the results of the Games, and offering prognoses regarding the next games. Almost all of them were smoking long red cazatl cigarettes, which rendered the mind incredibly lucid and accelerated the thought-processes. Many of them were holding conical cups without bases, into which White Guardsmen were pouring euphoric nolej. Thanks to nolej, there were hardly ever quarrels in the course of social occasions, even though frequently-opposed opinions were a permanent source of discord, duels and ambushes.

The rear section of the Council Hall was elevated by two steps. There, an immense iron table had been set up, capable of accommodating four hundred guests. Silver goblets had already been set out, containing precious wines from Lahoum and Zortal, the immortal hills of Venus, where renowned growers dedicated themselves to the selection and creation of ever-more-promising plants, and wines with ever-more subtle bouquets.

A White Guard opened the two battens of the main door, encrusted with quartz suns, and shouted: "Dal Ortog Dal, Navigator of Galankar and Malakorjal!"

Silence fell. Dal went in with apparent assurance, a slender silhouette with a metallic gleam. A few Housemasters frowned, but the nolej dissipated their ill-humor. They allowed themselves to substitute benevolent smiles.

Followed by Bor Talek, whose features were unexpressive and who was wearing an entire arsenal at his belt, Dal marched to the middle of the room, where several Sopharchs were mingling with the crowd. In an instant, the red-robed men had regrouped, and Karella started speaking.

"The ceremony will be brief," he said. "Let the godfather of Dal Ortog Dal's lineage present himself."

Zoltan detached himself from one of the silent groups. "Housemaster-Baron," said Karella, "confirm by gesture the resolution we have made."

Zoltan placed himself in front of Dal. His white cape, lined with green, undulated over a quilted tunic on which his antique blazon was displayed. *It's almost fashionable*, Dal thought.

"By the grace of God, by the dignity of your triumph, and by the most serene decision of the Sopharchy," Zoltan proclaimed, in a loud voice, "I present you with this Martian emerald engraved with your monogram. Keep it as the proof of your title, and let it be the first gift that you make to your eldest son."

Involuntarily, Dal searched with his eyes for the silhouette of Kalla. He discovered it next to the wife of a Knight, to whom she murmured something as she looked at him. Her face was pink and her eyes sparkling.

Dal took the emerald, bowed deeply and tried to begin the speech that he had prepared. His tongue remained paralyzed, in spite of the cazatl that he had smoked during the last half hour.

Karella smiled and clapped his hands. "To the table!" he cried. "The Knight will speak during the feast."

Dal was placed between Karella and the Sopharch's daughter, which provoked many jealous gazes.

As the terrine of crustaceans flambéed in nolej was served, Karella turned to Dal. He had to tap him on the shoulder to attract his attention, for Dal only had eyes for Kalla and had virtually turned his back on him. "It's time to give me your full attention now," he said. "You'll be able to enjoy the food and the joyful company that surrounds us afterwards."

Dal immediately turned round. "Accept my excuses, Sopharch!" he said. "Your daughter is so beautiful that I forgot the great respect I owe you."

"That's all right," said Karella, seriously. "Listen to me carefully, then, for I shan't raise my voice, in order not to be overheard by those who hate me. Know that I had commissioned certain of my most faithful Country Housemasters to find me a determined young man who could assume the risks of a perilous undertaking. You are one of them. That is how we progressively renew the ranks of the Knights, who are not exempt from the general regression of the nobility. It's also the case that the Stellar Corps counts increasingly on recent lineages…"

Dal entered with astonishment into the underside of politics.

"A short time ago," the Sopharch continued, "an expedition returned decimated, after having finally obtained, in the course of its journey, precise information on a matter that is of concern to everyone. I won't hide from you that I place very little confidence in that sort of quest, but the information brought back by the survivors is genuinely disturbing. It seems to prove that the legends are well-founded."

Karella savored the crustacean jelly. Dal was all ears, although he was holding Kalla's hand under the table.

"You'll command the next expedition," said Karella, abruptly.

Dal was now accustomed to miracles; the Sopharch's decision only astonished him slightly. The joy that overwhelmed him, however, was greater than that of his ennoblement. He squeezed Kalla's hand so forcefully that she had to choke back a cry of pain. "You have in me, Sopharch," he said, in a vibrant voice, "the most faithful and the most..."

"Not so loud, ardent Knight," Karella interjected. "I believe what you say. You will, therefore, be provided with a crew, in which I shall include your former adversary." He smiled. "As regards the Housemaster-Baron," he said, "you've probably guessed that the Housemasters chose him as a champion by reason of his incredible lineage—except for the few who take him for an impostor. But you're unaware that he is utterly loyal to the Council and will be an important trump card for us. Know that his telepathic gifts are artificial, and that the biophysics laboratories of Lassenia are responsible for them. In the course of the Games, not everything happens according to our wishes, but a fortunate combination of circumstances allowed you to be matched against a friend. In my opinion, you would still have come out level if the Housemasters had confronted you with one of the trouble-makers who abound in their midst, for the two final trials were as difficult for him as for you—but that's not important. Your physical and mental capacities, revealed in the course of hypnagogy, invite further training. You shall become a pilot and a captain."

Dal lifted a forkful of food unsteadily to his lips, and spilled it on his chin.

"You still have a great deal to learn…" said Karella

Kalla leaned toward Dal. "What is my father saying?" she asked. "You're not leaving on an Expedition, surely?"

Dal attacked the creamed haunch of venison. "Delicious!" he confided to Kalla, by way of reply. He leaned toward Karella. "I await your orders, Sopharch," he said.

The dinner continued without anything arising to destroy the apparent harmony of the guests. A few meters away from the group formed by Dal, Karella and his daughter, a plump priest seated between a Sopharch and a banneret was doing justice to the food and indulging in slightly excessive libations. His voice could be heard above the hubbub of individual conversations. He must have been repudiated by three-quarters of the clergy, for he was declaring loudly and clearly that, although salvation could only come from God, it was also necessary for Man to make a contribution, meriting it by his actions. Dal learned that the priest, who was called Noktor, had also been appointed to take part in the Expedition.

The night wore on in this manner, almost entirely in merriment, and dawn broke as the guests were taking their leave. Dal was more than half-drunk, and had to be separated from Kalla in order to avoid a scandal. He left the Palace proclaiming threats of death against Moniz and Melej, whose hiding-place no one had been able to discover.

After the excitement of the Games, Lassenia returned to its routines. Dal had had little opportunity until then to stroll around its streets and avenues, idle on the numerous bridges that bestrode the river or visit the singular north-eastern quarter situated near to the Stellar Port—quarters in which strange hotels received merchants from several solar systems, and where one sometimes encountered beings morphologically very different from humans.

The intelligent non-human races with which the Three Planets maintained commercial or cultural relations were, in fact, not very numerous. On the one hand, humans had not yet explored many systems; on the other hand, those it had explored often presented nothing but worlds devoid of life, or restricted to animal populations. Only twice had they made contact with species closely similar to humans, but at a lower evolutionary level—even lower than that to which humans had fallen back since the Blue War. Once, they had encountered forms of intelligent life that were reminiscent of large batrachians. They had limited themselves in respect to them with a kind of barter, and somewhat undeveloped exchanges of visitors. None of these races had the use of a Stellar Drive. Only the Akals—the intelligent batrachians—had colonized the planets of their own solar system, that of Regulus.

It was to the north-eastern quarter that Dal was taken with his crew, in order to use the eve of departure as a transitional phase, like a first contact with other worlds. On Kalla's advice, he had dressed in anonymous clothing. There were two reasons for that: firstly, to avoid a brawl, always possible in this quarter, where the Knights often got into quarrels with people paid by the Housemasters; and secondly, in order not to give the public the opportunity to mock a Knight without a blazon.

The question of a coat-of-arms had been the object of a debate, at the end of which it had been decided that Ortog's emblem would be constituted in the course of the Expedition, by Dal's calculated choice. That way, the arms of the future lineage would be justified by the actions of the first holder of the title.

As for the evening before the launch, it was spent in the traditional manner. Dal was, in any case, just as spellbound as any other member of the crew. After the second period of training that he had undergone, even harder than the first, he really needed a release.

The preparation for piloting and command had followed the followed the period of training that had been imposed on Dal with a view to the Games. It was all part of a program put into effect by the Sopharchy—a program whose unfolding had to be repeated for many others, since it was, at the end of the day, a matter of continually enriching the ranks of the Navigators with new elements still full of enthusiasm, on whose fidelity it was possible to count.

The knowledge to be acquired, along with the psychomotor conditioning, represented a sum of effort that it would have been impossible to complete successfully in such a short time if the method of hypnagogy under hibernation had not been employed, along with certain equipment that abbreviated the reactive apprenticeship.

Before embarking upon this preparation, however, Dal had had to undergo several series of tests, one of which had almost resulted in his elimination. It was a test of spatial representation in zero-gravity, in a transparent orbiting cabin. On that occasion, Dal had involuntarily revealed to the operators the sickness and fear that gripped him in confrontation with the stars, ever since the shock he had received in his childhood. A note had been made: *Psychosomatic syndrome, released by the conception of space. Candidate inapt to fulfil the functions of the Stellar Corps.*

Alarmed by this sentence, which made him a Knight bound to the Earth, Dal had made a special request of the Sopharchy, which Kalla had supported in self-defence, in which he had expressed the desire to be submitted to an entire battery of tests relative to his spatial sense. This wish had been granted; for three days he had struggled against horror and the worst organic disturbances. The results had not turned out to be entirely satisfactory, but he had reached the minimum requirement. As all the other characteriological, intellectual, neuromuscular and sensory factors were determined to be more than satisfactory, he had gone on to the seminary of Stellar preparation. None of it had been easy, by reason of that handicap—impossible to overcome without analysis—but he had succeeded very honorably. The Knight was ready to become a true Navigator...

They went into the most renowned tavern in the northeastern suburbs in little groups. Dal remembered, with a smile, the jealous scene to which he had been subject before his departure for barracks; Kalla was not unaware that the taverns of the periphery abounded with prostitutes—but Dal had no thought for anyone but her, and she was convinced of that, deep down...

The evening began in a thick fog of cazalt. Bor Talek did not relax his surveillance for an instant, and the entire night was spent in laughter and singing...but in the morning, one man was missing. They found out subsequently that he was Kallla's spy. The Sopharch's daughter had commissioned him to keep track of everything Dal did; he had hurried off to make his report at dawn, and collect his fee...

Chapter Four

*"Like the lightning that furrows the clouds depart
the vessels of the Navigators. And the icy darkness
of Space opens the maw of death for them…"*
Song of the Perfecti
Psalm XV, Verse 26

In the course of his accelerated training, Dal had once had occasion to visit the research laboratory of a specialist in gerontological medicine, Dr. Hafsen, who was also to go on the Expedition. He had then received some troubling details concerning the Malady.

"Although the curve of normal senescence, according to the Titan vestiges," Hafsen had said, "commences around 20 years of age, to decrease very slowly until 80, the curve of present-day humankind commences at 17 or 18—your age— and decreases according to two distinct slopes: one normally oblique until the age of 40, the other declining very rapidly after that age."

Hafsen had shown Dal statistics and graphs, and even old people of both sexes under observation. Some of them were no older than fifty; they were showing no obvious signs of senility, but their internal organs were performing their functions with decreasing efficiency: their lungs were very weak, their arteries laden with cholesterol, their livers sclerous, their kidneys nephritic, their hearts dilated…

"Either an essential organ stops functioning," Hafsen had specified, "or a simple fracture terminates in death, or a benign virus kills them within 24 hours. All our anticyclotoxic therapies are ineffective, as are preventative measures—diet, hygiene and so on…" He shook his head and concluded: "The cause must be genetic. The radiations of the Blue War have affected the structure of the DNA, even though the geneticists deny it."

No one knew which saint to pray to, for the geneticists were explicit. They based their conclusions on astonishing experiments carried out 60 years earlier. Frozen spermatozoa and ova had been found in storage-tanks on Titan, a certain number of which had been successfully restored to life, and half of them had been subjected to *in vitro* fertilization. The children thus obtained by slow ectogenesis had almost all lived, but had not aged according to the curve of the 22nd century, with which they were genetically contemporary, but according to the present-day curve. They were all dead. That anomaly could not have arisen from the artificial conditions of gestation, for it was known that the use of ectogenesis had been widespread in the 22nd century, and that the curves of senescence of test-tube offspring had been identical to others in that period.

Geriatric specialists like Hafsen were totally opposed to the hypothesis of a weakening of the vital potential of the gametes after a long hibernation, or that of the attainment of their genes during their transfer to Lassenia by the residual radioactivity. The gerontologists and geneticists therefore sent the ball back into one another's courts, and put the blame for their failures on one another. Dal conceived profound doubts as to the abilities of either party.

He thought about that slow depopulation. The Malady was even more prevalent in the Alpha Centauri system than on the Three Planets, and in the Terran colony's capital the average age of the population did not exceed 28, with a proportionate birth-rate.

Throughout the journey, and in spite of the profound joy he obtained from his role in one of the Expeditions of which he had dreamed for years, Dal stuck firmly to the vessel's opaque supplementary cupola, in order not to have to struggle against the sickness that would have restricted his efficacy. The mere fact of knowing that he was in space was sufficient to make him anxious, but he had been able to master his weakness by means of nolej. He had thus been able to show qualities envied by the second pilot, in spite of his qualifications. His command reflected justice and firmness, and discipline was not relaxed for an instant, without the slightest murmur of protest being raised.

In addition to Dal Ortog Dal, the Expedition comprised the second pilot, a Navigator by the name of Jern Tranis, who fulfilled the role of helmsman—or, rather, operator of the trajectory controls; Zoltan, the Housemaster-Baron, who was a specialist in mental communication—the Biophysics laboratories had not yet succeeded in amplifying the cerebral waves in anyone but him; the Reverend Noktor, whom Dal had noticed on the evening of his triumph: Bor Talek, who, of course, followed Dal like his shadow; and Dr. Hafsen, who was in charge of the infirmary. None of the members of this general staff was over 35 years of age.

As for the crew, it was made up of technicians specialized in disciplines as diverse as propulsion and dietetics.

Between the general staff and the crew were situated a group of three scientists who formed a separate group and had little contact with the officers save through the intermediary of Dr. Hafsen, who belonged to both groups: Horst, a zoologist; Bolene, a physicist/chemist; and Fayal, a geologist.

Finally, 20 warriors constituted the protective phalanx.

The *Solaris* had been thus baptized by Zoltan, a specialist in ancient cultures and a lover of exotic words. It was a ship of small dimensions, but exceptionally well-protected and well-armed. It was equipped with two drive-units: the G-motor, which was sufficient for medium distances, used the energy of gravitons and nullified gravity. As it shielded the navigators from variations in speed, no matter how immense, it was coupled with the MC-motor, which could institute prodigious acceleration and boost the *Solaris* to speeds far superior to that of light. The principle of the MC-motor got around the Einstein equations by means of the Malet-Cerenkoff effect discovered in the 20th century: in certain media, there are electrons that travel more rapidly than light *in those media*. It had, however, been necessary to modify the global mass-coefficient of the moving body in question in order to be able to generalize the MC-effect and apply it to interstellar propulsion. In fact, the Historical Gulf hid as many bewildering discoveries regarding the physics of matter as regarding the continuum, since the Langevin paradox had also been defeated, and cosmic voyages did not create any decalibration between Terrestrial time and that of a vessel.

The four light-years separating Alpha from the Sun were, therefore, covered in 37 Terrestrial days, in the course of which the technicians mingled with the soldiers to play Stall—a three-dimensional version of checkers, in which the movement of the pieces was variable—and to smoke cazatl.

During this interval, Dal had had several conversations with Jern Tranis Jern—particularly edifying conversations that he had not been able to have before the departure. Jern, the commander of the preceding Expedition, had gathered information on Alpha concerning the "Planet of the Archangels." He had steered his vessel toward Orion—as he had been advised to do by a Housemaster in Songa—but he had not succeeded in getting through a barrier-field, in which his spaceship had suffered terrible damage, causing the death of a large part of the crew. He had retained after the incident a sort of exhaustion of the will and a semi-amnesia that had prevented the command of the subsequent Expedition being entrusted to him.

Fortified by this lesson, the Lassenian specialists in interstellar navigation had taken the chance of providing the new vessel with the Blue Weapon. They hoped that its torrent of energy, which dislocated the structure of space, would succeed in piercing the unknown barrier. If it performed in a satisfactory manner, it would be necessary to take soundings of the space within the breach, at the risk of simply seeing the vessel disappear as it went through. Those soundings would be carried out with the aid of a makeshift instrument, for the necessary means of investigation were lacking; they would use the graviton-captor, with reference to the interdependence of space and gravitation.

All of that had been the subject of discussions between the two Navigators, but it was still necessary, in any case, to stop off at Songa in order to renew contact with their informer, for the exact point in the constellation of Orion toward which it was necessary to set a course had been lost.

Alpha 3 was a bizarre planet. Lit by two yellow suns that rotated around one another in a complicated ballet, it rotated around their common center of gravity, following a flattened ellipse, to which the pronounced inclination of its axis of rotation to its ecliptic added in submitting its capital to enormous variations of solar exposure and multiple violently-contrasted seasons. In Songa, the astronomical conjunctions were so strongly reflected in human character that it was practically impossible to find a truly equilibrated individual. The women did not change their mood on a daily basis but an hourly one. As for the colony's government, it was autonomous with respect to the metropolis, but subject to frequent and bloody modifications.

Forewarned of these disturbing particularities, Dal and Jern made contact by optiphone with the authorities as hey approached the planet, and checked the general state of mind telepathically before disembarking. The Expedition had had the good fortune to arrive during a period of relative calm. As it was common knowledge that the Navigators were in quest of an objective of value to the entire species in Songa, and as there were no pessimist priests there—nor optimists, for that matter—they were given a favourable welcome.

The Terrans had no intention of wasting time on Alpha 3, so they formed a party to go immediately in search of the Housemaster who possessed the information they needed. This party comprised Dal, accompanied, as always, by Bor; Jern, accompanied by his bodyguard Arkel; and Zoltan. Reverend Noktor remained on the ship, in order not to inconvenience anyone, and Hafsen kept him company.

At the Palace of Songa, the delegate of the Sopharchy received the travelers amiably, but apologized for his ignorance;
he did not have the slightest idea where Housemaster Markhart was to be found. Dal thanked the delegate for his welcome and declared that he hoped to discover the individual if
the authorities in Songa would lend him every assistance in his
search—of which the delegate assured him.

As they left the Palace, Zoltan entered into telepathic
conversation with Dal and Jeern.

We've just left the greatest knave in Alpha, he transmitted. *That man has delegated himself to represent the Sopharchy, as we know—but he's hostile to the Three Planets,
and thinks of nothing but breaking all links with them. That
was clearly legible in his mind. Markhart was given shelter
last year, in company with a priest. They were the sole survivors of an Expedition, and the priest died of his injuries.
Markhart's explanations were found to be confused, and he
was accused of the priest's murder. You, Jern Tranis, were
lucky enough to encounter Markhart before he was thrown in
prison.*

In prison! Dal thought.

*Yes—for having killed a priest, even though the people of
Songa hold Solarian priests in contempt. In reality, they seize
any pretext to imprison someone from the Three Planets. I fear
that the Blue War has scarcely modified the general sava-
gery...and I wonder sometimes whether the human race is
worth the effort of helping it to survive.*

"I'm sorry," said Dal, aloud. "For better or worse, that's
our role."

"I know," said Zoltan. "You're right not to question
that."

They had stopped in the shadow of a gigantic edifice that
must have been several hundred years old: a sort of warehouse
constructed in a substance whose composition had been forgotten. Since disembarking, they had been constantly surprised by the appearance of the titanic city, which had been
left untouched by the War, and whose immense buildings

were not at all reminiscent of the habitation units of Lassenia. The population, too, retained something archaic in its customs and its clothing.

I've contacted Markhart, Zoltan went on, *but I'm only getting a weak and vague response. He's exhausted by privations and ill-treatment, and I can't obtain any indication from him as to the place where he's being detained.*

Dal suddenly felt that he was confronted by a serious problem. Up to this point, he had tried to act in a certain way, and those who were capable of utilizing his good will had, by degrees, invested him with rank and the necessary powers. Now, he was the leader of the Expedition and, in spite of his youth, he was the one who had to make the decisions. If the Terrans manifested any hostility toward the colony, the delegate would immediately seize the pretext to beak off relations. Alpha, with its few millions of mostly untrained men, would never become a threat to the Three Planets, of course, but it might interfere to some extent with relations between Lassenia and other solar systems—for instance, by refusing local Terran agencies the right to store and transmit goods. In those conditions, the Sopharchy would not force the issue, considering that it was not appropriate for them to make war against a territory miraculously spared by the previous disaster. On the other hand, if Dal did not take the decisive action he had in mind, he Expedition would be compromised—and he could not bear the thought of a pitiful return.

"We'll have to attack the prison," he said, coldly.

The Terrans used their individual transmitter to ask the pseudo-delegate to put them in touch with a senior security-officer, on the grounds that he might be very helpful to heir enquiry. The delegate carefully concealed his irony in replying, and personally alerted the special commissioner to whom he sent them—with the result that, before they were introduced into the functionary's office, the latter knew exactly what false trail he was to put them on. What he did not know about, however, was the Housemaster-Baron's singular ability.

In the event, they took their leave of him politely, after a conversation stuffed from one end to the other with lies.

On their return to the ship, Zoltan revealed the information that he had extracted from the special commissioner. "Songa has no Relegation Unit comparable to the one in Lassenia," he said, "but 200 kilometres to the north, there's a well-guarded camp provided with all the commodities necessary to the torturers who command it. I've learned that the camp guards don't possess any spatial weapon that could damage our vessel, but they're equipped in a sufficiently modern manner, with coagulants and ultrasonic projectors. That, commander, will put many of your men in danger."

"With your permission," said Dr. Hafsen, in a dry and rapid voice, "I think I can synthesize a considerable volume of hypnotic gas aboard the ship, and store it under pressure in a reservoir."

"What gas?" asked Jern.

"Noctalium. A small amount in a cubic meter of air should provoke an unbreakable sleep for several minutes."

"Perfect," admitted the Reverend. "That way, we can preserve the lives of those on whom we're obliged to use force."

"In that case," Dal interjected, "would you care to get started on that synthesis without delay." As he spoke, he observed that Zoltan was having an effect; he had used the formal mode of address, which was spreading through the *Solaris* like a patch of oil.

At that latitude, at that time of year, daylight lasted for thirty-six hours. Dal left with five men for the residential quarters where he was, in theory, supposed to begin his enquiries. He perceived in the course of the visits he made that the social structure of Songa had very little in common with that of the Three Planets. The noblemen there were not very numerous and lacked authority, power being in the hands of functionaries of all sorts, as in the Solar System before the War. He only obtained negative or evasive answers, of course; according to all evidence, the inhabitants had been forewarned in some manner, and were intent on discouraging him.

He returned to the astroport as the second sun was setting, and waited impatiently for night to fall. Everything was ready for their departure.

In the darkness, the vessel lifted silently, by means of the G-drive. A few minutes later, it descended slowly into the beams of searchlights—and then its hull began too vibrate under ultra-sonic salvoes. That did not last long, though; while Dal had been putting one over on Songa, Hafsen had filled several reservoirs of noctalium, which he had opened over the camp. The anti-aerial fire ceased.

Powerful jets of air then dispelled the gas, and a command unit rapidly disembarked; they had less than ten minutes at their disposal. The cerebral waves of the sleeping Markhart were still guiding Zoltan's steps, though, as he accompanied Dal and his 20 men.

They went through an interior courtyard of large dimensions and entered the buildings by means of magnetic keys stolen from the guards. That enabled them to reach the cells, into which, for security reasons, the prisoners had been thrown on the vessel's arrival. Zoltan pointed out the one in which Markhart was to be found, and Dal threw him over his shoulder. Markhart was skeletal, and his face had the pallor of death.

The commando unit regained the ship without firing a shot. It took off immediately, and was soon out of sight.

In the pilot-room, Dal turned to Jern and said: "Too bad about the diplomatic complications—but there's a more immediate difficulty. Markhart became delirious as soon as he woke up. Dr. Hafsen is at his bedside, and Zoltan's trying to disentangle the information we need from the invalid's mental chaos. Alas, he can't seem to obtain anything whatsoever concerning Orion."

"I'll go join them," Jern declared. "I'm the one he talked to a few months ago; perhaps my presence will restore his lucidity."

As Jern left the room, the spatial radar revealed a launch that was approaching rapidly. The calling-lights flashed. Dal connected the receiver.

Songan launch to Lassenian vessel..." said a neutral voice.

Dal turned to the transmitter and said: "Lassenian vessel to Songan launch; I hear you."

"Message from the delegate to the Sopharchy. You have committed an act of aggression against a relegation-camp and contrived the escape of a prisoner. Our strength is insufficient to permit us to board you, but the Three Planets will be held responsible for your hostile act. All travelers from the Solar System currently on Songa will be considered as hostages until you return the prisoner to our custody. We give you one hour to decide. When that deadline has passed, the hostages will be put to death, and you will bear the responsibility."

"You're mad!" cried Dal. "If you massacre the travelers from the Three Planets, Songa will be razed two months thereafter by the Sopharchy, of whom you deceptively claim to be the vassals."

"We are aware of the sanguinary exploits of the Three Planets, but the Blue War did not reach us, and we have no fear of any kind of aggression. Over."

Dal irrupted into the infirmary, after having put the vessel into orbit. He stopped short. Jern was looking at him triumphantly. "I have the heading for our departure from Alpha!" he said, precipitately. "Markhart has recovered consciousness, and will continue to guide us."

Dal looked art him, bleakly. "That's a victory, and I congratulate you—but Markhart must leave us. A Songan launch has come after him. If we don't surrender him, they'll massacre thousands of people from the Solar System who are presently on Alpha 3."

"It's a bluff!" said Zoltan.

"I don't intend to verify their sincerity," Dal observed. "We have to return the Housemaster to them, in order to go in search of the goal of our mission. In the meantime, we'll warn the Solarians of Alpha that they have to return to the Three Planets. Songa has become an enemy city."

"Their attitude is ridiculous," declared Dr. Hafsen. "They don't have the strength."

Markhart signalled that he wanted to speak. "No," he said, in a hesitant voice, "they know very well that the Sopharchy has a horror of any sort of war or punitive expedition. It's better that I be put to death than pay for my life with the deaths of thousands of people."

"They'll imprison you again," said Dal, without any great conviction.

Markhart smiled resignedly. "I know them," he said. "They're mad with rage because you've tricked them, and they'll avenge themselves on me."

"But are they aware of what the information might mean for them?" Dal exclaimed.

"Vaguely. They don't understand much about the racial Malady, and don't accord much real importance to your efforts. Even more than the metropolis, they accept things as they are. They're brutes devoted to decadence. They're dominated by fits of fury or despair, which render them perfectly capable of exposing themselves to punishment. I think the astrophysical conditions of Alpha have had an influence on them even more disastrous than that of the Blue War on us. I'm originally from Mars, and I've made the journey several times. I've had the opportunity to compare them with the Solarians. They're all descended from unscrupulous individuals, and their heredity is burdensome..."

Markhart continued in this manner, edging imperceptibly toward delirium. By the time he was embarked on the lifeboat—an ironic title—he had fallen back into a profound stupor.

"Condemned in every sense," said Halfsen, when the lifeboat cast off. "The treatment to which he has been subjected has alienated his body and mind in an irreversible fashion. Only the shock prompted by Jern Tranis Jern's presence caused his brain to recover its lucidity briefly."

The lifeboat returned, devoid of any occupant. Dal set a course for Betelgeuse and summoned his general staff. "I've begun by freeing a man so that his life might be taken," he said. "That will be represented in my coat-of-arms by a broken chain on a sable field."

He asked to be left alone, and refused the nolej that was offered to him.

They remained under gravitic propulsion. Under the double cupola, Dal thought about Space, the presence of which he divined beyond the hull that contained a petty traveling universe: Space, with its billions of suns separated by abysms. He felt as if he were being watched by the void, of being cleverly steered to his doom by a formless and avid intelligence suspended between the stars.

"Our course will take us through the Great Nebula of Orion. Some space-travelers have observed singular disturbances in the indications of instruments within dozens of light-years of that nebula…"

He had spoken aloud, forgetting that the communication link to the helmsman's cabin was still open. Jern thought the words were addressed to him. "Are we making a detour, Captain?" he asked.

Dal started. He passed his hand over his forehead. "No!" he said into the interphone. "If we change course and the instruments malfunction anyway, we'll need to recover our heading visually. I'm afraid of making a mistake."

He cut the communication-link. He was not afraid of errors of parallax, but only the necessity of unmasking the cupola. The vessel continued to head for the constellation of Orion, whose configuration had not been noticeably modified by the change of angle represented by the voyage from the Sun to Alpha.

On the 75th day after the departure from Alpha, the stellar ship entered a region of space where the gravitic sensors began to give signs of erratic behaviour. Their wave-sequences were reflected and twisted laterally *by nothing* and provoked ridiculous responses from the servo-mechanisms. That resulted in a zigzag course, sometimes lateral and sometimes spiraling. The passengers only perceived this when Jern used the telescope to check the jerky needles of the trajectory-indicators. They reversed the MC-drive and stopped.

It was necessary then to unmask the cupola. With sweat on his brow, Dal saw an extraordinary landscape of red mist appear before him, as if he were sailing aboard a submarine borne by a current rich in pelagic mud. The light of a red star that seemed to be very close was reflected from innumerable particles of nebular dust. That was the supergiant Betelgeuse, two hundred and fifty times greater in diameter than the Sun. At the other extreme of the cupola, infinitely distant, was Rigel, an extremely hot blue star, whose radiation was fifteen thousand times as powerful as that of the Sun. Orion was sparkling in the red mist. It was quite evident now that the constellations seen from Earth were merely the projection, on an ideal sphere, of stars whose distances from the Solar System varied considerably.

The course was calculated. Dal, with his head in his hands, fought against himself while waiting for Dr. Hafsen to give him a sedative injection. When the remedy had been administered, he raised his head painfully and looked directly at the dust of worlds and the multicoloured stars.

"Head for Betelgeuse," he said, without closing his eyes.

As they drew closer to the giant star, the red dust thinned out and vanished. The clouds were so subtle, the density of molecule per unit of volume so slight, that the nebula vanished as one went into it. Distance alone rendered it visible.

They were still getting closer to Betelgeuse. Dal was permanently ill, only gathering his thoughts at the price of constant effort and a continual struggle against himself. Jern Tranis helped him as much as he could, but the depletion of his memory and will-power seriously limited the services that he could provide. After for days of that terrible tension, Dal handed command over to Zoltan and surrendered to Dr. Hafsen's care.

He was going into the infirmary when the Housemaster-Baron sent him a telepathic message of extreme urgency.

Captain, he said, *everything's going awry. I'm not prepared to face up to...I...*

Dal lost the thread of the mental communication. Reeling, he returned along the gangway, leaning on the walls for support, and set foot on the upper deck, where a vertiginous spectacle awaited him.

With his arms raised, the Reverend was standing in the middle of the room, immobilized in a silent invocation. Tranis had collapsed into the helmsman' seat, with his head in his hands. As for Zoltan, he was leaning against the instrument-panel and murmuring incoherently. Beyond the cupola, in the depths of space, all the stars were being displaced rapidly with such rapidity that they now formed mere lines of light.

On the brink of fainting, Dal threw himself toward the gyroscope controls, but remembered that they were no use, because the ship was in G-drive—which was why centrifugal force had not crushed the men against the hull, for the vessel was spinning like a top. In antigravity phase, that seemed impossible, but it must have been subject to the same deceptive movement before the metallic cupola had been opened. Immense external forces were acting upon the fabric of space here. Dal remembered the barrier-field with which Markhart's vessel had collided. He made a terrible effort of will.

"To your posts!" he cried. "Prepare to deploy the Blue Weapon!"

Groans emerged from the interphone. The sections of the crew seemed to be under great stress. One voice, however, took form: "Order carried out, Captain."

Jern had straightened up. Zoltan tore himself away from the panel. Noktor said: "I'll go to the crew-positions. They may need...comforting."

The Reverend's face was livid. He set foot on the ladder that led to the gangway between the cabins.

"I received a loud mental transmission," said Zoltan. "That fact..." He searched for words.

Dal projected the thought: *Yes, of course, Zoltan Charles Henderson cannot express himself in an approximate manner...*

"Of course," said Zoltan. "That fact doubtless derives from the special treatment of my neurons. The crew seems to have received the wave..."

"Attention!" cried Dal. "Couple the graviton captors. Note the density. You're to emit for one microsecond, and note the new density."

"Yes, Captain," said the interphone.

"Fire!" cried Dal.

At first, nothing happened, then: "Gravitational flux unchanged. Space restructures itself after the passage of the ray."

"Very well!" Dal felt that he was inundated with sweat. "Fire at will!" he shouted into the interphone. Addressing Jern, he added: "G-drive, automatic heading toward Betelgeuse."

The spaceship was surrounded by a blue halo, which caused the stars to fade. Little by little, their movement relented, and then stopped. The ship was stabilized again, its prow pointed at the red star.

Dal sat down in the pilot's seat. He was trembling, but he never took his eyes off Space.

"We've certainly crossed the barrier-field," said Jern. "That barrier seems to be similar in nature to the nebular forces that we've already encountered—but organized by some intelligence..."

"An intelligence," said the young Navigator slowly, "that opposes access to the region in which Betelgeuse is located."

"We've got in, though," said Zoltan, "and we're making progress in spite of it."

Chapter Five

*"Beyond light and shadow, beyond all human
conception, monstrous planets move through
the silence of Space...."*
Song of the Perfecti
Psalm XVIII, Verse 9

Jern raised his head. "The calculations," he said, "show that there's only one planet. It's orbiting 30 billion kilometres from Betelgeuse, and is in opposition at this moment, less than a light-hour away."

"A billion kilometres," said Dal. "Prepare to land!" he cried.

From the interphone came the noise of a receptacle falling and liquid spilling—then hurried movement, and murmurs.

"Order received, Captain!" said a joyful voice.

Zoltan smiled. Dal looked at him and cut the communication-link. "I prefer seeing them like this," he said. "They'll doubtless need the nolej that they're busy drinking."

The interphone signal blinked. Dal restored contact and heard the voice of the Reverend. "All's well, now," Noktor said. "The crew is on top form, thank God!"

"Thank you, Reverend," said Dal. He could not help adding: "Thank God, acting through the intermediary of nolej. Be careful of abuse—one has to be able to recognize danger in order to combat it."

As he concluded this speech, the spatial optiphone began to crackle. On the deck, everyone fell silent, holding their breath. Someone was attempting to enter into communication with the vessel.

The apparatus continued crackling, though, and no other sound emerged.

"There's a transmitter somewhere on that planet," said Jern, in a voice that he tried to keep level.

Dal looked at him, and allowed himself to be hypnotized momentarily by the blazon that ornamented Tranis's metallic costume: a purple sun of an azure field with three gold besants. He tore himself from that contemplation to launch himself toward the interphone. "Localize the transmitter installed on the planet."

"Yes, Captain."

Silence fell again. Nothing was audible but the crackling of the optiphone, which varied neither in pitch nor in strength.

"Transmission localized," said the voice of the radio technician.

Instructions as to velocity and heading followed. There was a pause. Dal set the automatic pilot according to Jern's results.

"Vessel in orbit," said another voice.

"Landing maneuvers commenced," said another. "Touchdown in four hours, at a point close to the transmitter."

The four hours passed slowly. At the command-post, Dal recovered gradually from the intolerable malaise that had been inflicted on him by the energy barrier and his visual horror of Space. He had left the cupola unmasked, but knowing that there was a planet nearby had virtually suppressed his anguish and vertigo.

A blood-colored crescent was growing solely on the optiphone screen. The crescent thickened, becoming a semicircle, and then an entire circle, which diminished in the other direction; the *Solaris* was orbiting the planet. Soon, it was entirely dark. It eclipsed the disk of Betelgeuse, which reappeared, and it all started again.

The planet was still growing. The crackling sound had increased in intensity, but the waves brought nothing more— nor attempt at oral or visual communication. The strangest thing was the coincidence of wavelengths; the crackling coming from the planet had been audible since the outset, without anyone having to try to capture it—which signified that the transmission from Betelgeuse 1 was coming over the usual channel. It was necessary to conclude that it demonstrated a *human* presence.

The metallic cupola was closed.

The starship rested, immobile, on hard ground. Preliminary measurements had already informed the expedition that the dense atmosphere was rich in oxygen, but almost devoid of nitrogen. That gas was replaced here by argon.

"That," said Zoltan, with the utmost seriousness, "is certainly the atmosphere that ought to be awaiting us, gentlemen."

Jern and Dal, to whom he was talking, looked at one another, nonplussed.

"A very ancient mythology..." Zoltan began, through pursed lips. He stopped, and made an evasive gesture, renouncing any explanation of the meaning of his joke, secretly indignant that the leaders of such an expedition should be ignorant of the legend of the Argonauts...

The preliminaries continued: measurements of atmospheric pressure, gravity...

This world is much more voluminous than Earth," Jern observed. "It must have a relatively low density—which, combined with its rapid rotation, explains why the surface gravity isn't much greater here than on Earth, in the zone where we've landed. I think the speed of rotation plays a considerable role, and that weight varies considerably between the equator and the poles.

"We won't need space-suits to protect us from the radiation," Dal observed. "Betelgeuse's radiation is weak in short wavelengths."

Dr. Hafsen came into the pilot-room just then. "For the moment," he said, I haven't found any pathogenic germs among the specimens I've examined—but it will be necessary to continue sampling the atmosphere and the soil before the result becomes conclusive. In the meantime, our polyvaccine will suffice."

The Reverend was displaying the exterior landscape on the screens. He made a stifled exclamation that attracted the attention of the other people present toward him. They went to stand beside him, contemplatively.

"Let's go and look at it at closer range," said Dal. "According to the calculations, we still have two hours before nightfall."

The air seemed extremely invigorating, and the temperature was mild, although a trifle cool. One inconvenience, however, was that the wind bore a heavy pestilential odor, which Halfsen attributed to traces of methylamine.

Dal had divided his men into two groups. The first formed a cordon around the *Solaris*; the second was distributed as sharpshooters. The specialists, who had spent half the voyage in discussion with the doctor, were summoned. Noktor took the lead, immediately followed by Zoltan. Dal, Jern and Hafsen came next, and the specialists brought up the rear. Two columns of soldiers, projectors in hand, flanked the troop. Bork Talek and Arkel, Jern's bodyguard, formed the rear-guard.

The most striking thing of all was the color of the landscape: a desolate expanse of rocky crags, with occasional crevices, which captured the red light of Betegeuse and cast immense shadows. It seemed that the entire world was covered in a bloody fluid, or that every part of it was reflecting firelight. That violence in the color of the ground contrasted with the softness of the sky, but harmonized disagreeably with the charnel odor carried by the wind. One expected to discover charred remains still surrounded by dying flames, and cadavers scattered around.

The humans headed for an object of large dimensions they had perceived at the edge of the plateau.

"It resembles a colossal statue," said Noktor.

"There's certainly a fault a little further on," Zoltan added, "or else we're approaching the edge of a cliff up there at the top of the slope."

"Listen!" Hafsen interjected.

They cocked their ears. In the far distance, they heard a confused concert of strange voices, so numerous that they only formed a single sound. Occasionally, they recognized melodic divergences in the chorus, but the ensemble was coming from so far away that it wove a sonorous fabric as light as gauze, whose shreds unravelled on the red wind.

"Be careful!" said Zoltan. "Those aren't human voices."

No one commented further. The soldiers seemed nervous. To one side, Bor Talek started a lively discussion with Arkel. Dal was overcome by a sudden fit of ill-humor.

"Bork and Arkel!" he shouted. "Get back to the column."

They obeyed, sullenly.

Zoltan came over to Dal then. "Captain," he said, in an excessively meek tone, "I would be grateful if you would allow me to make a suggestion."

Dal looked at him, frowning, and nodded his head curtly.

"My knowledge of archaeology," Zoltan went on, "leads me to draw a comparison. Incredibly ancient texts speak of a hero who had to conquer voices. That happened at sea. I observe that there are quarrels breaking out between us without any cause, and I fear that these distant voices might be responsible. As I say this to you, I'm forcing myself to be calm, for I would willingly speak to you with a disproportionate indignation and rage. Believe me, Captain, it would be salutary if we all wore helmets and cut out the environmental minutiae."

Dal stamped his foot on the ground, noticing as he did so that there was something abnormal about the gesture. He started to shout: "Retreat! Everyone back to the *Solaris*—and quickly!"

He brandished his coagulant with a ferocious expression. A concert of furious cries greeted his order, but everyone moved back to the vessel. Dal told the soldiers forming the cordon to go back in as well; they obeyed him, grumbling.

Once inside, that sort of collective dementia vanished abruptly.

"I was beset by ideas of murder!" confessed the Reverend, fearfully.

All the men looked guilty. Dal felt that he was in control of himself again, but he was disturbed. "That's one danger that out preliminary observations didn't reveal," he said, anxiously. "I'm very grateful for your intervention, Baron."

Zoltan smiled and bowed; that was the title he liked best, and Dal was not unaware of it.

"We'll take your advice," Dal continued, "and then we'll resume the interrupted exploration. Let's go to the clothing stores immediately."

They hastened along the gangways in single file.

Dal had ordered a second sortie, and the same troop advanced in good order. The sonic isolation conserved their peace of mind; the men were protected henceforth from exterior sounds, and could only hear the words of their comrades or their leaders, through the intermediary of the helmet antennae.

This countermeasure proved, in an incontestable manner, the role of the distant voices in the mental disturbances that had affected the commandoes on disembarkation.

Weight was slightly greater here than on Earth. Combined with the sloping ground, it produced a rather rapid fatigue. The primary objective was close at hand, however, and the little column soon reached it.

It was indeed a statue, but of such enormous proportions that everyone was disconcerted. *Someone* had sculpted it—or, rather constructed it—out of the same material as the ground, a black and slightly brittle stone, clearly different from the lighter-colored rock that cleft the surface. The megalithic work of art that loomed up, black against the fiery sky, had something sinister and formidable about it. The men surrounded it with a kind of religious respect, which Noktor did not encourage, but to which he too was subject.

Dr. Hafsen was the first to recognize the effigy. He was heard to murmur: "That's impossible…it makes no sense." He drew back, in order to be able to view the enormous statue all at once. Through the visor of his helmet, the expression on his face was indistinguishable. "There's no possible mistake, though," he added. He came back to his companions, who were waiting for him impatiently. "Have you realized," he said slowly, "that this is the image of a human embryo?"

A long silence followed Dr. Hafsen's words. Then the gerontologists specified: "A human embryo at approximately six months. The period at which the heart begins to beat—when it becomes legitimate to consider the fetus as a being endowed with a personal existence."

They were all now discovering in the form of the statue the visual illustrations of the elements of embryology with which they had been inculcated.

"How do you explain that?" said Dal, eventually, using the formal version of *you*. He was definitely taking on the idiosyncrasies of Zoltan's speech.

Hafsen made a gesture of ignorance. "There are two possible explanations," he said. "Either there exists a race closely resembling ours, for whom the prenatal form has a special significance—probably religious—or this was fashioned by Solarians. I'm leaning toward the second hypothesis, because of the transmission we intercepted before landing."

"Are they the same people, then?" asked the Reverend. "The ones who sculpted this, and the ones transmitting?"

"No. Remember the buildings of Songa. The civilization that preceded the Blue War was orientated toward the immense, the colossal. Nothing prevents us from thinking that this statue dates from before the Blue War. On the other hand, the customary channel on which we captured a crackling proves that the transmitter is a recent importation. It's only 50 years since the official exchanges adopted that wavelength."

A new silence descended. What Hafsen had said seemed perfectly rational, but it complicated everything.

"We have to find that transmitter," Dal cut in, "and also those who are making use of it—or, rather, who aren't making use of it. Let's extend our reconnaissance to the edge of the cliff first; it doesn't seem to be very far away."

The column resumed marching. Several men turned round to look at the enormous black mass that stood up against the flaming sky, and the most bizarre comments circulated through the ranks.

As they approached the edge of the plateau, they sensed the presence of a gulf: the presence of the void, the physical reality of space—the painful effects of which the young commander recognized.

They were within a few paces. Vertigo began to affect them. Without a word, they dispersed along the extreme edge, rendered mute by the spectacle that opened up before their eyes.

Dal vanquished his malaise and hoisted himself up on to the summit of a little spur of rock. Lying on his belly, he plunged his gaze into the immensity.

He was overlooking a gigantic abyss, at least four thousand meters deep. The horizon was a black expanse whose distant outline was undeniably reminiscent of the swell of a sea. That limitless expanse presented all the characteristics of an ocean; much closer, it was beating its slow and heavy waves upon an exceedingly pale-colored strand, which extended in a narrow band along the foot of the monstrous cliff.

Dal took off his helmet and let the wind strike his face. He had forgotten the noxious odor borne by that wind; even though he could no longer hear the dangerous concert of distant voices, he shielded himself again. Words resonated in his earpiece—the geologist talking to the physicist.

"An extremely ancient collapse," he was saying. "This planet has been subject to titanic upheavals."

"At least the ocean has partly dried out…but it's not water. It looks like some sort of bitumen from here. I can't see any sort of evaporation…"

"Captain!" said Zoltan. "You're well-placed—can you see the face of the cliff?"

"Vertical," Dal replied. "Smooth and sheer. It's an infernal landscape."

"An infernal landscape, you say? I see that you, too, have been struck by the ancient texts. Infernal is definitely the words that our ancestors would have employed."

Dal smiled behind the visor of his helmet. He was not displeased to have shown Zoltan that he had some notion of archaeology. The Housemaster-Baron was becoming irritating, though, with his extravagant knowledge. The smile left his face immediately, though: that sinister immensity was distilling a sort of horror, which he was anxious to escape.

Zoltan tore him out of it be replying to his thought: "I'm not unaware that I'm sometimes a trifle irritating, Captain. Excuse me—I feel as old as the Earth."

Of course…he was always forgetting that Zoltan was a telepath! In the final analysis, Dal thought, he was an enormous asset to the company, for they could rely on Zoltan, and he was capable of detecting any kind of treason in advance.

"Thank you!" said Zoltan, with a small laugh.

Dal abandoned the game and quit his rock. The majority of the Expedition's members had scarcely paid any heed to Zoltan and Dal's incomprehensible dialogue. They were petrified by the abyss, and the young Navigator had to repeat his orders before they would consent to carry them out.

They went back to the *Solaris* hurriedly. Night was already falling on the black ocean, and the darkening gulf gaped like the enormous mouth of a half-extinct oven. All the men retained the memory of that inhuman vision in their minds, and the troubling enigma posed by the gigantic monument was not easily erasable.

The vessel seemed to be asleep in the shadows.

Dal was determined that all of them men should be safe inside as soon as night fell. The daylight had revealed sufficient dangers for the crew not to be exposed to those of darkness.

113

The captain of the *Solaris* could not help experiencing a certain anxiety at the thought that unknown forms and living organisms—and perhaps a hostile human colony—might have been spying on the disembarkation without anyone being aware of their presence. That anxiety encouraged him to leave the vessel in darkness, thus avoiding any possibility of attracting the attention of enemies, if they had not already been informed of the human presence. However, he was no less determined to keep watch on the vicinity of the ship, in order to prevent any attempt at an attack under cover of darkness. For the sake of this second tactic, Dal decided to unmask the cupola—which permitted a field of vision much more extensive than that of the screens—and to deploy searchlights.

"That risks attracting…visitors," observed Jern, hesitantly.

"I've thought of that," Dal replied. "That's the reason we're here—and a little sooner or later…"

The vessel's general staff was standing on the catwalk that circled the large transparent dome. Around them, within a wide radius, the darkness retreated before the white light of the searchlights—a white light that was not of this world, dominated by the frequencies ranging from orange to infrared. The continual crackling of the optiphone had been switched off, and the catwalk reposed in a profound silence, only interrupted by a few brief words.

Dal was about to allocate the watches when the Reverend frowned and extended his arm. "Over there," he said. "I thought I saw…"

They turned in the direction he was indicating.

"What?" said Hafsen.

Noktor put his face to the window. "I don't know…a moving form. It's no longer visible."

Dal operated a rheostat. Outside, the beams of the searchlights built into the hull broadened out. The range of visibility decreased, but the immediate vicinity of the vessel was inundated with light.

"Oh!" said Zoltan.

Dal started. Something had passed rapidly through the light—something sleek, glossy and black. So far as they had been able to tell, the thing had been propelled by two large and powerful wings.

There was a breathless silence; then Noktor murmured: "Winged creatures... *the Planet of the Archangels.*"

"Hmm," said Zoltan. "The archangels of ancient religion didn't look like that, according to the descriptions given of them." He laughed. "For archangels were very precisely described," he added, "as if their inventors had really seen them."

"Who knows?" said the Reverend, pensively.

"Whatever it might be..." Zoltan continued.

There was a backward movement on the gangway, and fearful exclamations. Something of large dimensions had just struck the cupola with unexpected violence, clung there for a second and then disappeared. They had all been able to discern, clearly, two enormous black wings, and an elongated body surmounted by a vaguely human head, dotted with two white eyes devoid of irises.

"Your archangels, Reverend," said Zoltan, coldly, amid the general alarm, "are the offspring of a cross between a Mlol and a female pterodactyl..."

Dal had adopted the Housemaster-Baron as a role-model. He was in command of the expedition, but he was nonetheless an adolescent. He thought about Jaral Kerr. Models. He had even more need of examples: models of generosity like Jaral, of self-composure like Zoltan. He went to the interphone and put himself in communication with the laboratory. "Nel Horst," he said, calmly, "Will you please join us on the cat-walk."

"I'm on my way, Captain," said the zoologist's voice.

A minute later, Horst made the sign of protection, which Dal reciprocated.

"Nel," said the young Navigator, "There's a creature outside with regard to which I'd like you to give me your opinion."

Horst approached the transparent wall. Zoltan watched Dal surreptitiously, with an approving smile. *Something really might be made of that boy*, he said to himself, without projecting his thought. He knew that the zoologist's observations would not be very useful, in the present state of things, but that Dal had summoned him to create a diversion, especially for the benefit of Jern Tranis, who had obviously not succeeded in overcoming his distress. Jern had been sorely tried by what he had experienced in the course of the previous expedition—and even Zoltan had to admit that the general climate of this planet of blood and shadows was scarcely favourable to nervous equilibrium.

As it was necessary to wait for it, the winged monster did not reappear. For several minutes Horst searched the darkness, darting an occasional interrogatory glance at he other people present.

"Be patient," said Dal, negligently. "It will surely come back."

The cupola vibrated under the shock. Three huge black forms had just collided with it at the same time. They tried to get a grip on it, beating their wings angrily. Everyone could see the flat faces with the enormous white eyes, and the jaws equipped with a single trenchant blade, like those of tortoises—and nothing more.

Horst had leapt backwards. Beads of sweat were forming on his temples. "The...the worst hybrids on Earth are less hideous than that!" he said. He breathed out, and directed a terrified gaze through the cupola. "And they're probably not animals," he added.

Dal straightened up. "Why is that?"

Horst shook his head. "Haven't you noticed anything?" he said. He was short of breath.

"Explain!"

Horst pulled himself together. "Under the wings. They're carrying long shiny boxes attached beneath their wings. Either these creatures are domesticated, or intelligent."

"If they're intelligent," said Hafsen, "why are they hurling themselves against the cupola like that?"

Nel grimaced. "Perhaps they're disconcerted by the event that our appearance constitutes...I doubt that, though, since other Solarians must have landed here."

"Bah!" said Jern, without conviction. "They're dazzled by the light!"

Dal remained silent. All things considered, Nel's intervention had been productive, but it was not comforting. "It's necessary to make contact with them," he said, finally, "and as soon as possible. There's every chance that they're nocturnal, and that we won't encounter them in daylight. If they're intelligent, perhaps we can make them understand that we haven't come as enemies, and obtain some indication from them concerning...what we're looking for."

"The Prophet," Noktor put in.

"Yes, if such a person exists. If they really represent what legend calls archangels, let's not forget that the same legend claims that they are, in one way or another, connected with the Prophet. Guards, servants...how do I know? It's necessary to use them to attain our end."

"And if they're opposed to it?" said Jern.

"Come on, Tranis, pull yourself together," said Dal, as if Jern had said something stupid or incongruous. It was important that no one doubted the result of the search; they would need considerable trust to put themselves in the claws of these flying nightmares. However, as Dal did not want anyone to think that he had lost all lucidity and prudence, he added: "We have powerful weapons, and our men are trained and resolute. The members of this Expedition have been carefully selected, and the Sopharchy has armed the *Solaris* as no stellar vessel has ever been armed before. Set your hearts and minds at rest."

Contrary to what he preached, Dal was neither confident nor serene. He sometimes felt weak, to the point where he had already passed command to Zoltan once. Circumstances had constrained him not to abandon his post at that time, whatever his state of depression. On this menacing planet, he had succeeded in struggling against fear; he would succeed in facing up to the enormous responsibility that Kalla's father had placed on his shoulders. He fortified himself thus against doubt, but it did not happen without an ever-renewed conflict in which he was never certain of emerging victorious...

He turned to Zoltan. "Do you have the impression that a mental contact is possible?"

Zoltan pulled a face. "I tried, a few minutes ago, but I didn't get anything very precise. Nevertheless, I feel that Nel Horst isn't far from the truth in conceding them a psychic development superior to animal affect and conditioning. If you doubt your judgment, Horst, it's more probably in error by default than excess, for it seemed to me that it was as if I were bathing in a whirlwind of mental waves deprived of images. A—how can I put it?—a flux of abstractions. In my opinion, these creatures aren't merely intelligent—they're possessed of *advanced* intelligence."

Dal pushed back a rebellious strand of hair that had fallen over his eyes, Kalla had asked him not to have his head shaved. "Do you think you can obtain a better result if we venture outside?"

"No, Captain. The hull of the *Solaris* doesn't present an obstacle to exchanges of encephalic waves. It seems futile to me to expose anyone. Thus far, we may hope that they can't do anything to the vessel itself."

Noktor drew nearer. "You seem to be attributing bellicose intentions to them," he said. "That's not necessarily the case..."

"No, Reverend—but the problem remains."

"All right," Dal concluded. "We'll remain sheltered tonight, and we'll begin serious exploration tomorrow. Let's not forget the question of the transmitter."

The wall of the cupola resonated for some time under the impact of another giant bat. Dal switched off the searchlights.

Zoltan dreamed about vampires, and inadvertently transmitted his nightmares to some of the crew. It was necessary to distribute a special ration of nolej in the middle of the night. Dr. Hafsen explained that, in this particular instance, the amazing self-control of which the Housemaster-Baron gave proof was an inconvenience, in the sense that his repressed emotions gave themselves free expression during sleep. Zoltan's telepathic ability then served the function of an optiphone for thought, and the aftershock of his composure translated itself into a general terror. Hafsen presented his reasoning with an indignation and partiality so obviously exaggerated that he restored calm to the minds of the crew through the intermediary of laughter.

It was a fortunate result, considering that the nightmares were supplements by the dull thuds that often reverberated through the hull of the *Solaris*, giving rise to the image of flat-nosed faces with corneas as white as shrouds in the darkness: doors closed over superhuman intelligence…

The second half of the night—which lasted 17 hours—was filled with passionate discussions between Hafsen and the three academics. While the Technicians and the Guards continue their interminable games of Stall in the crew's quarters, Arkel and Bor Talek came to join the vessel's general staff, under the pretext that that they were attached to the two Knights and that they had, not a right, but a duty never to be apart from them.

They considered various possible methods of making contact with the winged creatures. The one that gathered most votes consisted of capturing one of them with the aid of noctalium and freeing it in order to use it as a go-between, after obtaining a few mental exchanges. No one was deceived by the apparent simplicity of this procedure.

"At any rate," Dal declared, "we'll undoubtedly be unable to try anything before tomorrow night. It's the transmitter that we must focus our attention on during the day."

The huge disk of Betelgeuse rose into the colorless morning sky.

The travelers left the ship again. The giant bats had ceased to manifest themselves before dawn, and Dal had decided to make the most of the long day at their disposal. He had decided to return to the statue first, because it had been impossible to examine it attentively the previous evening by virtue of the impending dusk.

A great silence hung over the landscape. The men were beginning to get used to the pestilential odor carried by the wind, and were thus able to make the journey without helmets. Dal remained alert, ready to give immediate orders if the distant voices should reach their ears again, but the silence was untroubled, and they reached the huge sculpted black without incident.

They were dispersing around the gigantic fetal form when an exclamation rang out, uttered by Noktor. "Come here! Come quickly! How did we miss this yesterday?"

They hastened to the Reverend's side. He was standing in front of one of the sides of the pedestal. Clearly picked out in the black substance by the as-yet-oblique orange light of Betelgeuse, engraved characters were distinguishable. On closer inspection, it proved that the pedestal was covered with them.

"It's unreadable," said Noktor, piteously. "It's a non-human language."

Zoltan leaned closer. "In spite of the great respect in which I hold you, Reverend," he said, "I don't share your opinion. It's the language that people usually spoke on the Three Planets before the Blue War. Some words and phrases therefrom are still in use in Songa."

This affirmation had a considerable effect. Zoltan was surrounded enthusiastically. "Can you translate it?" was the cry.

Zoltan smiled. Everyone was now using the formal version of *you*.

"It's not easy," he said, "but I think I can do it."

He became absorbed in reading the inscription. While he was studying it, Dal went around the pedestal, and stopped in front of other characters—other words—that were comprehensible!

"I've made a discovery too!" he announced. "Listen to this!" And he read aloud: *"Recording in grotto foot of cliff. Housemaster Markhart."*

This time, it was Dal who was surrounded. "Notice," he said, "how ill-formed the letters are. It seems that Markhart engraved this in haste."

"But why didn't he say anything to us about all this?" asked Hafsen, in astonishment.

"I think he'd also lost his memory," Jern suggested, "and was only able to retain the co-ordinates of the place where he'd landed. Consider my case—I too am incapable of remembering what I learned before my check, but if I didn't know that Betelgeuse was involved, it's probably because Markhart never pronounced the name. Something retains remembrance here, and one leaves with a memory emptied of its contents. Fortunately, those who have landed on the planet have left traces of their passage here."

There was a long discussion. Then they heard Zoltan's voice, from behind the stature: "It isn't as difficult as I thought!" he exclaimed. "But it's necessary to take immediate precautions!"

His voice drew nearer as he spoke. He appeared at the corner of the pedestal. His brows were furrowed. As he approached, he looked over his shoulder, then darted a glance at the sky. This conduct disturbed the men.

"Captain," said Zoltan, "I suggest that we go back to the ship, even though…well, I'll explain everything there."

"Retreat!" shouted Dal, who had confidence in Zoltan.

They all returned to the *Solaris* at a run. As the last man climbed in, innumerable black dots appeared in the sky.

The hull resonated under the impact of giant bats. In the command-post, Dal had the metal cupola replaced. Zoltan switched on the listening equipment and looked at his companions. A tide of strange cries emerged from the microphone—cries in which they were able to recognize something akin to syllables:

"Luc-touge…luc-touge…luc-touge…"

The first syllable, very brief, was followed by a sort of long wail, and then it began again: "Luc-touge…luc-touge…"

Zoltan cut it off. "The first colonists, naturally, called them *Luctouges*," he said. "Those creatures wiped out the immigrants completely."

He switched on the optiphone. On the screens, dense flocks of bats with livid eyes were massing their black wings in the bloody rays of Betelgeuse.

Zoltan turned the sound down but left the image. "Let's start at the beginning," he said. "But before anything else, you can see as well as me that the *Luctouges* aren't nocturnal…which won't simplify our exploration. On the other hand, I don't know why they haven't yet reduced the *Solaris* to dust. That might happen at any moment."

Noktor began to pray. Dal issued orders into the interphone. "Battle stations! Open up the large projectors! Bring the coagulants to bear!"

A sudden animation filled the vessel. Cavities resonated, sealed gunports opened with vibrations that extended through the sealed walls. An emotional voice emerged from the interphone, crying: "Ready, Captain!"

Zoltan shook his head. "You can give the order to fire, Captain," he said, "but I fear that it won't do any good. These creatures are practically invulnerable."

"We won't fire until they attack," Dal declared. "That would be irremediable."

Zoltan shrugged his shoulders slightly. "This is what I know…" he said.

He spoke, and everyone listened passionately, for what the inscription had told him finally cast some light into the Historical Gulf.

In April 4580 of the Solarian calendar, the Terran government mounted the first interstellar expedition equipped with the G-drive. Photonic rockets had already existed for nearly two millennia, but there had never been any news of those that had been sent forth—and the two immense vessels loaded with emigrants that had been launched with them had also disappeared into the silence of Space. That ignorance with respect to results, combined with the fabulous investment necessitated by the construction and equipment of such ships, had caused interstellar expeditions to be abandoned...until the G-drive had virtually abolished the relevant distances

In parallel, the laboratories of Earth had been conducting exotic researches in the field of biology. In 4560 or thereabouts, the treatment of non-viable human embryos had produced a kind of stagnation of the fetal state, compensated by a monstrous development of the embryonic brain. The experiment had only succeeded on a single subject, perhaps by chance, a conjunction of hidden causes escaping the experimenters and realizing the optimum conditions without their being aware of it. At any rate, a giant fetus had been obtained, with a brain more developed than that of an adult human. It had been kept in a tube filled with liquid nutrient, warmed and supplied with oxygen and assimilable molecules by a nuclear-powered servo-mechanism, which utilized whatever materials surrounding it for constant transmutation.

Thus freed of all dependence and any external contingency, the embryo had been installed in a room in the Principal Biology Laboratory of Kalinda, the Terran capital. The tube had been placed, along with the nutritive mechanism, in an exceedingly thick metallic envelope, which served as material for transmutation. That envelope had been supplemented by another, made of a substance proof against all known radiations, perfected by the same physics laboratories that had developed the marvelous nutritive servo-mechanism.

Why had they taken these precautions? It was because, after a certain time—about 4564—the immediate environment of the tube containing the fetus had been subject to singular phenomena: the displacement of objects, the appearance of luminous bubbles, the focusing of sounds at certain points in space...and also the birth of obsessive ideas in the laboratory assistants working in the vicinity, especially sinister ideas—including the inevitability of an imminent war that would be much more frightful than anything the Three Planets had ever seen. Now, at that time, the political balance between Mars, Venus and Earth had not yet taken a disturbing turn.

Five years later, the espionage services of Kalinda were reporting information that, although vague and truncated, nevertheless presented an extremely alarming character. It was rumored that the Venusian colony, which was very advanced economically and technically, had perfected an ultimate weapon.

Although the cold war of diplomats and spies continued, and military resources on Mars as well as Earth were at levels never previously attained, the laboratories of Kalinda decided to put the product of their research in a safe place, and had the giant fetus placed in the hold of vessel that was to carry emigrants in the direction of Betelgeuse.

The audience was hanging on Zoltan's every word. In the background, the faint lugubrious cries of the Luctouges mingled together. The Housemaster-Baron continued his story.

The vessel bore the name of the Terran capital; it was called the *Kalinda*. Its voyage proceeded without incident, and it made no intermediate landfall. Having arrived in the vicinity of Betelgeuse, it was perceived that the five habitable planets advertised by Earth-based instruments did not exist, and that there as only one world orbiting the red supergiant. Fortunately, it possessed a breathable atmosphere, and the pioneers established themselves there.

It was then that the Luctouges appeared. They annihilated half the colonists and almost everything they had built in a single day. The people had built a gigantic statue in the image of the fetus they had transported, following a crisis of religious mysticism that had contaminated all of the *Kalinda*'s personnel. The statue was neglected by the Luctouges, but they carried off the sarcophagus that had been placed at its summit, which contained the embryo. The people saw the swarm of aggressors fly away over the Black Ocean and dive into it, along with their idol. They were plunged into deep despair, and no longer had the courage to resist the further raids that followed.

The *Kalinda* was destroyed by radiations emitted by the Luctouges, which emerged from the shiny boxes they carried beneath their wings. The monsters adapted themselves with diabolical intelligence to all the parries that the survivors attempted, and the colony was soon wiped off the face of the planet. The expedition's psychologist was the last person to be killed, while he was inscribing the story of the Terrans' annihilation on the pedestal of the statue.

All gazes turned to the screens.

"There's nothing to hope for from them," said Dal, somberly. He clenched his fists and turned to the interphone. "Fire at will!" he ordered.

Nothing happened. The deadly rays departing from the *Solaris* passed through the clouds of Luctouges without killing a single one. Dal ordered a cease fire.

"It's as I feared," Zoltan observed. "The colonists of the *Kalinda* were better armed than we are, and they were annihilated. The Luctouges' radiation-emitter must also generate a force-field that protects them."

"Even the Blue Weapon might be ineffective against them," said Jern, his face taut.

"Nothing can resist the Blue Weapon," said Dal, peremptorily. He feared that a spirit of defeat was hanging over the *Solaris*, and was not overly optimistic himself as to the way in which things would turn out.

"But if they can destroy a spaceship, why haven't they attacked the *Solaris* yet?" ventured Noktor.

No one replied. Dread was infiltrating them, for they sensed they were presently subject to a delay—a delay that might end at any moment.

"Let's attack them first with the Blue Weapon!" said Dr. Hafsen, a trifle precipitately.

Dal thought about it. If he made use of the Venusian weapon and it had no effect, panic would break out almost immediately. On whom could he count, then, to prevent the Expedition from fleeing Betelgeuse without having fulfilled its mission? Furthermore, if the Luctouges had not yet attacked, perhaps they would remain in expectation for quite some time.

"No," Dal replied. "Only as a last resort. For now, it's necessary to explore the Black Ocean, since the inscription affirms that..." He suddenly realized what his words implied: subconsciously, he had understood the direction in which his research ought to be directed. Slowly, he concluded: "...Since the inscription affirms that the Luctouges carried off the embryo to the bottom of the ocean—which is to say that the 'Archangels' are holding beneath that ocean the 'Immortal Prophet' who predicted the Blue War."

There was an astonished silence; then a few exclamations were raised. Dal was pleased by the effect he had produced, for it constituted another excellent diversion.

Only Noktor seemed sceptical; he could not admit that the Prophet was, in reality, the product of a long-lost laboratory. "You all know," he said, "that I am not one of those priests of narrow and pessimistic vision, who raise obstacles throughout the Three Planets—but this time, think, you're skirting on blasphemy."

"What do you know about it?" demanded Hafsen—who, by contrast, found the hypothesis quite satisfactory. "Why

126

must a prophet be an adult, normally-constituted human being? Is it normal to be a prophet?"

Noktor launched into a theological argument, while Hafsen developed his own ideas, supported by biology. It was, as always, a quarrel of the deaf—but Dal rejoiced in it, for everyone seemed to be forgetting the Luctouges.

"Excuse me," said Zoltan. "It's equally necessary that you know what else I read on the pedestal of the statue."

The adversaries fell silent.

"Another vessel landed on this planet," said Zoltan. "In the year 4597, a vessel laden with emigrants from the Three Planets left Earth. That vessel reached Alpha Centauri, where the colony of Songa was founded. The people who originally composed it had been plucked from the shadiest districts and taverns. An iron discipline soon reigned there.

"The following year, a band of rogues captured one of the small police spaceships that Kalinda had just dispatched to Songa, and set off for the planet of Betelgeuse, expecting to find a flourishing colony there. The blackguards leading that company explored the planet with the aid of highly-perfected instruments that the police ship contained, discovered the statue, read the inscription and engraved another. These vagabonds boasted therein about their exploit and recorded their decision to go back to Kalinda instead of Songa.

"They must have escaped the Luctouges, and they were the ones who brought the legend of the prophet and the archangels to the solar system. The Blue War broke out in 4630 or thereabouts. The legend thus had time to spread everywhere…"

Noktor was thoughtful. "I remain convinced," he said, "that the prophet, whatever he might be, is inspired by God."

"Oh, that I'll concede to you, Reverend," said Hafsen, who could not prove the contrary and was not much interested in the question.

"Look!" cried Jern.

The screens were empty, and the cries of the Luctouges had died away.

"Let's take this opportunity to follow Markhart's indications!" said the young Navigator, who had not forgotten his own discovery. "Remember that Markhart, too, has landed here."

He sat down in the pilot's seat after giving instructions to the technicians. A few minutes later, the *Solaris* set down on the beach 4000 meters below.

Seen from that spot, the scene was even more surprising than when they had looked down into the abyss from the top of the cliff. The beach was several hundred meters wide, and was limited by the smooth wall whose summit was lost in the sky, almost out of sight. On the other side, waves of an extraordinary heaviness and viscosity bordered the narrow expanse of reddish dust: black waves, slowly seething.

"They're not waves," declared Fayal, the geologist. "The wind could never have the necessary violence to elevate this sort of bitumen. It's *boiling*."

Huge round objects, orange-yellow in color, were crawling along the "beach." They examined them on the screens, but Jern also switched on the sound. The dangerous voices that they had heard the day before were unleashed in the command-post with a noisy intensity. Jern immediately cut them off.

"It's these...mollusks that produce that sound," said Horst.

Hafsen raised his eyebrows. "Mollusks adapted to life in *boiling tar*, and which *sing*?" he said.

"I can't understand it at all," Horst said, regretfully, "but it seems so."

"And their voices provoke fits of rage in those who hear them?" completed Bolene, the chemist.

"As we have discovered at our own expense."

They watched the animals—but Dal raised his eyes toward the sky. "Let's make a sortie immediately," he said. "The Luctouges don't seem to be coming back. If they appear during our absence, the crew can employ the Blue Weapon against them. I'll give orders to that effect. Put on your helmets—wherever that choir comes from, it's necessary to protect ourselves against it."

He orientated the optiphone receiver toward the cliff, and pointed out a fissure that cut into its base.

"Than enormous hole is some distance away," he said, "but there doesn't seem to be another within visual range. That's undoubtedly the cave in which Markhart left his recording."

The company prepared to leave the vessel. Dal had given the order to get the Venusian weapon ready, and to fire if a flock of Luctouges appeared.

The expedition was brief. It was Bolene who found the transmitter, fuelled by a small nuclear reactor, on top of a mound of pebbles, with its antenna still deployed. For one reason or another, the crystal recorder was no longer in contact with the reader-head, which had interrupted the transmission. The crackling the *Solaris* had picked up obviously came from Markhart's transmitter. They took away the whole thing and regained the ship without encountering any resistance.

It was with great curiosity that Jern placed the crystal in contact with the reader-head; they listened religiously to the words that the Housemster had pronounced more than a year before.

Markhart had taken part in an Expedition financed by Mars, where he had been born. He had been invited to join it by the Navigator commanding it, and his participation had seemed advisable, in consequence of certain revelations that he had made to the Grand Council of Delegates on Mars.

During a voyage to Venus, the Housemaster had met a half-mad individual in a hotel in the astroport, who, under the influence of nolej, had claimed that the Immortal Prophet was to be found on a planet orbiting a star in the constellation Orion. He based this contention on secret Venusian espionage reports that dated from before the Blue War, and which he had discovered himself in the foundations of the ancient capital of Venus.

The man was drunk, and Markhart helped him back to his room. In the morning, he had disappeared. The Housemaster considered that it was his duty to communicate the information he had gleaned, true or false, to the Sopharchy, but he had made use of his planet's Council of Delegates as an intermediary, which had set up an Expedition without informing the Sopharchy as to its destination, doubtless in the slightly puerile hope of finally getting one up on the Terran Navigators.

The Expedition had taken four years to reach Betelgeuse, which it had explored belatedly after having roamed Orion and visited Rigel. It had eventually discovered the statue, but no one had been able to decipher the inscription on its pedestal. Markhart had left with the Expedition's priest in the lifeboat to attempt to gather further information, but, while they were exploring the foot of the cliff, he had received new orders from the vessel, which had been attacked by the Luctouges: the lifeboat being unarmed, and much less powerful in every sense than the ship, he was to limit himself to leaving a record of his passage, after having hidden the machine, and then beat a retreat.

The desperate Markhart had obeyed his captain's orders, and hidden the little space vehicle in the cave. However, at the moment when he and the priest were depositing the recording and the transmitter on the mound where Bolene had found it, mollusks had invaded the beach and their voices had resounded in the cave. Markhart and his companion had attacked one another savagely in the dementia provoked by those other-worldly voices, and the priest had been seriously injured. In a moment of lucidity, Markhart had dragged the inanimate reverend into the lifeboat, where he had waited for a long time. Finally risking everything, he had made the decision to leave the planet, adding a few words to his recording before departure, in which he declared his intention to revisit the plateau, even though the transmissions from the ship had been interrupted a long time before.

Markhart must have found the wreckage of the ship and engraved his own hasty inscription. He had escaped the Luctouges, and had doubtless been picked up by a cruiser from Songa. He was not yet imprisoned when Tranis had passed through the Alpha system, but he had not been able to enjoy his liberty much longer…

On the deck of the *Solaris*, a minute's silence was observed in memory of Housemaster Markhart.

Dal raised his head again. There was a fiery gleam in the depths of his gaze. He spoke rapidly, almost brutally, into the interphone: "Battle stations! Prepare for combat! Deploy anti-radiation measures. Blue Weapon at the ready."

He sat down in the pilot's seat. The *Solaris* took off, presented its prow to the Black Ocean, and set off over the surface. With its cupola entirely shielded, it dived into the boiling magma.

Dal let the ship run on, blindly, without the optiphones being able to pick up the slightest image or sound. Soon, they were travelling more slowly, as evidenced by the indicators on the control panel. Then the vessel came to a halt.

"Is this the bottom?" Zoltan asked, leaning over the dials as if they were able to tell him.

Dal made no reply, and tried to go back up a few meters. Impossible. He consulted the external viscosity indicator. The needle was moving toward the infinity symbol.

"Infinite viscosity…" said Jern, whose face was livid.

Bolene passed his hand across his brow. "We're…encased in the substance as in a solid," he said. "This frightful bitumen has solidified around us." Fear widened his eyes.

"But the Luctouges risk themselves here…" said Hafsen

"Perhaps they're the ones who have solidified the substance around us," suggested Horst.

Dal said nothing, and manipulated the G-drive controls. His back arched. He looked over his shoulder at his companions. "We're immobilized," he said. "The enormous power of the drive is inoperative. It's as if we've been sealed in a block of cement."

His rage surpassed his dread. Was the *Solaris*, then, going to terminate its Expedition in this lamentable and sinister fashion, without reaching its goal? Perhaps it would have been futile to reach the Prophet...perhaps the vessel would have gone back to Lassenia without bringing the Sopharchy the solution to the great puzzle...but who could tell? If the inscription had not lied, and the Embryo was still alive inside its double shield, what might one not hope of that enormous brain and its immeasurable psychic abilities?

Henceforth, the occupants of Solaris would have to live inside this habitable bubble inside an indestructible mass. That might last for years...

Hafsen thought of Koch bacilli, sealed in a calcareous husk by the lung they had attacked...

"To try the MC-drive," Dal murmured, "would destroy the ship for sure—and the G-derive still has no effect..."

"Perhaps we might try a high-powered ultra-sonic emission?" said Fayal. "It's not impossible that it might render the bitumen friable."

With a skeptical pout, Dal ordered the discharge. The *Solaris* was protected against the weapon—which, in these circumstances, might rebound against it. Nothing changed outside, though.

Dal hardened himself. He pronounced his words in a clipped tone. "Blue Weapon, one hundredth of a second burst. Fire!"

The screens transmitted a blue light, and the vessel seemed to fall abruptly. Dal sat up straight, while a flood of howls invaded the pilot-station.

"The Luctouges!" cried Noktor.

There was still nothing visible on the screens. Then the ship, whose fall had been braked by the anti-G screens, made a soft landing. Dal activated the external searchlights.

The *Solaris* was resting on an uneven ground. 100 meters above it there was a somber vault, from which a large hole had allowed a bitumen stalactite to flow, which had solidified before touching the ground. In spite of the clamoring of the Luctouges and the nightmarish forms whirling around on the screens, everyone on the deck breathed a sight of relief.

"We've just escaped perpetual imprisonment," said Jern, who still seemed very emotional.

Dal turned up the searchlights to maximum power, directing all those mounted on the cupola into a single convergent beam, and began a slow circular sweep.

Incomprehensible forms showed through the black flocks at intervals, which reared up here and there in an immense cavern, whose limits were indistinguishable but whose relatively low ceiling repeated the ululations of the giant bats in multiple echoes.

These structures occupied about half the available space in every direction. They were roughly comparable to tall frameworks of black tubes, concealing polyhedral niches with obscure orifices between heir components.

"I don't understand," confessed Horst, "how beings to whom the general opinion accords a fabulous I.Q. can live in rudimentary nests and express themselves by means of monotonous cries. Perhaps their intellectual development had steered them in other directions than concrete realization. Perhaps their cries don't constitute a language at all, and they communicate by means of a telepathy that is almost inaccessible, even to you Housemaster-Baron..."

Horst was only summarizing reflections that everyone had been led to stir up in himself. Dal lifted the *Solaris* a few meters off the ground and moved forward slowly, steering it according to the indications given by the screens.

"The great enigma in all of this is why they haven't destroyed us yet," said Bolene, in a low voice.

The Luctouges seemed to have gone mad. They were whirling around in an incoherent manner—or so it seemed. Occasionally, one of them came to grip one of the cells of the optiphone embedded in the hull, and its shining body veiled the corresponding screen momentarily, but then it moved away again with a somber howl. It was then possible once again to see the flocks gathered around the tubular constructions.

The cavern appeared to have no limits. As it advanced, the *Solaris* ran into an edifice of niches and tubes, which it smashed and demolished as if it were made of cardboard. White larvae emerged from it, floating down to the ground and crawling through the debris.

"They undergo metamorphoses," observed Horst, his scientific curiosity reawakening rapidly.

The *Solaris* passed through the midst of the shattered tubes and the disgusting larvae. The cries of the Luctouges were becoming strident.

"They're not accustomed to being attacked in their own realm," said Zoltan, whose fists were clenched. "They're content to destroy stellar ships as soon as they touch down. It may be that we're being protected in some manner; I can't believe that they haven't tried to annihilate us already, several times."

The thought of summarily destroyed Expeditions, and massacred immigrants and Navigators, filled Dal's heart with rancor. "Let's see if they're still insensible to coagulants and projectors," he said.

He gave the order to fire. A confused reddish light appeared on one of the screens. Dal steered the *Solaris* in that direction, smashed through a cathedral of tubes and passed on without remorse. The fleeing larvae did considerable additional damage; none of them remained still.

The light grew in intensity. Soon, the edifices became sparser. A vast and empty horizontal space appeared, hollowing out amid the structures something like a plaza in a city. In the center stood a cubic block, and on that block was a cylinder two meters in height and one meter in diameter. It was from this cylinder that the red luminescence was coming, which the explorers had noticed from some distance away.

"I'll lay ten to one that that cylinder…" Bor Talek began.

He fell silent. The *Solaris* had just stopped and fallen back gently to the ground, in the midst of the last constructions, and a singular malaise overtook the travelers. Outside, the Luctouges were flying around, less numerous than before, but not approaching the cylinder. Their clamor attained a pitch that set the nerves on edge.

"It's…the Prophet," said Noktor. He was trembling from head to foot.

The fearful voice of a technician emerged from the interphone. "What's happening, Captain!" said the man. "We're all going crazy with fear!"

Dal felt a chill in his face, as if he had been exposed to a glacial wind. He gathered his courage and replied, in a firm voice: "Nothing's happening. A simple general malaise. We're reaching the goal…"

He as about to add: "of the Expedition," but he fell silent. His voice had given way. He felt that his teeth were about to start chattering. He switched off the interphone and rose to his feet. Around him, in the brutal light of the pilot-station, he saw nothing but white faces and wild eyes. He straightened up painfully.

"We're going to make a sortie," he said. "We have to take possession of that cylinder."

"Oh, Captain!" said Jern, whose jaw was trembling. "We…the Luctouges…"

Dal clenched his teeth. "The Luctouges can't do anything against us, since they haven't been able to prevent our advance. They can only attack us with claws and teeth…or that trenchant blade which serves them as dentition. For our part, our radiations don't hurt them and using the Blue Weapon would risk destroying the cylinder. We shall therefore oppose them with the equivalents of their natural weapons…"

His voice broke. His spinal column felt like a glacial foreign body inside his back.

"The Navigators' vessels are well-armed," he continued, "as are the warriors who must make commando raids—but in case a warrior loses or damages his weapons in the course of a

135

battle, there is also a stock of long and trenchant blades in the holds." He looked slowly around the circle. "We'll put on anti-radiation armor and battle-helmets—and we'll fight with swords."

Bor Talek broke away from the group. He was very pale, but was not trembling. He addressed himself to Dal. "Lord," he said, gravely, "you can't fight before I've printed your family arms on your breast. On our departure from Songa, I took note of your choice and I've prepared the photosensitive stereotype. It will be sufficient for you to expose it on your breast. Another stereotype of reduced size will serve to mark the men of your phalanx. It will only take a few minutes."

Dal looked at him and said: "All right. Do it, in accordance with tradition."

Bor made haste. Soon, the white circle that Dal bore on his chest became a black circle. In its center was the purple sun of the Sopharchy, crowned by a gold chain that lacked one link. Above it was a Knight's silver coronet.

The operation was repeated on his anti-radiation suit and his space-suit. Bor then printed his own shoulder and went down into the warriors' quarters. When it was all done, Dal addressed his general staff.

"I can only lead my own men into battle," he said, "but if there are any volunteers, they will be welcome."

Everyone volunteered—even Jern, who had been so badly injured during his own Expedition. The Technicians could not leave their posts, though.

They were 30: Dal, Zoltan, Hafsen, Noktor, Jern, Bor, Arkel, Horst, Fayal, Bolene and the 20 warriors marked with the golden chain. Each of them had a long sword sheathed at the waist of his shiny armor, and the helmets on their heads concealed their pallor—due less to fear of the Luctouges as to the formless terror creeping around the cylinder. Dal thought about Kalla, lost at the far end of the universe.

They exited from the vessel through the large airlock, in order to be present in force from the outset. The Luctouges hurled themselves upon hem with terrible cries, their black covering the humans' square formation, bristling with swords.

Rays shot out of the weapons that the Luctouges bore beneath their wings. They rebounded from the Solarians' armor. The coagulants and the projector launched their own waves, which were absorbed by the invisible field with which each Luctouge as surrounded—but the trenchant jaws attacked the garments and helmets, trying to rip through the armor. Whirling swords replied to the rushes of black wings and the whirlpool of livid eyes, and the monsters' protective fields did not prevent the blades from doing their bloody work. The green blood of the Luctouges soiled their wings, which beat like leathery foliage around the humans. Momentarily, there was something like a current of murderous thought, which paralyzed the Solarians—but the nature of Luctouge intelligence was too different and too distant from the human psyche for the attack to attain its objective, and the combat resumed, harsher and more ferocious still.

Numerous monsters were lying dead or fleeing in oblique and awkward flight, but there were always more to replace them, and the humans were gradually becoming exhausted in the face of that enemy, whose ranks filled up as soon as the swords opened breaches therein. Already, three warriors had succumbed to the radiations after their armor had been damaged. Horst fell in his turn, then Jern. Hafsen carried all of them back to the ship, and retraced his steps, piercing two monsters with his sword.

Progressively, the humans were advancing toward the cylinder—and, as they got nearer, the Luctouges were abandoning the battle. Thirty meters from the cylinder, the Solarians recovered their breath; the enemy was massing between them and the *Solaris*—which, in the midst of the tubular vegetation and the eddying wings, was reminiscent of a cetacean starred with luminous eyes.

Between Bor and Zoltan, Dal Ortog dropped his sword and fell forwards. They caught him, and saw the hideous wound he had sustained in his shoulder. They were all moving as if in a dream, between the red light and the white beams of the *Solaris*. The fear had left them, but an invisible and gigantic hand had gripped their thoughts. The howls of the Luctouges only reached them now through a universe of dark cotton wool crawling with lights.

"The Captain is wounded," said Zoltan, in a soft voice. "I'm taking his place. Ten men get hold of...the cylinder. Dr. Hasfsen and I will carry Dal Ortog."

Abruptly, the universe of cotton wool seemed to explode. The cries of the Luctouges drew nearer, and then died away. A giant voice thundered in the skulls of the Solarians, but it remained unintelligible. Moved by a strange impulse, Noktor and Zoltan came together and turned to the cylinder, their arms raised, palms open. Hafsen had laid Dal on the ground and was dressing the wound that the radiations had hollowed out terribly.

"Wait, solar cells!" said the gigantic voice. "There is no point in taking possession of me, for your hands would be empty before the end of the voyage. For 350 years, I have been meditating, and listening to the confused rumor of animals and plants, rocks and humans, and also the subtle and dangerous intelligence of those who stole me from humans. The latter know nothing of the long voyages that you have conceived and undertaken, but they are an integral part of their world and are not unaware of its meaning. Cease this carnage; the creatures that you are fighting are powerless against you, by virtue of the mere presence of your ultimate weapon. Like you, they are fragments of a vaster entity. The Being that is being born in the Solar System is comparable to the one that lives on Betelgeuse. Thrown into the bosom of the Spatial Void, you are the spermatozoa of the Solar Being. Content yourselves with bearing Its life from world to world."

The cylinder emitted a brighter light.

"By virtue of my fetal nature," said the silent voice, "I am plunged into the bosom of the collective consciousness. Every human is a cell and the human race is the noble tissue of the Solar Being, of which animals and plants form the rest of the body. The human race is the brain of that which it calls God, which did not create its universe but was, by contrast, created by it when the ultra-violet radiation activated the first nucleo-proteins. Little by little, the Being is acquiring an increasingly profound degree of consciousness, as the evolution of its cells produces more favourable results. The internal liaisons of its immense body are consolidating and it is establishing within itself—on a level that you cannot comprehend, but which I can attain because the prenatal individual consciousness is still at the archetypal source—a metabolism analogous to that of your bodies, an equilibrium."

The cylinder was now emitting a scarlet light that the eye could not sustain.

"The Solar Being has struggled perpetually against the maladies inherent in its nature, which are maladies of equilibrium and adaptation to its progress. Your Blue War constitutes the last of these redoubtable infections. In a single stroke it has broken the planetary ecology and attained the noble tissue of the Being to such a degree that its entire equilibrium is now condemned. It has attempted, by a flare of natality, to cure itself of that critical state, but the vital potential in each ovule had been too profoundly injured. The directive tissue of the Solar Being is in full degeneration and the existence of its cells is increasingly brief. While that tissue is dying, the vulgar tissues of vegetable and animal races is proliferating and producing, by mutation, another dominant race, which will, for the Solar Being, be akin to the graft of a new brain. Solar Cells, if you wish to survive, you must proliferate before the others and distribute your semen in Space. In this exceptional period, natural methods are futile. Employ ectogenesis at an accelerated rate, and your race will, by courtesy of the general equilibrium of the Being, recover the normal potential of its gametes."

The light decreased considerably.

"Solar Cells," said the Prophet, then, "I have answered the question that was haunting your minds. Leave me to me meditation now, in order that I may continue the transformation of my body into energy and I can dissolve myself once again in your collective consciousness."

Dal uttered a groan.

"We have to get him back to the ship right away," said Dr. Hafsen.

Zoltan and Noktor turned round slowly. The priest had an ecstatic expression on his face; Zoltan open haggard eyes, as if he were emerging from a crisis of delirium.

Dal moved slightly. Hafsen lifted up his head. The injured man looked at the physician with eyes already veiled by death. They all surrounded him and leaned over him. A beam of light extended from the ship to rest upon the alarmed group. Luctouges howled from the edge of the darkness.

"Kalla…" groaned Dal, in a sigh. "I place her safety in your hands, Zoltan and Bor…" He breathed in, with difficulty, then continued speaking: "I fainted…during which the Prophet's voice echoed in my mind. Did you hear it too?"

"Yes, Sire! Yes Captain!" Noktor and Zoltan replied, at the same time.

"You will convey the Prophet's words to the Sopharchy. Swear that you will devote yourselves to the immense task of extending the application of ectogenesis on the Three Planets…"

"We swear!" cried twenty voices in unison, already pierced by tears.

Dal took another deep breath. "I would like," he said, in a scarcely-audible voice, "an Order of Knights to supervise the equipment and its functioning everywhere…"

"They shall be called the Order of Perfecti, Captain," said Zoltan, who felt a large lump, impossible to swallow, moving up and down in his throat.

"That's enough!" said Hafsen, brutally. "The patient's still alive. It's more urgent to care for him that hear his last wishes."

They picked Dal up, with the utmost precaution, and his men made a rampart for him with their bodies and their weapons. The return journey was, however, easier than they expected. The Luctouges howled in the depths of the darkness, but not a single one attacked the Solarians. The Prophet was undoubtedly keeping them at bay.

Dal was laid down on a table in the infirmary, and Dr. Hafsen immediately put him into hibernation.

"I can't do anything else for him," he said. "Only the central clinic in Lassenia is sufficiently well-equipped to attempt to save him. I hope the hibernation will permit him to survive until we get home." He turned to Zoltan and Noktor. "Make a record of the information you have received," he added, "in case you progressively lose the memory…"

The *Solaris* smashed through the vault, passed through the Black Ocean and drew away from the planet. It did not encounter the energy barrier emitted by the Luctouges; the Prophet had destroyed the amplifiers.

On board, an adolescent lay suspended between life and death. His coat-of-arms and his sword had been laid on his body.

Thus returned to Kalla Karella, more rapidly than light but inert and without voice, Dal Ortog Dal of Galankar, Knight-Navigator of the Stellar Corps of the Three Planets, and Founder of the Order of Perfecti.

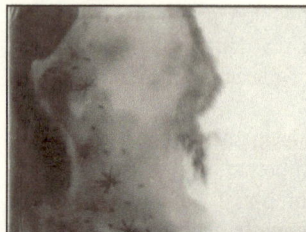

ANTICIPATION
FICTION

KURT STEINER

ORTOG ET LES TÉNÈBRES

FLEUVE NOIR

Part Two: Ortog and the Darkness

Chapter One

A brutal gust of wind stung the streaming trunk of the cypress. In the dusk, a black bird flew off like a stone from a sling. Its beak bore two canine teeth.

The forest outside the village was being cut to ribbons, and the cypress was one of the first guards to be wounded. Centuries-old trees had been uprooted from all over the world and replanted here, where their funereal foliage had found better employment. The tempest continued to assault them stubbornly—but it required something much more powerful to fell mutants that synthesized silica.

With the cries of the wind and the implacable sound of the rain was mingled a slow music, whose fragments came from the extreme end of the pathway. It was a tragic and despairing music, which beat the forest night and day, like a sea. That was deliberate, for in the distance, in the cold mist, stood a black stone mausoleum whose fronton bore a prestigious seal. It mass loomed over the rocky debris; its summit surpassed those of the highest trees. Armed with the best techniques drawn from the past, thousands of men had built it in a few months—and for two years, now, the monstrous cone had addressed its reproaches to the Heavens and the Earth. Lightning sometimes struck it, with a furious detonation, but was only a spark so far as the edifice was concerned; it assimilated the energy to assure its permanence.

Behind the curtains of the rain, violently ripped apart by the east wind, the entrance to the monument appeared. The soft light perpetually bathing the interior emanated from its triangle, and that greenish yellow light colored the nearest raindrops coldly, battling the steel blue distilled by the invisible sky. In the gigantic circular hall that occupied the base of the cone, peace reigned; diffused outside, the music was only distantly audible there, along with echoes of the tempest; a strange acoustic technique rendered it almost soundproof. Around the perimeter, statues and frescos bore witness to that, with their human representations fixed in meditative and dolorous attitudes, their hands over their ears and their eyes closed.

There was nothing there but withdrawal and refusal, isolation, negation and reproach. On the contours of those faces of flint and amber; in the folds of those garments of schist and silver; on the golden trinkets of the statues; on the soft or abrupt tones of the frescos—where the eyes, by contrast, were open and haggard, staring into dark infinities; on the enamel and the red copper of fuming incense-burners emitting a perfume of resin and moist earth, ran the same cavernous light, produced by billions of animalcules nourished by air and water vapor. It ran as far as the basalt flagstones that reflected the inverted image of everything that it had touched, outlining another cone filled with liquid stone, into which it seemed astonishing that one did not sink.

In the center, like an island, with its immobile reflection around its base, stood a circular pedestal supporting an open sarcophagus, in an upright pose like that of a sentry. A wall of blue light issuing from the ground surrounded it, a seemingly fragile obstacle, but one whose ominous wavelength disclosed its murderous nature.

In front of this transparent drapery stood a man dressed in an iron-grey costume. His arms were folded, his head bowed, and his forehead striped by a long blond lock of hair. He was Lord Dal Ortog Dal of Galankar, Knight of Malakorjal and Navigator of Lassenia—and the sarcophagus that loomed over him contained the body, petrified by death, of Kalla Karella, the daughter of the Sopharch.

Frozen in his meditation, Dal Ortog let his memories flow freely. Two years already! He had returned, injured but victorious, from a mission that Sopharch Karella, the wisest member of the Assembly of Sages, had assigned to him. Sheltered, cared for and saved, it had been necessary for him to receive, like a hammer-blow on the head, the news of the death of the person who had been constantly in his thoughts. During his absence, Kalla had died of the very Malady for which he was bringing back a curative mechanism.

Still under the influence of the long hibernation in which he had spent the return journey, he had initially refused to believe in such an injustice. Then he had lacerated his bed and fled his therapeutic cell to bruise his bare fists against the bronze doors of the institute for the preservation of bodies. Knight-Navigators had subdued him in order that his treatment might be completed.

Since then, his directives had been put into operation. The Malady of the human race that was making its members die prematurely was known to be caused by an ecological disequilibrium. It was known that the Terran biosphere—which is to say, the ensemble of its living creatures, plant, animal and human—formed something akin to a vast organism, of which of each individual was a cell. It had been learned that humans played the role therein of nervous tissue, which could not survive with less than a minimum number of cells. The war of the Three Planets, which had occurred two centuries before, had almost annihilated humans by virtue of the use of an ultimate weapon: the Blue Weapon. Thanks to his transgalactic quest, Knight-Navigator Ortog had brought back the solution to this problem: a considerable augmentation of the birth-rate by the development of ectogenesis—the maturation of fetuses *in vitro*, outside maternal wombs. For that purpose, Ortog had founded the Order of Perfecti.

Thus, the progress of the genetic Malady had been arrested—but too late for the man who had saved the race. The only person who was necessary to him, he had been unable to preserve. Then, he had demanded that Kalla's body, frozen at minus-20°C, should be placed in a suitable tomb. The Assembly of the Sopharchy, the College of Priests and the aristocracy of Housemasters and Bannerets had all—willingly or un-willingly—facilitated the mobilization of workmen and artists for the construction of the mausoleum. And since his recovery, Dal Ortog had gone every day to that place without hope, which he had ordered to be constructed in the vicinity of the village of his birth, the hamlet of Galankar.

An hour aboard a helix was sufficient to cover the hundreds of kilometres separating Galankar from Lassenia, the capital. Today, as every other day, Dal Ortog Dal reflected that his membership of the caste of Knight-Navigators, the elite corps of spacemen, the armed nobility and guardians of the security of the Sopharchy, had not preserved him from the greatest of disasters: mourning the person who had given his life meaning.

Had he not the right to think of himself a little now? Was the gratitude of humankind sufficient to fill and legitimate the remainder of his days? He sometimes reached the conclusion that it was all he had lived for, and that it had usurped his existence. Perhaps he had only been destined to play the role of savior, a single cell simultaneously privileged and condemned within the vast organism of which he had brought back the notion. If that were the case, his role was complete; he had nothing more to do but retire to the wings. Only the Knight-Navigators had the right to deploy the Blue Weapon; why not turn it on himself? A glacial light: the annihilation of space. No more Ortog. His work would live on; his pain would die.

Dal felt like a bow stretched to breaking-point. He knew that he no longer had the strength to bear this daily torture much longer. Undoubtedly, he ought to freeze the memory of Kalla as he had frozen her body, and chosen someone to replace her from among the myriads of young women of Lassenia and elsewhere—but Kalla was unique. There was nothing he could do but join her.

Dal straightened up, and passed his hand over the perennially-rebellious lock of hair that always striped his face. *Why not get it cut?* An automatic thought, like a tune sounding at the most inopportune movement, which obsesses and parasitizes the mind—but there was only one thing he had to do: march toward the sarcophagus and through the barrier of blue light. No weapon was necessary.

There was a muffled footstep behind him. He turned round, and saw a priest in a black robe, with the hood pulled up. The garment shone with a thousand droplets of water that it had retained—minuscule diamonds like those seen on the plumage of aquatic birds after a dive. Tall and thin, the man was reminiscent of a heron.

There was a long silence. Two people stood as if immobilized in a transparent gel, and the cone above their heads, in an eternal light.

Dal shook himself. "Who are you?"

The priest bowed. "I belong to the Central Temple, Lord. My name is Brother Alban."

"What are you doing here, Brother Alban?"

"I need to speak to you, Lord."

"Let's not bother with titles," said Dal Ortog, impatiently. "Do you think this is an appropriate place for a conversation?"

"It is, Dal Ortog Dal. No one but you comes here, and it's desirable that no other ears overhear what I want to tell you."

"Go on, then—get to the point. I have to leave soon for Lassenia."

The head beneath the hood shook. "I saw you take a step forward. Dare you affirm that you would have gone back to your apartment in the Navigators' quarter if I had not intervened? I know how great your pain is, and I suspect that you have been ready to leave us for some time, leaving it behind you like an empty garment."

"Go on," said Ortog, coldly.

"It's a long story," Brother Alban began. "You know that not all priests are hostile to the Sopharchy and the Navigators. Among your allies are numerous seekers brought to the temple environment by certain mysticism, but who work on the scientific plane, like the geneticists before your departure and your discoveries. The Central Temple has concealed a biophysics laboratory for nearly 100 years, in which the borderlands of death are studied."

"What do you mean by that?"

"Our research hypothesis was not the existence of a god, nor the permanence of a soul, but the survival somewhere in the cosmos of the mental phenomena that accompany life. Phenomena that present a fundamental contradiction: the apparent necessity of a physical support—that of the brain—and the impossibility of being situated other than in time. In what kind of space do thoughts take place?"

"There is no thought; there is only speech. Someone who believes that he is thinking makes micro-movements of his tongue and his larynx, and that so-called thought is merely a complex reaction to external or internal stimuli. There's no real difference between that and the cry of a bird or the flutter of a fish's fins. The mental phenomena of which you speak are merely an illusion born of nervous circuits. At the most basic level, pleasure and pain themselves represent peripheral reactions in which consciousness is uninvolved. We're no more conscious than an acid confronted with a base—but that offends one of our regulatory mechanisms, which is called pride."

"Even if that is so, Lord, it does not prevent the arrangements of electrons that I call thought or consciousness from leaving fields of force in the universe, like a hollow imprint, when the neurons return to dust. We hold to the theory that the imprint in question continues to react with the energy-currents of the cosmos. The Reverend Physician Gallego said, in my infancy: 'Death is a decimal point punctuating eternity.' We have declared that a dead person is the negative of a living one, and have decided to take a new print therefrom."

Ortog shrugged his shoulders, with bitter scorn. "Superstition served with rational sauce," he said.

"Not as much as you think. At any rate, the efforts of geneticists offer no weapon against the Malady. If we cannot retain the living, it is necessary to retrieve the dead."

"You've lost your mind Brother Alban. I authorize you to withdraw."

"Not before I've finished—then, you can act as you see fit. You can have us all imprisoned or exiled, we who form the secret College of Necrosophs."

"All right. I'll give you two more minutes."

"Our research was at the point of conclusion when your success removed our initial goal, but our endeavors were so far-reaching that we have pursued them with the same passion as at the outset. I made a personal contribution to an improved method of exploring the confines of life. Some of us engaged on that course and brought back information. The end of the journey is within sight, but it requires as an experimental subject of a calibre that none of us possesses. You are perhaps the only man who has never been seen to retreat."

Ortog smiled ironically. "And yet," he said, "I refused interstellar voyages several times. It was necessary that I overcome my terror of space."

"Are you ready to overcome your fear of the beyond?"

"I don't fear what doesn't exist, but I refuse to engage in a senseless enterprise."

"What if there were a faint chance for you to make contact with the person you have lost?"

Dal clenched his fists. "No stupid arguments! Go set your bird-trap somewhere else, and let alone a subject that I can't bear to be raised!"

Brother Alban bowed silently. "I have a more selfish reason, Dal Ortog Dal. You have been in hibernation for several months, and although you retain no memory of that period, you might be better armed than we are for an initial plunge."

"Why don't you have yourself put into hibernation?"

"Time is pressing, Lord. Some priests are enemies of the Necrosophs. The Sopharchy will only support us if the Knights listen to us. Now, I understand from what you say that we cannot count on them all. That's why I am permitting myself, Dal Ortog Dal, to take advantage of your grief to make an ally of one."

With the back of his hand, Dal pushed the hood back to the necrosoph's neck, revealing an angular face with jutting jaws and a stubborn forehead. The shaven skull gleamed in the yellow light of the animalcules. "All right," he said, "you don't lack courage and I'm not averse to your cynicism. I promise to think about your proposition. Go in peace."

Brother Alban bowed once again and turned on his heel without another word. His sandals scuffed the floor as he disappeared through the triangular door, and the rain swallowed him up.

Pensively, Dal took a few paces, returning to the pedestal that supported the sarcophagus. Visionary nonsense! How had he had the patience to listen to it until the end? Utterly desperate as he was, he must still retain a solid and flammable nucleus of hope for any such idle talk to be welcomed with so much interest.

But for the arrival of Brother Alban, though, this would doubtless have been Ortog's last day on an Earth more inhospitable than the most desolate asteroid. That was of little importance…one day more or less! However, Dal sensed that his thoughts had taken another direction. It seemed impossible, at present, for him to surrender himself to a definitive gesture. Slowly, he headed for the door in his turn.

Night had fallen, but the squalls of rain had not diminished in violence. In the overcast sky, toward the north-west, the powerful beacon lights of a helix were just vanishing. His mission accomplished, the necrosoph was returning to the Temple. Ortog returned to his own vehicle, whose dimmed lights were shining feeble 100 meters away, at the end of the cypress-lined pathway. Other cones of an even deeper darkness, the large trees with branches infiltrated by silica crystals opposed to the non-mutant plants a mineral immobility. The wind did not shake them, any more than if a giant hand had sculpted them in obsidian—and Dal Ortog thought that they made a suitable guard for Kalla.

As soon as he was aboard the helix, he engaged the automatic pilot and let it carry him toward the capital. Seated in the warm cabin, he looked through its transparent walls and the gloomy void through which it moved like a bullet. Only the streaming water, which the vehicle's speed separated into three symmetrical rills, provided evidence that there was anything outside but that absence, that lifeless darkness. Sometimes, a forked lightning-bolt appeared, lighting up a universe of raindrops following horizontal trajectories, but Dal could not even hear the thunder, whose echoes did not pass through the soundproof walls of the helix. It was an inhuman environment, but one that it might be possible to explore, if the necrosophs were right.

No, it was that ridiculous hope, without foundation, beginning to speak again. The necrosophs were nothing, could not possibly be anything, but charlatans. He was entitled to wonder whether all that might conceal some political maneuver, telecommanded underhandedly by the nobility: the Housemasters and the Bannerets, with the collusion of the priests opposed to the Sopharchy. The future would relieve those doubts, however; no power was able to attack the Knight-Navigators head-on, but someone might perhaps attempt to sap their influence by means of a provocation in which he himself might serve as the bait. The subversion would have to be well-sustained, because, for the present, the balance was unequal. It was not by calumny or any other sly accusation that anyone could get rid of the phalanges equipped with the Blue Weapon.

The helix set down in Lassenia's aeroport annexe. In spite of the storm, a snowflake could not have settled on the ground more gently.

Chapter Two

In the hall, three men were waiting for Dal. Nothing made them stand out from the crowd, but they were dressed like laboratory workers. They invited the Navigator to go with them to the University—provided, of course, that the Lord had no objection. Dal smiled; relationships between Navigators and researchers were entirely amicable, and there were no other two groups in the population whose communication was more straightforward and less constrained by etiquette.

"Gentlemen professors," said Dal, with his sad smile, "I shall be honored to accompany you to those venerable buildings."

The three men smiled in their turn, but with the reserve that Ortog's mourning required. A vehicle conveyed them rapidly to the Psychophysics Building. From the outset, Dal felt his interest awakening; what they had to tell him was closely connected to the conversation he had just had with the Necrosoph, and the result that they wanted to communicate to him overlapped with his own thoughts and what Brother Alban had claimed.

"You've chosen your moment well," he observed.

"Yes, we know," said one of them. "You're alluding to Brother Alban?"

Dal frowned. "How do you know about that?"

"Oh, it's quite simple. For five years we've been shy with respect to the geneticists, but we've been working with the best minds in the priesthood. Necrosophy and biophysics are virtually synonymous."

"Then why these mysterious procedures, since the word can be used here with me, in the laboratory and among you?"

"We never understand Brother Alban completely, but I think he wants you to be impressed by an intervention in the solemnity of a place that invites confidence."

"He's succeeded, in part," said Ortog, shaking his head. "At least, if you're standing surety for him…"

"To a degree, and only to a degree," one of them hastened to say. "Alban is something of an *inspired* seeker…and we're rather suspicious of that category. We think that considerable progress has been made, and that it's possible to go further, but we don't have any certainty as to the result."

"In sum, you believe that we can probe, to some extent, the regions that extend after death, but you won't prejudge what might be found there?"

"Not even that. We don't know if those regions exist or not, but we're in favor of a probe."

Dal remained silent momentarily, looking at the ground. Then he said: "I assume that if I go to the Temple tomorrow morning, I won't find you there?"

"No. Communications with the necrosophs remain as secret as their research, for the moment. I must emphasize the fact that ours are of a more biological order, but they're based on comparable theories regarding the relationship between living beings and the cosmos; we've arrived at the conclusion that every organic system can be compared to a sequence of stationary waves that persist after the disappearance of its generator, which is taken in relay by the nearest electromagnetic field, by virtue of phenomena of the same kind as induction. That conclusion remains materialistic, while proposing a model of survival after the death of bodily tissues. What the necrosophs say isn't much different, underneath their metaphors, but they have a faith in the exactitude of that hypothetical interpretation that we don't share."

"I think I'll go to the Temple tomorrow," Dal said, "if only for further information."

"We can already show you one or two recent experiments," declared the biologist who expressed himself with the greatest confidence. He stood up, along with his two assistants. One of them opened a cage from which the other took a little hybrid mutant, the fruit of the Blue War. It was a dog with a human head, which started repeating mechanically:

"Let me go! Let me go!" It punctuated its pleading with sharp bursts of idiotic laughter. It was laid out on a board and anesthetized.

"This," said the biologist, "is a male cananthrope that has learned to navigate this maze." He pointed to a structure about a meter high, which occupied part of the laboratory. "I shall kill it, after connecting up the electrodes of the electroencephalograph, and having placed it in a beam of ultra-short-wave radiation, which is reflected here, in order to be received by this receiver. There!"

The assistants had already shaved the head of the cananthrope and connected the electrodes. The electroencephalograph began registering alpha, beta and delta rhythms. At the moment when the cyanide injection was given, the electrical trace became flat; there was no longer any cerebral activity. The hybrid was dead—which was confirmed by other tests, including an intravenous injection of fluoresceine, the disappearance of the electroencephalographic signal being an insufficient criterion.

One of the assistants then took hold of another cananthrope, which was in an adjacent cage, and connected electrodes to it in its turn, which were similarly linked to the short-wave receiver.

"This time," the biologist said, "we won't put them in contact with the recorder. Instead of transmitting, they'll receive. This experiment could have been carried out a thousand years ago, if receivers have been available sensitive enough to register signals at a very low intensity."

The second subject was freed, and taken to the center of the maze. "Needless to say," the experimenter added, "this one has received no special training." He had scarcely completed the sentence when the canathrope appeared at the exit from the maze. "You can draw your own conclusion," he said. "In the barbaric atomic era, it might have been said that the second is a medium who has been visited by the phantom of the first. In that era, strangely, they spoke of the 'specter' of a magnet."

"Papa! Papa!" appealed the cananthrope, while it was being replaced in its cage. It fell silent, in order to assemble the letters of the alphabet in the midst of its excrement.

Dal looked at it uneasily. "Is that our probe?" he asked.

"No, it's merely the proof of mental activity outside the neurons. In my view, that's already a result. One knows that one has made a real discovery when one brings into the domain of physics a phenomenon previously belonging to the realm of metaphysics. It was once the same for questions of 'time' and 'space', or even 'matter' and 'energy'—but that's no longer relevant to us."

Dal did not reply. He was wondering whether what remained of Kalla was dancing somewhere in an undulatory eddy, nourished by radiations—and whether *that* might be thinking about him.

An order became audible through the window of the laboratory, which was on the ground floor. Then there was the brief flare of a blaster and the sound of someone running away. Dal raced to the window and opened it. A man was lying in the bushes. He wore the white uniform of the guards, with the sun of the Sopharchy on his breast. Other guards were arriving.

The University quarter was sealed off, and all the outbuildings where practical work was done were searched, along with all the audiovisual halls—but no one was found. Then the Security Forces arrived, whose men began their enquiry. The enquiry got off to a bad start, though: the tracks that were found under the laboratory windows were the clawed footprints of a bipedal hybrid.

Dal went to confer with the Security lieutenant. "It requires a rather intelligent animal to handle a blaster," the latter said. "They do exist—some citizens employ them as domestics."

"They can't be very numerous," Dal observed, shivering slightly as he thought about the experimental subjects he had just seen.

155

"No, Sire, but numerous enough to complicate our task and reduce the possibility of a result."

That was a warning, combined with an excuse. Dal understood that he ought not to expect anything to come out of the enquiry. He took his leave of the lieutenant, then of the biologists. He understood now the precautions taken by the necrosoph. Someone was interested in the work—someone who had sent a hybrid equipped with a weapon—and doubtless also with a sensitive recording device.

As he left he met the lieutenant again. "Do the tracks extend over a long distance?" he asked.

"No, Sire. They stop after a few meters."

"That doesn't surprise me. They must have sent a flying hybrid."

He abandoned the lieutenant, who opened his eyes wide and struck himself on the forehead. The affair did not interest Dal overmuch, though; he did not belong to the Security Forces. Each to his own work.

It was very late when Dal arrived at the Palace, but for him, all doors in Lassenia were open day and night, especially the most important. He was taken to Sopharch Karella, who was finishing—not without disgust—a legal document arranging the reallocation of the provincial Bannerets.

Karella had passed the landmark of 60 years of age—a rare thing. He did not know whether he would benefit from the efforts made on behalf of general longevity, but that ignorance did not interfere with his intelligence and the characteristic methodical nature of his work. Like all Sopharchs, he was simply dressed in a red robe tightened by a belt. His office offered the singular spectacle of a chaos in which no one other than him could find anything. He waved his hand to invite Dal Ortog to sit down. In spite of his daughter's death, he considered Dal as his son.

"The inquiry is in its early stages," he observed.

Dal raised his head. "You know already, Sopharch?"

"If information were delayed, we would already have been replaced by some dictator or other with private interests..."

Dal smiled, but only with one side of his mouth. "Oh!" he said. "If you know..."

The vertical wrinkles disappeared from the Sopharch's forehead. "Yes, the Housemasters and the priests. The Bannerets are less dangerous."

"Perhaps not all the priests," Dal amended.

The Sopharch looked at him hard. "You're thinking about the necrosophs?" he said, softly.

Dal made no answer. "You really do know everything," he said.

Karella shrugged his shoulders and placed his slender hand on the ocean of sheets of psychosensitive paper over which he was leaning.

"Fifteen years ago—you were still a child then, like Kalla—I called on their help myself. Kalla's mother had just died. She was thirty years old. I wasn't yet a Sopharch; I was only an obscure gerontologist buried in his research—but there's no secret science. The whole University knew about the necrosophs' research, although it didn't let anything filter out. There's no secrecy between specialists in different disciplines—if there were, research would make no progress. It has never been otherwise."

Dal was listening, suddenly mobilized. "And?"

"Nothing. My wife is dead, and she has remained dead. The necrosophs were unable to do anything about it."

Dal understood the echoes of Karella's grief, but did not share them. He observed a moment of silence, and then went on: "In that era, their work had not borne fruit. Perhaps that's the reason why they weren't yet surrounded by spies from outside the university."

"You think that if the spies have got involved, it's because the work has progressed?" said Karella.

Dal was silent momentarily. Then he said: "That makes sense. Someone has just importuned me at the mausoleum, and then some other faction listened in on the words of those who were waiting for me at the aeroport. Do you know the results of the recent experiments in biophysics?"

"Yes."

Taken aback, Dal struggled to retain his self-control. "And you don't believe in them?" he exclaimed. "You think that because your wife hasn't benefited from their research, your daughter is definitely excluded? Because you're a Sopharch, you think that a simple Knight can't nourish the hope that has escaped you?" For the first time in his life, he burst into sobs.

Karella got up and came toward him. "I make no difference," he said, placing a hand on his shoulder. "Pull yourself together, Dal Ortog Dal. I made you a Knight myself. It doesn't become you to behave like a child."

Dal got up in his turn, and passed his hand over his face, as if his tears had been something shameful. His voice became firmer. "I don't believe in anything," he said, "but I've never given up hope."

When Dal Ortog left the Palace, it was snowing. Dal decided to go back to the Knights' quarters on foot. Fortunately, there were few people about in the streets; Ortog was famous, and everyone bowed very deeply as he went by. It cost him the return of innumerable bows. The snow was falling in dense clusters, though, and the pedestrians were making haste.

By virtue of contradictory association, the snow reminded Dal of the shiny black robe that Bother Alban had worn. Whether it was the impossible hope that was struggling in his mind like a fly in a spider's web or the sudden plausibility that the laboratory had conferred on the necrosoph's words, Dal could no longer maintain the bleak numbness of the heart that had kept him apart from everything for so long, even while he was engaged in the difficult task of organizing the Order of Perfecti and the supervision of ectogenesis. Something was now seething in the depths of his being: an impatience to know more about the disquieting work of the necrosophs and biophysicists, whether it might end with an exorbitant communication between the living and the dead or with the definitive collapse of a mistakenly fortified hope.

The two Knights guarding the gateway presented arms—simple blasters—as he approached. On their shoulders, however, they also bore the frightful Blue Weapon. He interrupted the military ceremony with a gesture, and chatted to them for a few moments. His breast was still ornamented with his now-celebrated armorial badge: the broken chain over a red sun. The other Knights had their own, and the sight of the group, motionless beneath the plasma searchlights, retained the breath of those who passed close to them.

Dal soon shook his snow-powdered hair and took his leave. He passed through the great courtyard and immediately went to his apartment, where he ordered a light meal. Then he searched his hologrammatic magnetophone reels for those which treated the subject of death. He only possessed the ones from the encyclopedia, but had had no need of any works of art or human documents. He spent hours with them before sinking into an agitated sleep.

Very early the next morning, Dal left for the Temple. Again, he went on foot, in order to prepare himself for the trials that might await him. Before he had succeeded in that, he was accosted by a priest in a brown robe, who invited him to follow him. They both went around the edifice and went into it by a little door that opened into an alley. At that moment, another priest was passing the end of the alley; he continued his route along the avenue, and went into the Temple in his turn, but by the main entrance, under the arcades.

Behind his guide, Dal went down a staircase that led to a subterranean corridor. In the middle of the corridor there was an opening in the wall. Dal was then shown into a room of vast proportions, which was a laboratory. He was left there—but he did not have to wait long. Brother Alban appeared, with his hood pushed back. He was smiling humorlessly.

"Peace be with you, Sire," he said bowing. "I wasn't sure that I'd see you today."

Dal looked at him. "I spent some time yesterday with the biophysicists from the University..." he began.

"I know. Did they have more success than me in convincing you?"

"I'm reserving my judgment."

"Prudence is always honorable."

"What about you?" said Dal, a trifle brusquely. "What more have you to show me?"

Brother Alban raised a hand. "Have a little patience," he said. "First, know that we're conducting our own enquiry here into yesterday's events." He darted a glance toward the door of which Dal had just made use, and lowered his voice. "We know that the wolf is in the sheepfold," he said. "The hybrid that killed the guard certainly belongs to someone in the High Priest's entourage. If you're ready to attempt the experiment, it has to be now. I fear that sabotage might lead to its postponement or—who can tell?—its suppression."

Dal had the strange impression that his will had nothing to do with the reply he made. "I'm ready."

"Good. Follow me."

They went into another room. Dal stopped on the threshold, petrified. The room was almost entirely filled by an enormous machine that was vaguely reminiscent of a starship fitted with a gondola.

"The necroship," said Brother Alban.

There was a cigar-shaped spinde that reflected a metallic gleam. Cables extended from the spindle supporting a sort of primitive boat. Nothing else was visible.

"Are you making fun of me?" Dal asked, suddenly becoming aggressive. "What is this ridiculous assemblage?"

Brother Alban beckoned him to come closer. "This ridiculous assemblage," he said, "is the fruit of a century of stubborn effort, undertaken by generations of numerous and skillful crews. It's necessary that the voyager not be placed behind any material object, including an operator. As for the superior part of the...vehicle, it contains the drive-units."

"The drive-unit?" Dal repeated, weakly.

"It's not a matter of a voyage through space or time," Brother Alban said, "but it is a matter of a voyage. To say *voyage* implies propulsion, of whatever sort—and yet the necroship will remain here, even when it is displaces."

"What do you mean?"

"We've already sent it to where it needs to go, but without a passenger, by means of a...sort of automatic pilot. It was duplicated. Its replica drew away from it, went through the walls and disappeared. On its return journey it reappeared, and the two necroships fused into a single one."

Dal did not reply. He waited for more.

"We've also sent it forth with a passenger on board—a little hybrid."

Again, Dal thought about the hybrids in the laboratory. "And?"

"Between the moment of duplication and that of fusion, the subject was nothing but a cadaver. It came back to life thereafter, without our having attempted any kind of reanimation."

"Was the subject duplicated too?"

"We're not sure, because it was very difficult to observe it at that moment, but it's highly probable. On the other hand, we have to confess that we're entirely ignorant of the nature of that double, and...the place—I have no other term—where it goes."

Dal studied the necroship. The whole adventure was pure folly. Had it not been for Kalla's death, he would have brought all the necrosophs before a tribunal for fraud. One would then have seen, in the course of the trial, whether there was anything serious in their claims. In his present situation, however, he had to enter into their mysteries. He now understood how a clever crook can easily succeed in duping a man blinded by grief.

161

"Let's get on with it," he said, bad-temperedly. "Do I climb into that barbaric fishing-boat?"

Brother Alban raised his arms to the heavens. "Not so fast! For you, I want a gradual approach, taking all possible precautions."

"What else is there?"

The necrosoph led him to a part of the room where there was a table laden with papers.

"You might still take me for a trickster, but what I'm telling you is true. These are the cards of sleep."

Dal leaned over, frowning. Alban put his hand on the cards.

"One of us made these first designs—for the necroship might perhaps be used as an oneiroscaph, a syncoplane, a psy-chobathys…"

"What is this jargon?"

"It's not ours—it's the biophysicists'. We prefer term like 'gondola of dreams,' 'explorer of unconsciousness' and 'chariot of the seven agonies'."

"That's no less obscure."

"It's just words. The important thing is to know whether a region exists in which dreams unfold—a region common to all humanity, and animals too, and perhaps even to plants. We call it 'the World of the Objective Unconscious'."

"What verbiage! How does this concern me?"

"You'll begin with a short voyage to this unknown land. You can see for yourself that our cards are covered with white patches. If all goes well, you'll advance some way into the unconscious, and you'll bring information back to us regard-ing your swoon—but you won't get past the oceans of Coma. The Agonies will be part of your true expedition. They lead to forbidden territories—the wild savannahs of death."

"But why do I need all this apparatus to explore dreams? It would be enough for me to go to sleep!"

"Wrong. You would only have the memory of your own dreams. A sleeper is blind to the dreams of other sleepers—except in rare cases of the interpenetration of dreams, linked to telepathy. Aboard the necroship, you'll be displaced into the midst of the dreams of millions of beings, with their characters, their events and their scenery. As for the inferior degrees of consciousness, the necessity of such a vessel for exploring them, and bringing back memories of them, has not been demonstrated."

"I've already told you that I don't like the term consciousness—but that hardly matters. Show me how to operate your machine."

They approached the gondola, which was floating, sustained by its cables, a meter above the ground. Dal looked up. "How is that enormous mass suspended in mid-air? An anti-gravity device?"

"No. The ship is in an unstable state, between being and non-being. Its weight merely equilibrates the centrifugal force of the Earth's rotation. It remains motionless wherever it is put. In a very deep valley it would fall; on the summit of a mountain, it would escape Earth's gravity. At this level, it's like a body immersed in water—a body that has the same density as water. You've seen toy submarines?"

"Yes."

"We think that—in a purely analogical sense—it moves in a comparable manner through those regions in which it has to travel." He leaned forward, over the edge of the boat. "Do you see this dashboard?"

"I see it."

"It has several circular plates. Each of them has a hollow imprint of a hand with five splayed fingers. You only have to place your own hand in these imprints, one after another. Don't touch the last on one the right—that's the one for definitive travel."

"What are these two levers under the plates?"

"The one on the left controls the drives, the one on the right the horizontal and vertical tiller."

"What about coming back?"

"You apply the back of your other hand to the same imprint in which, on departure, you placed the palm of the first—but you have to keep it there."

"Good. Let's not lose any more time."

"One more detail. Do you see the bottom of the gondola?"

"Yes—a sort of platform, like the ones on which coffins are displayed."

"You couldn't have put it better. That's for the body."

"The body?"

"The sailor's body. In the course of the voyage, your double will be at the controls, but your body will be lying here. For the first trip it will simply lose…the awareness of things. After the second departure, it will become a temporary corpse. I have to tell you that even the preliminary voyage isn't free of danger. Everyone knows how courageous you are—reckless, even—but the adventures you've undergone have nothing in common with the one you're undertaking now. It's necessary that it be of your own free will, knowing in advance that you might not reap any benefit. On the contrary—you're risking your life, and, at the very least, your reason."

"Enough talk. Can I get in?"

"Go."

While they were talking, a group of necrosophs in black robes had entered the room and formed a semicircle around them. He leapt over the side of the gondola, which bumped into the floor, dragging the enormous cylinder down.

"I told you it all weighs practically nothing," said Brother Alban. "At present, it weighs as much as you."

Dal sat down, disconcerted. He looked around, and placed the palm of his left hand in the imprint borne on the first plate.

Everything around him became blurred, and vanished.

Dal was sitting on a chair in a kitchen. It was the seat of the gondola, but, at the same time, it was a chair in a kitchen.

It was the house in Galankar where he had lived as a child. He was very small, and was eating pumpkin soup. The table was confused with the dashboard. *Don't put your hand in the last plate on the right*. Fortunately, that was difficult to do, because he had to put his left hand into it, by virtue of the position of the thumb.

Facing him was a window. It was open, but what was visible through it was not what should have been visible. No valley, no herd of megatheria—an immense grey plain and, in the sky, a fleet of gigantic galleys with their triple rows of oars.

Dal shook his head and shrugged his shoulders. He swallowed a spoonful of pumpkin soup. He had always loved it. The apocalyptic armada could not make him forget it.

I'm in one of my own dreams, he said to himself. *This isn't a good way of utilizing that marvelous machine.* He raised his head. Superimposed on the ceiling was the outline of the spindle. He seized the left-hand lever and pulled it gently toward him. He felt himself moving forwards. Splitting the wall and shattering the window, a single bound took him into the heart of the armada of triremes, which were fraying before his eyes as if they were made of smoke.

He was floating over the grey plain now. A pink sun was just disappearing behind an incredibly close horizon. Beneath him, he saw a monument in the form of an anvil, surrounded by a crowd of tiny individuals. Manipulating the vertical tiller to his right he descended.

In the twilight, fires lit in a circle fought against the last rays of sunlight. One of the tiny individuals was standing motionless in the center of the terrace that crowned the monument. He saw the necroship and shielded his face with his folded arms. At the same time, the others assaulted it with interminable ladders. They soon invaded the terrace and formed a circle around the man. Dal saw that the man was pierced with arrows, and that blood was running from his wounds, forming a pool on the ground. Momentarily, he wanted to go all the way down to rescue him—but the man was dreaming. What would be the consequences of such an initiative? Dal abandoned the idea.

He started talking to himself, lisping like a baby. *That's a funny plate, over there, on the right... but the big people have forbidden anyone to touch it. The big people think nothing of spoiling your games.* Twisting his body, Dal advanced his left hand.

He leapt 20 years forward and snatched back his hand as if he had burned it. He had become a Knight-Navigator again, in charge of a redoubtable machine. He activated the drive and was instantly at the far end of the plain. There, the ground was dotted with mounds, as if an enormous mole had been digging tunnels there. He descended further, skimming the surface, and stopped in a sort of bubble in which a woman in rags was scolding a man with a low brow. Whose dream was he in? The man's or the woman's? The dream of someone else, perhaps, who was dreaming both of them? But where was that other? He saw him: a bearded individual who was putting his head through the wall of the bubble in order to watch, and who waved a fist at him.

Dal had the impression that he had committed an indiscretion, and moved off again over the ground, straight ahead. He re-emerged on the flank of a mountain, in a furnace.

He was in a forest that was on fire, but the flames did not burn him. It did not appear to be the same for a man who was rolling in the embers as he tried to escape them. Dal heard his silent cries—those cries that one utters in dreams. The man saw him and, in spite of his apparent suffering, grabbed handfuls of firebrands, which he hurled at the necroship. This time, the hull of the gondola began to redden, and Dal hastened to place his hand on the second plate in the dashboard, hoping that the next region would be less inhospitable. As he withdrew his hand, an immense flock of bats flew across the sky and disappeared.

He was on a high deserted plateau, swayed by a glacial wind. An immense hand was outlined on the horizon, with the index-finger cut off. What remained of it was reaching for a charcoal sky, in which echoes of discordant music lingered. The titanic hand was surrounded by effluvia, and Dal knew that he must not get too close too it, lest it close upon the fragile necroship and turn it into a shower of debris—but if he kept his distance from it, the regions of light unconsciousness, in their solitude, seemed less hostile than those of dreams. Even so, Dal decided not to remain there any longer. He placed his hand on the third plate.

He was a few meters from the surface of a waveless ocean, whose liquid seemed to have the consistency of glue. From time to time, a viscous form emerged in part, to sink into it again immediately. Dal moved over that surface without noticing anything else. He dared not operate the vertical tiller so as to dive into it. That would have been like entering a coma within a coma.

He travelled in this manner for a long time, without seeing anything else. Gradually, he felt that he was running into a damp indifference, in which preoccupations and projects became blurred. Why make an effort? Why try to do anything at all? What was the point of the vain agitation that had led him into this place of origins, this antechamber of oblivion—what was the point, if not to lose himself in it forever?

He had to mobilize all his energy to place the back of his hand in one of the imprints.

"Did you have a pleasant voyage?" asked Brother Alban.

Dal leaned his hand on the edge of the gondola, and immediately snatched it back; it was red hot.

Brother Alban came closer. "What happened?" he asked, leaning forward.

"Oh, nothing!" said Dal, with difficulty. "A man threw a handful of flaming branches at me…"

"Ah! Good!" said the necrosoph. "One has to be careful of dreamers. In circumstances like that, it's necessary to take action."

"How?"

"Shout at them. They wake up and disappear."

Dal looked at him suspiciously—but Brother Alban's expression was serious.

"What about the other regions?"

"They're no more restful," Dal admitted. "At any rate, if all that didn't happen solely in my imagination, I have to admit that the vessel works…one way or another."

"Is your imagination capable of burning the gondola?" Brother Alban asked.

Dal did not answer, and got out of the boat. Brother Alban took him to the card table. Tapping them with his fingers, he said: "You'll find that everything you've seen is, in a sketchy fashion, already contained here. Tell me about your journey."

Dal obeyed, as faithfully as he could.

"Setting aside the beginning," said he necrosoph, "which was your own, look at what is on the first card."

Dal examined the card In the middle of large white zones, he found the delimitation and summary description of what he had seen for himself."

"The forest on fire, for example, is always there. There aren't always two people quarreling in the bubble in the ground, but the bubble is always there—and so on. It's like a stage-set established once and for all, in which sleepers display their dreams. I ought to warn you, in passing, that you didn't reach the region of true nightmares—but you were on the frontier. Others have stopped in the domain of erotic dreams, where they have routinely found themselves at odds with those who happen to be there. It's one domain where travelers are unwelcome."

The necrosophs had left, having work to do elsewhere.

"I utilized the second and third plates," Dal recalled. "According to you, I was then exploring the depths of syncope and coma. How was my body?"

"At the end, you were really in a coma. You came out of it abruptly, as one does."

One of the necrosophs reappeared. "There's a man here," he said, with an alarmed expression. "I don't know how he found the way to the laboratories."

Brother Alban straightened up anxiously. "What does he want? He isn't hiding anything?"

"He arrived abruptly and asked to speak to Knight Ortog. He says that he's a Housemaster-Baron, and that his name is Zoltan Charles Henderson de Nancy."

"What!" cried Dal. "He's back! Let him in!"

Brother Alban looked severely at the necrosoph who had brought the news. "So you don't know the Housemaster-Baron, even by name? The Knight's companion-in-arms?"

The young priest hung his head. "I... Yes, of course... But..."

Zoltan came into the room. He was a tall man, whose upper lip was adorned with a fine moustache—an affectation that had fallen out of fashion centuries before. His eyes shone with an extraordinary brightness. He came toward Dal and the two men shook hands—an equally outdated custom. In addition to his bizarre name, however, Zoltan never behaved like anyone else. He knew things about the past that even the Sopharchs did not know, and spread around himself a sort of superstitious dread. It was even worse when he did not hide his telepathic power—then, some fled.

"I wish you good day, Ortog," he said. "I can't tell you how glad I am to see you again."

Brother Alban remained silent. He shook his head. The Housemaster-Baron always expressed himself in an extravagant fashion; people did not understand half of what he said. At that moment, Zonltan turned to him. "Good day, Abbé," he said. As usual, Brother Alban did not understand, but he returned the greeting, as politeness demanded.

"Good day to you too," said Dal, ceremoniously. "So you've returned from your tour of inspection of the Order of Perfecti on Mars and Venus."

With Zoltan, there was no question of using the informal form of *you*. The polite plural had been virtually lost in the

Blue War, but Zoltan had never been cured of it. He addressed everyone as *vous*, and if anyone could not reply in the same manner, he had to learn. Zoltan had a horror of vulgarity and the disgusting familiarity of language. He prided himself on his immemorial origins, and added to his authentic title of Housemaster that of Baron, which had no significance for anyone, but which he treasured more than the former.

"Nasty places," Zoltan remarked. "Those people conduct themselves with a culpable nonchalance. I thought of having a large number of them executed, in order to accelerate the birth-rate…"

Dal smiled vaguely; he was aware of Zoltan's generosity.

"But let's leave that subject," said the Housemaster-Baron. "I permitted myself to undertake small psychological probe in order to discover where you were, my dear Ortog. On this occasion, I learned some very strange things."

Dal's face darkened. "Yes," he admitted. "A crazy endeavor."

"Crazy if you depart alone," Zoltan replied, "but I've nothing urgent summoning me. Would you deign to accept the collaboration of my sword? Death is an adversary worthy of me!"

Dal straightened up with a glimmer of joy. "Let your sword aid mine, then. I'm grateful to you, Henderson! But first I must warn you about the dangers of such an expedition."

"I know," said Zoltan. "It was fatal to the man who attempted it before you…"

"What?" said Dal, suddenly attentive. "Someone has tried it before?"

"It's a trifle legendary," said Zoltan. "A fabulously old story. I'll tell it to you someday."

"Permit me to interrupt you, Lords," said he necrosoph, coming forward. "The Housemaster-Baron could not have put it better in speaking of his sword. We had decided to furnish the Knight with a weapon, but the only one that has any chance of being effective in the course of this voyage is the Blue Weapon. Now, one cannot transport it as it is, for reasons inherent in the method of...displacement. It was therefore necessary to make it into another of similar power, and that is why I tempered the Knight's ardor. I shall therefore give orders that—under the high authorization of Dal Ortog Dal—two blades should be forged in the crucible that gave birth to the Blue Weapon."

"We shall go together, Brother Alban," Dal concluded. "Otherwise, you would not even be able to get close to the Edifice of the Terror, where the laboratories of war are located."

The Edifice had been built a long way from Lassenia. It was a rather derisory precaution, for if a catastrophe were to occur, it would have annihilated such a surface area that nothing would have remained of the continent, but it was necessary to satisfy public demand.

In order to be visible from afar and to discourage any approach, the laboratories were crowned by a roof of vast height, at the four corners of which red searchlights blinked day and night. They were so formidable in their power that it was easier to look at the sun. Even that was insufficient, though; the edifice was flanked by four bell-towers with immense steeples, where eight huge bronze organ-pipes founded expressly for that purpose played an incessant carillon at full volume. The howling tocsin of their brazen bellies bent the trees in the countryside and put the most monstrous hybrids to flight.

It was into this apocalyptic atmosphere that Dal, Zoltan and the necrosoph advanced, deafened and blinded, toward the doors that were permanently guarded by phalanges of Navigators with hearts of iron. There, the sound was held at bay.

Dal parted the flaps of the cape that he had thrown over his shoulders, displaying the golden chain on his breast—but that did not satisfy the Navigators, even though they knew him well. He had to pass through the psychogram chamber, which occupied a barbican.

"That's all right, Ortog," said the commander of the phalanges. "You may go in, as may your friends." He adopted a flinty smile to add: "I recognize the famous Housemaster-Baron. How are things in the Solar System?"

Zoltan was several meters away and had not heard. Nevertheless, he replied: "Ticking over, Sire, ticking over."

The Navigator looked at him with some slight astonishment, but no more. He was an athletic individual, with a face as grey as is uniform—a face in which two sea-green eyes shone almost as brightly as Zoltan's. "Thank you, Henderson," he said. And long live the Sopharchy!"

"Long live the Sopharchy!" repeated Brother Alban, as he passed before the Navigator's suspicious gaze.

"One moment," the officer said to Ortog. "You've brought a priest?"

"I'm capable of anything," Dal replied. "Don't worry—he's a friend of the Sopharchy."

"There are still some among them, then?" remarked the officer, curtly.

"A few," Dal confirmed. "One rarely encounters them."

The Navigator shrugged his shoulders. "How can you remain on his damned planet, Ortog?" he said. "It's only two months since I returned from my last mission, and I'm already yearning for space."

Ortog looked at him and smiled. He understood completely. "Would you like to be an itinerant overseer?" he said. "You'd assist in the productive application of ectogenesis on the two sister planets?"

The officer's face suddenly took on a hint of humanity. "I'm at your disposal."

Dal took a psychosensitive card from his jerkin, and pressed his thumb on it momentarily. "Take it," he said. "Have yourself replaced tomorrow and request an audience with Sopharch Karella. Repeat my words to him. Tomorrow evening, you'll be in space."

The Navigator stiffened as he took the card and bowed. "Thank you, Ortog!" He stood aside to let them pass.

No one could get close to the crucible; it could only be contemplated from afar. A gravitic barrier surrounded it, but a human form was vaguely discernible within it.

"The temperature inside the crucible isn't very high," said a physicist. "3000 to 4000 degrees. The protective suit that the smith wears can support 5000 to 6000."

Dal craned his neck. "It really is a forge," he said.

"Of course. No manufacturing process can work with fragments of cerulite, whose particular radioactivity makes spations explode. They have to be fashioned as a mass."

"But that's absurd," said Dal, shrugging his shoulders. "You'll be telling me next that nothing but a wheelbarrow is suitable for some space vehicle!"

The physicist made a gesture of helplessness. "That's the way it is—we think it had to do with the fundamental irregularity of human movement. A machine can be programmed to vary the energy of its impacts continually, but that wouldn't do. The result isn't viable unless the entire process is governed by hazard, as occurs with human muscles. I assume that it's something to do with the probability curve representing the integration of the fibrils."

Dal shook his head, but continued his contemplation. Wading through the molten metal, the smith, whose protective suit was equipped with a cylindrical helmet, rained forceful blows upon an anvil constantly cooled by a jet of liquid air, in order to prevent it from melting. With the aid of pincers, he held a piece of mineral more flamboyant than all the rest, which was deformed by the hammer-blows.

"Very well," said Dal, finally. "We require two swords."

"Made of cerulite?" queried the physicist, amazed.

"Yes. We're leaving on a voyage, and we can't carry the Blue Weapon in its current form, as a rifle."

The physicist reflected. "It's the scabbard," he said, "that will pose problems."

"Why?"

"Because, if you carry it without a scabbard, you're going to damage the space-time around you, and you'll be gradually destroyed yourself. It's necessary that the scabbard be similar in nature to the traditionally-employed rifle.

Zoltan moved closer. "Can't we fashion a gravitic scabbard, like the barrier surrounding the crucible?" he said.

"Yes, undoubtedly...but it's at your own risk and peril. That hasn't been tested."

"Ortog will take the risk," Zoltan replied, "and I the peril."

And the swords were forged.

They were back in the room where the necroship was. Evening had arrived, but there was neither day nor night in that subterranean room. The preparations were being concluded. Standing next to the gondola, Dal and Zoltan were fastening their black shoulder-belts.

The gravitic scabbards resembled ordinary scabbards, but their contours were unclear and their weight varied continually. Inside, the redoubtable power of the cerulite sword was dormant. The Housemaster-Baron and the Knight had tried them out in a valley; Dal had cut down a sequoia with a single stroke, while Zoltan had sent the top of a rock, ten meters in diameter, flying through the air. It was not necessary, though, to employ the swords in hand-to-hand combat. To hurl their force against a distant enemy was sufficient to annihilate that enemy in a nanosecond, and by describing a semicircle one could exterminate any army.

The travelers had to challenge death, though. Each of them was also equipped with an energy-shield. This was not a screen produced by a generator attached to the belt. It had been necessary to manufacture the shields, and their charge would only last for a limited period. They were rectangular in shape, tapering at the bottom into V-shapes. Dal and Zoltan passed the straps of the large shields over their left shoulders, thus crossing over the ones supporting the swords. Round helmets with repulsive power were placed on their heads. And in the bright white light, shining upon their costumes and their helmets, the colors of the coats-of-arms painted on their shields burst forth.

Brother Alban raised his arms and formed his hands into a cup above his head. "In the name of the Global Mind of the Biosphere," he said, "I bless your expedition. May you come back soon, and victorious!"

Dal and Zoltan bowed, and Zoltan turned to Dal to say: "Do you know what I remembered just now?"

Dal shook his head.

"A dream, Ortog. A dream I had last night. In that dream I was solemnly dispatched on a mission to discover the existence behind existence, and I departed for a universe starred with mirrors, in which I saw myself from behind. It was this morning that I made telepathic contact with you, and found out about your project. It seems to me that my path was already laid out." He turned to the necrosoph. "What do you think of that, Abbé?"

Brother Alban raised his eyebrows. "It's the path of wisdom, Lord. The Global Mind was certainly the divine messenger of that dream."

"Thank you, Abbé. Are you coming, Ortog?"

They climbed into the black boat, and, one after the other, placed their hands on the fourth plate.

The huge spindle, the cables and the gondola were also slowly duplicated. An image as light as vapor was detached; it headed for the wall, where it gradually dissipated. The human forms at the controls were momentarily distinguishable, and then there was nothing.

Accompanied by two necrosophs, Brother Alban moved the inert bodies of Dal and Zoltan. They laid them out on the boat's platform, in the large gutters formed by their huge shields. They unbuckled their swords and placed them on their breast, with their hands folded over the pommels. Then Brother Alban stepped back, raised his hands in the form of a cup above the prostrate forms, and pronounced a ritual formula.

The bodies were motionless, their chests no longer rising and falling, their hearts no longer beating. Zoltan and Dal were no longer anything more than corpses.

A biologist came into the room; over his white suit he wore the black robe of the necrosophs. "Oh! They've already gone!" he said, looking at the gondola. "Have you thought about food-supplies?"

Brother Alban pointed to an amphora and a jar that had been placed at the stern of the boat.

"Perfect—but follow me into the small laboratory. I'll show you an interesting curve. Whatever happens, they won't be back within two or three minutes."

Brother Alban consented, and followed the biologist. The other two necrosophs accompanied them. The ship remained alone with its two cadavers, travelers in nothingness.

Then, with infinite precaution, a priest in a brown robe emerged from another door. He was the same one who had gone past the entrance to the alley that morning. Half-concealed by the folds of his robe, he was carrying a blaster. Within an instant, he was beside the gondola, looking down at the bodies.

As faint as a breath, words escaped his lips. "So here are the heroes, idols of the Navigators and refuge of the Sopharchy. Her are the men who set themselves against the Temple and scorn the Housemasters. Here you are, weaker than insects. You had to listen to that madman Alban and his crazy friends in the accursed laboratories. We shall see whether Alban's sacrilegious science will permit him to achieve the resurrection of cadavers dead twice over, whose bodies have been destroyed by a blaster—for I heard them mention two or three minutes. They need a brain whose cells are still viable. I'll make sure that these bodies are useless."

He raised his head to look at the great hull of the necro-ship, and a cold smile appeared on his lips.

"What an effort to kill two men! What a scene!"

First, he aimed the blaster at Zoltan's body.

Chapter Three

Slowly, the necroship advanced along the road of the Seven Agonies, which led to the gates of death. In the gondola, Dal was at the controls. Next to him, Zoltan was surveying the surroundings. His right hand was on the pommel of his sword, and his left was shielding his eyes, for they were entering a region of thick cloud pierced by the rays of a hidden sun.

Wild music mingled with somberly-toned choirs was audible. Perhaps it was one of the last echoes of the life they had just quit. Perhaps it was the voice of the icy worlds for which they were headed. Upright, immobile and silent, their heads held high and their eyes gleaming, like Siegfried and Parsifal at the frontier of Valhalla, the Knight of Galankar and the Baron de Nancy were heading into battle.

Then, amid the fanfare of trumpets and ox-horns that pierced the clouds, behind the wild choir of a million tortured voices, the monstrous rhythm of a drum as big as the Earth began to thunder. The clouds were torn apart; the men were passing over the summits of mountains that loomed over the country of the First Agony.

The ship lost height. Dal plied the tiller, as he had done during his first voyage, but in vain. The ship was no longer responding to the controls. It was rapidly drawing nearer to a howling crowd that covered the ground like a sea. The music and the choirs were extinguished. Nothing remained but the continual hammering of the cosmic drum, the echoes of which resounded from the nef's long spindle.

Zoltan drew his sword and positioned his shield to protect his torso. Dal abandoned the useless controls and did likewise. They placed themselves back to back, a living fortress covered by their shields, before which shone the malevolent glow of the Blue Swords.

At that moment, the gondola brushed the ground.—and it was as if an enormous wave swallowed it. Armies of hollow-eyed men, lacerated everywhere, brandishing the bloody stumps of limbs, rushed upon the sailors, trying to snatch their weapons away, to cut them into pieces and pound them into pulp. They were decimated in the first attack; the swords made horrible gaps in their ranks; hundreds were simultaneously cut in two. Zoltan cut and thrust, and a gigantic hole appeared in which nothing any longer moved. Dal rested his sword momentarily and manipulated the tiller. The ship finally obeyed, freeing itself from its besiegers with keen avidity. With one bound, it rose up into the cloudy sky, pursued by an immense howl of rage.

Dal and Zoltan resumed their positions.

"Small fry. What do you think, Ortog?"

"We've fought the agony of all the wounded of the world, Henderson. We were prey—but I'm waiting for the real attack."

Dal increased their speed. In front of the ship, a vast black cloud hid the sun, whose rays made its circumference shine as if it were fringed with carbuncles. Dal pointed the ship toward the cloud, and accelerated its progress further. The spindle pierced the vapor and flared up in the rays of sunlight. They arrived like a thunderbolt over the side of a mountain. It was necessary to slow down abruptly, and the travelers fell forwards over the necroship's dashboard. When they got up again, the gondola was resting on the ground. Thousands of men bearing frightful burns were crawling toward them. Others were running, trailing tatters of charred flesh behind them. All of them were reaching for the ship with hands clenched like vices. They were there within seconds—but Dal and Zoltan had reformed the fortress.

"That's inconvenient," said Dal. "I feel as if I were burning myself."

"It's true. We're among the inhabitants of the Second Agony. It's necessary to hold them back."

The swords whirled again, slicing through the repulsive mass, but Dal sensed the temperature rising incessantly. "Let's retreat," he said. "Although we haven't been burned yet ourselves, the ship is at risk of damage."

"You're right," said Zoltan, without pausing in his frightful windmilling. "I don't want to break down in this region."

Dal slung his shield over his back and returned to the controls. The ship tore itself away from the burned men, who were uttering long throaty howls. Within a few seconds, the temperature had returned to normal.

"Oof!" said Dal, sponging his brow.

"It's all going well," Zoltan declared, gaily. "I'm very curious to learn how the compassionate people of the Third Agony will conduct themselves."

"Look!" was Dal's only reply.

The ship was floating over a somber lake whose shores were invisible. Blanched and bloated faces were, however, slowly emerging from the surface. Myriads of shipwreck victims emerged in this fashion, rising up to waist-depth, silently extending their arms, convulsed by the horrors of suffocation. Many of them grabbed hold of the edges of the gondola, drawing the ship toward the black surface. Dal and Zoltan had already begun cutting off the arms with wide-ranging sweeps, but the blades also cut the surface of the water, provoking immense waves, which splashed over the side of the boat. It was necessary to start baling with the jar and the amphora, and the food-supplies and drinking-water were lost.

Dal finally succeeded in gaining height, just as he and Zoltan were beginning to choke.

"Let's make haste to meet the inhabitants of the Fourth Agony," said the Knight. "I'm eager to challenge death."

"We're already challenging it," Zoltan reminded him. "Take care—its face is still masked, but that's what's attacking us."

"Let's say that I'd like to see it uncovered."

"Do you think, then, that it will be an entity—an enemy that responds to its name?"

"If that's not the case, we'll crush it."

"Very good, very good! If we crush death, we'll exceed our aim. Anyway, it's not as easy to crush an abstraction as a nominal enemy. No, Ortog, were going to enter death alive. A very ancient poet said: 'Must these evils lie in wait for you? Yes, or everyone would go to Heaven alive.' Well, that what we're going to do. So we shall know what its mask hides without it having to remove it. In the meantime, here are those you summoned just now with such enthusiasm…"

It was necessary to form the fortress immediately; the necroship had just touched down on the shore of the lake. From the edge of a nearby forest ran a host of men and women of leonine appearance, with amputated limbs, who surrounded them, howling. At that moment, they perceived that the titanic drum was still beating in the clouds. Again, it as necessary to send such limbs as the wretches retained flying through the air—not without the two sailors of the Shadows being inundated by their foul blood.

"Lepers!" breathed Dal, disgustedly.

"Bah!" said Zoltan. "I'm sicker than they are." And he continued to carve valiantly.

Dal suddenly cast off, and they were both thrown backwards. Brushing the tops of poisonous trees, they floated far away from the nauseating beach. Fungoid vegetation, ocellate thongs and livid filaments hung from the braches of trees with soft black leaves, whose branches were shaking, even though there was not the slightest breath of wind.

Suddenly, the filaments and the thongs whistled over the spindle of the ship, dragging it toward a clearing covered in reddish mud. The swords cut into the tangle, but a multitude of men with pain-contorted faces sprang from the ground and the trees, bent double, with their hands clasped over their stomachs. Dal and Zoltan were gripped by violent pains in the belly and torso, headaches and cramps, vertigos and nauseas.

"The Fifth Agony is that of the poisoned!" said Zoltan, painfully.

They struck out again, but they understood that, with each new enemy, their efforts were becoming weaker. They were no longer as great as those of their aggressors, against whom they had to defend themselves, whose frightful pains they felt in their turn. It was, however, necessary to fight in order not to be drowned by that human tide.

Dal cut the last filament, simultaneously cutting a hundred men in half, just as he felt himself losing consciousness. He saw that Zoltan was atrociously pale, and that he was no longer gripping the hilt of his sword—but the ship finally pierced the clouds, and the inhabitants of the Fifth Agony were already no more than a memory.

"Our shields can't protect us against that sort of attack," said Dal, breathlessly, having closed his eyes briefly.

Zoltan had calmed down. "Our real shields," he said, "are inside us."

Then an extraordinarily violent wind got up, which bore the ship away without Dal being able to keep control. The ground flew past beneath the gondola so rapidly, that they could no longer perceive its details—and straight ahead loomed up a giant mushroom surrounded by an unsustainable light. Night fell immediately—a profound darkness in the bosom of which the ship made brutal contact with.

"That was one of those primitive nuclear explosions," Dal observed, in surprise.

"Yes, some people—some small groups, rather—still use them, as soon as the Navigators take their eyes off them. They're only playthings, but they're murderous..."

"Look out!" Dal cried.

From the depths of the darkness, the phosphorescent outlines of a vast number of mutilated combatants were emerging. Dal and Zoltan struck out without delay, for they were already feeling radiation-burns. As the swords flashed, the mortally-wounded arrived, preceded by the screams of a thousand fearful voices. Lightning-flashes lit up the night, dispersing the phosphorus glow of faces pitted by gamma rays. The Blue Weapon finished them off, but Dal had greater difficult in leaving this time; it seemed that the radiation had damaged, or at least slowed down, the functioning of the drive.

The opaque clouds dissipated. Only light clouds haloed with radiance remained before a bright sun. The sunlight was that of a high chalky plateau, immense and deserted.

"We've got through the Sixth Agony," Dal recalled. "We're coming to the last."

"We must be very close to it," Zoltan put in—and he burst out laughing, for no apparent reason.

Dal looked at him anxiously, then moved the vertical tiller.

Fissures split the ground, which was fuming in the hot sunlight.

"Can you hear the drum?" Dal asked, tilting his head. "That sun isn't our sun. It's a drum. That's what we can hear. What we take for light is only sound. It's a star of death that's radiating noise in every direction." And he too burst out laughing, as he contemplated the individuals who were hoisting themselves out of fissures and approaching the oat: men in rags, with haggard eyes and twisted faces.

Zoltan suddenly took on a taut expression. "They're mentally ill, Ortog! The Seventh Agony is dementia. It's futile to fight—flee immediately, or we too will be…" He burst out laughing and raked his face with his fingernails.

Ortog recovered consciousness briefly—for the instant necessary to get off the ground and climb like an arrow toward the zenith. Zoltan looked at him dully.

"Are you all right?" Dal cried.

Zoltan's gaze became focused. "The worst enemy of all," he said, slowly, "is delirium—and our internal shields can't always protect us from it…" He leaned over the side of the gondola. The madmen were dwindling in the distance—but it was as if a solar eclipse was beginning; night fell again, as dark as the aftermath of the explosion. There had been no explosion though; there was nothing to explain the victory of the darkness.

The necroship was now flying at an increased speed through a terrible darkness, compared to which a winter night would have seemed like a summer morning. Their hearts embraced by the thickness of that darkness within the darkness, the paladins pressed their shields against their bodies.

"I'm beginning to miss the Agonians..." Zoltan said—but the words were carried away by the black wind, while the spindle of the necroship bristled with St. Elmo's fire. The atmospheric tension would have drawn screams from less battle-hardened men, but they remained silent.

Dal finally said what they were both thinking: "This time, we're entering into Death."

The silence was formidable. The violet plumes surrounding the necroship still projected a feeble glow some distance away, but that only served to display the absence of everything: an inhuman desert over which pitch-blackness closed again—and yet, Dal could see that Zoltan was pointing toward the prow.

"Can you see that?" he said.

Dal opened his eyes wide. They were speeding like an arrow toward an immense tree, entirely plunged in a feeble glow that bathed it like stagnant water.

"Can you see now what it has on its branches?"

Dal made out huge bats, hanging head-down like bunches of grapes.

Before the swords had been forged, Dal had described his first expedition through the lands of Dream to Zoltan. Zoltan reminded him of it. "Didn't you see a large flock of bats at the moment you left the regions of Dream?"

"Yes."

"It was those. They've been noted by the author of a work of the greatest antiquity. Every time one of those bats takes flight, a man has a dream. I wonder which of them was in flight when I had the dream that decided me to accompany you. Hold on—look!"

In the distance, behind the vessel, a large flock of bats roe up at once and disappeared into the darkness.

"That ancient author," Dal remarked, "must have made the same journey that we're in the process of making..."

"No. Poets have a direct grasp of nature. They divine many things without hang seen them."

They both knew, however, that they were only engaging in this conversation to avoid the horrific pall that was extending the renewed obscurity over them again.

"If it's like this until the end of the voyage," Zoltan declared, "We won't have learned very much."

Dal did not add that, if that were the case, it would be a terrible failure for him. He had not launched himself into this glacial adventure in a mere spirit of discovery, but to attempt to make contact with Kalla, the woman he loved, and who had died without waiting for him...

"Perhaps we've skipped a stage," Zoltan continued. "We should undoubtedly have passed through the world of nightmares before encountering the Agonians."

"No—nightmares are situated well before that. They're between dream and syncope. I've followed the whole of that route."

"Perhaps, then, the gates of Death are closed to us because the ship sustained damage in the course of the battles..."

Gradually, a titanic wall emerged from the darkness in front of them, of which they could perceive neither the top nor the bottom. There was nothing but the enormous wall: a cyclopean prohibition of further progress; an infinite barrier dividing two infinities.

Dal slowed the ship down as much as he could, but it was still animated by such a velocity that they were bound to crash within seconds into that inconceivable wall. Instinctively, they raised their shields to protect themselves. Their shields developed their own wall of energy, against which matter dissolved.

As the ship arrived like a bullet, Zoltan had the courage to ask a question: "What happens when an irresistible force meets an immovable object?"

"A false problem," said Ortog. "A contradiction in..." He feel silent. He had seen an opening, and he plied the controls with as much skill as he had formerly used to steer his starship.

They passed through.

The necroship was still slowing down. It began drifting lightly in a grey shadow, above an uneven ground. Slowly swaying at the end of its cables, the gondola seemed more than ever a kind of primitive boat, and Zoltan was not at a loss for one of his references to a past known to him alone.

"According to a very old mythology, a certain Charon…"

"Oh!"

Dal extended his arm, pointing with his index-finger. Zoltan perceived forms beneath them. There were three of them, which paused as the ship passed over: three human forms clad in armor that was both cloudy and bright at the same time. The details of their shape were indistinguishable, but the whole was sufficiently clear for the travelers to be able to observe an incomprehensible phenomenon: the forms were simultaneously visible from the front and in profile.

"Do you see what I see?" asked Dal, smiling.

"I assume," said Zoltan, "that you can see them from the front and the back…oh!—no, from the front and in profile."

"No," said Dal, whose view had just changed. "I really can see them from the front and the back at the same time…which is to say…"

Everything was constantly changing. Soon, they could see the three individuals from every side at the same time—which was extremely disconcerting, and made them feel ill. Already, though, the ship had passed over them, and they were lost in a mist as thick as that of autumn evenings on Earth, in the world of Life.

They continued their progress through the same mist, which sometimes broke up, allowing them glimpses of rocky ground below, and a greenish, sunless sky above. A glimmer to their left, however, caused them to think that a dawn was about to break. Dawn, in the universe of death—a dawn in which anything was to be feared.

More human forms emerged, more distantly, and disappeared—but they too had paused in their march.

"One really might think that they're wearing armor," said Dal. "Is that because…because they're dead, and yet the dead can still make war?"

"Perhaps they're going to tell us…"

Dal did not reveal the conclusion of his thought. If it were a matter, one way or another, of dead human beings, whose forms subsisted in this word, Kalla must be among them. And if she were here, Dal would not turn back before having found her. That might take a very long time, and demand a great deal of courage.

"But there are two of us to carry out the search," said Zoltan, and added: "Oh! Pardon me for not having warned you that I had made contact…"

The sky turned emerald green, and soon became a violent yellow. A white sun rose over the horizon of the plain, dissipating the fog.

"So," said Zoltan, "the Beyond resembles a planet with its own sun. It all seems to obey the same cosmic laws as those familiar to us."

"Unless it's merely an appearance. What about that wall we came through?"

"What if that were mere appearance?"

Dal made no reply. They were overtaking columns of armoured silhouettes, which stopped as they passed overhead—but there was not the slightest hostile gesture, merely a pause. They were seen, and their presence constituted an event—that was all.

When they had melted into the distance, Dal lost altitude. "We need to make contact," he said. "But how?"

"Go forward, then," Zoltan proposed. "Look at what's in front of us."

In the distance, a vague form was quivering in the sunlight. Dal drew nearer to it. It was soon an immense edifice,

186

ponderous in form: like a gigantic cube whose faces were not quite at right-angles to one another. The ship continued its approach, overtaking yet more columns, which were heading for a vast circular opening yawning in the wall of the edifice—such a large opening that the ship seemed like a bat at the entrance to a cave.

"Let's go in with the columns," Dal decided. "There's no reason for them to bar our way now, when they haven't done so before."

"Perfect. But perhaps it's their capital—let's be vigilant."

The ship floated into the opening, and the columns interrupted their march again to look at it—but then they started off again, immediately. A long corridor extended before the travelers, which became narrower as they advanced—but the entrance had been so vast that it took a long time for them to find themselves cramped for space. The nef's spindle brushed the ceiling of the corridor, even though the gondola was very close to the luminously armored individuals. The latter merely raised their heads as they passed over, but did not slow down.

"Such indifference to something disquieting," Zoltan remarked. "After all, we must be as strange to them as they are to us!"

"Undoubtedly—but we're still going forward. Who shall we ask? They don't seem to have a leader. Oh, too bad!"

He stopped the ship, which remained motionless in the narrowed corridor. "Hey!" he cried.

There was not the slightest result. "They're deaf!" he said.

"You know," said Zoltan, "if they don't react to the sight of us, there's not much chance that they'll do so on hearing us."

"That's true," said Dal, ill-humoredly. "Let's go on into the heart of this citadel, which seems to be swallowing soldiers as an ant-eater swallows ants…"

The corridor had become too narrow, though. The exterior light had given way to a scarlet twilight. It was in that bloody light that Dal and Zoltan had to take their machine back. They turned round.

Behind the ship, the corridor had the same form as it had in front. It was continuing to draw in. There was no trace of an opening.

It was the anger brooding in Dal that burst forth, not the dread. "Ah! So it's a trap! A lobster-pot! But I'm too big a fish for such a small basket. And since we can neither go forward nor back, let's go forward!"

He got the ship under way, slowly. "After all, we're the impalpable double of the necroship. We can pass through all obstacles."

Zoltan said nothing, but he pulled a face when a frightful grating sound was heard, accompanied by a rain of green sparks. The spindle of the ship raked the ceiling, while the armoured individuals beneath the gondola ducked. Dal stopped—but his rage had increased further.

"Let's leave the tub here!" he cried. He leapt over the side, his shield on his arm.

Zoltan did likewise without saying a word. He had to hurry to catch up with him; Dal was already in the midst of the columns.

There, they had a much clearer sight of those surrounding them. They were human in form, but their faces were hidden by a sort of helmet without any opening for vision. It was not their natural form—that seemed evident at every movement, at the level of articulation, for their limbs and their throats were protected by the same shiny material.

The columns were advancing in a compact mass, however. It soon became impossible to progress at the same time as them. Dal and Zoltan stopped, leaning against the curved wall, still amazed by the lack of attention paid to them. Ahead of them, it was like the depths of a seashell lit by a fire; behind them, an identical scene.

"It must be an illusion," Dal said, eventually, gradually calming down.

"But, my dear chap," Zoltan remarked, tapping the pommel of his sword, "The ship didn't say so…"

"I didn't go back," Dal recalled.

"I advise you not to. It's a good bet that things would have turned out the same way."

"But what can have happened?"

"I don't know on what principle the trap—which doesn't seem to be affecting these people overmuch—works, but I think it's effective. I imagine its some sort of geometric semi-conductor."

"In that case, it's necessary to find someone who's capable of reversing its direction. As retreat is impossible, let's continue going forwards."

They looked back again, waiting for a gap in the disciplined crowd.

"Do you see those who are arriving?" Dal asked.

"Yes. One would think that they were coming through the walls of the funnel. They appear abruptly."

"And in front of us?"

"The same thing. They disappear through the other wall. How can they exist between two cones with interpenetrating summits, the communal part of which is a trap?"

"Perhaps it's only a trap for the ship. We shall see."

A vacant space appeared between two columns. They stepped into it. To see them advance thus, preceded and followed by those bellicose forms, one might have thought that they were under strong guard, or that they had been given a guard of honor. It was neither one nor the other. They gave rise to no more emotion than a helix passing over houses in Lassenia.

When they reached the point in the corridor where it seemed impossible to walk on without ducking, they did as the column did: they went through the wall without sustaining any damage. Then, an unexpected spectacle was offered to their gaze; they found themselves in an immense tunnel, circular in section, where the armoured individuals were deployed in numerous lines without being able to advance any further. In front of them, other lines barred the route: ranks and yet more ranks of black armor, from which the fiery light threw constantly changing random reflections. And between the first lines there was a space covered with extended bodies: a space furrowed by silent lightning-bolts.

"They're fighting one another!" Dal exclaimed. "We'd better stay back!"

"Undoubtedly, undoubtedly…but who wants you to fight?" asked Zoltan.

"No one. We'll try to separate them. It's the best chance of making contact with either side."

"We can try," aid Zoltan, skeptically.

They had little trouble carving a path through the lines. Those among whom they arrived were marking time, or advancing very slowly, and their ranks cleared as they suffered losses. The travelers, therefore, reached an open space in which chaos reigned: a crossroads on which adjacent tunnels opened, within which the battle was continuing.

It was not easy to stand between the adversaries, for the combats were becoming individual. They did it, though, and tried once again to attract attention—without succeeding. All that they achieved was to be grazed several times by the lightning-bolts the enemies were exchanging.

"Let's find another strategy," Dal proposed, standing aside.

They took refuge in a crack in the wall at the entrance to one of the tunnels. Very close to them, a duel began between two adversaries whose helmets were decorated with incomprehensible symbols. They were exchanging lightning-bolts, which departed from the end of a rod that each held in his hand. At each blast, the length of the rod diminished, as if it were composed of pure energy, which was being liberated in fractions. The bolts were striking the enemy, surrounding him in a halo of light, but the armor seemed to be an effective protection. Each of them therefore, was aiming at the joints where the pieces of the other's armor fitted together—without hitting them. They seemed to be equal in strength; although they were both skillful, they displayed an equal agility in avoiding the adverse fire.

The combatant in white armor soon had nothing between his fingers but the fragment of an inoffensive baton. He took a new weapon from his belt, avoiding a rain of thunderbolts. As he moved, though, something fell to the ground: a triangular object that emitted a faint light. Dal bounded forward and grabbed it. Then he retreated to his shelter, rejoining Zoltan—who had drawn his sword.

The white helmet and the black helmet turned toward them at the same time. The two enemies had ceased their duel. They advanced on the intruders together.

"Ah!" Dal shouted at them. "We exist now! Come and get it, then!" And he waved the object, which was very heavy and warmed his hand slightly. Faced with this challenge, the two adversaries pointed their weapon at the travellers with a single movement. Zoltan and Dal raised their large shields. The lightning-blasts sprang forth.

There was a deafening explosion. The assailants were lifted from the ground and thrown back ten meters, while Dal found himself brutally plastered against the wall. His shield had become red hot. Zoltan had to let go of his almost immediately.

The black helmet had been knocked off by the shock, and the tottering being—the humanoid—was revealed. It was a strange sight, that face which could be seen from several angles at once: an entirely human face, whose features were confused by the omnivision. The other was writhing alongside him, though, and aimed his weapon again, profiting from his enemy's weakness. The armor came apart, and the humanoid fell, a black patch in the middle of his forehead.

"Oh!" Dal exclaimed, indignantly. "What treachery!" He bounded out of his shelter while the victor was getting up— but the being had no time to point his weapon; Dal was upon him, and drove his sword through the shiny breastplate. A new explosion resounded. There was no more enemy; in his place was a luminous vertical line, whose glare faded away, and which disappeared completely.

Petrified, Dal stood still, staring at the place where the line had vanished. Not far away, the duel were ceasing. With three steps, Zoltan was next to Dal.

"Your shield, damn it! Your shield!"

Dal raised his shield, mechanically, and they both retreated to their shelter.

"Oh well!" Dal sighed. "We now know what effect the Blue Weapon has in this world—and also how the force-field of our shield behaves."

"And I think you've had an important effect," Zoltan added. "Look at them all."

Everywhere, the soldiers on both sides had stopped fighting. Several of them advanced toward the two men in hiding.

Suddenly, Dal looked at Zoltan, with an alarmed expression. "Where are we?" he said. "What are we doing here?"

Zoltan furrowed his brow and closed his eyes momentarily, then said: "Who are these people?"

The soldiers continued to draw nearer.

"Let's protect ourselves," Dal said. "They seem hostile."

They raised their shields—but their minds were utterly disturbed. One of the humanoids in black armor pointed his weapon and fired. Zoltan and Dal were flattened against the wall by a detonation, and the assailant hurtled into the others, knocking a dozen to the ground.

The explosion had ripped apart the veil that had extended over the voyagers' memories. "Oh! I remember!" Dal exclaimed, relieved. He saw that it was the same with Zoltan. "Is there a weapon against memory?" Dal murmured. He shook his head. "We wouldn't have recovered so quickly," he said. "No—there's something else."

The assailants had formed a semicircle, and suspended their attack, but they had not mingled their ranks to any great extent. Two white suits of armor advanced, their weapons extended. Dal, who remembered the effect produced by the Blue Weapon, took a step forward to meet them, brandishing

192

his sword. The bold pair retreated, and threw themselves into the ranks of their enemies, who riddled them with lightning-bolts. One of them succeeded in getting away; the other fell. Immediately, there was a general stir in the white-armored host, which mobilized the others—but the combats were not resumed. They all turned toward the two voyagers.

"Yes," said Dal. "I think I've got hold of something that's equally important to both sides." He addressed them: "I didn't know how to make contact with you, but now it's you who no longer know what to do. Come on, then, come closer, so that we might make peace! Or, if you want war, well, you shall have it! We have what we need to fight! I am Dal Ortog Dal of Galankar, and I've crossed the void between the stars! And this is Zoltan Charles Henderson de Nancy, who has also crossed the void between the stars, and who also knows how to capture thoughts at a distance, without the aid of words! Come on, you cowards, you hypocritical dogs—attack again, and I shall strike you with this blade, and none of you will escape! Or let the wisest among you agree to talk: I shall give this object to the one who offers me the best deal!"

Thus spoke Dal Ortog, in the excited ardour of his youth. Zoltan, however, leaned toward him and said: "They have ears, but I don't think the sound of our voices reaches them. I'll try to establish telepathic contact with them."

He straightened up and stared at the nearest one. At the same time, he projected his thoughts into Dal's mind. If he could capture these creatures' thoughts, he would thus serve as a relay, and they would both receive the mental communication. That took some time.

Then, there was something like a shell-burst, which made them both shiver. The humanoid spoke to them. "Who are you, and where do you come from, flat things?"

"Flat things!" exclaimed Dal, indignantly.

"Ssh!" said Zoltan. "Let him go on."

"We thought that you were a publicity projection, obtained by a new method—but you are living beings, since you have killed one of us, and you have stolen the Key."

Zoltan transmitted a response: "How can we kill you, since you are dead?"

There was an overlap, a mixture of fluid thoughts, then: "Who told you this madness?"

"We come from the world of Life. What can you possible be but dead men?"

"*This* is the world of Life: the world of volume. You are flat animals—semi-living things. Give us the Key."

Zoltan studied the white suit of armor, and cut the contact, re-establishing it with a being in black armor.

"Whose side are you on, flat things?" said the latter.

"That depends," Zoltan retorted. "We have the Key. Would you like to have it?"

The soldier took a step forward. Dal raised his sword. The soldier stepped back. "Yes," he said, "certainly."

"To whom does the Key belong?"

"To us."

Zoltan returned to the first one. "To whom does the Key belong?"

"To us!"

"Someone's lying," Zoltan concluded. "We'll keep the Key."

Desperately, Dal turned to Zoltan. "We've gone the wrong way," he said. "We aren't in the land of Death."

The black-suited individuals were visibly communicating among themselves, as were the whites—but nothing was audible.

"Wait," Zoltan said to Dal. "How can we be sure that the dead retain the memory of their anterior life? Ours, that is. If that memory escapes them, and they have a particular kind of existence here, would they say anything different? The greatest of liars is a dead man who declares that he is dead. A sincere dead man stays silent, or claims that he is alive. All the rest is merely ghost stories, and the dead don't return. It's necessary to go in search of them where they live, and that's what we're doing."

A black and a white came forward, empty-handed. Zoltan capture the thoughts of the white first.

"We're the messengers," he said. He pointed to the other. "And they're the fallen."

Zoltan looked at Dal. "This is reminiscent of all the old religions," he said. "We've happened upon a battle between angels and demons. Something must once have filtered through from their world to ours—perhaps an accidental telepathic communication."

"At this moment, you're in the prison of the fallen," the messenger continued, "and the Key that you have is that of the prison. You must give it to us, or we shall take it by force."

"What will you do with it?" Zoltan asked.

"They are rebels who have killed their guards. You are foreigners. Go back to your flat world. Give me the Key."

"Enough," said Zoltan. "Your weapons are too weak. We'll trade the Key for something valuable."

Dal turned to Zoltan. "This is the moment," he said. "Relay my thoughts." And he thought intently of Kalla's face, her voice, and all the forms of thought personal to him.

"Put us in contact with the being that we have just described," Zoltan transmitted hereafter.

It was as if a wall came down in front of them.

"We have your vehicle—the flat spindle. We'll give you that for the Key."

"He's side-stepped the demand," Zoltan said to Dal. "That's a good sign. Otherwise, he would have made his ignorance manifest—but he's not an honest dealer." He spoke to the messenger again. "I've told you what I want," he said. "It's that or nothing. We'll get our ship back ourselves and keep the Key."

"Be careful. We have other weapons than this one."

"Oh, really? Well, let's see them."

The messenger retreated, disappearing among the others. Zoltan addressed the black suit of armor then. "So you're one of the fallen?" he said. "Fallen from what? And the others—the messengers—whose messengers are they?"

"We've fallen from the estate of the messengers—and the messengers claim that they're the emissaries of the Great Power."

"Everyone talks about God, one way or another," Zoltan said to Dal, "but no one will show him to us here, any more than in Lassenia."

"We want the Key," repeated the fallen.

"Of course," said Zoltan. "When one is in prison, that's the first thing one desires—but can you give us what we ask in exchange?"

"If it's in our power, yes."

"Off we go," said Zoltan to Dal.

Dal remade the mental portrait that he had already composed. The portrait was accompanied by an affective atmosphere so sad that Zoltan felt all his jokes coming apart.

"That being exists," said the fallen. Dal uttered an exclamation. "But it—she, rather—is a messenger."

"Where is she to be found?"

"I don't know, but there is someone who can undoubtedly tell you."

"Who?"

"The Weaver of Echoes."

"Who is the Weaver of Echoes?"

"He's our leader. He's here. He was born in prison."

"Take us to him, and you shall have the Key."

The reply was accompanied by an ambience of restrained joy. "I'll take you to him, but it will first be necessary for us to form a guard, and you might even have to fight."

"Yes, I imagine that the messengers will react. Well, we're waiting."

There was a great commotion among the black suits of armor. Many of the fallen resumed the battle unexpectedly, wreaking carnage among the messengers. Others took advantage of that surprise attack and localized victory to form an escort ten ranks deep, weapons in hand.

Then a cohort of white-armored figures appeared, carrying an enormous disk, dull in appearance.

"We must flee immediately," said the fallen. "They intend to employ the Mirror of Negation here—it will destroy everything."

Dal and Zoltan were preparing to follow the escort, which was moving back in an orderly fashion, when they all through themselves on the ground, along the walls. The voyagers had not hade time to quit their refuge, though. A black ray had just emerged from the center of the mirror—a ray that drowned everything it encountered in obscurity. They ray began to sweep slowly around the subterranean crossroads, and Dal and Zoltan saw, to their horror, that wherever it passed, no one remained—merely a hole whose depth was inestimable.

Dal sprang out of his retreat. In three bounds he was in front of the line of messengers that was preceding the machine. He was welcomed by a rain of lightning, and fell back in the midst of explosions—but the entire first line had collapsed. Dal got up again, holding his shield up, and his sword made a wide sweep. Twenty messengers were transformed into luminous lines, which writhed momentarily and vanished. The operator of the Mirror of Negation turned the weapon toward Dal as quickly as he could, but the Navigator was already underneath it, and slashed at it with powerful thrusts.

The result was frightful. The light changed from red to greenish yellow and a shrill whistling sound resounded through the tunnels. The mirror disappeared in a flash of darkness, cleaving through the walls of the tunnel for hundreds of meters.

Dal fell backwards, unconscious. Zoltan, however, was already running to his aid, supported by the escort that had just been formed. The Blue Weapon carved through the messengers, who had been thrown into disarray by the obliteration of their superweapon. The fallen completed the carnage with lightning-bolts.

Dal had a slight wound on his arm. He recovered consciousness with his back against a fragment of the mirror.

"Ah!" he said, faintly, to Zoltan. "I think I've broken their crossbow!"

The losses were counted. They were high, especially by virtue of the mirror. There were too many enemy cadavers to count, though; the swords had caused a substantial fraction to disappear. As for those that the fallen had killed, they were littering the crossroads. There were also all those that the mirror's explosion had disintegrated.

"You had a certain amount of luck, my dear chap," said Zoltan, in an emphatic voice. "One might say that you exposed yourself. The crossbow didn't do a bad job of annihilating people as it broke, and you were immediately underneath it—but if you hadn't attacked, none of us would be here to comment on the battle."

Dal got up, grimacing. Zoltan had already mopped up the blood on his arm and applied one of those little bandages that cause a wound to scar over in less than an hour.

"What about the ship?" he said. "We ought to be able to see it from here. They were telling the truth when they claimed that it was in their power. How shall we get back?"

"Don't worry. We've given them proof that the Blue Weapon is even more powerful than their mirror, which must represent the best they can do here, in respect of military materials. We can deal with them at our leisure when we wish. Look—not one of them remains! I'll wager that they're already on the plain. Besides, there's no conclusive proof that they had the ship in their possession. If it's still in the common part of the two inverted cones in the entrance corridor, it's quite possible that we wouldn't be able to see it from our present position."

Zoltan helped Dal to stand up, to sheath the sword that was beginning to destroy the ground where it had been abandoned, and to readjust the shield. Then he added: "When you've recovered Kalla, my dear chap, you won't ask so many questions."

Dal looked around, hopefully, and they followed the escort into one of the lateral tunnels. The fallen with whom they had concluded their bargain was by their side. Zoltan resumed telepathic communication.

"Why did you fall, by the way?"

"I don't know. None of us knows—except perhaps for the Weaver of Echoes. If he consents to tell you, you'll know too."

"Damn!" said Zoltan. "They don't know why they're in prison. They're born here; they die here. What is this regime? They're charming, these messengers!"

"How can Kalla possibly be among these tyrants?" Dal wondered.

As the communicative link was established, the fallen heard that. "What's a tyrant?" he asked.

"It's a messenger," said Zoltan, briefly, "but not necessarily a messenger…"

From time to time, the travelers observed the beings they could see from all angles at the same time without moving. They could not succeed in doing so. Zoltan ended up communicating to Dal a thought that he had been harboring for some time. "This is doubtless the land of the dead, but where we are is certainly a four-dimensional space. There are several reasons to think so."

"I can see the first," Dal said. "It proves that it's a matter of four spatial dimensions, without counting Time—which might not flow here as it does in our world."

"Exactly. What is that proof?"

"The Blue Weapon annihilates space, and the beings struck by it are reduced to a line. The weapon has taken away the three dimensions of our space, and the only one that remains to them is the supplementary one. That line eventually disappears in its turn, because it's inviable."

"Yes, I've interpreted that in the same manner. A further proof is that we can see these beings from several angles at the same time, as certain painters might have represented them before the Blue War. The reciprocity of that proof is that they see us as flat beings."

"Evidently. We have one dimension less than them. We must have the same effect on them as a two-dimensional being on Earth."

Zoltan had not broken the communication-link, so their companion began to transmit. "Your notion does, indeed, explain several things. That's why we took you for flat projections over a long distance. Comparable ones already exist, over a short range—and even projections that aren't flat."

"Yes, in four dimensions, as we have three...the only ones we know in our world."

"But I can't see the relationship between the dead and the fourth dimension," Dal said.

"And yet," Zoltan said, "that might also explain a great deal. We'll know more, I hope, when we've been introduced to this Weaver of Echoes. I doubt, though, that he'll be able to explain a few troubling analogies regarding this particular world of the dead and the world of four dimensions."

"What do you mean?" said Dal, interestedly.

"Well, these messengers and fallen, and the situation of the fallen—which seems to me to be unending, with no remission.....I wouldn't be particularly surprised if I were to discover that the fallen were imprisoned because they went in search of a certain merchandise that we call Knowledge..."

"What about this God, this cosmic mind?"

"That's another story. It's the kind of idea to which the combination of hope and anguish gives birth in very world. There are certainly infantile personalities everywhere that need to believe in something larger than themselves—but that has nothing to do with a certain form of survival linked to physical planes and higher mathematics: planes that must have corresponded with ours on occasion, leaving traces of information that have been transformed into legends in the course of the ages. I'm saying this because I'm here. If the necroship hadn't brought us here, I wouldn't even believe in the existence of this world, but there has to be an explanation for objective facts...

"Survival, too, has always seemed to me to be a consolatory idea, reserved for the anxious who commit suicide out of fear of death. It needed you to be Dal Ortog to give me the chance of discovering my mistake…"

The continued on their way without speaking. Neither their guide nor their escort hesitated—and yet, they had never encountered a maze so inextricable. Corridors and yet more corridors, of every length and every diameter—and always the same red light, which ended up making them feel sick. Sometimes an inclined plane appeared, which descended into the ground, or, by contrast, seemed to be climbing toward the sky. Often, they passed one or several openings pierced in the wall of a tunnel; through those openings they could see families occupied in mysterious tasks. The men were dressed in black fabrics; the women were distinguishable by their hair, which reflected all the shades of the light from red to scarlet, pink to purple and carmine to vermilion. Pensive children could be seen standing still in front of some of these windows, staring at the opposite wall.

The guide transmitted his thought: "It's said that, in the beginning, the prison only had four large corridors, pierced in an immense mass of matter. It was enough that the messengers had imprisoned them—but the prisoners multiplied, and they were obliged to hollow out other, narrower corridors, in every direction. The long road that we have to follow is the result of that. Even the messengers, at present, are incapable of finding their way through these ramifications. When they undertake an expedition against us, they always remain in the fringes of the first corridors. They know that if they were to advance they'd soon go astray, suffer defeat, and get cut to pieces. But we have to stop them, because their dearest desire is to infiltrate everywhere, in order to control us completely, and they were doing that gradually, maintaining guard on the positions they've taken. It was those guards we got rid of—an action that occasioned the expedition in which you got mixed up."

He stopped, and so did the entire column. "We're calling a halt. The cells of the great vault are still a long way off, and it's necessary to rest and recuperate." He pointed into a circular hall, at the entrance of which they had just stopped. "This is one of the energy gardens."

Dal and Zoltan looked at one another, then studied the floor of the hall, which disappeared beneath a carpet of cloudy spirals.

"Are we going to eat spirals?" asked Dal, anxiously. He was hungry, and even if the ship had been within reach, there would be nothing to be found there, since the food and drinking water had been lost during the battle with the inhabitants of the Third Agony.

"Come on—and don't be embarrassed: you're invited guests."

Zoltan went to the first bed of spirals. He plucked one of them circumspectly, but it escaped his grip immediately, falling while rotating. He caught it again, trying to hold it in both hands, but the effort was wasted.

For the first time, Dal laughed frankly. "How do you expect to hold four-dimensional objects made of pure energy in your three-dimensional hands?"

"It's intolerable! These absurd lettuces will pay for that!" He threw himself into the middle of the garden, under the reproachful eyes of the fallen—but he soon came back. "It's all right. It's sufficient to touch them. The energy is directly absorbed through the skin. I feel much better."

Dal went closer then and verified that Zoltan was correct. Their hosts, however, conducted themselves in a more traditional fashion: they were eating. Sitting in little groups, they had laid down their weapons and were chatting among themselves telepathically.

The pause lasted for some time. Even though Dal had not yet handed over the Key, which he kept in one if the pockets of his uniform, the alliance with the fallen no longer seemed to be in question. They had been accepted.

They set off again through the eternal corridors, alongside excavations in which an entire people was at work. The cells of the great vault were well-protected. No stranger to this region would have discovered it without years of searching, and perhaps never—and yet they finally bumped into a powerful guard, which barred the tunnels. The guide undertook negotiations, while the escort and the guardsmen fraternized. They passed through, accompanied by a contingent of guardsmen.

There were yet more corridors swarming with black breastplates, in which all the clefts in the wall were occupied by soldiers. There were no more families, no more women or children. Then came the great vault: an immense hall with a hemispherical ceiling, divided into a great many sections by walls of various heights.

The guide preceded them, was absent for a few minutes, and then returned.

"The Weaver of Echoes is waiting or you."

They followed the route pointed out to them, crossing the entire hall of the great vault. As they went forward, the light dimmed. They finally ended up at a dwelling whose dimensions they could not determine, for it was plunged into a gloom that was too intense. Facing them, they saw a long curtain, ceaselessly stirred by a slight breeze. The curtain shone with a thousand colors, but so weakly that it could not illuminate the surroundings. Next to it stood a motionless human form that they could scarcely make out.

Zoltan established communication and immediately received a question: "Who are you?"

This time, Zoltan decided to play it straight. "We came from another world than yours. It's a world whose inhabitants are mortal, and our researchers have constructed a machine that permits entry into the universe where our dead live. We've arrived in yours."

An absence of thought, and then a reply: "We are also living beings that die, but we have no knowledge of an anterior existence. However, some among us know that there is a world vaster and more complex than ours. We are all familiar with its manifestations, but the messengers have always said that those manifestations are of a supernatural order, and that they emanate from a unique power."

"That's exactly what the priests of our own universe say," Zoltan replied. Then he addressed himself to Dal: "We've doubtless already died once, when we quit a two-dimensional state to assume our present form—but we're unaware of it, in the same way that, when we only had two dimensions, we did not know hat our former condition was that of geometric points. And when the people of this world die, they become five-dimensional beings…and so on. Death is the acquisition of a dimension."

Zoltan was half-joking, but the Weaver replied: "Perhaps you're right. It was on account of research of that sort that our ancestors were imprisoned, and it's because we're continuing it in secret here that the messengers are trying to take total control of the labyrinth. But they're a long way from accomplishing that—especially if you're in possession of the Key."

"We have it, and we're willing to make a pact with you if you can give us information about the woman or whom my friend is searching."

"I know. I've been informed, and the portrait of the person you mention has been communicated to me precisely. She exists, but the portrait is woefully insufficient. She is all that and much more."

As if to himself, Dal said: "Yes, undoubtedly…she has an extra dimension now." Via Zoltan's relay, he addressed the Weaver: "Can you tell me where I can find her?"

"You've been told that she's a messenger. I don't know about that. What I do know is that she resides between the two mountains of the exterior world, in the direction of the star—and, naturally, on the strip of habitable land. Now, the Key!"

"I can see that you're a man of your word," said Dal, "but I need some supplementary information. Here the Key, anyway." He took out the triangular object and offered it to the Weaver, who took it.

"I'm very grateful to you," he said. "You can't imagine how important this Key is to us."

"Yes, yes," said Zoltan. "We know that it's the Key to your prison. In your shoes, I'd grant it the same importance."

"First of all," Dal continued. "What is the exterior world? I have my suspicions, but I'd like confirmation."

"It's the space that extends outside the labyrinth. It's the world inhabited and governed by the messengers. I'll explain the rest of what I said to you. It's necessary for you to go as far as two high mountains, marching in the same direction as the star, to find the residence you seek. It will be dangerous, for she's important and strongly guarded."

"It will doubtless take a long time," said Dal, pulling a face.

"No; our world is very small—but it's all desert, except for a narrow strip where the habitable countries lie. At any point situated inside that strip, the star can be seen passing the zenith."

"Ah! Only the equator is inhabited," Zoltan translated.

"But how do you know this, if you were born here and have never left?" Dal asked.

"I have many secret visits, made by messengers who sympathize with us—one among them, in particular...who knows the person you want to find."

"How?" cried Dal, seized by jealousy. "What is this...this individual?"

"Oh, you'll find out. She'll tell you the story of her adventures herself. What is worrying is that...step further into the light, stranger."

Dal did so.

"Yes, he resembles you somewhat, even though you're flat. Or, rather, you have something of him..."

"Oh?" said Dal, nonplussed. "But I'm not dead! It can't be me, transported into this world..."

Things were getting complicated. Zoltan judged that they did not have time to dig more deeply into this new problem, and changed the subject: "Why are you called the Weaver of Echoes?"

The dark form got up and reached out to touch the curtain that was still floating nearby. "Look," he said. "This tapestry ends here—but it continues in all the cells of the great vault. I'm the one weaving it."

"And what is this tapestry?"

"It contains the memories of everyone living in the labyrinth, by means of a complex disposition of the woven threads and the colors. Everyone comes to see me and tells me everything new that they have to say. Especially the researchers…for imprisonment has not discouraged them."

"And why weave the tapestry? It resembles, in principle, certain machines that we make."

"Because our worst punishment is not imprisonment, but the incapacity to conserve our memories in our own heads. By that means, the messengers thought they could be forearmed against our endeavors, for no effort can succeed without memory; everything that is learned is fragmentary, and loses its significance. A great collective memory was required. I am its constructor and depositor. That's why I'm called the Weaver of Echoes."

The light brightened. Zoltan saw that the Weaver resembled him.

Chapter Four

As he had done with respect to Dal, Zoltan tried to evade the problem posed by that second resemblance. The hypotheses already constructed were obviously too simplistic, but this was not the time to revise them.

At that moment, Dal was struck by the resemblance, and exclaimed: "But you too have points in common."

"Really?" the Weaver transmitted. "As this concerns me, and you're flat…"

"Yes," said Zoltan. "I believe my face has elements of yours. And yet, I am present myself in this hall…" He turned to Dal. "Would you mind if we talked about this later? Since disembarking in this world we've already gleaned information and devised theories. Other information will come along that will modify and complete our notion of things."

Dal nodded his head. "As you wish," he said. "But if beings can exist here that resemble living people in our world—you and me, in this case—there's no longer any proof that there's a relationship between our dead and their living. The woman we're talking about might have no connection with Kalla, save for a fortuitous resemblance."

"No, Ortog. These resemblances are too improbable to be coincidental. Stay confident—we'll get to the bottom of things." He turned back to the Weaver of Echoes. "Don't you think that it's now time to act?" he said. "We won't take advantage of your hospitality any longer. We have to get back to the exterior world. We ought to do that together, as allies."

"Well said, stranger."

The Weaver imparted a sequence of subtle movements to the multicoloured work of art that he held in the tips of his fingers. These movements were transmitted along the entire length of the interminable curtain, in all probability continuing beyond the walls of the cells to some sort of guard-post, for it took less than a minute for a group of armed men to appear. In spite of their multiple appearance, Dal and Zoltan thought it more appropriate to call them men than fallen.

The guards received orders and left just as rapidly. Their leader then addressed his guests. "We have a language," he said, "that you can't understand—a very ancient language that has fallen into disuse. Like the messengers, we can express ourselves directly by means of thoughts, but not as easily as them."

"By what means are they able to take away your memories?" Dal asked.

"They make use of our own discoveries in the domain of mental function, which they have improved. It's unpleasant to see ourselves robbed and shackled by that which belongs to us. I think they have perfected a device based on principles that we discovered—a device whose energetic emissions inhibit a series of psychological mechanisms."

"Nothing is written for eternity," Zoltan declared. "Can we go now?"

"Yes. Go back the way you came—the guards are waiting for you. I'll join you later. We'll have to fight, and I can't do that without exposing myself unreasonably. On the other hand, I know that the messengers have your ship in their possession; it's necessary to get it back—we'll help you do that."

"May I be permitted one last question?" Dal put in. He perceived, with satisfaction, that he had not needed to use Zoltan's psychic relay. "This...this messenger whom I resembles—what is his..." He hesitated, fearful of the reply, but continued: "What is his relationship with the person I seek?"

There was a hesitation of the Weaver's part, but he finally replied: "They were going to live together, but it hasn't happened yet."

Dal felt a lump rising in his throat. So Kalla had only died to throw herself at the head of someone else, in the universe where she had finished up?

Involuntarily, Zoltan had followed his thought. "You're forgetting two important points," he said.

"Which are?" said Dal, angrily.

"Firstly, if it really is her, she has lost her memory of her anterior life. You can't reproach her for anything."

"And secondly?"

"Well, take note that she has been seduced by a messenger who resembles you. I can't believe that's a matter of chance. Once again, these correspondences are too extraordinary for there to be no coherent links."

Dal fell silent momentarily. What comfort was it, that Kalla displayed a certain constancy in her inclinations? "What does it matter to me that my rival is also my twin?" he said.

Zoltan shook his head. "Don't you think that you're going a little too quickly? We still only have a few fragments of information about this world and the events that unfold here. If you want to know more, we must go. Are you coming?"

"I'm all yours," Dal declared, reluctantly.

They hastened to reach the vicinity of the subterranean crossroads where the battle had taken place, and did so much more rapidly than they had reached the cells of the great vault. The Weaver of Echoes joined them then, at the head of a column so numerous that its far end was lost in the depths of the corridors.

"What doomed the messengers," the Weaver said, "is that they've blocked the entrance to the labyrinth in order to impede any contact; it wasn't sufficient for them to forbid any emergence. That's why they were obliged to bring the Key, and that's how it fell into your hands.

"So the same key works in both directions?"

"Yes—there's an electrogeometric circuit that can be interrupted from either side of the exit."

"At any rate," said Ortog, "It was only interrupted for us: the ship was unable to get through."

"The spindle that contains the drive, undoubtedly," said Zoltan.

The Weaver approached the wall where there was a rectangular hole of no great width, and introduced the key into it, which fitted into a slot.

"But how did they get out?" Dal exclaimed.

"One of them must have another Key. It's sufficient to place it in the slot momentarily and get out quickly after recovering it. So far as we're concerned, there's no need to take it out. It can stay here—but we'll need another, to place outside, in order to get back in. After all, this is our city, even though it was originally our prison. Besides, I know that the thought of getting out frightens many fallen..."

He left them in order to exhort his troops. Many soldiers were hesitating and pausing before the funnel-like tunnel. The ranks finally got under way, with a good deal of reticence. The Weaver came back.

"It's necessary to understand them," he said. "So long as it's a matter of fighting messengers who have intruded here, they give proof of courage, but the external world is a redoubtable mystery to them. They were born here, and have never gone out—and the only information that arrives from outside comes directly to me. It's recorded in the tapestry of echoes, and is forgotten if it's divulged. I'm able to retain my memory by reason of my function, but I'm alone in that. Even I require continual recourse to the tapestry."

"Now that you mention it," Dal remarked, "we had an episode of amnesia when we entered the labyrinth."

"Yes," said Zoltan. "Just as the battle began."

"Then you have also been subject to the influence of messengers—but you come from another world, and the influence was only partial."

The advance guard had already disappeared into the exit cone. Dal, Zoltan and the Weaver went into it at the head of the main body of troops, who had to be encouraged by word and gesture. Dal and Zoltan brandished their shields, the effect of which was too recent to have been forgotten already. There were silent shouts, and everyone resumed their forward march.

When they reached the common part of the two opposed cones they met elements of the advance guard retreating toward the tunnels. Many of them were wounded, supported by heir comrades. Others were covering their eyes; they seemed to have suffered a violent shock.

According to the reports made to the Weaver, it appeared that the sortie had run into two obstacles: on the one hand, the presence of an armed company of messengers, and on the other, the brightness of the sun: a glare unknown in the tunnels in which the fallen had spent their lives.

"Do the messengers have other mirrors?" asked Dal.

"That's the worst of it," said the Weaver. "They've deployed two of them, which can cover the exit with their crossfire.

"That's fine. Tell your troops that we'll take care of the mirrors. As far the sun, you'll have to make them understand that its light is what the messengers have withheld from them, and that the right to that light is exactly what they're fighting for. The presence of a numerous army shouldn't frighten elite troops that have just put part of that army to flight. Thy can make inroads into it if they adopt a solid wedge formation with a great many ranks tightly packed." He interrupted himself to add: "Of course, that's only advice given by a stranger accustomed to battles. It's up to the Weaver of Echoes to lead troops that know him and will follow him."

The Weaver seemed to appreciate this politeness, and gave his orders in the course of a harangue that ended with further acclamations. Dal and Zoltan went through the ranks, which parted respectfully in front of them.

"All the same," said Zoltan, "It's going to be a hot affair."

They emerged into the light, swords in hand, well-protected behind their shields. The plain was covered with white suits of armor, which threw off thousands of bright reflections. To either side of the exit from the labyrinth, the Mirrors of Negation were immediately aimed at the travelers.

"You take the one on the left," Dal said to Zoltan. "I'll take the other one."

With heads bowed in order to be better covered, the set out to advance slowly, their swords thrusting. Behind them, the black suits of armor were set in motion.

Lightning-bolts flared, but the voyagers knew their effects now and they were braced behind their shields. They only took one step back, carving the air with their sword in front of them, in the direction of the first line of enemies, as thy had done in their battles against the Agonians.

They were dealing with troops who had not taken part in the previous engagement inside the labyrinth. When they saw the first three rows of troops transformed into luminous lines scarcely visible in the sunlight, and then disappear, discipline broke down completely, the foremost ranks turning on the spot and knocking over those behind them. They moved over the lightning-generators abandoned by the soldiers. Dal and Zoltan had to trample over bodies that their weapons had not touched. The messengers that Zoltan as fighting regrouped, however, and attempted a maneuver intended to surround him. They were pushed back by the fallen, leaving hundreds of victims strewn on the ground.

At the same moment, however, Dal was touched by the sinister black ray. At first, no more was seen of him. Then, as the ray cut out, the Weaver saw him, lying motionless on top of his shield. A fissure had formed in the ground around him. Immediately, fallen ran to his rescue, under the threat of the black ray, which was not fired. Zoltan felt his calmness abandon him. He rushed forward, annihilating the enemy ahead of him, and opened up a furrow into which the fallen hurled themselves. Before the operator of the second mirror could aim it correctly, he shattered it into smithereens with his sword, in a terrifying black explosion.

Behind the other mirror, the operator was dead, killed by the reflection of the ray from the shield. He had not disappeared entirely, but he had enormous holes in his body, through which the pedestal of the mirror was visible. As for Dal, he slowly recovered consciousness.

The army of messengers was fleeing toward the horizon. The fallen had only suffered slight losses, and their booty was considerable. They now possessed a Mirror of Negation, which would already suffice to guard the approach to the labyrinth if it were placed in the opening.

Zoltan came to make sure that Dal was not badly hurt. "This is what I propose," he told him. "I'll accompany the army of fallen that is setting off in pursuit of the runaways, in order to recover the ship. They can't have taken it far, for they obviously have no vehicles. They're doubtless hauling it behind them, pulling it by the gondola's cables. As for you, why don't you follow the Weaver's advice and set off in search of Kalla. We'll meet back here, if you wish...."

Dal only had enough strength to nod his head in assent, and was then left alone on his shield.

The sun seemed to be immobile in a green sky that was almost white. The sun itself was entirely white, but not blinding, It did not seen hot either. It was a very bizarre sun. One had a desire to see it at closer range, which was doubtless impracticable. Dal looked at the sun, and felt his strength returning gradually. No, it wasn't hot, but its light was charged with some unknown potential: rays as penetrating as cosmic rays, or perhaps neutrinos. The fallen, in their dense prison, must have received these regenerative corpuscles, even though its luminous rays had been stopped by the walls.

Dal stretched his limbs. He must not be idle much longer. He was not wounded. He felt no pain. Kalla was waiting.

He sat up on his shield. Was Kalla waiting? Was it her that the Weaver had talked about? He had to find out. He stood up.

The two armies had disappeared beyond the near horizon. Yes, as the Weaver had said, this world was quite tiny. Dal got his bearings. The sun was rising on his right. He drew an imaginary vertical line from the sun and positioned his sheathed sword on the ground in the direction of the foot of that line. Then he waited until the sun had changed its position significantly, in order to find out which way it was moving relative to the sword. He waited for some time. Then he traced a line on the ground at right-angles to the sword on the appropriate side, picked up the weapon and his shield, and followed the direction he had obtained. Thus, he was sure of not turning his back on the equator.

He marched for a long time through a stony desert, whose pebbles presented the same disturbing characteristic as the world's inhabitants: one could see their hidden sides clearly. The sun was now to the left, in front of him. It was rising slowly into the sky. By the direction of his course, he saw that he had not gone the wrong way.

The shield was weighing heavily upon his shoulder, though, and the blade on his hip. He made haste to reach the equator, which he would recognize because the sun would then be to his left...provided that he reached it before midday.

As these thoughts crossed his mind, he saw that meager shoots were appearing in the ground. The labyrinth must be on the edge of the equatorial strip that was favourable to plants. On turning round, he could still see its summit. He felt discouraged, however, by the thought that, in spite of the smallness of the world, it would take him a long time to reach his goal.

He was now advancing through brushwood that reached his waist: aggregations of plants with pointed brittle leaves. When he stepped on the stems they made a noise like broken glass. He looked at them more closely, stopping to do it. Something bumped into him from behind. He turned round swiftly, his sword already in his hand.

It was a plant with red transparent leaves, which was swaying on its roots in a hideous fashion. He recoiled. Another plant lashed out at him. He refused to fight with these aggressive vegetables and resumed walking, increasing his pace—but the brushwood, by virtue of some mysterious subterranean communication, began to slow him down: a stem wound around one of his ankles; a thorny branch suddenly barred his passage at face height.

Why, he said to himself, *this couch-grass is getting in my way!*

He was reluctant to open up a wide path with sweeps of his sword. He simply put his shield in front of him, which moved the vegetables aside—but they immediately attacked him from the rear. His jerkin was already torn at the shoulder. When a thorn pricked the place of his recent wound, he did not hesitate any longer: he began to scythe ahead of him with the sword-blade, opening up a path through which ten men could have moved abreast.

Then a slight noise rose up around him. On either side of the path, little berries exploded, spreading clouds of greenish dust. Dal guessed that he ought not to breathe in the clouds. He started running, whirling his weapon, and the clouds themselves disappeared beneath the cerulite blade. Finally, he emerged from the zone of hostile plants, reaching a forest that screened out the light. He could still see the sun, though, as a bright patch on the foliage. The patch was now very low, but almost directly to his left.

Placid trees at last, he thought.

He heard a growl close at hand, and suddenly felt a chill. He stopped. Something had just emerged from the ground in front of him.

It was a sort of mole, ten feet long with a white transparent body. Its beating heart was visible, along with the viscera and the circulatory system. Vapor was forming around the animal, rapidly hiding it from Dal's sight, in combination with the clods of earth that it was throwing up in every direction. A horrible cold emanated from the apparition. Dal stepped back in order not to lose consciousness, and in order not to have his limbs instantly frozen.

The beast soon emerged from the mist it had produced, however. It headed straight for Dal. He moved back again, among the scattered tree-trunks, covering himself with his shield—but the shield could not protect him against the cold.

The beast drew nearer. Shivering, Dal took a step forward, then a second, and then a third. He attacked the animal with sword-thrusts just as he felt his knees begin to give way.

The beast started melting with extraordinary rapidity, and ended up being transformed into a luminous line, which soon disappeared. Dal fell to his knees. He dropped his weapons in order to warm himself up with appropriate movements. Around him, the icy vapor dissipated. The only remaining evidence of the encounter was the mountains of earth that the mole had flung out of the ground, and the tunnel through which it had arrived. Fearful of the irruption of another similar animal by the same route, Dal went around the enormous hole and hastily continued on his way.

The Weaver forgot to mention the encounters to which I've been exposed, he thought.

It would have been possible to attack from afar, making use of the sword's action at a distance, but that would have obliterated a part of the forest, and he did not want to attract attention. What would he do, if a powerful company of armed messengers surged forth, supported by two or three Mirrors of Negation? There was no reason to believe that the army engaged in the battle of the labyrinth was the only one at their disposal.

Very soon, the sun was directly to his left. Dal changed course, taking a direction at right-angles to the one that he had followed thus far, in order to march along the line that separated the equatorial strip into two halves, with the sun behind him. Close by, however, he heard a continuous sound. He advanced a few meters, in order to see what was making the noise. He parted a vegetal curtain. Unlike the nutritive spiral, the stems could be seized; they possessed four dimensions, but they were not made of pure energy.

There was a river running in front of him, and he understood immediately the part that it might play: he could construct a primitive raft, for the current was flowing in the direction he needed to go. On the raft, he would reach the two mountains the Weaver of Echoes had mentioned rapidly, without tiring himself out. First, though, he had to ascertain the nature of the liquid; he had no intention of launching himself upon a river of acid that would dissolve his raft in a matter of minutes. He picked up one of the bizarre pebbles with which the ground was littered and threw it into the liquid, which had a very viscous consistency but was nonetheless limpid.

The pebble was not dissolved in the midst of an explosion of bubbles. It scarcely sank before it shot off like an arrow, carried off by the current.

That simplifies things, Dal thought.

He fixed his sword and shield as securely as he could, tightened the neck-strap of his helmet, and leapt into the river. He had the impression of falling on to a cushion, and remained seated on the liquid, which slowly bore him away. *The current's only rapid in the middle*. He moved as best he could into the middle of the river. There, he was borne along at such a vertiginous speed that he could no longer make out the vegetation along the banks clearly.

On turning round, Dal could still see the sun behind him; the river was following the equator exactly. He wondered if it might go all the way around the world—of it might be a watercourse devoid of a source or a mouth, whose current was linked to the rotation of the planet. At any rate, the current was still carrying him at the same crazy pace. Dal was beginning to find the voyage tedious when he glimpsed the summits of two mountains rising up from the horizon, situated to either side of the river.

He began to draw nearer to the bank, and his speed diminished. When the mountains finally seemed quite close, he displaced himself again over the surface of the liquid, which was as dense as mercury, and began drifting slowly along the bank.

The wild plants had disappeared, giving place to implausibly flat and circular vegetables, which oscillated and rotated about their axes when the wind blew. Dal set foot on ground that was apparently civilized, and started walking through he plantation. In the distance, toward one of the mountains, which seemed quite close—a deceptive impression that he had had since quitting the watercourse—helicoid buildings were outlined. Dal imagined Kalla standing beside one of the elliptical windows that dotted their surface, plunged into a meditation on this world in which she had recently arrived— perhaps thinking of him...

Madness! he told himself. *If, by some miracle, she's really here, she has lost her memory of terrestrial life, and me along with it.*

He shivered. How should he conduct himself if he met her? In order not to frighten her, he should introduce himself as an unknown stranger making a visit. He should stifle his sentiments in order to mount an efficacious plan. Was it necessary, then, to draw up plans coldly when one found someone who had disappeared, and was now living mortally on a world with no link to the preceding one?

At the moment for which he had waited so long, which had motivated his crazy voyaged, Dal found all his assurance slipping away. The idea of meeting a stranger was a sharper pain than the grief he had experienced at her loss. But he ought not to allow himself to be overwhelmed by such sentiments. It was now or never that he had to react against them. He put on a brave face, and accelerated his pace.

A silhouette loomed up not far from him, among the circular plants, and fled. Before it disappeared, Dal recognized a messenger, clad in a loose-fitting garment, blue in color. As it could not be one of the fallen, it had to be a messenger. The Weaver had not mentioned any other group among the population. Dal perceived others, all of whom fled as he approached. He suspected that his presence had been signaled, and prepared himself to receive armored soldiers that would surely be dispatched against him—Kalla's guards, perhaps?

He could not go into her home as an enemy. It would be impossible for him to present himself to her after annihilating her guardsmen. He decided not to use his sword against anyone who might attack him; he would only protect himself with his shield, forcing them to retreat toward the house, so that he could at least request admittance without having killed anyone.

He continued walking, and finally saw the first soldier in front of him. Others would presumably follow. He passed the strap of his shield over his neck and held himself at the ready. The messenger came forward swiftly, a lightning-generator in his hand. Dal continued straight ahead, preparing to endue the shock. Ten paces from the enemy, he was surrounded by sparks, stepped back, and then resumed his march. The messenger fired again. Dal reeled. The closer to the source one was, the more violent the discharges became. They were not really lightning-bolts. It did not matter; he had to reach the buildings.

The soldier did not retreat, though. Dal wondered whether he would get close enough to push him back with the shield. Assuming that no others would arrive to support him in the next few minutes…

He continued straight ahead, and received a discharge that knocked him flat on the ground. He got up, thinking: *I could make him disappear with a single gesture. Kalla is already among my enemies, since I'm allied with the fallen—but no; it would only make the situation worse.* He launched himself forwards.

Taken by surprise, the messenger was thrown to the ground in his turn. Under the shock of the impact, his helmet came off and rolled on the ground. Dal stopped, astounded.

The messenger had long blonde hair. It was a woman—whose face, in certain features, was irresistibly reminiscent of Kalla's.

A foreign thought thundered imperiously in Ortog's mind: "Get away from here, miserable imitation, simulacrum, effigy! You dare to caricature the form of Garal the Noble!"

Dal remained silent. His own thoughts were so chaotic that it would have been impossible for him to reply. The telepathic gift of messengers was not a revelation for him, but this torrent of abuse was the last thing he had expected. The woman got up, picked up her helmet, and advanced toward him."

"What bold image is this, that dares to raise a hand against the daughter of the Master of Ellipses?"

Dal flinched. That rarely happened. His arms sagging, inconvenienced by his shield, he spoke in thought: "I...I've come in search of Kalla."

There was a pause, then: "Who is Kalla?"

In spite of his distress, Dal recognized a femininity common to all worlds: curiosity was overcoming anger in his enemy."

"You are!" Ortog transmitted, with the energy of despair.

There was a longer pause, and then: "It's me you're looking for? But my name is Ifliz, not Kalla. Your mind is desiccated by the desert wind, and you're confusing water with salt. Where do you come from, appearance?"

"I come from a world more distant than I can explain. But who is Garal the Noble?"

The woman looked at him darkly, and let her helmet hang down from her extended fingers. "That's none of your business—but how have you succeeded in usurping some of his facial features?"

"Have I something in common with Garal, then?"

"Garal the Noble." She leaned forward. "You remind me of him—but, in spite of your brutality, you can't be entirely evil."

Dal saw a tear run down the strange face in which Kalla's features were so present that he felt his own eyes becoming moist.

"What has he done to you?" he asked, gently.

She straightened up. "Get away from here, I said. Go back to your flat world, and never come to disturb me again." Suddenly, she frowned. "Might you be him? He's capable of deforming himself to add to my displeasure, and using even worse treachery to get to me."

"I'm Dal Ortog. Don't you recognize me?"

"Dal Ortog?"

"Doesn't that name strike any chord? I wish your memory were like a pool, and that memories were laid down there like a sandy bed. I wish I were a fallen stone, raising clouds of memories. I don't want them to dissipate."

"What are you saying?"

"I'm saying that you are Kalla, but that you're unaware of it—but abandon this fallacious name of Garal…"

"Garal the Noble, fallacious? It's not for you to insult him. I've allowed you too much liberty in your madness." She threatened him with her weapon. "You've found your doom. Move—and don't try to resist."

Dal gave up on the argument—but he had not made the journey to renounce its goal. He said nothing more, and resumed walking toward the buildings. This Garal was evidently the messenger of whom the Weaver had spoken.

Dal's mind was in turmoil. He was in an another world—the one that some people on Earth called *the* other world—and it was a planet, with its sun. On this planet, he had met someone who reminded him of Zoltan, then a woman reminiscent of Kalla…and he resembled someone else too, who behaved like a rival. Thus, the universe of death was populated with beings linked in some strange fashion with those of Earth, alive or dead. What difference was there between those who resembled the living and those who resembled the dead? There had to be one. The converse would be incoherent: if such resemblances existed, it was not by chance, and for reasons of "symmetry" one could not imagine a vast irrational mixture.

Dal awaited events. For the present, he was the prisoner of the person he had wanted to recover beyond the tomb—or the prisoner of a double of unhuman dimensions. He wondered whether disappointment had now taken the place of grief within him…but no: everything that reminded him of Kalla was welcome.

They approached the buildings: a large cylinder flanked by two helical towers. Other, smaller constructions stood not far away. A battalion of armoured messengers greeted them.

In response to a gesture from Ifliz, they grabbed hold of him. They dragged him away, and she vanished from his sight. When he was shoved into the edifice, he had already been deprived of his sword and his shield—but he had noted that the soldiers who had taken charge of them had gone into one of the towers.

He was led along a series of inclined ramps to a large room, where he was taken to a couch set in a corner. He was left there, without the round window or the vertically-sliding door being closed and without any guard being mounted.

Incredulously, Dal listened to the soldiers' footsteps dying away along the corridors and the ramps. He had the impression of being a guest rather than a prisoner—but that impression changed radically when he decided to go and look through the open window. Indeed, he had scarcely taken a few steps before he began to choke. He moved rapidly toward the window, then toward the door; the further he went, the less able he was to breathe. Staggering, with his face swollen by the onset of asphyxia, he returned to the corner of the room where he had been left. Immediately, his lungs easily filled with air.

How could the messengers maintain a sort of bubble of respirable air in the midst of an unbreathable atmosphere in this fashion? The method was, at any rate, more effective than bars, chains and guards. These people were knowledgeable in matters of imprisonment.

Dal lay down on the couch, which seemed to him to be a bed in a large room, although it was no more than a bunk in a cell. He realized suddenly that he had been fighting and travelling without preserving his strength, and that he was exhausted.

He went to sleep, but he did not dream. The dreams of this world were not for him.

When he was woken up, he had no idea how long he had been asleep. A glance toward the window told him that the sun had scarcely changed position in the sky. Either its progress was incredibly slow, or he had only been asleep for a few minutes.

The two messengers who had come for him took up position to either side of him and urged him forward. Remembering the suffocation he had experienced, he manifested a reluctance to follow them, but soon saw that they were breathing quite comfortably. In those conditions, why surrender himself to their surveillance? He might as well give them the slip, recover his weapons, find Kalla—not Ifliz—and attempt to re-engage her in a dialogue...even an uncertain one.

He escaped them with a single bound—and clutched his throat with both hands as he opened is mouth. He understood, and came back. The respirable bubble accompanied him in his movements, provided that they were in conformity with his guards' desires. Going anywhere else would result in asphyxia. He became docile. He thought of telling them that he now had the liberated fallen behind him; that was a trump card that he might be able to use to put an end to this odious method of coercion.

They went through suspended courtyards, along more slanting ramps and more corridors, passing people in cloaks who followed them curiously with their eyes. They stopped in front of a circular door.

The door opened on a vast hall topped by a cupola. It was a glass-paned cupola, which let in the light generously. Dal thought about the cells in the great vault, out there in the depths of the labyrinth, to which he fallen had been relegated. Here, he was in a palace where masters resided. Here, there was a right to sunlight. The more contact he had with the messengers, the more antipathetic he found them. Ifliz was, however, definitely a messenger. That thought depressed him.

Several individuals were standing in motionless groups. They were not talking. They were content to look at one another, in order to exchange their ideas directly. When Dal entered, framed by his guards, everyone turned to look. One of the individuals detached himself from his group and approached. The others followed him at a short distance, soon leaning on low columns that seemed to serve as tables or sitting down in softly-molded armchairs. The setting, the light and the petrified individuals in their white garments all combined to give Dal the strange impression that he was being examined by malevolent statues.

"I'm the Master of Ellipses," transmitted the first messenger to approach. "How did you defeat my army, when you come from a world without consistency?"

Dal looked the messenger straight in the eye. He could see the back of his interlocutor's neck at the same time, but that no longer troubled him. "Why that absurd and bombastic name?" he transmitted, insolently.

A murmur of indignant thoughts resonated in his mind—a confused murmur, from which the silent voice of the Master emerged: "The ellipse is the symbol of wisdom, because it has two foci in equilibrium."

"What have you to do with wisdom," Dal retorted, "who imprison and kill half your subjects."

"I'm patient and you intrigue me," the Master replied, "so I shall answer you. If you are alluding to the fallen, know that they sustain subversive theories and pursue dangerous research. It's in the name of the general interest that they have been punished."

"The general interest has always served as a pretext for extending the reach of particular interests. That's not the conduct of a sage, but that of a tyrant."

"Very well—I'm already weary of indulgence. Now you'll reply to my questions."

"Mine first," said Dal, curtly. "You don't have control of the situation. I've freed the fallen, and they're my allies. My companion possesses weapons identical to mine; he is supporting the prisoners whose memories you have stolen."

"Shut up. I can sweep that derisory army away, and I shall if it has the folly to attack me. Why did you come here?"

"I've told you: I've come to ask you some questions. They are the only reply that I can make to yours. I belong to a mortal people. Some among us have found a method to enable me travel into the universe of our dead, and I have arrived here. Instead of finding our dead, I have encountered living beings that resemble us. What does that signify? What is the relationship between this world and ours?"

There was a pause, and then: "You bear a strong resemblance to Garal, who was called Garal the Noble, but has since turned traitor, deserter and blasphemer. He has set off on a forbidden voyage. On his return, he will be one of the fallen."

"What voyage? For what destination?"

"That's not your concern."

The murmur had resumed. There was mention of "analogy," and another voice qualified it with the term "scandalous." The mental hubbub intensified.

Dal forced his own thought through the parasitism: "And why," he said, "does your daughter Ifliz resemble the fiancée that I have lost? Dare you claim that there is no relationship between your world and mine?"

There was another silence, and then, as if regretfully: "Garal and the fallen believe that we are all linked in some manner with a universe different from ours, but which is not yours. They claim that certain catastrophes originate in that universe, although we attribute them to laws as yet unknown in this one. That's the reason for their exile, for their experiments risk multiplying these catastrophes, even though their interpretation of their nature is false."

"False? How do you know? If you admit my existence, you must also admit that of my universe. Why not another? Are there any other means to discover the truth than experiments, incursions and voyages? How can an unchanging faith be sufficient for you? Isn't it the simple reflection of fear? But doesn't the greatest danger reside in ignorance?"

"You talk like the fallen, and like Garal. I don't have to debate with some paltry flat being who has come from a world of smoke to give me lessons in wisdom. We'll resume this interrogation later. Take him back to his cell, but let him wander around the palace if he wants to, in order that he doesn't imagine that he represents any danger to us."

The messenger turned his back on Dal. The guards turned around, with their prisoner.

Having been taken back to his cell, at first Dal remained seated on the couch where he had slept. He had he impression of holding a tangle whose threads were being unraveled without his involvement. He could see the ends of some of them quite well, but that did not serve to illuminate the whole scheme.

I'm free to move around the palace, he said to himself.

He got up, anxious in spite of everything; the memory of his suffocation was painfully present in his mind. Cautiously, moving very slowly, he drew away from the spot to which he had been riveted a short while before. It was true; he was now free in his movements. Another thought occurred to him. *They're very imprudent; their pretension has blinded them.* In reality, he could not do very much, disarmed as he was—but it was, after all, better to be half-free than a prisoner.

The corridors yawned before him. He headed in the direction opposite to the one in which he had earlier been taken, hoping to discover, at the hazard of the courtyards and the ramps, a communication with the tower where he confiscated arms were. He did not rate any such hope very highly, but it was necessary to have some motive in order to act. The thought of running into Ifliz only gave him partial pleasure; such an encounter could only increase his despondency.

He went past a sort of game-room, in which two groups of messengers were throwing a sharp-edged disk which sailed from one team to the other, whistling. The players intercepted it with little round shields, from which it rebounded to fly in the opposite direction. Some players displayed arms or faces that were extensively scarred. He went on, amid general indifference. Later, he went past people bearing trays full of bizarre nourishment: multicolored disks and spirals, which were fuming—and after that, stiff-necked individuals carrying cylinders.

The palace turned out to be much larger than he had initially imagined. He soon entered a zone that was increasingly deserted, in which the light gradually dimmed. It was necessary for him to watch where he put his feet, in order not to fall from one ramp on to the next one down, for there was no wall, banisters or guard-rail. After a fairly long interval of that semi-blind march, he realized that he was lost—although, of course, he was only lost from his own viewpoint, not that of the Master of Ellipses, who would doubtless be able to discover him rapidly if he so desired.

He went past rooms drowned in profound darkness, where the glances he darted revealed nothing at all. Then, as his pupils adjusted, he vaguely perceived forms lying down on lines of beds. All of them had a mineral immobility. Sleep? Catalepsy? Meditation? They might have been philosophers, invalids or workers at rest. He resumed his hazardous march.

The light became slightly brighter: a pale light, which seemed to spring from impossibly-angled ceilings. There was a circular courtyard, which was like the bottom of a well; high above, the sky was visible. People were assembled in the courtyard. As he approached, Dal felt his mind filling with discordant music, mingled with olfactory impressions, colored visual sensations and collisions of vague and contradictory sentiments. The closer he approached, the more refined and precise all that became. He was soon prey to pain, joy, rancor, desire, hope and discouragement—and all these sentiments gradually adapted themselves to his personal situation, alimented by his problems and conflicts. It was as if they were visualized, echoing in all his senses. It was music, painting and theater all at once, whose elements he provided himself. His entire personality—heart and mind alike—was instantaneously multiplied and actualized.

His present situation, however, was not conducive to being enjoyed as a mere actor-cum-spectator. He felt himself being simultaneously impelled toward murder and suicide. A few more minutes, and he would have had to rush upon that contemplative crowd in order to pay them back for the harm

227

he had suffered—those who were partially responsible for it as well as the others who were unconcerned with it. He retreated, shivering, and went back into the corridors.

At the end of another ramp he arrived at a terrace inundated with sunlight—a sun still low over the horizon. Another multitude of people were sitting on the ground, facing a messenger in a white cloak. The thunder of a thought exploded in his head:

"You are the messengers of the omnipotent Spirit, who has power to do us harm as well as good, who sometimes manifests himself in sudden darkness or cyclones inside closed dwellings. You must know that He is powerful in recognizing the signs of His power, and not seek like the fallen for some external cause of sacred manifestations.

"Whoever follows in the tracks of blasphemers will be accursed, exiled and fallen. By our arms, he will be struck. By our voices, he will be expelled. By our minds, he will be detested. By our hearts, he will be hated. But you, who are the messengers of the primal power, shall dwell in innocence and felicity. Thus you will spend a long life, entirely occupied with concern for His grandeur and glory, and you will enter without dread into the annihilation of death.

"Whoever seeks in death another life will waste his time in the course of his existence and neglect the obligations for which he is in this world. But the just, who, on the contrary..."

Dal retreated again. The preacher's delirium told him little about the orthodox ideas of this universe—ideas that, as he already knew, mingled contradictory principles in a strange manner. He continued on his way, into the depths of the palace.

The ramp that he had followed soon led to an opening: the doorway of an enormous pyramidal hall. He went in.

A soft light reigned there, revealing walls hollowed out with a vast number of niches formed like seats. These niches filled the walls from bottom to top, and there was a slanting ramp beginning at the door that led to that top. It wound around the room many times, serving the niches like a long walkway serving the cells of a beehive. Dal embarked upon it.

As soon as he reached the first niche he understood their purpose; he was in a library. His mind had automatically received a whole sequence of information regarding the manner of consulting telepathic works on history, science, religion, literature, music, technology, medicine, and so on.

He opted for recent history, saving the completion of his theoretical knowledge of less urgent subjects for later. He hoped that he might find something related to Ifliz. That was not impossible, for Ifliz was the daughter of the Master of El-lipses—an important official of some sort, who ought to figure large in the chronicle.

First he had to climb half way up the edifice. As he passed each niche, a silent voice invited him to acquaint himself with a long series of works, instructing anyone who desired to consult them to sit down and concentrate on a title and a particular issue: he would immediately be given a reading from the relevant memory-recording.

What a treasure for the fallen! Dal thought—but nowhere was the name of Ifliz mentioned. Dal was about to select a more general subject, one more likely to give him a means of getting to grips with his situation, when the voice offered him a communication from the Institute of Ellipses on "The Brilliant Intervention of Garal the Noble," followed by "Hypotheses Concerning the Treason of Garal and the Motives for his Detestable Voyage."

Dal immediately installed himself in the seat hollowed out in the wall, and concentrated his mind on the title of the communication.

"We shall not repeat," said the interior voice, "the chronicle of the great upheavals. Let us merely recall the deadly dawn that saw a much closer sun shine down, and the more precipitate days that followed. Let us remember that many people died, that the circular river emerged from its bed, that the subterranean animals appeared along the fertile crown, and also that the hostile plants extended far beyond their customary zone. An era of desolation began, and disorder took our world in its grip, as we might crush a fruit."

Involuntarily, Dal thought of the Blue War, which had provoked disasters in his own universe that were trivial on a cosmic level, but undoubtedly frightful on a human level.

"Then," the silent voice went on, "Garal the Noble had a dream…"

Zoltan, too, joined me in consequence of a dream, Dal thought, without being able to draw any conclusion therefrom.

"…A dream in which he saw himself duplicated, and in which one of his two facets was asleep. The dreams of the sleeping Garal were fueled by those of the double dreaming twice over—and the second Garal thought in symbols untranslatable for someone awake, but eloquent for the first. And Garal the Noble woke up, saying: 'It is necessary for the alternation of days and nights to recover its former rhythm. For that, it is necessary that the celestial forces recover the equilibrium that maintained the equivalent in question'."

Dal was transfixed by the idea of the double, which corresponded so closely with what had happened to him in this universe.

"Now, Garal the Noble had just been appointed to the chair of Spatial Structure at the University of Ellipsa. Moving the planet was a task too formidable for the technical methods already envisaged to accomplish it within the necessary time-frame. It was up to Garal to devise his own."

There was a slight interval at this point—a pause that gave the listener time to commit the beginning of the communication to memory.

"Then," the telepathic recording went on, "Garal posed the problem in terms of space-time rather than mere gravitation. He mobilized all the Mirrors of Negation, and made the calculations necessary for their appropriate orientation and the determination of the exact moment of their activation. When the day arrived, a crown of mirrors was disposed around the world, and a chain-reaction was established. The black rays swept the universe, twisting certain preferential sectors of space into gutters. The length of the day was immediately extended, and the traces of the cataclysm effaced."

There was a further pause, during which Dal wondered whether the perturbations of this universe might have been engendered by the Blue War. What would have happened on Earth if two-dimensional people had annihilated vast surfaces?

"After this repeal of cosmic events and their scientific reparation, we arrive at considerations of a political and personal order. Garal the Noble's brilliant intervention had conferred a great deal of authority upon him, to the extent that he seemed to have a right to build disturbing hypotheses. He claimed that the revelation that he had had while asleep had been bestowed on him by an external intelligence belonging to a race other than our own. He went so far as to stray dangerously close to the errors of the fallen regarding the mythical existence of an invisible population responsible for all miraculous manifestations. The Master of Ellipses summoned him and demanded that he put an end to the diffusion of these ideas, which were likely to disturb public order. He condescended to speak to him as one equal to another, in taking account of the exceptional role that the accused had played, and had difficulty in addressing the necessary remonstrations to him, for Garal was the man who enjoyed the favors of Her Wisdom Ifliz, the Master's daughter."

Dal thought that Garal had not been far from the truth, but that he must have made a mistake with regard to the persons responsible. What the preacher had said about cyclones inside closed dwellings, and sudden darkness, could undoubtedly be assimilated to the cosmic upheavals. Dal remembered his conversation with Zoltan, and thought that Garal had divined the existence of a five-dimensional world, but that he was unaware of the three-dimensional universe.

"Then Garal, whose popularity had rendered him arrogant, decided to devote his efforts to the exploration of his imaginary world, exactly like the fallen in the depths of their labyrinth. To the prohibitions of the Master of Ellipses, Ifliz joined her prayers and reproaches, but nothing could deflect

231

Garal from his determination, and he was declared fallen. An enquiry found that he had been in communication with a secret agent of the fallen, lurking in the depths of their prison, and soldiers surrounded the Spatial Structure laboratories."

Dal drank in the internal voice avidly. The more information he obtained regarding this universe, the more he discovered the reflection of his own, as if in a mirror.

"But Garal had constructed an energy-wall around the laboratories against which the troops hurled themselves in vain. The utilization of the Mirror of Negation was proposed. Garal had only been sentenced to disgrace; he had not been condemned to death. Moreover, there was no proof that the mirror's radiation would pass through the energy-wall established by the guilty party. It was therefore necessary to wait for the powerful fallen to emerge of his own accord. When the barrier was raised, however, Garal had vanished. On interrogation, his assistants declared that he had made a sudden departure; he had gone into a chamber whose sole issue he had sealed, and that chamber was empty when it was reopened. The room was carefully searched without anything being found, until one of the searchers determined that there was a cleverly concealed trapdoor. It was opened, unmasking a well, at the bottom of which Garal's body was found. It presented all the signs of death, but had not decomposed."

A death like mine, Dal thought. *He has departed without a necroship to explore the higher universe.*

"Surveillance was therefore established around the well in which Garan the fallen is asleep. Perhaps he is dead; perhaps he is making an inconceivable voyage—but the Institute of Ellipses has declared him dead, in order not to encourage subversive ideas. Listener, take care not to fall into an interpretation that might lead you into disgrace!"

Dal got ready to leave the audition niche. Analogies were accumulating, but without sufficient coordination to provide the elements of a coherent explanation. As he got up, however, the voice resumed its discourse; the communication had not finished.

"As Garal has quit the world behind, so he has quit his friends and relatives. At this news, Her Wisdom Ifliz came to reflect at the funereal well, where the proximity of her severed lover shook her confidence in life and her sense of responsibility. She set off in a vessel on the circular river, in order to find the point at which the sun is at the zenith. Knowing that long exposure to its perpendicular rays was toxic, she adjusted the speed of the vessel to that of the star, thus receiving the flamboyance through an entire period of the planet's rotation. The suicide attempt was unsuccessful, however; multiple passages beneath the zenith become dangerous over time, but a single prolonged exposure does not have the same result. Ifliz returned to her father's palace, once again meriting her title. Thus, one can and should address her in thought with the honorific 'Her Wisdom.' "

That was the end. Dal waited for a moment longer, then got up and left the audition niche. His brain was ringing like a church-bell and his heart beating like a drum. It seemed probable that Ifliz's suicide attempt had caused Kalla's death—and even if the two events were not related as cause and consequence, that did not mean that there was no other link between them.

Dal went slowly down the long ramp that wound around the pyramidal hall, and regained the door of the...of the what? Of the Pathotheque? He tried to get his bearings, but he was well and truly lost. Then began a long period of wandering around the ramps, halls and courtyards.

He did not find the preacher's terrace again, nor the theater of musical painting, nor the absurd games room, but he did find a semicircular space whose straight wall had a large rectangular opening that overlooked the plain and its cultivated fields from a great height. Dal went to it, crossing the deserted semicircle, and began studying the expanses over which the sun was rising at a snail's pace.

He saw a cloud of dust appear on the horizon, which approached quickly enough for him soon to be able to make out the details of black suits of armor, arriving in myriads.

233

Chapter Five

The messengers had not built any fortifications around the residence of the Master of Ellispses. Why would they have done so? There was no political opposition, and the fallen had been sealed in their immense labyrinth for generations. They might, of course, escape from it, but the scorn in which they were held had not encouraged prudence among the messengers. Dal wondered, however, how the masters of the world had been able to neglect the most elementary precautions in this respect, once they had been informed of the event. Such an attitude rested on a flagrant underestimation of the adversary's strength. To be sure, they had the Mirrors of Negation—but what about the travelers' Blue Weapon, the courage of the fallen and their numbers?

The army drew nearer. Dal soon perceived that, with respect of armaments, the attackers were not in such an inferior position. Several mirrors were visible in their midst, which they must have captured from the retreating enemy. If they made use of them first, they might volatilize the residence before the messengers could bring theirs to bear. Dal suppressed a slight shiver. Without his shield, he felt like a crab deprived of its shell. Even if Ifliz was not Kalla, he feared for her, as if the eventual death of Ifliz would be a second death for Kalla.

Resistance was being organized, however. The grating murmur of armor was audible from the depths of the halls and ramps. From the vast bay where he was standing, Ortog was able to observe the establishment of an uninterrupted double line of defenders, in the midst of which threatening mirrors were being deployed at regular intervals. That presumably only represented the first lines of defence; numerous well-armed soldiers would probably come to reinforce them.

By way of response, the black army began to split up. In a long, sinuous movement, the columns executed an encircling maneuver at a considerable distance. That seemed to imply that the range of the mirrors was relatively restricted, and that the fallen did not intend to expose their radiant artillery from the start, because it was too weak for an immediate duel. They had doubtless judged that the isolation of the residence constituted a more profitable and less perilous strategy.

Thus, the plain gradually disappeared beneath the black forms, which distance transformed into upright insects. To have arrived so rapidly, the rebels must have employed the same means of locomotion as Ortog. The Knight-Navigator imagined the circular river entirely covered with black suits of armor, passing like a whirlwind before the fearful eyes of river-dwelling messengers.

Dal remained motionless for a long time at the semicircle's great bay window, where the echoes of the tumult accompanying the organization of the defense were still audible. The burning chagrin that gripped him with the sensation of his impotence was succeeded by a torpor. He had the impression of having retreated to an observatory, and having yielded to an expectant somnolence. In the distance, the black army was now deployed, but its combatants remained motionless. Much further away, other mirrors were vaguely discernible, which were doubtless ensuring the safety of the rearguards. Much closer was the double line of white suits of armor, also motionless. It was like the preparation for a siege within a dream: the petrified confrontation of two Manichean armies, like a formidable memory or a prophetic evocation of things to come. It bore no resemblance to anything that was possible, or present—and yet, a wave of cold hatred passed over those multitudes, presaging carnage.

A voice suddenly sounded in Ortog's troubled mind. "Well, Sire, are you still in this world or already in another? Given the curiosity that I know you have, I know you're capable of going in search of the death inside death."

Zoltan always behaved bizarrely, but he had the precious gift of being able to exercise his telepathic powers at long distances.

"I'm alive," Dal replied, silently. "Or, rather, I'm continuing to live the death of which you speak, Henderson." A smile strayed across his face. An uninformed observer might have taken him for a madman prey to his chimeras.

"Very well," said Zoltan, from the depths of the plain. At present I'm among the fallen who are investing strange buildings. Where are you."

"In those buildings, stupidly taken prisoner. What has become of the necroship?"

"Near the labyrinth, under strong guard. We took it back from the messengers, but I decided not to use it, in order not to expose it to any risk. The Devil only know what would become of it under the black ray, and it's our only means of returning to Lassenia."

"You did well—but what's happened here has only intensified the mystery of this world and its relationship with ours. My twin is asleep here, as I am asleep in the Temple; like me, he's exploring another universe. I've encountered another Kalla, who does not know me, but whom my double has pushed to a suicide attempt. All that's very obscure. The despot of this place doesn't seem ready to shed any light on anything. He's known as the Master of Ellipses, under the pretext of equilibrium…"

"Ellipses are nothing but vicious circles, my dear chap. We'll prove that to him by attacking. I assume they've taken away your armaments?"

"I allowed myself to be disarmed by the second Kalla." His mind darkened. The second Kalla! Was he taking it for granted that Kalla was really dead, and that Ifliz was a complete stranger?

"Come on," said Zoltan, half-mocking and half-paternal, "pull yourself together. I'm convinced that we'll resolve this enigma, and that your voyage won't have been futile."

Dal made an effort to rally himself. "Great cosmic upheavals have occurred in this universe. They seem more recent than the Blue War in ours, but I think the flow of time is different in the two worlds, although the two sorts of duration are doubtless linked by a mathematical relationship. Garal, my twin, was able to remedy these upheavals by unimaginable methods, but his actions seem no stranger to me than what I did myself to combat precocious death on our own planet..."

He stopped short. The violet light that inundated the plain changed slowly to bright green, and then to dark green. The black suits of armor began to mill round in a chaotic fashion, while the messengers' lines broke up. An immense whirlwind of seemingly-black sand rose up between the two armies, darkening a part of the sky. The phenomenon was accompanied by a strident whistling that the ears could hardly bear. Zoltan's thoughts began to go astray, maladjusted. Dal was now only receiving something like a radio-transmission distorted by fading and atmospheric interference.

"What's happening? The Apocalypse? Are you still..."

A howling blast of red lightning emerged from the base of the whirlwind, and thrust into the sky like a sword. It began to rain sand, which spattered the transparent material of the huge bay. Instinctively, Dal recoiled. Inside the semicircular space, however, a great wind sprang up: a tornado from nowhere, which caused Ortog to totter, and eventually to fall.

Dal got up again, with difficulty, struggling against the violence of the wind. He remembered what the preacher had said about the one "who sometimes manifests himself in sudden darkness or cyclones inside closed dwellings." Was this a natural phenomenon, or was it really being caused by some redoubtable entity?

The worst thing about the cataclysm was the silence. The rustlings of armor were extinct; the whistling from outside had diminished by degrees in both pitch and intensity. It now disappeared, giving way to a deceptive peace, further belied by the gradually-dying hurricane. Outside, the frightful green light continued to drown the landscape. It colored the interior of the semicircular space with a deathly hue.

With sweat on his brow, Ortog contemplated the spectacle of the end of the world. It seemed to him that he was learning to read the time on a clock without hands, to speak without an alphabet, to scream in mid-yawn—but Zoltan's thoughts returned, clear with every passing second.

"Have you witnessed such a phenomenon before in this part of the planet?"

"No," said Ortog, "but it appears that it happens from time to time. The messengers attribute it to a sort of God who does not promise an afterlife, although the fallen have made an empirical study of it."

"Yes. The Weaver has told me about prodigies of this sort inside the labyrinth. Whatever its cause, its sows panic on both sides."

"Have you been able to keep a nucleus of the fallen in hand, at least? The Weaver of Echoes and his guards, for example?"

"The latter have no need of my encouragement. If they're frightened, they scarcely show it."

"It's not the same for the troops surrounding me. Their ranks have splintered everywhere, and are only re-forming slowly. If your army had been closer, you would have been able to launch a sudden attack."

"There's too much panic among the fallen, and the elite guard is not sufficiently numerous. I have another idea, since the messengers are showing themselves to be at least as vulnerable."

"What?"

"Are you free to move around, and able to summon a messenger by telepathy?"

"To move round, yet, but I'm lost in the residence. I don't know about the summons. I'll try. What's your plan?"

"Try to contact the Master you mentioned to me. Tell him that the cataclysms are definitely linked to our world, and especially to our presence in this one. Make him the following proposition: we'll leave as soon as we've resolved the problem of doubles, on condition that he lifts the punishment of amnesia from the fallen."

"What about Kalla?"

"She's part of the problem."

"I have another idea. I'll offer to make contact with Gar-al, in order to reveal the mechanism of the prodigies."

"How will you make contact with your double?"

"By using the necroship again. It was you who made me think of it jut now, when you said to me: 'I know you're capable of going in search of the death inside death'."

"He'll refuse; research of that sort is strictly forbidden. Your voyage would be sacrilegious."

"There are underlying political reasons for that. It might be sufficient for such an attempt not to be surrounded by any publicity to win the Master's eventual approval—but the stumbling-block is elsewhere. He'll refuse to lift the amnesia, in case the messengers are swept away by the fallen."

"Perhaps a treaty can be agreed by both sides; the messengers' superiority with regard to the mirrors might serve to guarantee its faithful observance. What do you think?"

Dal reflected, while staring out into the plain, where the light was gradually resuming its normal hue. "I'll try."

He turned his back to the huge bay, the landscape and the armies that were forming up again. He went across the semicircle, and set off along a ramp in search of any messenger with whom he could communicate.

Courtyards, ramps, halls, corridors—they were all empty. After what seemed to him to be a long time, though, Dal happened upon the library again, just as a silhouette emerged of it, drawing away along the corridor. He increased his pace, caught up with the messenger and overtook him. Then he stopped in front of him, trying to attract his attention and capture his thoughts. Unlike Zoltan, he was no telepath, but experience had proved that contact was possible, if the messenger so desired.

A dialogue was established.

"You're the one who comes from another world," said the messenger, more as an observation than a query.

"I need to communicate with the Master of Ellipses. I might be able to make myself useful to you all."

"The Master doesn't grant audiences, especially in the present circumstances."

"This is, however, the moment for him to grant me one. Time's pressing. I have good reasons to think that some kind of catastrophe will occur if my companion and I don't return as quickly as possible to my own universe. If you have any influence with the Master, urge him to listen to me."

"I don't have any more influence on him than anyone else. I'm only the attendant in charge of the library."

"That's all right. At least serve as my guide—I'm lost. When you've taken me to the part of the building where the Master can be found, I'll make sure that he listens to me."

"You're very presumptuous, flat dream—but it doesn't matter. Follow me."

They set off. The messenger found his way easily through the labyrinth, which was as inextricable as that fallen's, and they soon reached a large gallery bordered by two lines of soldiers in white armor.

"I'll leave you here," said the guide, silently. He drew away along the gallery and turned the far corner. Dal was alone in the middle of the motionless suits of armor. No one paid any heed to him. He went to plant himself in front of one of the soldiers, and stared at him, in spite of the queasy feeling that the sight of a being that one could see from all sides at once always provoked. The messenger did not react. Dal threw himself forward, head lowered, and grabbed him round the waist. There again there was a disagreeable impression of gripping something only half-palpable. Ortog had already wondered how he could take hold of a four-dimensional object. It must be that the usage of the necroship conferred something akin to a transitory supplementary dimension on its passengers, sufficiently real for contact to be possible, but not sufficient to give the voyagers an appearance of volume in the eyes of the people of this world.

The struggle was rapid. The messenger succeeded in drawing his weapon, and Ortog fell backwards amid a lightning-flash. He lay there briefly, shocked; the power of the fulguration had been reduced.

When he came to his senses, several messengers were supporting him in front of an opening that put the gallery in communication with a small triangular room. A messenger without armor was standing in the middle of the otherwise-empty room, alone. Ortog received his thoughts. "It's not enough for you to retain a certain amount of liberty. You have to take advantage of it to attack my soldiers."

"I had to attract attention. I need to speak to the Master of Ellipses."

"Tell me what you have to say to him. I occupy a high rank."

"No. Take me to him. It's urgent. My companion and I have to leave in order for the prodigies to stop."

"We could also put you to death—but only the Master can make that decision." The messenger advanced, and signalled to Ortog to precede him.

Dal started walking, with difficulty, framed by the soldiers. A brief walk took them to the room where he had already met the Master. The latter was still there, surrounded by messengers with whom he was in mental conversation.

Dal heard in his mind: "This one again! What does he want?"

The Knight formulated his proposal. A silence followed—an absence of thought—and then: "I authorize you to retrieve Garal, if you're capable of doing that—which I doubt—but your companion must stay here as a hostage. As for the problem of the relationship between your people and ours, it's no more to me than an interesting illusion. Finally, with regard to the amnesia of the fallen, there can be no question of abolishing it. For that insane request alone I ought to condemn you to death. I have spoken. Give him every facility to carry through his project, as soon as you have his companion in safe custody."

The Master let it be understood that the conversation was over.

Dal was taken back to the room in which he had first been imprisoned. A soldier was posted by the opening, with orders to contact him when Dal desired to do so. The semi-prisoner went to the previously-inaccessible window; beyond the glass, the two armies could be seen in formation, having reconstituted their ranks.

Dal searched for Zoltan's thoughts, but the Housemaster-Baron was out of range. If he had to go all the way to the ship, it might be a long time before their plan could be put into operation; either he would have to go on foot, or he would have to go all the way round the planet on the circular river. It was a very small planet, but that certainly represented an exceedingly long journey.

Laughter sounded in Ortog's mind. "The necroship is on its way. It's quite close."

Dal started. "How did you do that?"

"Easy! I induced our excellent fallen to tow along the river it by its cables. It will be here before the sun reaches the zenith."

"I should hope so. It seems to be stationary, so slow is its movement. But are you aware that the Master—that word stings me—wants to keep you as a hostage while I try to find Garal, my double in lethargy?"

"I followed that vaguely. That doesn't bother me."

"It greatly displeases me—but I see no means of avoiding the man's demands."

"I've spoken to the Weaver of Echoes about the eventual lifting of the amnesia. What do they say on your side?"

"The Master of Ellipses threatened me with death when I put that condition to him."

"Too bad. We can force him to do it. If you find Garal, he'll doubtless be on our side. He can offer us useful support."

"There's another obstacle. When you bring the ship here, the Master might not keep his promises, and have the vessel destroyed."

"I still have my sword and my shield. Besides, I've had two mirrors placed in the gondola—not without difficulty, it seems. At any rate, the necroship is now a warship, doubtless vulnerable but with terrible fire-power."

"I'll wait for you, then. Let me know when the ship arrives."

"You can count on me."

Dal darted a final glance over the plain, then headed for the soldier on sentry duty. The messenger had his orders, for Dal received his thought: "What do you want?"

"Take me to Ifliz. I need to talk to her."

The messenger hesitated momentarily, then said: "All right. I'll take you to her."

Outside Ifliz's apartment, it was necessary to negotiate. Ifliz was not seeing anyone, especially strangers responsible for the liberation of the fallen. Ifliz did not understand her father; she would have condemned them on the spot. Dal sent word that he proposed to find Garal. That immediately unleashed an even more extravagant anger—then, without transition, he was shown in.

Again, he had a lump in his throat because of the resemblance she bore to Kalla: an absurd resemblance, like those that strike you in dreams between dissimilar objects that are nevertheless linked in some obvious manner—a relationship that awakening obliterates. What would be the effect of returning, in the present instance. Would there, in fact, be a return

Dal had difficulty formulating his thought. It was no more than a desire: that of embracing this unhuman being in order to search desperately for the presence of Kalla within her. But the deception of death was waving a lure before his eyes: a simulacrum of Kalla, like a foreign body that had arrogated a few of her facial features.

Dal reacted. "I know about your relationship with Garal. I know how you came to be separated."

"You've come here as a spy. Your resemblance to him merely augments my scorn."

243

In spite of the insult, there was now a certain reserve in Ifliz's thoughts, and something melancholy in the affective color of the communication. This was not the imperious Amazon he had run into previously, but the equivalent of a forsaken woman.

"Chagrin and spite are dictating your words. I'm neither angry nor resentful, for I understand you—I who am searching in you for the one I have lost."

"Spare me your pity, and renounce your madness, or I'll have you thrown out."

"I'll say no more about that subject, then. What I'd like you to tell me is the exact role that the sun plays with regard to the organism. Why is it dangerous to be exposed to it?"

Ifliz remained devoid of any detectable thought momentarily. "It's both life and death," she said, eventually. "Life when its rays are oblique, death when it passes the zenith and its rays are vertical."

"But it passes the zenith every day!"

"Every day, at that moment, its harmful effect takes us a step closer to destruction."

"A kind of aging?"

"Perhaps. Before that, though, there's a day when something happens that enriches us. That's the moment when we become adults, and that has to be celebrated."

Dal reflected. It seemed to him that these words were providing him with a key, but he could not see the form of the key and did not know what door it might open. An idea occurred to him. "You're an adult?"

"Since a little while ago."

The revelation was on the point of exploding. "And Garal?"

"Not yet."

The curtain was torn away. Ortog's thoughts ran on with vertiginous speed. "I see it now," he said. "In our world, old superstitions have made certain people believe that, when we die, our spirits depart for a land where we become shadows. It's the opposite that's the case. We're shadows while we're alive—your shadows. The rays of your sun project these shadows into our world, which seems to you to be flat, as we appear flat to your eyes. We also have a sun that projects our own shadows on the ground, but they're two-dimensional shadows deprived of life."

"What is this rambling?"

"A picture of the truth. As the rays penetrate you, you become more transparent to their unknown particles. That's our aging, because we're your shadows. One day, you no longer project a shadow in our universe. That's our death—it corresponds to your adult state. Your enrichment is the integration of your shadow with your body. That's our arrival in your world."

"So you're Garal's shadow?"

"Undoubtedly, since he's the person I resemble—but Kalla was your shadow, and it was you who killed her by exposing yourself as you did. Now, she's within you. You were Ifliz, a stranger; you're now Ifliz and Kalla, intimately fused." A profound despair took hold of him. "And if that's the case, I've lost Kalla forever, for that which is made can never be unmade."

Dal felt a thrust of compassion emanating from Ifliz. Had he succeeded in moving that which was within her of Kalla, of awakening in that phantom of Kalla some trace of the memories that death had removed from her? But no—it was only the fleeting compassion of a fundamentally different being.

However, Ifliz said: "There's something in me that is struggling against my indifference with respect to you." A blur, a moment of interference, and then: "That confirms what you say—but it's so insane that I can't believe it."

Ortog sank into bleak a dejection. An idea occurred to him: if Kalla was now out of reach, there was nothing more for him to do but die—and by virtue of that death, he would melt into the personality of Garal. If the latter could regain Ifliz's love, Dal would regain Kalla. They would be united through the intervening individuals...a derisory consolation, since he would no longer be himself, and would have lost all personal memory.

He started. He must not abandon himself to despair; there was no proof that his interpretation of things was the expression of the truth. Before anything else, he had to find Garal. "Will I have authorization to go to the well where the voyager is sleeping?"

"You undoubtedly will have, but I don't want his name to be mentioned."

"And if he comes back to you, will you send him away?"

"He's put himself outside the law. He has disobeyed my father. He's one of the fallen."

"And is all that sufficient to obliterate the affection you had for him?"

A mental silence, like a barrier; then: "What does it matter?"

"If I'm linked to him, and if Kalla is in you, your problems are mine. First, though, we must put an end to the war between the messengers and the fallen. If my theory is correct, many of those among you have involved themselves in it before attaining the adult state. Many of those will be killed, causing premature death to an equal number of human beings in my universe. I'm the only one who wants to do something about that fatal mechanism of echoing death."

"And you think you can do that?"

"Garal will have to help me. The pain of seeing Kalla enchained in this world won't prevent me from legitimating my voyage by protecting my race. I'm all the more duty bound because I'm responsible for this confrontation. It's only afterwards that I can decide my own destiny."

"These thoughts honor you, but the fallen must return to their prison and their leaders must be punished."

"I'm the foremost of those leaders. Garal is the second. Of what are the fallen guilty, if their ideas are correct and their research valuable?"

"That's not for me to decide."

Dal did not insist. Ifliz could not rid herself in a single instant of the familial and social conditioning that had made her a messenger, with all the prejudices belonging to that class. He concluded: "I'll take my leave of you, I'm very grateful to you for having seen me. In your presence, not only have I felt as if I had found something of the person of whom I came in search, but you have helped me take a great step forward. I think that I now hold the end of the thread that will repair the link between our universes. I shall go to see the man you want to hate...."

She only replied to his thought with an incomprehensible tumult of contradictory sentiments. He knew that he had made inroads into her confidence and called into question the resolutions dictated by self-respect. The women of hyperspace cast shadows in their own image.

Without raising any obstacle to Ortog's desire, the soldier who had been attached to him led him to an outlying part of the complex, in which Garal's laboratory was situated. They were so close to the periphery that there was a double cordon of troops along part of the walls. Above their heads, in the distance, Dal could see the first ranks of the immobile black suits of armor. It was a redoubtable siege: the fallen covered the plain like an ocean of congealed tar.

Dal went into a square courtyard, preceded by his guide. In the center of that courtyard stood a sort of small outbuilding, similarly square—at least, Dal interpreted the forms in that fashion, although human language was powerless to describe them. There was a messenger to either side of the door. Each of them held a serpentine instrument, the function of which the voyager guessed; he could not hear anything, but the complex elements of a cascading rhythm arrived in his brain, accompanied by color sensations. It was like a rainbow across a curtain of rain agitated by the wind.

"Musicans?" Ortog queried.

"I don't know what you mean—but the Institute of Ellipses has authorized the rebel's relatives to place two celebrants next to his tomb. Night and day, they perform a commentary on the life of Garal the Noble before his fall."

Dal thought of Kalla's tomb, far away on Earth. His brow furrowed. He opened his eyes very wide, in order that the first tears would dry up quickly. "Let's go," he said.

Inside the edifice, the well was dark. The soldier made a gesture and the walls of the pit lit up. A few meters lowers down, Garal's body was lying. Dal stepped back. He knew that the messenger resembled him, but he had not yet seen him. The common points of their features introduced a hallucinatory familiarity between faces that were simultaneously more foreign and more distant than those of a human and a hybrid.

"No one knows whether he is dead or whether he has departed on a forbidden voyage?"

"No one."

Dal knew, though. The more he thought about it, the more his theory of shadows seemed to explain the facts—and in this instance, Garal could not be dead, because his death would have claimed Dal too. He concentrated his thoughts in the direction of the inert body. No response. Garal was further away than he imagination could place him. This confrontation served no purpose, but Dal would have regretted it if he had not bothered. The Master of Ellipses had assumed that the encounter would be vain; that was why he had tolerated it. What he did not know was that it fortified Dal in his conviction and gave him the strength to verify it.

"Good. Take me back to the central building—the part next to the tall tower."

He retained a clear memory of the place where his armaments had been deposited, and did not want to be far away from it, in case something happened that would help him regain possession of his sword and shield. But what had the messengers done with them? Might they have thought of subjecting them to analysis? Awkward attempts of that sort might end in a gigantic catastrophe that would destroy the buildings and both armies.

Just as they arrived at the foot of the tower, Dal received a mental communication from Zoltan: "Sire, I have to tell you that the ship is ready to go."

"Already!"

"Finally, you ought to say. I've been begging them to make haste, and the delay seemed quite long to me. No matter—can you alert the blackguards to my arrival, in order that I won't be greeted by one of their damned black rays?"

"I'll take care of it. Be so good as to resume contact shortly." Dal then addressed himself to his guide: "My companion is ready. He's on his way. Can you do what's necessary to protect him?"

The soldier in white armor seemed undisturbed. "I have instructions to give orders in that respect. Be patient—but don't try to get into that tower; you'd lose your life in the attempt."

He drew away. Dal remained alone on the esplanade. There was no movement in the buildings, and no evidence of life. One might have thought them abandoned, although they would presumably disgorge armed combatants ready to withstand an assault if the double line of defense was breached.

Between two buildings, Ortog saw that line open to form a corridor. The messenger was coming back already. "Your companion may advance—but the maneuver must not involve any trickery, or you'll both be executed."

Dal made no reply. He waited for Zoltan's mental transmission. It soon arrived: "Will flower-petals be strewn along the route I must take? Will triumphal music rise up as I pass by?"

Dal smiled weakly. "Not exactly, but you're expected. Be careful about your slightest action; these people don't feel safe, and they're capable of opening fire without rhyme or reason."

"Damn! I'll stay on my toes."

Silence fell. Dal moved toward the point where the defensive line had opened, and stood still at the entrance to a corridor formed by the white suits of armor. In the distance, the ranks of the black army parted. The spindle of the ship emerged from behind a hillock and advanced into the gap. The mirrors placed in the gondola were visible. Between them was Zoltan, whose torso bore the crossed shoulder-straps of his sword and his shield. In the sunlight, which was finally increasing, the black spindle glinted occasionally. The ship advanced in this fashion at low altitude, menaced by the mirror that the messengers aimed at it. It slowly crossed the expanse of no-man's-land and moved into the corridor, whose living walls drew apart in front of it. When it was in the plaza, it settled on the ground, and Zoltan got down. Soldiers immediately surrounded him and disarmed him.

Dal came forward, addressing himself to the individual who seemed to be in command. "It's possible," he said, "that a hostage does not have the right to keep his weapons—but I'm departing on a voyage where I shall have need of them: a voyage the Master has authorized me to attempt. Will you return mine to me?"

"Take these—yours are in the hand of the mirror technicians."

"That's what I feared. The slightest mistake on their part could annihilate half the world."

"They're not unaware of that. They understood it from the first moment. Now you may go."

Dal buckled on Zoltan's sword and passed the shield's strap over his shoulder. He shook the Housemaster-Baron's hand, and addressed himself once again to the messenger in charge: "If my companion is answering for me, you are all answering to me for his head. If the slightest harm has come to him when I return, I shall give the fallen the signal to attack and annihilate everything within range."

He had omitted to mention that the presence of Zoltan and Ifliz would prevent him from doing as he said, but his words did not seem to the messenger to be an empty threat, for the latter replied: "A hostage is not a convict. However, not only must you come back, but the fallen must not attack in your absence. If they do so, the hostage will be executed as soon as their attack begins."

Dal shrugged his shoulders. "You all talk about nothing but executions..." He addressed himself to Zoltan; "What did you say to the Weaver?"

"I told him to postpone the attack. They'll maintain the siege in the meantime."

"What if the Master of Ellipses' reinforcements attack them from the rear?"

The officer stepped forward. "I understand," he transmitted. "Why do you slow down the unfolding of your thoughts by expressing them materially? With regard to the reinforcements, they have orders simply to threaten the besiegers."

"All is for the best, then," said Zoltan. "I wish you good hunting. May you return promptly."

Dal raised his arm. "See you soon, Henderson!"

He climbed into the gondola and placed his hand in the final imprint. If the necroship could travel from three-dimensional space to hyperspace, why should it not travel from there to the world of five dimensions?

To the amazement of the messengers, the vessel was duplicated. The second form became wispy and disappeared, while the first remained motionless in the same place. In the gondola, Dal Ortog was inert. Zoltan laid him down, with some difficulty; his body now had a corpse-like rigor. Somewhere in the succession of nested universes, Ortog's double was sailing in quest of the person whose shadow he was.

Dal was moving slowly over a troubled terrain formed of greasy yellow clay. Something told him that it was a cemetery on a planetary scale—a cemetery with neither graves nor mausoleums, pleated into hills that blocked the horizon. A sickening charnel-house stink advertised mass burials, or some vast collective profanation perpetrated by some casual genocide. He was entering into the sort of nightmare that cadavers undergo, learning to suffer the second death that awaits the inhabitants of coffins, trying to extract the square root of death.

251

The immense horror gradually melted into a grey monotony. Dal prudently steered the necroship into it. The vessel seemed to be slowed down by a viscous resistance.

Without any transition, the clouds were rent apart. The ship and its gondola were now floating in the heat of a pale void splashed with light. From a hundred different directions came a giant pulsation that was almost unbearable, like the pounding of hammers on anvils of flesh—and in the violet-tinted distance false dawns trembled, vague threats of light that disappeared immediately.

What was this formidable wall? The Knight adjusted the shoulder-strap of his shield, as if wrapping a garment around himself in the bosom of a storm. He recognized the trademark of the titans of the void who built infinite ramparts to isolate worlds.

The wall was very close. Dal took the ship higher. Like an enormous toy submarine, the black vessel brushed the wall. Was that an opening? No—a niche, a crevice. As he passed by, Ortog saw nameless things escaping from it, which took flight in hideous clusters, howling. What forms of life—or what forms of death—burrowed in this fashion between universes?

The wall went by monotonously. Like a wild beast in a cage roaming back and forth in search of an exit, Dal steered the ship in every direction: no opening. Wrath accelerated the pulse-beat in his temples, drowning the cold fear inspired by the rampart. He took matters into his own hands and brought the mirror in the prow to bear.

Instantaneously, the black ray struck the wall. His heart full of hope, Dal saw a crack extend from the point of impact. He maneuvered the unfamiliar weapon again, and the crack became a rift. A third shot, and it widened further—but the black ray became grey, then colorless. Its energy was exhausted. Dal drew his sword. He moved closer to the rampart, orientated the spindle of the ship parallel to it, and climbed up on to the rim of the gondola. He thrust.

In a terrible gout of flame, splinters of cerulite went flying. The ship pitched at the center of a blue halo, while a series of enormous explosions extended their overlapping echoes. Shaken like a feather in a hurricane, Dal Ortog almost dropped his sword as he clung on to the gondola's cables. He had closed his eyes in order not to be blinded.

Little by little, silence was restored. The glare of the explosion no longer penetrated Dal's eyelids. The combat of matter and energy had ended.

He opened his eyes again: the Blue Weapon had cleaved through the infinite rampart; a breach had been opened in it, through which an entire fleet might have passed. He moved the ship away, while his eyes were burning and his ears buzzing. He lined up the spindle, and went through the great barrier like an arrow.

As he went through the obstacle, Dal initially feared that he might have made an error. What if he had gone the wrong way? What if he were returning to Earth? This might be the same wall as before, approached from the opposite direction.

What awaited him on the other side, however, immediately proved the he was not on a false track. To keep his hands free, he replaced his lightly-pitted blade in its scabbard; piloting the ship required his full attention.

The vessel was moving forward into an incomprehensible space. He had the impression of being both inside and outside that space; it seemed both empty and full; vast deformable entities showed both their backs and their fronts. In comparison with that space, a Möbius ring was nothing but a segment of a straight line, a Klein bottle a triangle, and the messengers and the fallen mere Chinese shadows. As for Dal, he felt different; he deduced that he had acquired a further provisional dimension—a sort of officially-sanctioned passport.

He had entered another universe as vast as its predecessors. How could he find his way around it? How could he find the route that would lead him to Garal? While drifting through the formless network that surrounded him, he reassured himself by thinking that the planet of the messengers and the fallen was only one world in hyperspace, and yet he had arrived there straight away. Lines of force presumably linked homothetic beings, and he could not fail to meet up with the one who served as his destiny. He therefore let the ship continue in the direction it had already taken—if one could speak in terms of direction in a place where everything that was below was above, and everything inside outside…

He saw the sky through the ground, and it seemed to him that at the same time, he was looking down at the ground, through which he could see a second sky. Distracted by these insane observations, he did not notice until the last moment the approach of a bifurcated form distantly reminiscent of a human being. There was a crackling sound, and he suddenly felt very heavy, while the ship and its gondola were enveloped by a multicoloured bubble—but the assault stopped there.

If he had been considered as a flat shape in the preceding world, this one ought to make a line of him. At a superior level, he would be a point, and would pass completely unperceived—but here, already, the weapons deployed against him revealed themselves to be far too powerful; they were ineffective. He concluded, with satisfaction, that there was no need for him to make war in this foreign universe.

He had to retract that notion, however. A second offensive followed, which was extremely disagreeable: an impression of being crushed. Were these beings using a gravitic weapon?

The third attack was so painful that Dal unsheathed his sword and thrust at a distance. In a blue flash, the living form became a motionless surface, which was reduced to a line and soon disappeared.

Other forms converged on him. More bubbles formed in succession; the impression of being crushed and rent apart was renewed. Dal staggered to the stern mirror and activated it. The black ray began leaping from one form to another—but the effect was different. The forms exploded in spheres of darkness, dissociating into a thousand elements that went through the ground. The aggressors retreated and vanished. Dal assumed, however, that he had better move rapidly; it was inconceivable that beings as complex as these would not possess weapons adaptable to three-dimensional biology. Even if he were invulnerable, the ship would end up being damaged and he would remain a prisoner in this chaos. He accelerated the ship.

The confusion that served as a landscape fled around him at a crazy velocity. He perceived that he had no need to steer the vessel to avoid obstacles; it went through them without difficulty and without wreaking the slightest destruction.

Suddenly, structures began to appear—angular, bubble-like and honeycomb-like—which seemed to signal the intervention of an intelligence: that of the aggressive beings that Dal had been constrained to annihilate in order to stay alive. It was a regrettable situation, but he could not embark on efforts at communication while he was being used as a target.

Dal moderated the speed of the ship, which came to a standstill next to a wall of the transparent architecture. It was, indeed, reminiscent of a dwelling. As he studied it, however, Ortog was obliged to yield to the evidence: it extended prolongations in every direction and did not seem to be delimiting any functional volume. No organized construction attained such obvious absurdity. And yet, it was there that strange thoughts imposed themselves on his mind.

"You can apply all your methods of torture," said the strange mind, "but you won't get the secret of my voyage out of me. You're hidden, but you're prowling around me, waiting for some error on my part—a lapse in vigilance, or an involuntary thought—but I've already told you that my transportation was the result of a certain state of mind, not the employment of a machine or a mathematical formula." There was a pause, and then: "So you can continue to act blindly upon my universe, unleashing unnatural phenomena there—but others will come to my aid, who are doing so at this very moment. We shall invade you and you shall be at our mercy." There was another pause, followed by a more tentative and less resolute thought-sequence. "Who's there? There's a life-form close by different from my jailers. Who are you? Your thoughts don't have the tortuous form that they effect. No more is it a mind like mine. What are the strange images that I see stirring within it?"

Dal projected his own thoughts as best he could toward the iridescent interior of the honeycomb: "My name is Ortog. I come from a universe different from both yours and this one. Are you not Garal?"

"How do you know me?"

"I've been in your homeworld. I'm here to take you back to it. How are the inhabitants of this world retaining you?"

"Their structures have an isolating function. I'm in a kind of cage."

Dal took out his sword. "Stand back," he said. "I'm going to try to break through the walls of your prison."

"Impossible..." The transmission weakened. "They have one dimension more than there is in my own universe."

Dal raised his weapon. "Well then," he concluded, "they have two more than in mine..." And he thrust.

The bluish flame erupted, with a racket like an entire horizon tearing apart. The wall of bubbles was transformed into a thin screen, animated by vague movements. Through that screen, Dal saw Garal: an image if himself, hewn by a sculptor with omnivision.

The screen became increasingly transparent and its ripples diminished in amplitude. The inferior and superior zones vanished; there was no longer anything more than a horizontal line, as taut as a vibrating string, which melted in its turn.

The messenger came toward Ortog. "How flat you are!" he said, mentally. "But don't you resemble me?"

"Indeed. We'll talk about that later. It's more urgent to avoid an attack."

Garal gestured toward the ship. "What's this?"

"The vehicle that brought me here. Get in without delay."

"But how can I get into a flat image like this machine?"

"Do you see these mirrors?"

"I recognize them."

"Don't they have as many dimensions as your body?"

"Yes, since they're from my universe."

"Then you can do as they have done, and get into the gondola. I think that it's acquired an infinitesimal part of your supplementary dimension during my sojourn there. On my planet, there are certain objects that are very flat, but have three dimensions nevertheless." He looked at Garal curiously, then added: "But if you prefer your own method of travel, we'll meet again in the company of the Master of Ellipses…"

Garal hesitated. "This thing seems inconceivable to me. I think I'll go back by my own means." He stood still momentarily, then adopted another pose, standing still again. "No," he said, eventually. "I fear that this world is a trap for me in more than one sense; I was able to get into it, but its entire constitution is isolating when it comes to returning. Its inhabitants had no need to imprison me. I'll go with you, then."

"Good."

Dal toppled the mirror from the prow, whose energy was exhausted, on the side of the gondola, and showed the other one to Garal. "Get ready to repel any attack from the rear. I'll open up a pathway for us ahead." He tapped the pommel of his sword.

Garal stared at it oddly. "That's a powerful weapon you're carrying."

Dal smiled proudly. "It's capable of destroying Mirrors of Negation."

Garal shook his head—all of whose faces were simultaneously visible. "I'll content myself with the mirror."

Dal assumed a determined expression. "That's also a fearful weapon."

Garal had some difficulty hoisting himself into the gondola. He succeeded, however, and installed himself next to the stern mirror, Ortog maneuvered the ship to take the direction

257

opposite the one that he had followed in coming. He put his hand in the imprint, in the reverse sense.

Nothing happened. In front of them, a proliferation of multicoloured structures had filled the whole visible space. Forms with a million unintelligible contours were moving within these structures. Without taking the gondola down, Ortog aimed the sword. The obstacle split apart, and a large part of it was blasted into luminous powder. The ship set off like a bullet.

As they passed through, they suffered the impact of gravitic weapons, and nearly lost consciousness. Gsaral, however, had strength enough to launch a fan of black radiance, which contrived a massacre as it cut through the remains of the barrier. While traversing the tangled network, they saw flames bursting forth far behind them, whose bases were deep black and whose extremities were dazzling white. The flames died out, and a thick incandescent fog crept through the inextricable geometric jungle.

Then it all disappeared.

The necroship was floating once again in an ocean of cloud.

The mist was something animated by internal currents that gave birth to dark superficial eddies. It presented a surface tangled by immense prolongations, unsoundable valleys and fleecy summits, whose features the ship traversed at an immeasurable speed. Some clouds that seemed to emerge from infinity with the speed of light revealed themselves to be stationary with respect to some other nebulous formation racing to meet them—and among these moving points, which served as fallacious reference-points and deceptive beacons, the mariners of the darkness ended up not knowing whether they were even moving.

Once, they passed within a short distance of a blurred form as dark as black crystal, half melted into the fog. It was so reminiscent of a shipwreck in the lightning-flash of a storm that Dal put his hand as an eye-shade and watched it for as long as it was visible. What sailors, come from what universe, were lost in that rightful cloud? What unhuman cadavers were manning that dismasted sailing vessel, drawn along by unknown currents?

Although he was a stranger to any machine of that sort, Garal examined it too, and Dal picked up something in his thoughts akin to a surge of surprise and anxiety. Dal was not unaware that the messengers, like the fallen, were not devoid of sentiment, even though they controlled their emotions better than humans. He remembered Ifliz: her imperious character and her ability to feel pain.

There was very little piloting for Dal to do. He tried to make mental contact with the messenger. He obtained it, and told him the reasons for his voyage.

"Mine was scientific in nature," Garal told him, without repeating what Ortog had learned from Kalla. "I believed that the celestial upheavals were caused by the beings we have just quit. Some time afterwards, I had a dream, in the course of which a mysterious communication was established between my mind and a foreign mentality that was also in sleeping state. The dream was full of people who were dying prematurely, in the wake of a terrible war. On awakening, by some unfathomable hidden mechanism, I found the means necessary to restore the disrupted equilibrium of our universe. The individual with whom I had communicated could only have been one of those who took me prisoner."

Dal shivered. He remembered his long period of hibernation, but he had forgotten its contents. Garal's declaration tore away the veil with which his memory had enveloped itself. He relived the dreams that had populated his artificial sleep; he knew that he had thus made contact with a foreign intelligence: that of Garal. But he did not say so yet.

"And from the journey that led to my detention," Garal continued, "and the journey you were able to accomplish by means other than mine, I've learned something important: we, the messengers and the fallen, are only the shadows of the beings that you have encountered, and with whom we have engaged in combat."

Ortog could not hold back his thoughts. "You've made an error, but you've found the truth. The person with whom your mind made contact was me—and you were able to do that because I am your shadow, as you are the shadow of a life-form that possesses one dimension more than you. When I die, I shall be integrated into your personality, and you will become an adult. When you die, you will do the same at a higher level—that of the beings we have encountered. As you believed that you had made contact with one of them, however, you thought that they were the origin of the perturbations exported to your universe, when it was my own race that was responsible for them. The great conflagration you mentioned took place in my universe; it resounded from space to space, through the dimensions."

Garal's thoughts remained out of reach.

"However," Ortog added," that's not the case with the prodigies that are occurring at present, which I have witnessed myself. These seemingly-impossible events are certainly provoked by the inhabitants of five-dimensional space, where the repercussions of the changes you have contrived in your own universe have been felt."

"Perhaps you're right."

Dal had a bright idea. "Do you know the leader of the fallen, the Weaver of Echoes?"

"Yes. It was our conversations that determined my voyage, after incurring the wrath of the Master of Ellipses."

"Do you know whether he has attained the adult state?"

"He hasn't attained it, but he was born long before me, and was on the point of getting there when I left."

Dal felt a chill. If this whole shadow ballet reflected a reality, Zoltan was in mortal danger.

The ship continued on its cloudy course. Ortog projected his thoughts: "My companion is the Weaver's shadow. We must make haste."

What could be gained by hurrying, though, unless the Weaver could be shielded from the sun's rays? And how could he be shielded without removing him from his planet, since the radiation even penetrated the labyrinth? And Zoltan's problem was that of all human beings; it could still be called destiny.

There is a connection between all the worlds, Dal mused, *such that every event in one is correlated with a different event in another. Thus, the Blue War provoked a catastrophe in hyperspace, leading to a more rapid rotation of planets—for there are doubtless others that the one on which I landed. That acceleration resulted in a more frequent passage of the sun through its zenith, which resulted in a premature arrival of adulthood of the messengers and the fallen, and thus of premature death among human beings—but the application of ectogenesis in my world was merely the translation of what Garal accomplished in his own in slowing down planetary rotation. Analogous processes must have unfolded in the fifth dimension—and perhaps beyond...*

"All that is possible," thought Garal, in reply.

Ortog's mind remained vacant momentarily. "We're all caught in a net in which each element of the mesh is as large as the cosmos, and however microscopic we might be, we can never escape that net."

They drifted in the silence of thought, all communication suspended. In the depths of the mist, the lights were drawing away. Others appeared directly ahead of them; they were in front of the mighty wall, where the breach seemed half scarred-over. The hole was still enormous and negotiable, though, and cloudy currents were rushing into it tempestuously. The ship was drawn into it, whirling around without Dal being able to control its trajectory, with the result that it nearly precipitated the travelers into the frightful void separating two infinities.

The tempest of mist suddenly calmed down, however; through gaps in the clouds, a flamboyant horizon appeared.

Slowly, the vessel descended on to a plain covered with black suits of armor. It approached a group of buildings circled by white suits of armor.

In the middle of a courtyard, the necroship's double was waiting. There was a slow and silent fusion. Ortog's rigid body was reanimated.

Garal had vanished.

Dal got to his feet. Standing beside the gondola, Zoltan watched him, his arms folded. "Just in time," he said. "These fellows are about to come to blows."

Involuntarily, Dal darted a glance at the sky; the sun had almost reached the zenith. Then he noticed Garal's absence.

"Come on—we have to go to the well."

Zoltan leapt into the gondola, and Dal immediately covered him with his shield. The surprised soldiers were too late raising their weapons: the lightning-bolts struck the shield. The necroship was already rising above their heads. Dal, who knew the way, steered it rapidly to the square outbuilding. As it got there, Garal emerged, walking unsteadily. At the moment of return his body had been reintegrated. Ortog called out to him by means of thought.

"Come with us. I'll set you down among the fallen. You're in danger here."

Garal hesitated, then hoisted himself into the gondola as soon as the ship had lost enough height. The Master of Ellipses then surged forth from a nearby building, surrounded by a group of armed soldiers. In front of them was Ifliz.

Dal understood that the situation had become desperate. He leapt to the ground, seized Ifliz in his arms and lifted her up. He was acting purely on impulse, absurd as his actions were. On board, it was Garal who took hold of Ifliz.

"Lend me your sword," said Zoltan to Dal.

"What are you going to do?"

"You'll see." He addressed himself to Garal. "Where's the transmitter that provokes amnesia in the fallen?"

Garal understood and replied promptly: "Behind that building, between my old laboratories and the Institute's. It's in a little tower—you can see the top of it from here."

"Henderson!" Ortog cried—but Zoltan had already leapt down.

He ran toward the soldiers, whirling the blade. Half of the messengers were transformed into luminous lines. Behind them, a helical column collapsed, cut in half—but other white-armored individuals were flooding into the empty space. Zoltan disappeared behind Garal's mausoleum.

The ship was surrounded by lightning-bolts. Ortog was obliged to maneuver to escape the attack. The spindle rose up and steered toward the place where Zoltan had disappeared—but the latter's thoughts exploded in Ortog's mind: "No! Go put Garal under the protection of the Weaver, and come back right away."

Dal hesitated, then obeyed, reluctantly. The vessel soared high into the air, above the messengers' lines of defense. The no-man's-land had melted away; the fallen were advancing, twenty ranks deep. In the wind that had got up, long fragments of the Weaver's tapestry were floating, serving as banners. Dal headed for the longest of the oriflammes. The black suits of armor parted on all sides. The ship went down.

Garal looked at Ifliz, and Dal overheard their dialogue.

"Come with me. I now have proof that the fallen are right, and that the have been unjustly persecuted."

"No. You preferred your research to my company. You won't act any differently in future. I'll oblige this flat being to take me back to my own people. Goodbye."

Garal did not insist. He got out of the gondola. Before heading toward the Weaver of Echoes, however, he said: "The battle that is about to take place will decide our destiny. Don't take any risks. I want you to live, for I shall never forget you."

The ship rose up, departing for the residence of the Master.

As he approached the enemy lines, Ortog saw a blood-red flame leap up in the midst of the buildings, which surpassed the tallest of them. An abrupt explosion, followed by a long whistle, struck his ears, and the ship oscillated in a furious blast of wind. While he crouched over the control's Zoltan's thoughts arrived to reassure him.

"There! Those who live in forgetfulness don't know how lucky they are. I've just given them back the torments of memory. Would you care to collect me at the foot of the ruins?"

"I'm on my way."

But Ifliz threw herself at the controls. Ortog had all the difficulty in the world shoving her away, and then preventing her from hurling herself over the side. He finally succeeded in steering the ship. Behind him, Ifliz lay prostrate.

It was certainly a question of ruins! A crater had opened up in the ground. Not far away, Zoltan was holding a numerous troop of messengers at bay. The vessel drew nearer. As it began to descend, several soldiers managed to take up a position behind Zoltan.

Ortog tied to warn him. "Look out!"

But the lightning-bolts had struck home. Hit in the back, Zoltan dropped his sword and fell. The other messengers inundated him with furious fire. Terrified, Dal saw Zoltan's body shrivel up before his eyes.

From the depths of the zenith, the sun inundated the battle with its rays—and the Weaver, who was raising his banner...

Chapter Six

Crushed by amazement and grief, Ortog had abandoned the controls. The ship remained stationary, as if suspended above the cohorts—but it soon came under fire from the messengers, and Dal protected Ifliz with his shield, covering himself as best he could.

He had to get away; one or other of them might be hit at any moment.

Dal could not perform the necessary actions, though. In spite of the shock that he had just suffered, and against which he was not yet capable of struggling, he was thinking about two extremely important things. On the one hand, either the sword that Zoltan had dropped would, in the not-too-distant future, degrade and destroy the ground with which it was in contact, or the messengers who would take possession of it would not fail to make us use it, with redoubtable awkwardness. On the other hand, the second sword—the one that was already in their hands—similarly represented a considerable danger to the entire world.

The ship swooped down like a bird of prey on the soldiers, who scattered.

Ortog leapt to the ground just as a messenger threw himself toward the sword. He seized it cleanly, but had to catch Ifliz round the waist again as she tried to escape. Covered by the shield, they hoisted themselves aboard; the soldiers hesitated to launch their lighting-bolts, for they had recognized the daughter of the Master of Ellipses. Dal took advantage of that to maneuver the ship, which was out of range in the blink of an eye. Ortog's teeth were clenched at the idea of abandoning Zoltan's body in the midst of is enemies, but there was nothing he could do about it. It was not in this universe that the Housemaster-Baron would receive a sepulchre worthy of him.

The ship passed over the buildings. It headed straight for the tower into which the second sword had been taken. Not far from the building, Dal brandished his weapon. The tower collapsed—but a blue gleam soon appeared in the rubble, which became flamboyant. In the midst of that halo, the color of tempered steel, a point emerged more luminous than the sun. Dal closed his eyes, as he had done before the wall. The air around him became intensely hot; a tornado rose up. The ship was carried away like a feather.

Cautiously, Dal—who was holding on to Ifliz, crouching at the side of the gondola—opened his eyelids slightly. He was already a long way from the residences, which were ablaze in a dazzling blue furnace. Beneath him, the plain inundated with black suits of armor was visible. The fallen had been attached in the rear by the previously-summon reinforcements, but they were holding them off. The black rays of mirrors were crisscrossing through the battle, which was bristling with lightning-bolts. Here and there, fragments of the tapestry of echoes were no more than simple flags; Zoltan had sacrificed his life for the slaves who would never have need of such sacrifice again.

Disabled, the ship was still drawing away from the planet at a vertiginous speed. Ortog was not inconvenienced by any rarefaction of the air; the notion of void had no more existence in hyperspace than in the nameless places to which it had granted access. The world of the messengers and the fallen was soon no more than a little luminous bubble in the diffuse glimmer of space; then it became a dot. Sparkling, the ship continued to bury itself in an increasingly bright light.

In the distance, another world appeared, also orbiting the unknown sun. Ortog saw it grow as he drew nearer to it, and made out variously-colored patches on its surface. Perhaps its surface was divided up into continents and oceans; perhaps there were mountains and valleys to be found there. Undoubtedly it harbored a population. That of the solar system from which Dal came was still much reduced by comparison with the figure it had attained before the Blue War, but it represented a number of individuals far superior to that of the messengers and envoys combined. If every human were the shadow of a hyperspatial being, many of those beings must be located on a planet other than the one that Dal had explored. As for the extraterrestrials of three-dimensional galaxies, they correspondent to the hyperspatials of homologous galaxies, situated far from the sun whose rays were bathing the ship, but in the same space.

Ortog passed too far from the planet to learn any more about it. He tried, however, to take advantage of its attraction to unblock the vessel's controls. It was in vain. He turned to Ifliz. She was still prostrate, staring into infinity.

At that moment, he noticed a strip of plastic dangling beneath the dashboard. It was emerging from a small orifice and fell at his feet just as he as about to grab old of it. He picked it up. It had writing on it. Ortrog read;

Report of microcomputer. Analysis of radiation-field. Presence of corpuscles of increasing density. Nature bears no relationship to three-dimensional subatomic particles. Action stimulant to all life-forms foreign to hyperspace. Progressive necrotizing effect on autochthonous life-forms. Conclusion: exceedingly dense field of Bions mutational effect on human beings. Increase of exchanges, with acceleration of processes of elimination. Considerable augmentation of potential of cellular survival.

Dal set down the reel of plastic. Only one phrase remained engraved on his mind: *necrotizing effect on autochthonous life-forms*. It was by exposing herself to these radiations that Ifliz had attempted to end hr life. The abduction of which she had been the object had succeeded where she had failed. By trying to recover Kalla, Ortog was in the process of killing Ifliz.

He looked at her, searching for her thoughts. There was no communication. She was still leaning against the side of the gondola. Dal had the impression that he saw her less distinctly. He too remained motionless, not knowing what to do.

The wind was whistling through the cables: a ridiculously faint wind by comparison with the velocity of the vehicle, which ought to have been disintegrated by the friction of air molecules, in view of its speed—but the drive's energy-field was serving the function of a screen. Around Ifliz, that slight wind, like a spring breeze, contrasted with the peril to which Ortog had exposed her—but Ifliz's fate could only move Dal superficially. In his eyes, she was merely Kalla's receptacle. He had hoped that, after the return, she might lose a dimension and that he would recover Kalla—but what would happen if she died before then?

He went back to the control panel, trying desperately to turn around. It was impossible. The explosion had damaged the vessel.

He set his hand in the imprint reserved for the passage from one universe to anther. The ship continued its course toward the sun, through the rain of Bions.

Ortog looked at the star, and was not dazzled. He remembered his desperate gesture, when he had abducted Ifliz as if he were seizing Kalla. He remembered the thoughts that had besieged him thereafter, until the recent past. He had the somber impression that his reasoning amounted to a deadly sin, which had been hidden from him by his anxiety. He was convinced that he had committed a fatal error, but he did not know what it was.

With a formless anxiety, he watched the sun grow ahead of him: an impossible sun whose proximity would not kill him. He thought about Ifliz, about Kalla, about Zoltan's death—and gradually stopped thinking about anything. His mind capsized, as if invaded by consciousnesses other than his own.

As he came closer to the sun, he felt depersonalized. At first, he was someone else: an unknown man whose ideas, memories, projects, pain and sorrow he assumed—then a different being, devoid of ideas and projects, dominated by emotions and impulse: an elementary being, which loved tearing living flesh with its teeth. He was also something slow and dull in its existence, in which thoughts no longer moved, and emotions were reduced to a sort of plenitude in an environment of liquid nourishment, in a bath of radiation—and again, a semi-living thing blindly led by tropisms, scarcely informed of the chemical reactions it engendered around it. Then he became a molecule, of turbulent atoms and a sheaf of protons, and a flux of neutrinos that traversed the universe, making a mockery of obstacles.

When he recovered his own identity, his closed eyelids were traversed by a horrible light that suddenly diminished in intensity. He opened his eyes slightly and saw Ifliz lying motionless in the bottom of the gondola. He threw himself toward her and tried to reanimate her with awkward gestures, methods contrived for human beings. He did not even succeed in determining whether or not she was still alive.

Around him, everything had changed. He had entered into a zone on departure from which he could see space and its world behind him. In front of him were moving landscapes, constantly changing and overlapping, like the result of multiple superimpositions. With its fiery speed, the runway necroship had gone through the surface of the sun, and that sun was nothing but a star.

Space disappeared from Ortog's sight. Meanwhile, the necroship slowed down, without its passenger being subjected to any inertial effect. Dal sensed that he was surrounded by a thousand presences that jostled his distress. The vessel continued too burst through unintelligible images, and ended up settling gently in a place where semi-darkness reigned.

The ambience that bathed the place gripped him by the throat, as if he had abruptly found himself in mortal danger. No peril became obvious, however. There was only an atmosphere of violent menace emanating from everywhere.

With his hand on the hilt of his sword, Dal looked around. The vessel was resting on something that might pass for ground, followed at a short distance by nebulous walls. It resembled a cave. As he moved to the side of the gondola, he saw that Ifliz's body had moved. She was still alive. Hope was born again in Ortog's heart. The Bions were doubtless only emitted by the surface of the sun, and Ifliz's physiology had been able to fight against their deadly properties. Dal, by contrast, felt wearier than he had at the moment when he had received their maximum radiation.

This was no time to feel weary, though. Gradually, Dal understood the nature of the threat that surrounded him. Accustomed to telepathy by his communication with Zoltan, and then with the messengers and the fallen, he recognized, as an evident truth, that he had entered into the mind of a being that had recently killed, and was preparing to commit a second murder.

He did not try to get to the bottom of the relationship that existed between the nebulous cave and the foreign mind. There was a tension in the air, as at the ends of a condenser. Nourished by hatred, indignation and desire, the homicidal impulse grew. At the same time, an opposite impulse merged, compounded out of pity, remorse and dread. Negative pole, positive pole: in which direction would the spark go?

Dal got down from the gondola on to an elastic surface. In front of him, a luminous fog, blood red in color, seemed to muffle the walls of the cave. Behind him, a vivid yellow light streamed from the ceiling. From that sunny light came an impression of relaxation and appeasement, from the red light a current of violence and fury. Dal advanced toward the bloody light, holding his shield in front of him.

The light flowed around him like a stream of scalding water. He could not help crying out in agony and flinching— but behind him, the two light-streams melted into an orange mass in which a million nuances battled. He advanced again, and his shield seemed to drive the scarlet fog back. The pain, however, was so intense that he lost ground again. In the center of the cave, the necroship was surrounded by effluvia that borrowed all the shades of ruby and gold.

The sunny light withdrew, infiltrated by madder-red. Dal reached the prow on the ship, where the blood was triumphant. In spite of the burning heat, he advanced. A drapery of gold refreshed his shoulders. Offensive flames writhed against the nebulous wall. Behind the ship, however, there was no longer anything but conflagration. He had to fight on, while simultaneously protecting Ifliz again that dreadful influence. Torn between two anxieties, he drew the sword that had so often defeated his enemies; would it reveal itself to be ineffective in this inconceivable place, against an immaterial adversary—or, on the contrary, would it provoke such catastrophes that Dal would lose his own life along with the unfortunate Ifliz?

Raising his arm high, like a torch, Ortog headed toward the fiery light. The blue phosphorescence of the blade mingled with the ferocious reflections. At first, Dal could not see clearly that the situation had been modified, for he was sheltering behind his shield, but he soon realized what effect the sword was having and abandoned his protection. The red fog climbed along the wall, toward the place where the bright light had emerged, while the latter ran over the ground and disappeared into the wall from which the burning light had flowed. When that separation and exchange was complete, the sword alone dissipated the darkness, which began to resemble moonlight.

At the same time, the presence of the murderous mind vanished, along with the internal conflict in which his passions had been engaged. A bleak coldness took possession of the fleecy walls, which began slowly to draw away from one another, while the vault gradually retreated to an inestimable altitude. Ortog deduced that the atmosphere of violence had been directed against him, and that he had just escaped a dire peril.

He got back aboard the gondola and tried once again to return to his own universe. He was unsuccessful again. However, the ship was now obedient to the ordinary controls. As the limits of the cave had retreated into infinity, and the surrounding space was entirely occupied by the chaotic images he had already encountered, Dal slowly got under way. Ifliz's shape, which had been indecisive for some time, became more precise, at least in part—those features that were normally accessible to three-dimensional eyes. Thus, Ifliz bore an in-

creasingly close resemblance to Kalla. Ortog's hope streng-
thened when he saw that she was still breathing But what, then
had been the error that he thought he had committed? Perhaps
it had only been an unfounded apprehension.

He steered the ship toward a dark point that he took to be
an orifice in the surface of the sun into which he had penetrated undamaged. Once in hyperspace, finally removed from
that source of witchcraft, he would surely be able to get back
on track.

He reached the dark spot, which was not an orifice in the
surface but another bubble of formidable dimensions. When
he penetrated into it, he gripped the sides of his head with his
hands, so violent was the psychic impact that he had just sustained.

It was a voice like that of the ocean on stormy evenings,
a voice more profound than that of a hurricane, more moving
than that of a million beings carried away by a tidal wave.
Perceptible within it, all at the same time, were an infinite
number of unfinished sentences, fragments of thunderous
echoing speeches, rivers of groans and cries of agony, sym-
phonies made of squeals of pleasure, all of it confused with
animal calls, the grating of sprouting plants and the rustling of
sap—and, further away from the intelligible, the continuous
bass-line of electronic transfer in the bosom of viral molecules.

And through that apocalypse of fused and integrated life,
one terrible voice made itself clear, booming in the Knight-
Navigator's brain. It said:

"I am the Being of beings; I am One formed by the union
of all. I exhaust myself in combating other collective giants, in
order to postpone my fusion with them in an entity of a superior order. While my cells are in perpetual conflict and unaware of my existence, I refuse to become a cell, in order to
conserve my identity..."

The voice was so fantastic that Dal feared that he was
losing his mind. Painfully, he activated the controls of the
ship, which went through the dark bubble in which the im-

mense litany was still resonating. It finally emerged, scattered images and found itself in hyperspace again. Behind the vessel, the frightful sun slowly diminished, bombarding the necroship with its dual-action Bions.

As Ortog felt his own potential for frantic life growing stronger in, his passenger sank deeper into unconsciousness. Meanwhile, Ifliz was gradually losing her original characteristics; she was turning into Kalla, in a fashion so alarming that Dal abandoned the controls to protect her with his shield, hoping to isolate her by that means from the radiation that was killing her. It seemed that it was not without effect, for she showed some signs of life again—but not enough to reply to Ortog's pressing questions or react to his hectic embraces. In his pain, he cried out: "Have I come to snatch you from the world of death only to expose you to it again, without even having returned you to life? Will you give up the struggle and abandon the man who has undertaken the most terrible of voyages for your sake?"

Then he turned toward the ever-more-distant sun and waved a clenched fist at it, insulting it: "So it's you, Mind of the galaxy—or, at least, one of those who haunt it! You are the one of whom my companion in arms, Henderson de Nancy, dead forever, said that you were once named God! But you have no creatures—they, on the contrary, are the ones who have created you by their union! Instead of a sense of harmony, you are only the essence of war and egotism; instead of knowledge, you are ignorance, for you do not know that one of your cells knows your nature! And what is your power but a miserable weakness, when you only survive thanks to the discoveries of that cell, without which humankind would have become extinct, causing your disappearance? And this is the recompense that you reserve for him: a second death for the woman whose resurrection I have already contrived!"

Ortiog interrupted himself then in order to improve Kalla's protection. As the dying woman had entirely lost the physical characteristics of Ifliz, he conceived an idea that made him shiver with dread. If Kalla had become a Terran again, the

Bions had killed Ifliz and could only hasten the recovery of the woman who had replaced her! But if that reasoning was false, and Dal exposed her to the particular bombardment, he would surely finish her off. No, he could not take such a gamble, in which he had more to lose than to gain.

In any case, for the first time, Kalla seemed to be regaining consciousness. She opened her eyes and looked at him, with a gaze still imbued with darkness. Her mouth opened. Dal heard it pronounce his name.

No words could describe the violence of the happiness that suddenly snatched Ortog from his apprehensions. For the first time since his departure, he found Kalla as she had been before her death. For the first time, it seemed that the insane quest was on the brink of triumph. He persuaded himself that he must immediately isolate the resurrected woman from the unknown influences of the universe with which she had blended. He left her momentarily in order to try once again to get back to the Earth.

It was with a rapidly beating heart that he placed his hand in the imprint—the mold whose surface opened a door toward a negative of existence, or, rather, brought back to life those who had withdrawn from it.

A nearby planet disappeared. Distant constellations flickered, erased by a hand on the scale of a hundred nebulas. The necroship shook, and its gondola swayed at the end of its cables. Enormous detonations resounded; lightning-bolts flashed, as long as the diameter of a solar system. They drifted in a limitless place in which enormous white-glaring clouds sped by. Dal recognized that space beyond space, that sky between skies, whose menace had to be overcome in order to traverse the dimensions. In the bosom of that furious chaos, a human being was only a dismantled molecule, a disintegrated atom. By comparison, a shipwreck in a tempest represented a haven of peace.

Dal went back to Kalla.

She was just as she had been on the day when he had met her for the first time, in Lassenia. She had the same expression in her eyes, interrogative and seductive at the same time: two tiny windows open on an adolescent world. But there was a gleam there as pale as it was dazzling, for she was born of the tomb, and the gondola was for her a second cradle.

Dal lay down beside her and lifted up her head, passing his arm under the nape of her neck. She huddled against him, looking at him without saying anything. He could see that she was still very weak, but knew that the memories of her life had not been lost, since she had recognized him.

With the burning violence of lava boiling within a volcano, he felt carried away by an immense need to be united with her, to fuse with her into a single being over which death would no longer have any leverage. He recognized the perfume of her skin, which he had never forgotten, and was overtaken by a great urge to protect her, as if she were a dead flower that he had taken out of a locket, and which had miraculously come back to life in the water of a specially-prepared vase.

Dal dreaded that she might not still retain the more extreme marks of her love, but the gaze that she fixed upon him contained a testimony more eloquent that words. He gradually allowed himself to be convinced by her appeal, and they were united, in the midst of lightning-flashes.

Above their heads, the spindle of the ship masked a portion of infinity, and the gondola carried their bodies like a fragile boat. In those symbolic instants, Dal received the greatest gift that life could bestow, multiplied a hundred times by the chagrin and hope that had consumed him for so long, and multiplied too by the wild joy whose effects Kallla showed him. It was like a coupling of gods, the outburst of which held back the menacing clouds.

Tearing apart the vapors and cutting through the lightning-bolts, they went through a fissure in the second titanic wall like an invulnerable bullet. As they passed through, the obscure forms of existence lurking in the cavities of that endless wall—the moving things sheltering in the frontiers of being and nothingness—hid themselves within their wings, whimpering; or, as death draws away in terror from manifestations of life, they departed in sinuous trajectories, leaving wakes of fire behind them.

Dal pulled away from Kalla, though. The ship was following the road of the Seven Agonies—which had metamorphosed into a contractile tunnel—in an inverse direction. Ortog, semi-conscious, felt with terror that he had left a place softer than swansdown, more peaceful than dreamless, serene, protective and reassuring sleep. In front of him there was nothing but tearing, crushing and choking. He had to pass through the narrow door of rebirth, with all the heart-rending constraint that implied. It was so long and so painful that he lost consciousness.

In the great hall of the Temple, the necroship is almost motionless. At the most, it is agitated by a slight tremor, since the murderous priest has fired at Zoltan's body. The Housemaster-Baron's face has taken on a grey tint under the deflagration of the blaster, whose discharge has simultaneously charred the edge of the gondola.

The murderer, too, is motionless, his hand trembling as he aims the weapon at Ortog.

That hand pulls back, as if retained by a force superior to that of his muscles—and, slowly, it rises toward the face of the guilty man. The blaster is aimed at the priest's temple.

The hand falls back. It threatens Ortog again—in vain. The adverse force is greater. The arm bends. Again, the priest puts the blaster to his own temple. A silent illumination, and he collapses, thunderstruck.

The duplicate necroship materializes through the wall. Slowly, its indecisive form fuses with the one that awaits it. Its voyage has lasted less than three minutes, in Earthly time.

Dal's body is reanimated. He stands up. The somber flame of the world of Death is still shining in his eyes. He sees beside him the charred body of Zoltan, and then the corpse of the priest a few feet away. His gaze becomes keener and more rapid. He looks around for Kalla—but she, whom he brought to the very fringe of life, has been unable to complete the final stage of the journey. Dal suddenly understands, and while his heart is twisted in his breast, his mind clears.

The terrible apprehension that pursued him had a real basis; in the same way that Ifliz survived the deadly actions of the Bions for a long time, Kalla did not vanish with her—but Kalla was the shadow of Ifliz, and, as such, could not survive without the body that gave her existence. A shadow without a screen, she was able, thanks to the Bions, to conserve her recovered form and personality, but only for a few moments—the moments that permitted him one final act of love.

With longer exposure to the radiation, she might perhaps have become a viable shadow, definitively detached from the condemned body of Ifliz. By refusing the gamble, Dal has undone what he had done. He has lost Kalla forever.

The false star of hyperspace, the source of all the latter's living emissions, contained those of the priest who killed Zoltan here, at the moment when the messengers were killing him in the Beyond, at the moment when the Weaver of Echoes crossed the Bionic mutational threshold.

Ortog's last duel, therefore, was situated in the mind of the priest, obliging the latter from the inside to spare him and commit suicide. He has thus saved his own life, without knowing it. Also without knowing it, however, he has lost Kalla as soon as he had found her.

Dal cannot bear this new loss. He draws his sword, in order to plunge it into his breast. On contact with him, however, the blade that slices through universes shatters into pieces, which fall to the floor.

A blue flame fills the Temple hall, annihilating the necroship. Debris rains down from every direction on the howling necrosophs. In Lassenia the Great, people marvel, and assume that it is a comet-strike.

Alone in the midst of ruins, Dal Ortog Dal of Galankar remains standing. He has lost his companion in arms. He has lost forever the lover who momentarily lived again. He no longer has any reason to exist, but he can no longer expect his days to end; his voyage into death has granted him a derisory immortality.

A shadow forever detached from the body that gave him life, he will remain alone for tens of thousands of years. He will be no more than an animated statue, whose despair is not on a human scale.

Through the ruins of the Temple, he stares at the Sun, which is descending toward the distant forests.

THE END

Bibliography

Fleuve Noir "Angoisse"

Le Bruit du silence [*The Sound of Silence*] (No. 13, 1955)
Pour que vive le Diable [*Long Live the Devil*] (No. 17, 1956)
Fenêtres sur l'obscur [*Windows onto Darkness*] (No. 20, 1956)
De Flamme et d'ombre [*Of Flame and Shadows*] (No. 23, 1956)
Le Seuil du vide [*The Threshold of the Void*] (No. 25, 1956)
Les Rivages de la nuit [*The Shores of Night*] (No. 27, 1957)
Je suis un autre [*I Am Other*] (No. 29, 1957)
Les Dents froides [*Cold Teeth*] (No. 31, 1957)
L'Envers du masque [*The Other Side of the Mask*] (No. 33, 1957)
Les Pourvoyeurs [*The Purveyors*] (No. 35, 1957)
Sueurs [*Sweat*] (No. 37, 1957)
L'Herbe aux pendus [*The Herb of the Hanged Men*] (No. 39, 1958)
La Marque du démon [*The Mark of the Demon*] (No. 42, 1958)
Lumière de sang [*Blood Light*] (No. 44, 1958)
Syncope blanche [*White Faint*] (No. 45, 1958)
La Village de la foudre [*The Village Struck By Lightning*] (No. 47, 1958)
Le Prix du suicide [*The Price of Suicide*] (No. 48, 1958)
La Chaîne de feu [*The Chain of Fire*] (No. 52, 1959)
Dans un manteau de brume [*In a Shroud of Mist*] (No. 57, 1959)
Mortefontaine [*Deathfountain*] (No. 59, 1959)
Glace sanglante [*Bloody Ice*] (No. 64, 1960)
Le Masque des regrets [*The Mask of Regrets*] (No. 68, 1960)

KURT STEINER

LE SEUIL DU VIDE

ANGOISSE

Éditions
"FLEUVE NOIR"

KURT STEINER

LE VILLAGE DE LA FOUDRE

ANGOISSE

Editions
"FLEUVE NOIR"

Le 32 Juillet

KURT STEINER

★

ANTICIPATION

Éditions
"Fleuve Noir"

Fleuve Noir "Anticipation"

Menace d'Outre-Terre [*Menace from Beyond Earth*] (No. 124, 1958)

Salamandra (No. 131, 1959)

Le 32 juillet [*July 32*] (No. 146, 1959)

Aux Armes d'Ortog [*Under Ortog's Arms*] (No. 155, 1960)

Les Improbables (No. 269, 1965)

Les Océans du ciel [*The Oceans of the Sky*] (No. 315, 1967)

Ortog et les Ténèbres [*Ortog and the Darkness*] (No. 376, 1969)

Les Enfants de l'Histoire [*The Children of History*] (No. 388, 1969)

Le Disque rayé [*The Scratched Record*] (No. 424, 1970)

Brebis Galeuses [*Black Sheep*] (No. 596, 1974)

Un Passe-Temps [*Pastime*] (No. 944, 1979)

Others Books:

Alerte aux Monstres [*Alert, Monsters*] (*as Kurt Wargar*) (Flamme d'Or, Visions Futures No. 6, 1953)

Du Sang jusqu'au coude [*Blood Up To the Elbows*] (Faucon Noir, 1953)

Manuel du Savoir-Mourir [*How To Die Manual*] (*As André Ruellan*) (Horay, 1963)

Tunnel (*as André Ruellan*) (Robert Laffont, Ailleurs & Demain No. 25, 1973)

Les Chiens [*The Dogs*] (*as André Ruellan*) (Titres SF No. 1, 1979)

Mémo (*as André Ruellan*) (Denoël, Présence du Futur No. 390, 1984)

Grand Guignol 36-88 (Fleuve Noir, Gore No. 62, 1988)

On a tiré sur le cercueil [*They Shot at the Coffin*] (*as André Ruellan*) (Denoël, 1997)

Big Crunch (Rivière Blanche No. 2063, 2009)

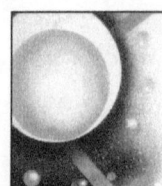

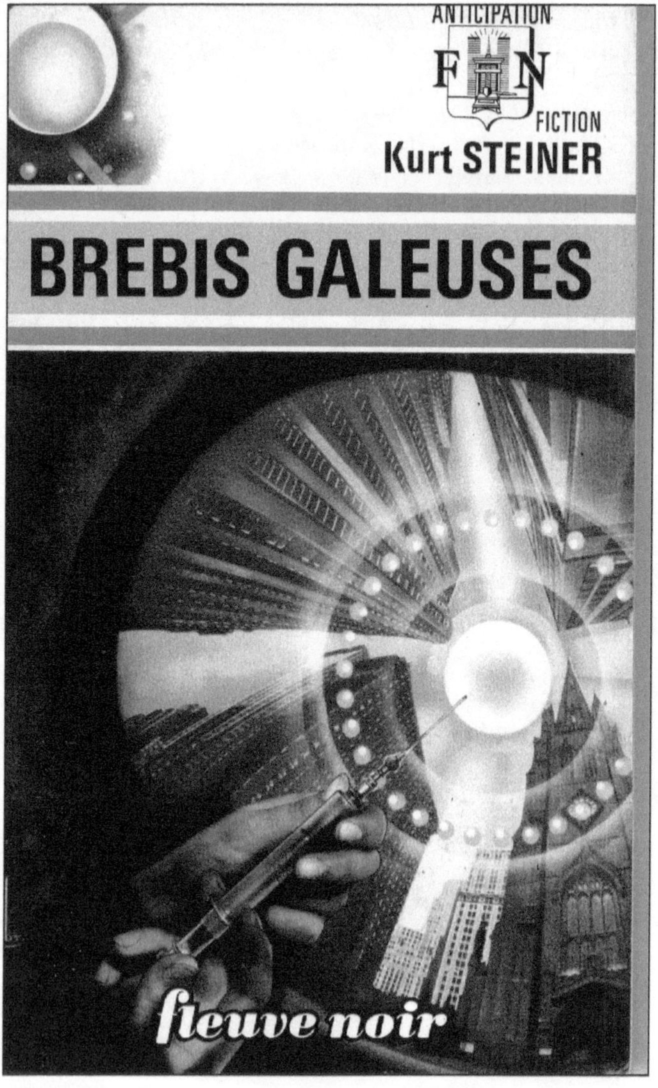

ANTICIPATION
FN
FICTION
Kurt STEINER
BREBIS GALEUSES
fleuve noir

Filmography

Le Distrait [*The Daydreamer*] (1970)
Le Seuil du vide [*Threshold of the Void*] (1971)
Les Malheurs d'Alfred [*The Troubles of Alfred*] (1972)
Les Grands sentiments font les bons gueuletons [*Big Sentiments Make for Good Sports*] (1973)
L'Ombre d'une chance [*Shadow of a Chance*] (1974)
Hu-Man (1975)
L'Ibis rouge [*The Red Ibis*] (1975)
Infidélités [*Infidelities*] (1975)
Le Roi des bricoleurs [*The King of Handymen*] (1977)
Les Chiens [*The Dogs*] (1979)
Paradis pour tous [*Paradise For All*] (1982)
Divine enfant [*Divine Child*] (1989)
Il gèle en enfer [*Hell Freezes Over*] (1990)
Ville à vendre [*City for Sale*] (1992)
Bonsoir (1994)
Noir comme le souvenir [*Black As Remembrance*] (1995)
Vidange [*Tune-Up*] (1998)
La Bête de miséricorde [*The Beast of Mercy*] (2001)
Les Araignées de la nuit [*Spiders of the Night*] (2002)
Touristes? Oh yes! (2004)
Grabuge! [*Destroy!*] (2005)
Le Deal (2007)

TV :
Billet doux [*Love Note*] (1984) (*mini-series*)
Sa Majesté le flic [*His Majesty The Cop*] - *episode* Série Noire (1984)

BLACK COAT PRESS

M. Allain & P. Souvestre. *The Daughter of Fantômas*
Anicet-Bourgeois. *Rocambole*
Guy d'Armen. *Doc Ardan: The City of Gold and Lepers*
Aloysius Bertrand. *Gaspard de la Nuit*
A. Bisson & G. Livet. *Nick Carter vs. Fantômas*
Félix Bodin. *The Novel of the Future*
Comte de Chousy. *Ignis: The Central Fire*
Lucien Dabril. *Rocambole*
V. Darlay & H. de Gorsse. *Lupin vs. Holmes: The Stage Play*
C.I. Defontenay. *Star (Psi Cassiopeia)*
Charles Derennes: *The People of the Pole*
Harry Dickson. *The Heir of Dracula*
Sâr Dubnotal. *Sâr Dubnotal vs. Jack the Ripper*
Alexandre Dumas. *The Return of Lord Ruthven*
J.-C. Dunyach. *The Night Orchid: Conan Doyle in Toulouse*
J.-C. Dunyach. *The Thieves of Silence*
Paul Féval: *Anne of the Isles*
Paul Féval. *The Blackcoats: The Companions of the Treasure*
Paul Féval. *The Blackcoats: Heart of Steel*
Paul Féval. *The Blackcoats: The Invisible Weapon*
Paul Féval. *The Blackcoats: The Parisian Jungle*
Paul Féval. *The Blackcoats: 'Salem Street*
Paul Féval. *Captain Phantom*
Paul Féval. *Gentlemen of the Night*
Paul Féval. *John Devil*
Paul Féval. *Knightshade*
Paul Féval. *Revenants*
Paul Féval. *Vampire City*
Paul Féval. *The Vampire Countess*
Paul Féval. *The Wandering Jew's Daughter*
Paul Féval, *fils. Felifax, the Tiger-Man*
Emile Gaboriau. *Monsieur Lecoq*
Arnould Galopin. *Doctor Omega*
V. Hugo, Foucher & Meurice. *The Hunchback of Notre-Dame*
O. Joncquel & Theo Varlet. *The Martian Epic*
Jean de La Hire. *Enter the Nyctalope*
Jean de La Hire. *The Nyctalope on Mars*
Jean de La Hire. *The Nyctalope vs. Lucifer*
Steve Leadley. *Sherlock Holmes: The Circle of Blood*